RAVE REVIEWS FOR EDWARD LEE!

"A horror extravaganza . . . Lee's twisted tale has an outrageously paranoid surprise that will keep fans of cover-ups and conspiracy theories reading to the final sentence."
—*Publishers Weekly* on *Monstrosity*

"The living legend of literary mayhem. Edward Lee writes with gusto, guts, and brains. Read him if you dare."
—Richard Laymon, internationally bestselling author of *Darkness, Tell Us*

"The hardest of the hardcore horror writers."
—*Cemetery Dance*

"Lee has penned some of the wettest, bravest terror this side of the asylum."
—*Hellnotes*

"A demented Henry Miller of horror."
—Douglas Clegg, award-winning author of *The Hour Before Dark*

"Adventures galore."
—*Publishers Weekly* on *City Infernal*

"Utterly intriguing."
—*Horror World* on *City Infernal*

"Lee is a writer you can bank on for tales so extreme they should come with a warning label."
—T. Winter-Damon, co-author of *Duet for the Devil*

"Lee pulls no punches."
—*Fangoria*

NEW IN TOWN

Why would Walter dream such a thing, such an *awful* thing?

He was standing on a street corner in a city, but it was unlike any city he could have ever imagined. The midnight sky was ruby-red, the low sickle moon was black. He could only see these features, though, by looking straight up because the buildings lining the street must've been hundreds and hundreds of floors high, skyscrapers unlike any he'd seen. He got dizzy just looking up. *Do they even make buildings that high?* he questioned himself.

"They do here," a little girl said.

She was skipping down the street, smiling at him. Walter almost fell over. Her pigtails flipped as she skipped. She wore black-strapped shoes and little white socks, a bright red-and-white checkered dress. Deep lines ran down her gray, wizened face. The girl was mummified.

She was playing hop-scotch but the squares weren't formed by chalk, they were formed by long, odd bones. She couldn't have been more than seven or eight. "You're in the Mephistopolis, you're in Hell," she told him. . . .

EDWARD LEE

INFERNAL ANGEL

LEISURE BOOKS   NEW YORK CITY

For Christy Baker & Bill Agans.
thunk.

LEISURE BOOKS ®

January 2004

Published by

Dorchester Publishing Co., Inc.
200 Madison Avenue
New York, NY 10016

ISBN 0-8439-5203-2

The name "Leisure Books" and the stylized "L" with design are trademarks of Dorchester Publishing Co., Inc.

Printed in the United States of America.

Visit us on the web at www.dorchesterpub.com.

ACKNOWLEDGMENTS

Though in debt to many, I need to acknowledge the following for their support, inspiration, and friendship. Tim McGinnis. Dave Barnett, Wendy Brewer, Rich Chizmar, Douglas Clegg, Don D'Auria, Tony & Kim Duarte, Dullas, Tom Pic, Bob Strauss, Wrath James White, and Bel Wilson (& Harold). Much gratitude also to Amy the Maémaè and Scott, Charlie, Darren, Cowboy Jeff, Julie, Kathy, R.J., and Stephanie. Thanks additionally to Teri Jacobs for cool names, music, and impetus for cryptography. Thanks to Jeff Funk and Minh.

Inestimable thanks to —, —, —, —, and —. I am forever in your debt.

INFERNAL ANGEL

Prologue

The metropolis sprawls. The moon is black and the sky is the color of de-oxygenated blood. Screams rip down streets and through alleys, carried by malodorous winds. The people of this place trudge the sidewalks back and forth, to home, to work, to stores, etc., just as they do in any city. There's only one dissimilarity.

In *this* city, the people are all dead.

What . . . is this place? Cinny wondered. She lay in a stinking alley, flat on her back as if dropped there. Cut-off jeans and a holey t-shirt that read MOTORHEAD. A tiny tattoo on her ankle affirmed NOWHERE LEFT TO GO BUT DOWN.

What am I doing here? she thought, but the thought speared her mind like an ice-pick. She tried to think back, couldn't remember. All she knew was this:

I'm in a city . . .

1

It was too big for St. Pete, she knew. She turned tricks there all the time, when Harley Mack was either in jail or too strung out to deal ice. Cinny would do anything for Harley Mack—and she had, literally, *anything*—because she knew the only thing keeping them together was their mutual addiction to crystal methamphetamine. Her eyes opened wider, then she shrieked when something chittered alongside. A rat—a big one. She saw its shadow slip away into a pile of garbage. The animal looked the size of a puppy.

Cinny tried to get up but couldn't yet. Her heart was beating funny—it did that a lot lately, when she smoked too much crystal at once—and her mind continued to reel, not just from the toll the drug was taking on her but from her confusion. Some john must've knocked her out and raped her; it happened all the time, a hazard of her profession and one she'd long since learned to live with. The fuckers were too cheap to fork over the twenty-five bucks, so they'd just hit her in the head with a blackjack or something, then dump her somewhere later. That must've been what happened. *Some trick jacked me out and dumped me here.*

But—

Where, exactly, was *here?*

She peered harder out the mouth of the alley, leaning up now on her hands. No, she wasn't in St. Petersburg and she knew as well that this couldn't be downtown Clearwater. This city was too big for either of those. *Tampa,* she realized. Right now Cinny was looking at some big buildings, and there were plenty of those in Tampa. It just seemed a whole lot of trouble, though. Why would a psycho john drive her all the way from St. Pete to Tampa just to rape her?

She thought back harder, her heart still beating funny,

beating slow. Then some memories began to emerge, recollections that dashed her previous suspicions: *Wait a minute . . . I wasn't turning tricks tonight. I was with Harley Mack. We were breaking into that place—it was a pharmacy or clinic or something . . .* The memories continued to jell. Harley Mack had gotten wind of a local medical clinic that had a lot of Dilaudid and other synthetic smack stored in its pharmacy vault. That kind of stuff went for big money on the street these days, so he and Cinny had broken into the place . . .

But that's all she could remember.

Gotta get up, gotta get out of here, she told herself. She'd remember the rest in time; the actual events that had led to her being in this stinky, rat-infested alley weren't important right now. She had to find Harley Mack. She had to get up and get going, and hitch a ride back home.

Get up, get up, get up! she was yelling at herself now, but she was still so dizzy and racked out, any movement sent her senses reeling. She sighed and lay back down against the slimy pavement, tried to settle down and catch her breath.

Then she heard the sound.

What's . . .

A vigorous, wet smacking.

The sound emanated from her left side; she quickly turned her head.

"Who are you?" she shrieked when she saw the man sitting there.

He sat against the alley's wall, dressed in rags that reeked. A homeless bum. He was loudly eating food and looking right at her at the same time. Eventually he said, "My name is Edward Teller." His yellowed eyes went briefly wide in some secret enthusiasm. "Have you heard of me?"

Cinny squinted. *God, he stinks!* "No," she replied.

"You're not very well-educated, are you?"

Cinny chose not to answer the ridiculous question. So what if she actually had dropped out of school in the seventh grade? Who was he to insult her? *At least I'm not a stinky bum!*

"I built the Fat Man with Oppenheimer," he said.

"Huh?" Cinny said.

"Then I invented the hydrogen bomb."

You're crazy, Cinny thought. She saw street people like this all the time; they were all nuts, they were schizos.

Then he said, "Excuse me, my foot itches," and he pulled off a corroded tennis shoe. The stench that wafted up was the worst odor Cinny had ever encountered in her life. Her sinuses seemed to swell shut. Clumps of something fell to the pavement when he peeled off a sock; it took Cinny a moment to realize what the chunks were: pieces of dead flesh, white as paraffin. In fact most of the flesh on the bottom of his foot had peeled off with the sock. Toenails yellow as a YIELD sign stuck out inches long, out from under which grew parasitic green mold.

Cinny was reeling at the stench. "Put your shoe back on!"

"Oh, of course. You're new here. You're not acclimated to such things yet."

What did that mean? The smell was so awful it made her teary eyed, like tear gas. "What city is this?" She tried to get through to him. "Is this Tampa? I don't know where I am."

"It's not Tampa. It's the Mephistopolis."

Cinny peered at him again. "It's . . . *what?*"

The bum shrugged. "You're dead. You died and went to hell."

Jeez! she thought now. This guy really *was* crazy. But even beyond the impossible abstraction, Cinny knew she wasn't a bad person. She'd done things in her life that were

4

bad but they weren't her fault. The meth made her do those things.

Her mind trailed back. Sure, she'd helped Harley Mack set up her first husband, Barny, but Barny had beaten her, he'd nearly killed her a few times, so Cinny had slipped Harley Mack the key to the trailer one night and he'd killed Barny with a hubcap mallet and made it look like a burglary. He'd also killed the dog and Barny's mother, who'd happened to be visiting; then there was the neighbor who'd seen him go into the trailer—old Mrs. Hollis, who was, like, ninety or something. Harley Mack had had to beat her head in too because she was a potential witness. But *Cinny* hadn't done those things, Harley Mack had, so why would Cinny go to hell for his crimes? Turning thousands of tricks wouldn't condemn her to hell, would it? There were prostitutes in the Bible, at least that's what she'd heard. And then there were her two babies. She'd sold them both for meth money to an "adoption broker." He'd promised her that the babies would go to good, wealthy parents who'd give them a better life than Cinny could. It wasn't *Cinny's* fault that the broker was lying and that he'd actually sold them to some underground research lab where they did experiments with infant brain tissue. *The broker would go to hell, not me!* she thought.

It didn't matter anyway. She wasn't in hell, she was in Tampa, and she had to find someplace to hitch a ride back home. She could care less what this nutty old bum was saying.

This time Cinny made a concerted effort to get up. She tried to put her feet down against the pavement—

But couldn't.

Then she started screaming. By now her eyes had acclimated to the alley's darkness and she could see why she couldn't stand up.

5

Both of her legs were gone from the knees down.

"Sorry," the bum said. "I couldn't help it."

He continued to eat, lips smacking. He was gnawing ravenously on her left calf, like a big turkey leg. Her right calf and most of the foot connected to it had been consumed to the bone. It lay glistening beside the bum.

Cinny screamed so hard she saw stars, but in between the stars two figures approached. They seemed hulking but quick, as if homing in on her horror. Were their eyes alight through lids like chisel-slits? She could make out no details, only the most vague fragments of features. Heads like silhouettes of anvils, with protrusions, like horns. Hooks for hands. Grins akin to black holes full of nails. That was all she could see, and all she needed to.

But it must be a nightmare: there were no people like this, not really. It was all those years of meth that made her see these things. They weren't monsters, they were just men, and her mind was making her see the rest.

One of the men slammed her down immediately; Cinny's stumps flew up, and her back arched as her shorts were torn off. Something hot and inordinately large penetrated her. Above this most primitive rape, black chuckling fluttered. Cinny continued to scream until the second man, kneeling attentively beside her, jammed two very long fingers down her throat. Reflex bid her to bite down hard on the fingers but that just seemed to urge more chuckling. She began to convulse, the screams quickly replaced by vicious gagging. When the fingers pressed down against the very back of her tongue, Cinny spontaneously vomited. Her attacker seemed to receive great pleasure from this act.

When he withdrew his fingers from her throat, Cinny could breathe again; her chest heaved. She was still being methodically raped by the first man, and through her horror more reflex emerged. She began to scream again, from the top of her lungs:

"HELLLLLLLLLLLLLLLLLLLLLLLP! POLIIIIII-IIIIIIIIIIIIIIIIIIIIIIIICE! WOULD SOMEBODY PLEASE CALL THE POLICE?"

The chuckling rose. The bum remained where he sat, having just finished the last morsels of his meal, and he calmly informed her: "I hate to tell you this, but those two men *are* the police . . ."

Cinny convulsed harder when a mouth as big around as a fry pan closed over her face. Her screams for help were smothered now, and inhaled. Then the rows of teeth bit down and ate her face off her skull as an eager child might eat all the icing off a cupcake at once, and though Cinny never saw it, due to the dark, a metal sign stood up straight at the end of the alley, yellow with black block letters, spelling CITY MUTILATION ZONE.

Isobel would be typically referred to as a Hierarchal She-Demon, and less typically as a multi-bred species known as *Demonus belarius.* Everything human was all the rage now, especially in art and physical fashion. Feminine viewpoints differed little between here and the Living World. Isobel stood in the salon's annex, tall and appraising in her sunglasses, chiffon dress, and high heels made meticulously of Ghor-Hound bones. She slipped the sunglasses up over the diminutive horns in her forehead, looking up at the runway.

"So how is the Grand Duke these days?" Isobel was asked. The woman who made the inquiry was a petite Troll with lovely carmine-spotted skin and elegant three-fingered hands—the salon's manager.

"The Grand Duke is just fine," Isobel replied, though this response didn't quite equate to the truth. Being a concubine for a member of the Unsacred College of Cardinals brought lofty social status for someone such as Isobel, but the status only lasted as long as the fascination. Isobel feared that Grand Duke Pilate was growing bored with her body of late; hence, she felt compelled to do something about the matter quickly, a few nips and tucks, a few maintenance spells, etc. Most of the other concubines in the Duke's harem were human—he had a thing for them—so Isobel thought it only logical to try and follow their example, starting with Hell's equivalent of a breast implant. Without the Grand Duke, where would she be? *Gotta keep my man happy,* she resolved. "Yes, yes, he's just fine," she went on. "But a little enhancement couldn't hurt, now could it?"

"Then you'll simply *love* our latest models. I can't wait for you to see them!" The Troll spoke with great enthusiasm because Isobel, as a Hierarchal, was always regarded as a priority patron. The Troll passed Isobel a flute of blackish wine made from the finest aged Brooden blood. "One's a bona fide succubus from the Lilith Subcarnation Institute. And the others are brand-new acquisitions from the Ramirez Agency—"

"I'm looking for something human," Isobel interrupted.

"It's all the rage these days!" the manager exclaimed, batting crystal-red eyes the size of billiard balls. She leaned over to whisper, even though no other customers occupied the salon. "It just so happens that yesterday we signed on two absolutely stunning human women, whom we've reserved especially for our favorite buyers such as yourself."

"Show them," Isobel said, sipping her wine. "Just the humans. I'll pass on the succubus and half-breeds."

"Of course!"

The manager snapped her fingers and an instant later, two reasonably well-fed human females traipsed out onto the runway. Both were nude and well-curved, one a strawberry blonde, the other a brunette with the most stunning sea-green eyes.

"Marvelous," Isobel whispered to herself. A nine-foot-tall Golem made of polluted riverbed clay had brought the pair of models out. It stood behind them dead-faced, arms crossed. *The Duke would love those!* Isobel thought in glee. This glee, of course, she couldn't express vocally because that would've been unrefined. In truth, Isobel was desperate to keep her man's eyes off of the other concubines. *If he gets sick of me, it's the end of the line.* The Grand Duke had no *ex*-concubines; when he tired of one, he had his chef prepare her as marinated satay to be served at the next orgy.

"Yes, marvelous," Isobel repeated.

"The blonde?" asked the proprietor.

"No, no. The brunette."

"Very good!" Next the Troll gave a single nod to the Golem, and the Golem nodded likewise. One arm shot around the brunette's neck in a split-second, lifting her kicking and screaming off the runway floor. With the long curved knife in its free hand, it neatly sliced off both of the woman's breasts. Her screams sounded more akin to some kind of high-rpm machine with bad bearings.

I'll look ravishing with her breasts! Isobel thought. "Oh, and the irises, too," she hastened. "I simply adore those sea-green eyes."

The manager nodded again, and next the Golem was expertly removing the brunette's eyeballs from their sockets with a specially made ocular retractor. The eyeballs and severed breasts were then passed to a waiting surgeon dressed in a black mantle and hood.

"And don't worry," the giddy Troll prattled on, "our transfigurists are all licensed. They're the best in the district." She put her dainty, clawed hand at the small of Isobel's back and gently urged her toward the surgery suites

9

in back. "The procedure's completely painless. You'll be out of here in a jiffy! With brand-new human breasts and irises!"

"I really can't thank you enough," Isobel replied. "And I'll be sure to tell all my friends about your fabulous salon."

Isobel was led into the back, where the transfiguration would take place. Eventually, the Troll-woman returned to the showing room. Eyeless, breastless, and now too deep in shock to scream, the brunette shuddered on the runway.

The Troll sternly instructed the Golem: "Now cut this bitch's guts out and call the diviners. Then sell what's left to the pulping station down the street." She clapped her hands sharply twice. "And be quick about it!"

The Golem nodded.

Hell is a city.

It stretches, literally, without end—a labyrinth of smoke and waking nightmare. Just as endlessly, sewer grates belch flame from the sulphur fires that have raged beneath the streets for millennia. Clock towers spire in every district, by public law, but their faces have no hands; time is not measured here in seconds or hours but in atrocity and despair. In the center of this morass of stone and smoke and butchery and horror stands the 666-floor Mephisto Building, where Gargoyles prowl the wind-blown ledges and from whose highest garrets the innocent are hung from gibbets and left to rot for eons. The lone occupant of the very top floor looks down upon his dominion and smiles a smile that is brighter than a thousand suns. Here, yes, everyone is dead yet everyone lives forever.

Welcome to the Mephistopolis.

Welcome to the city of Hell.

Welcome.

Part I
Etherean

Chapter One

"You would do that? For me?"

The voice which had spoken the words was incalculable. Words like light, a vocal utterance like a caress.

The response to these words was nearly as luminous. A simple, resolute "Yes."

In a sense they were merely two men in a room.

"Verity and reckoning," the first man said. His face could not be viewed. Could it have been that he was too beautiful to be perceived? "Is this all that we are? Two men in a room?"

"Much more than mere men," the second man said. "I will prove that to you."

"You'll die, my friend."

"I'll die gladly, for your glory."

The first man opened a door studded with jasper stones,

13

revealing the parlor of atrocity within. "She reminds me of Mary," he whispered.

The second man looked in, where a lovely Demoness wheezed, locks of long hair dripping wet and hanging over her face. Hands corded behind her back, she gagged on her knees, before a tub of water. A cloaked Warlock knelt right behind her and suddenly thrust her head into the tub, held her down. She convulsed. Bubbles of air exploded in the water, and still the Warlock kept holding her down. Eventually she went limp and died.

"Watch," the first man said.

The Warlock pulled her out and let her collapse to the scarlet-carpeted floor. Dark words flowed from his lips, an incantation in the most secret of vocabularies. Shards of dark light seemed to flit about like butterflies, and then all at once the Demoness heaved, expelling blasts of water from her lips, and her heart which had stopped only moments ago began to beat again.

"It's a Resuscitation Spell," the first man said rather proudly. "The idea titillates me. They kill her, then bring her back to life, kill her, then back to life, over and over. I can't resist the symbol of that. It's so . . . rapturous."

The second man watched the striking demon-woman fully regain consciousness. She briefly screamed, and her head was plunged back into the water.

"Kill her, then back to life, kill her, then back to life."

"And, yes, she does," the second man remarked. "She looks just like Mary."

They walked back into the main hall, their footsteps silent as death on tiles of amethyst and agate. The first man went and opened a hinged, iron-framed window of stained glass. The mosaic depicted an orgy of monsters at the summit of Calvary, while three victims of crucifixion helplessly looked on. His eyes drank in the wondrous red night outside, watched a Griffin sail by, reveled at the endless vista of buildings and smoke. "All that out there, and just us up here," he whispered.

"All that out there is yours. And so am I," the second man said.

"Yes. You are my most blessed."

An acolyte in white robes entered, bearing a large wicker basket. The basket was set down, then the acolyte bowed and left, his face sewn with pearls and diamonds. The first man approached the basket and withdrew from it a newborn Imp. Its huge eyes looked back at the man in total love.

"So beautiful, so innocent..."

"Not much innocent is ever born here," the second man said.

"Oh, but you're wrong. Everything is innocent at first. Even you and I. Even God was innocent once, wasn't He?"

"I...don't remember."

The first man held the infant creature closer, looking at it as a father would. "Like this, this joyous creation here in my hands. The longer it lives, the more of its innocence it loses. It becomes corrupt. But now, right now, this instant." The luminous voice fluttered. "It's perfect undefected pure clean innocence." He smiled at the second man, passed the infant to him. "What's wrong with me, my friend? I don't have the heart anymore."

"I'll be your heart," the second man affirmed. With no hesitation, he threw the infant out the window, knowing it would likely be devoured by Griffins long before it hit the pavement 666 stories below. "I will be your heart, and I will be your mind, and I will be your might—in the Living World. I promise."

The first man maintained his smile, a tear in his gemlike eye. "Really?"

15

"Yes."

"But you'll lose everything."

"And you will gain *everything,* as you should. Let me be just a drop of the ink that you use to rewrite all of human history."

"And for all of this that you will do for me, you ask nothing in return."

The second man bowed as if ashamed. "I ask only . . . that you remember me."

From the open window, the most distant howls could be heard; it sounded sweet, serene. Clouds a sickly green parted, to reveal the coal-black moon.

"Go now. And I will—I will remember you forever."

The second man left the room. He was a Fallen Angel from the House of Seraph, and his name was Zeihl. The other one's name was Lucifer.

Chapter Two

(I)

Two cops, on routine patrol. Well, not actually routine, not tonight—or at least not by any standard that would be called typical of modern law enforcement. Ryan and Cooper were partners, the quiet town of Dannelleton's only two midnight-to-eight cops, routed through the dispatcher of the county sheriff's department. Cooper keyed the mike, standing just outside their patrol car's open window. "County dispatch, this is Unit 208, we're 10-6 at the 600 block of 76th Avenue on a TCD violation."

"Roger, 208. You want us to run a make on the vehicle?"

"No, don't bother," Cooper replied. "He's a local. We got it covered. We'll call back when we're 10-8."

"Roger, 208. Out."

TCD stood for traffic control device, and what Officer Cooper had just related to the dispatcher was a complete lie. No one had run a red light, and they weren't really at the 600 block of 76th Ave. They were pulled over on a long dark back road just out of town. "Hurry it up, will ya, man?" Cooper complained to his fastidious partner. "Somebody's gonna see us out here."

Ryan was just as lean, mean-eyed, and cocky as Cooper . . . but a little more whacked in the head. "Out here in the boondocks? Relax." Then he looked down at the driver of the mint '68 Camaro that they'd supposedly "pulled over" for ignoring a "traffic control device." "What do you think, Dutch? My partner's over there dumping in his pants. You think anyone's gonna see us out here on this shit-hole road in the middle of the night?"

"You better hope not," Dutch said back, his arm crooked out the window. In his other hand he hefted the sizeable bag of crack cocaine that Ryan had just given him. It had taken Ryan and Cooper all night to shake down all those dealers for the stuff. "What'll happen to me if I get pulled over by *real* cops?"

Ryan shrugged. "You'll go to prison for ten years, and that'd make me very disappointed."

"I didn't know you cared."

"I don't. I just don't want to have to go to the trouble of finding a new bag man to buy all this crack we rip off of clockers and whores." Ryan ripped out a loud belly-laugh.

"Would you guys quit yacking? Jesus Christ! We have to get out of here!" This latest complaint hadn't come from Cooper, it came from Dutch's passenger, a brown-around-the-edges beach tramp by the name of Arianna. She was Dutch's squeeze, very attractive in her own way, yet a spoiled blond pain in the ass just the same. "Dutch, give the guy his money so we can get out of here."

"I'll second that motion," Cooper remarked from the cruiser. "Suppose a county sheriff or a state cop drives by?

We get caught out here, our fuckin' asses are fuckin' *fucked*."

Dutch grinned. He had a gold front tooth, which he thought of as stylish for a mid-level crack mover. Crack was hard to get down here; everything was pharmaceuticals and crystal meth, due to the virtual multitude of rednecks. In the crackburgs, Dutch was The Man. "Here ya go, Deputy Dawg. Call me on my cell when you got more for me."

He passed Ryan a band of fifties. Ryan's thumb flitted over the band's edge like a deck of playing cards. "Thanks, amigo, but I'm thinking that maybe this isn't quite enough."

Dutch's golden smile disappeared. "Yo, yo, that's not cool. Three grand's what we agreed to. Don't be pulling any Dirty Harry on me."

"No, I mean I'm just thinking that maybe we could go for a little benny on the side. You know. A little something to jazz up another lonely night for a couple of hard-working officers of the law."

Dutch smirked and opened the bag. "You want a couple rocks, you should've said so." He proffered two wax-pale nuggets of the drug. "Put this in your pipe and smoke it. It'll definitely *jazz up* your lonely night."

"We're fuckin' *cops,* you moron," Ryan reminded him. "We don't smoke that shit. I'm thinking that maybe we could go for a little of *that*."

Ryan's eyes shot past Dutch, to Arianna, who was doing her lipstick in the mirror behind the sun visor. The following silence seemed to give her a nudge, then she glared at Ryan and then at Dutch.

"No way, Dutch!" she complained. "I'm sick of spreading my legs for every chump you buy product from."

"That's *Officer* Chump to you, little miss," Ryan said.

"Come on, honey," Dutch passed it off. "You used to do it all the time. It's good business, it's how things are done."

This response was clearly not what Arianna wanted to hear. Her tone of voice turned into a bray: "Goddamn it, Dutch. The old days are over! You promised I wouldn't have to do shit like that anymore." But even Arianna, way way deep down, realized that her objection was a bit unreasonable. When you were a drug-dealer's girlfriend, part of your function existed as a deal-sealer. It was part of the turf and she knew it.

And she'd sealed many, many deals for him and others in the past.

"Sweetheart, how about a little slack?" Dutch asked next. "It's not that big a deal, is it? Ryan and Cooper are prime business, and it's only fair we keep 'em happy."

"Fine!" Arianna spat, ludicrously crossing her arms to cover her $2500 implanted bosom. "*You* fuck them!"

Ryan leaned over and looked at her. "Hey, Arianna, I've been meaning to ask you. You still have that outstanding warrant going on in Hillsborough County? What was the name you used there? Francine Rauder? Aiding and abetting the transport of controlled substances, harboring a known felon? That's a five-year hitch, baby. It would really suck if Hillsborough ever found out what your real name is."

"Shit on a stick," Arianna conceded. She climbed into the Camaro's cramped back seat, peeled off her top and peeled off her hot pants. "Come on," she griped to Ryan. "I ain't got all night, and I hope you've got rubbers."

Ryan grinned. On the job? He *always* had rubbers.

"Are you out of your mind?" Cooper nearly wailed. "Ryan, what in the name of fuck are you doing?"

"I just got us some ring-a-ding, partner. Hope you don't mind sloppy seconds."

"What part of WE HAVE TO GET THE FUCK OUT

OF HERE don't you understand? You want to boff the tramp, do it off-shift."

"Hey, did he call me a tramp?" Arianna took exception, nude and spread-legged in the back seat.

Cooper's rant went on, "Jesus Christ, the dispatcher thinks we're in town right now. What if we get a call?"

Ryan opened the door, was about to get into the back of the Camaro. "Cooper, you're being paranoid. At this hour we're not gonna get a call—"

"Unit 208, this is dispatch," the radio suddenly crackled. "I have a priority call. Proceed immediately to west end. Investigate multiple civilian complaints of fires and screaming. Code Two."

Ryan never had a chance to get into the back. "What did they say? Fires and—"

Cooper was close to flaking out; he grabbed the mike. "This is 208, I.D. 8. Please repeat."

"Investigate multiple civilian complaints of fires and screaming. Code Two. Abandon your current 10-6."

"Did you get a 20 from the call?"

"The computer went out when the calls came in. You're at 76th Avenue, right?"

Cooper stalled. *No, actually we're not at 76th Avenue,* he thought. *We're out in the sticks selling crack to a dealer.* "Uh, roger, dispatch. We, uh, don't see any fires or hear any screaming, but we'll check it out. What'd the fire station say?"

"We couldn't raise them. The entire phone net seems to have failed all through Dannelleton."

"Did you call them on the radio?"

"Radios are out, too. Maybe the tower's down. Get back to us ASAP, let us know if you need any assistance from the sheriff's department."

"Roger," Cooper tried to sound official. "208, out."

Ryan and Cooper just gaped at each other. "Fires and screaming?" Ryan repeated. "In Dannelleton?"

"That's what she said. Now let's go!"

Ryan was about to break for the cruiser. "Ring-a-ding" had just lost its priority. But then he stopped; his head tilted up and he sniffed the air. "Hey. Do you smell something?"

"Yeah," Dutch cracked. "I think Arianna just farted."

"I did not, you asshole!" she shouted from the back.

Ryan jumped in the cruiser, Cooper already at the wheel. He lead-footed it out of there. It would take them fifteen minutes to get back to town. "Fuckin'-A right, I smell something," he said to Ryan. "Something in the air. Something burning."

Cooper almost had the speedometer pegged by the time they were only a few miles away from the town limits. Was it fog that suddenly obscured everything, or smoke? "What else did dispatch say?" Ryan kept asking. "The phones are all out *and* the radio isn't working?"

"Yeah. Something's seriously fucked up," Cooper eloquently stated. "How can all the phones in an entire town go out all at once?"

"Maybe a transformer or something caught fire." Ryan had no idea what he was talking about. "Maybe one of those, you know, phone terminal buildings."

Just then Dannelleton PD Mobile Unit 208 roared past a long drab brick building with barred windows and poor exterior lighting. High fences surrounded the property. The large sign at the front gate read simply DANNELLETON CLINIC, which sounded unassuming enough, like an HMO facility or a chiropractor's. It was actually a private and very expensive in-patient ward for the mentally ill, which local parlance had long ago dubbed "The Rubber

Ramada." Ryan watched the obscure facility pass in a blink.

"You know what I'll bet happened?" he proposed. "I'll bet someone busted out of that nut hatch and got into town, set something on fire. There's some hardcore psychos in that place, like that girl I keep hearing about."

Cooper thought on it. In the meantime he had to slow down to barely twenty miles per hour on account of the fog or smoke or whatever it was. Indeed, it smelled like smoke, but much else, too. It smelled atrocious.

"You know, you may be right," Cooper finally said. "That girl, the lawyer's daughter, Heydon. They've had her locked up in there for over a month is what I read in the papers."

"I remember hearing something about that too . . ."

"One of those Goth chicks. Piss-yellow hair and screws in her face, that weirdo shit. They won't give her a trial date until she's had a full psych evaluation, but if you ask me they're taking their sweet time."

Details of the case began to surface in Cooper's mind. "Yeah, yeah, she lived on some big estate with her father in southern Virginia. The father was a big fancy lawyer or some shit."

"Right, and she burned the entire estate down . . . with her father *in* it. For the money. The guy was worth millions."

"I'm not exactly grooving on the coincidence," Cooper admitted, plowing through more fog. "We're driving hell for fuckin' leather to town on a fire call, and we've got some chick in the Rubber Ramada being evalled for setting a fire."

Ryan glanced to Cooper. "Not cool. What did you say her name was?"

(II)

"Cassie."

"No, I mean your *full* name."

"Cassie Heydon.

"Age?"

"Twenty-two."

"Date of birth?"

"October 26, 1981."

A pause.

"Last time we did this, Cassie, you mentioned that there was some significance to your birth date. Do you remember?"

"It's the date of the execution of Baron Gilles de Rais."

"And who is Gilles de Rais?"

"He was the Marshal of France by order of King Charles VII, and the sergeant-at-arms for Joan of Arc. He sold his soul to the devil, and he eventually became the most notorious satanist of the 1400s. He butchered hundreds of children."

Another pause.

Somewhere, a clock was ticking.

The process was called narco-analysis: the patient—or suspect—was polygraphed while in a drug-induced hypnotic state. It provided an invaluable therapeutic tool; it didn't matter that anything the patient—or suspect—said couldn't be used in court, it was the divination of the modern world. It divined the truth. A trained pathological liar could beat one of the systems, but between the galvanic sensors, the voice-stress analysis, all the computer cross-references, and the very latest hypnotic drugs—no one could beat *all* of the systems.

Dr. Morse was the facility's chief clinician, and he looked

the part: studied, poised, a trimmed beard with no mustache. But as smart as he was, the eyes behind his spectacles looked confused. He pulled R.J.—his therapeutic director—aside, speaking lightly. "What do you make of this?" he asked the younger technician. "This is just like the MMPIs and the Thematic Apperception Tests."

"She's delusionary," R.J. said. He nearly glowed in his starched, bright white pants and shirt. He looked the way one might expect a psychiatric technician to look—except for the Notre Dame hat on his head. He continued, "It's just—"

"She's delusionary but not delusional. She's not sociopathic, and if this were all a psychotic break, the tests would've shown that by now. It's one thing for a patient to believe her own delusion, but . . ."

R.J.'s conjecturing gun-metal gray eyes narrowed. "I know. Absolutely no psychopathic personality traits and she's not lying." He seemed to shrug off the unsaid implication. "It's just something we haven't seen before. We'll figure it out."

Both men looked back at the patient. Cassie Heydon. Young, attractive, something strangely radiant in spite of the moody dark blouse and skirt—and in spite of the fact that she was in a deep somnambulistic trance. Even unconscious, she seemed to be waiting for them, giving them their time to consider more of her perplexities. Yet either hypnotized or in a full waking state, she would insist she was telling the truth.

The polygraph was insisting that too.

Perfectly straight hair, collar length and bangs, so blond it was nearly lemon-yellow. Candy-apple red highlights. There was something loud about her Gothy appearance yet her face couldn't have been more serene.

The Embassador lie-detector was wired to a bank of

CPUs which evaluated and scrutinized every response including thermal reactions, diastolic blood pressure, vocal inflection, and heart rate. R.J. knew they could go on with this all night, and it wouldn't matter—the results would be identical to the first three sessions.

Dr. Morse pinched the chin of his beard. "You don't think she did it, do you?"

"Burned her house down, murdered her father for his inheritance?" He looked Morse right in the eye. "No, I don't. And neither do you."

"I . . . suppose you're right."

A few minutes later, R.J. was reseated at the console, Morse standing aside.

"Cassie? Can you still hear me?"

"Yes."

"Did you murder your father?"

"No."

"Did you want to inherit his money?"

"No."

"Did you burn your house down?"

"No."

"Do you know who did?"

"Yes."

"Who did?"

"A subcarnation. They do it with Machination Spells. It was a succubus sent by Lilith."

"Who?"

"Lilith is the Kiss of the Apocalypse, the Whore Madonna. She's the mother of harlots and all abominations of the earth. She tried to burn our house down herself the first time, but that didn't work. So she sent another succubus."

"To burn your house down?"

"Yes."

"Why? To kill your father?"

"No, to destroy the house. The house was a Deadpass. Like a door, or a portal. To the Mephistopolis."

"The—"

"A Deadpass is a doorway to Hell. Certain kinds of people can go through the doorway. People like me."

R.J. kept his eyes on the readout screen. The computer, thus far, had detected not a single negative impulse.

"People like you," R.J. repeated after her. He glanced down to his notes from the last session. "And you've said that you're an . . . Eth—"

"An Etheress," Cassie said blankly. "I'm a living person who can go to Hell and come back. Any time I want . . ."

Cassie kept the memory, clear as a picture in a locket. In fact, she *had* a locket, a silver locket on a silver chain—with her sister's picture inside. Cassie yearned for that locket, yearned to see the image of Lissa, even though an identical facsimile of that image gazed back at her any time she might look in a mirror. Cassie and Lissa were identical twins; only two traits told them apart; one, their hairstyles (Cassie's short cropping of highlighted bright blond, and Lissa's long velvet mane of black, with a snow-white streak on the right side) and two, the tatts: a petite barbed-wire tattoo encircled Lissa's navel, while Cassie had a petite half-rainbow around hers.

There was one other difference now, of course. Cassie was alive, and Lissa was dead.

Cassie kicked off her sponge ward slippers and lay back on the thin-mattressed cot. Unconsciously she reached up to her bosom to touch the locket—an incessant reflex—then muttered, "Damn," when she remembered that her hosts had taken it, along with her watch and wrist purse and a few other belongings, and locked it all up in the property vault when she'd been admitted. "Sorry, we can't let you keep all that," the instatement nurse had sternly told her. "Your records from Washington list you as a type-one suicide risk." Cassie winced back a wave of sarcasm: "I just want the locket, just the locket. It's got a picture of my sister in it. Jeez! How could I possibly kill myself with a *locket?* And I'm not suicidal, for God's sake." The nurse frowned, flirting with a chuckle; her eyes shot to Cassie's wrists, which were heavily lined with old scars.

"Really?" Now it was the nurse's turn to be sarcastic. She flipped through the swollen stack of Cassie's old D.C. psychiatric records. "Suicidal tendencies are often hereditary. Did you know that? Doesn't it say somewhere in your records that your sister committed suicide?"

So much for the locket.

And the memory.

Wide awake or in the deepest dreams, the memory would not stop haunting her. Lissa had been less stable than even Cassie could imagine. That night in the Goth House, it had been Lissa's boyfriend, Radu, who spiked Cassie's drink with some disorienting drug. Was it really Cassie's fault? She blamed herself—for being so drunk at the club in the first place—but her therapist had spent a year trying to get her to see that Lissa's suicide wasn't the result of anything Cassie had done. She'd been drugged. And when Radu had started kissing her in the storage room, Lissa had walked in at the same moment. Believing that her boyfriend was cheating on her with her own sister was too much for her fragile psyche to bear, so Lissa had promptly shot herself in the head, only after doing the same to Radu. Her face hot pink and streaming with tears, Lissa's last words to Cassie were: "My own sister . . . How could you do this to me?" and the next thing Cassie knew, there was an ear-splitting bang and her sister was a corpse in her arms. Brains and blood spattered the walls and most of Cassie's face.

In herself, Cassie supposed she knew she wasn't really to blame for Lissa's suicide—yet the guilt perpetuated all the same, like an arcane infestation, a psychic cancer that had gone full-blown metastatic. It didn't matter that she'd been tricked, it didn't matter that she'd been intoxicated and then drugged. The awful fact remained: Lissa had killed herself because she thought Cassie had betrayed her.

That was all that mattered. And that was the memory that cursed her to this day. Hence, her plight. If Cassie ever did any one thing in her life it had to be to confront Lissa face to face and tell her she was sorry for what had happened, and she knew she would spend the rest of her life trying to do that—which, to a layman, would sound absurd, as absurd and as crazy as the doctors of this psychiatric hospital thought she was. How could Cassie come face to face with a person who was dead and in the grave?

Unfortunately, that was the easy part. Cassie had quite a bit of experience hanging out with dead people.

"This is Xeke and Hush," Via introduced last year when Cassie had discovered the three transients living in her attic. Via was probably eighteen or twenty, slim but curvy, and with a demeanor that seemed not really butch but definitely tomboyish. What took Cassie most aback was the girl's appearance: shiny leather boots and black-leather pants, a studded belt, a deliberately shredded black t-shirt under a black-leather jacket. Not Goth but more like late-'70s punk. Buttons on the jacket confirmed the estimation. THE GERMS, THE STRANGLERS, a button of Souixsie and the Banshee's THE SCREAM. White haphazard letters on the t-shirt read SIC F*CKS!

Via was one of the dead people. "This is Cassie," she finished the introduction. "She lives here with her father."

Cassie didn't even move her head to look back at them; only her eyes darted. Xeke, the male, was dressed similarly: late-'70s British punk and appropriate buttons and patches (BRING BACK SID! and Do You Get The KILLING JOKE? and the like). Were it not for her shock, Cassie would've been struck by how handsome he was—lean, toned, dark intense eyes on a face like an Italian male model's. Small pewter bats dangled from his earlobes, and his long jet-black hair had been pulled back into a masculine ponytail. Xeke's eyes appraised her as though she were iconic, and the same went for the third squatter, the other girl. *What did she say her name was?* Cassie thought. *Hush?*

"Hush can't talk," Via said, "but she's cool."

Cassie felt far away as she listened; she felt detached from herself. Her throat clicked as she tried to speak. "Yesterday . . . when I first met you. You said you were dead."

"We are," Xeke replied matter-of-factly.

"We can guess what a shock it is to you," Via continued. "It'll take you some time to get used to."

"All three of us are dead," Xeke said, "and when we died, we went to Hell."

People living in my house, Cassie thought numbly. She and her father had been living in the old southern antebellum house for several months now. Her father had suddenly retired from his lucrative law practice in Washington, D.C. His wife, Cassie's mother, had left him for another, richer man several years ago, and Cassie's father viewed the move as the only real option now: getting Cassie out of the city would likewise get her away from the memory of her sister's suicide. No more therapists, no more anti-depressant drugs, just a new and different environment, fresh country air and lazy hills and farmland to look at instead of traffic jams and skyscrapers. It seemed to work—at least at first.

The house they'd moved into was an old plantation estate called Blackwell Hall—brooding, dark, a clash of architecture. But Cassie had loved it; it fit her eccentric tastes.

Until the day she strayed up into the attic and found these people there.

Dead people, she thought.

She didn't contemplate any of it now. It was either true, or she was insane. Period. Instead, back on the day of their first meeting, she followed Via, Xeke, and Hush down the stairs.

"We'll just prove it to you now," Via said, "and get it over with."

"Then we can really talk about things," Xeke added.

Hush looked back over her shoulder and smiled.

Yeah. I'm following dead people down the stairs.

"Blackwell Hall is the strongest Deadpass in this part of the Outer Sector," Via was explaining.

"Deadpass," Cassie stated.

"It's because of Fenton Blackwell—"

"The guy who built this section of the house, in the '20s." Cassie latched on to the familiarity. "The Satanist who . . . sacrificed babies."

"Uh-hmm," Via verified.

Xeke laughed when they got to the next landing, his mirthful eyes on Cassie. "Jeez, you must think you're losing your mind about now."

"Uh, yeah," Cassie said. "The thought has occurred to me more than once."

"Just be patient. Follow us."

When they went down the next flight of steps, Via advised, "Don't make an idiot of yourself, Cassie. Remember, *you* can see us and hear us—but *they* can't."

Cassie wasn't sure what they meant until the four of them marched into one of the dens, where Mrs. Conner, her father's new housekeeper, was busily waxing some antique table tops.

Cassie stood there, looking at her.

The older woman glanced up. When her eyes met Cassie's, there was no way that she couldn't have seen Via, Xeke, and Hush standing alongside of her.

" 'Mornin', Miss Cassie."

"Huh—hi, Mrs. Conner."

"Hope you're feelin' better. Your Pa said you had a spell yesterday."

Via laughed. "Your *Pa!* Jesus, what a hayseed!"

Mrs. Conner didn't hear the comment.

"Uh, yes, I'm feeling a lot better," she replied.

"She's got the hots for your father," Via added.

The remark startled Cassie. "What?"

Mrs. Conner looked back up. "Pardon, Miss?"

"Uh, er, nothing," Cassie said fast. "Have a good day, Mrs. Conner."

"You too."

"Your father's got the hots for her too," Xeke said through a grin.

"That's ridiculous," Cassie replied.

Mrs. Conner looked up again, a bit more oddly. "What's that, Miss Cassie?"

Instantly, Cassie felt idiotic. "Just, uh, er—nothing." *My father,* she wondered, *has a thing for Mrs. Conner?* The notion was absurd, but then—

So was the notion of dead punk rockers occupying her house.

"I told you to be careful." Via chuckled, leading on.

"Something smells good," Xeke said.

It did. Via was leading them into the kitchen, and when the four of them entered, Cassie saw her father puttering at the range, clumsily wielding a metal spatula. When he glanced—and noticed her sheer, short nightgown—he cast her a fatherly frown. "You trying out for Victoria's Secret?"

"Relax, Dad. No one's going to see me," she replied.

"No one except us," Xeke piped in. "Your daughter's got some smokin' hot bod, huh, Dad?"

He and Via laughed out loud.

Cassie's father clearly didn't hear them, or see them.

"You feeling better?"

"Fine, Dad. I was just out in the sun too long yesterday," she tried to placate him.

"Well, good, 'cos you're just in time for a Cajun catfish omelette."

"Sounds a little too heavy for me," Cassie said.

"Hey, Dad, look!" Via exclaimed. She walked right up to him, hoisted her black t-shirt, and flashed her breasts.

Bill Heydon didn't see it.

"So what are you going to do today, honey?" he asked, searching for the pepper grinder.

Xeke chuckled. "Yeah, *honey?*"

Shut up, Cassie thought. "I don't know. Probably wander around."

"Yeah, Dad," Via chided. "She's gonna wander around with the dead people living in your house."

"Well, remember. Not too long in the sun this time." Her father tried to sound authoritative.

"I won't."

"Still don't believe us?" Via asked her.

"I guess I do," Cassie answered, then immediately thought *Damn!*

More laughter from her cohorts.

Her father looked at her. "You guess you do *what?*"

"Sorry. I was thinking out loud."

"That's a sign of senility, you know." Now her father was dropping pieces of catfish into the fry pan. "You're too young to be senile. Me? That's another story."

"Hush?" Via said. "Show her."

The short mute girl in black drifted across the kitchen. She grabbed Cassie's bare arm and squeezed, to verify it to Cassie. Then she grabbed her father's arm but—

Hush's small hand seemed to disappear into Mr. Heydon's solid flesh and bone.

"All the way now," Via instructed.

Hush stepped *into* Bill Heydon's body—and all but disappeared.

He suddenly shivered. "Damn! Did you feel that cold draft?"

"Uh, yeah," Cassie said as an afterthought. Her fascination gripped her as she watched Hush step back out of her father's body.

"If you don't believe us *now*," Via said, "then you've *really* got a problem."

"Tell me about it," Cassie said.

Another funky look from her father. "Tell you about what, honey?"

Damn! Did it again!

More laughter.

"Come on, *honey*," Xeke said. "Let's get out of here before your father thinks you've completely lost it."

Good idea. This was getting way too confusing. "See ya later, Dad," she bid.

"Sure." He gave her another look, shrugged, then returned to his cooking.

She followed them out, back toward the atrium-sized living room. Hush smiled at her and took her hand, as if to say, *Don't worry, you'll get the hang of it.*

Cassie had no idea where they were taking her. Via led the way down the hall. Her leather boots thunked loudly on the carpet, but by now, Cassie realized that only she could hear them.

"Down here," Via said at the door. "We can talk better down here, in the basement."

"So," Cassie deduced once they were down. "You're ghosts."

"Nope." Xeke sat on the cold stone floor, lounging back against the basement's long wall of tabby bricks. "Nothing like that at all. We're living souls. We're physical beings."

Hush sat beside Cassie on a row of moving boxes; she leaned her head against Cassie's shoulder as if tired, her black hair veiling her face. Via remained standing, walking back and forth.

"How can you be living souls," Cassie asked, "if you're dead?"

Via answered, "What he means is that we're living souls in *our* world. We're physical beings in *our* world. In your world, though, we're subcorporeal."

"What's that mean?"

"It means that we exist . . . but we don't."

"But we're not ghosts," Xeke said. "Ghosts are soulless projections. They're just images left over. No consciousness, no sentience."

Cassie considered this. "If that's true, then what are you?"

Via took off her punky leather jacket and dropped it in Xeke's lap. By her attitude and gestures, it was clear that she was the leader of this little group. She began to diddle with the safety pins holding the tears in her t-shirt together. "It's a long story, but here goes. First, you gotta understand that there are Rules. We weren't really bad people in life, but we were fucked up. We couldn't hack it. So we killed ourselves. That's one of the Rules."

"No ifs, ands, or buts," Xeke said.

"If you commit suicide, you go to Hell. Period. No way

around it. If the *Pope* committed suicide, he'd go to Hell. It's one of the Rules."

Cassie touched her locket, felt something shrivel inside. Her sister, Lissa, had committed suicide. *So she went to—*

Cassie couldn't finish the thought.

"This house is a Deadpass. Fenton Blackwell, the previous owner, committed atrocities so extreme that they created a Rive—that's, like, a little hole between the Living World and the Hellplanes. If you're like us—if you can find one of the holes—you can take refuge in the Living World."

"But no one in the Living World can see you," Cassie figured.

"No one. Period. That's another one of the Rules."

Cassie began, "Then how come—"

"*You* can see us?" Xeke held his finger up. "There's a loophole."

A dense silence filled the narrow basement. Via, Xeke, and Hush were all trading solemn glances. Hush held Cassie's hand and squeezed it, as if to console her.

Cassie looked back dumbfounded at them all. "What is it?"

"You're a myth," Via said.

"In the Hellplanes," Xeke went on, "you're the equivalent of Atlantis. Something rumored to be true but has never been proven."

Via sat down next to Xeke and slung her arm around him. "Here's the myth. You're a virgin, right?"

Cassie flinched uncomfortably but nodded.

"And you were never baptized."

"No. I wasn't raised in any particular faith."

"You've genuinely tried to kill yourself at least once, right?"

Cassie gulped. "Yes."

"And you have a twin sister who *did* kill herself." Via

wasn't even asking anymore; she was *telling* Cassie what she already knew. "A twin sister who was also a virgin."

Cassie was beginning to choke up. "Yes. Her name was Lissa."

More solemn stares.

"In Hell, you hear about it the same way you hear about the angelic visitations here, like these people who see Jesus in a mirror, or St. Mary on a taco," Via went on. "Stuff like that. You hear about but you never really believe it."

"It's all written down in the Infernal Archives," Xeke said. "The Grimoires of Elymas, the Lascaris Scrolls, the Apocrypha of Bael—the myth's all over the place. We've all read about it, and never really believed it either. But you're real."

"And the myth is true," Via said. "You're an Etheress."

The strange word seemed to flit about the basement like a trapped sparrow. "Etheress," Cassie repeated.

"Just like it says in the Grimoires," Via continued, "you're a physical bond in the Etheric Realm, something that's created by astronomical circumstances. Two twin sisters, both virgins and both suicidal. One commits suicide and one survives. Both born on an occult holiday."

Now Cassie frowned. "Lissa and I were born on October 26. That isn't any *occult holiday*."

Via and Xeke laughed out loud. "It's the date of Gilles de Rais's execution," Via explained.

Then Xeke: "To the Satanic Sects, it's their most powerful day of worship. Makes Halloween and Beltane Eve look like a sock hop."

Via spoke louder now, her voice echoing. "You're an Etheress, Cassie. You're very very special."

Cassie didn't understand. *Very special? Me?* She'd never felt special in her life.

"We'll show you how special you really are," Via said.

Xeke: "As a true Etheress, you have powers..."

Powers, Cassie thought.

Then Via went on, "And one of those powers is the ability to enter Hell anytime you want."

Cassie's eyes widened in the mounting confusion.

"You're a living person, but you can enter the realm of the dead..."

"We'll show you," Via promised. "We'll show you the city..."

It was nothing she could have ever expected. Why should she? Cassie didn't even believe in the existence of Hell—until now, of course. There were some surprises.

They left the garage through the side door, stepping out into the sultry night. The chirrups of crickets throbbed loudly. Moonlight made the woods fluoresce. They wound around to the front of the house, which faced south. "You said we're going to the city," Cassie stopped them.

"That's right," Via replied. "It's called the Mephistopolis."

"You're talking about Hell, right?"

"Oh, yeah," Xeke answered. "Home, sweet home."

"Sort of," Via amended. "See, we don't live there anymore—we can't. We're XR's—ex-residents."

"Same as fugitives," Xeke explained. "In the city, there are two social castes: Plebes and Hierarchals. We're Plebes, commoners, and as XR's we're not allowed to reside in the city anymore. We're considered criminals because we haven't conformed. That's why we have to live in a Deadpass, like your house, or the Deadpasses in the other three Outer Sectors. It's a bitch, but if we stay in the city too long, the Constabularies get wise to us. We wouldn't last very long if we tried to stay in the city limits."

Via could read the confusion on Cassie's face. "Believe me, it's easier to just learn as you go. You still *do* want to go, don't you? Remember, you don't have to."

"I still want to go," Cassie said testily. "I just want to know exactly where it is we're going. Hell? Hell isn't supposed to be a *city*. It's supposed to be a sulphur pit, a lake of fire, stuff like that."

Xeke chuckled. "It used to be—several thousand years ago when Lucifer was cast out of Heaven. But just use your common sense. Take New York City, for example. What was New York City several thousand years ago?"

"Woods, I guess," Cassie said, still not getting the point. "Just . . . land."

"Right, undeveloped land. So was Hell when Lucifer first arrived; it was just a hot plain, a wasteland."

Then Via put it this way: "Just as human civilization has evolved over the past three or four thousand years . . . so has Hell."

Xeke: "And just as God's creatures have developed here on Earth, Lucifer and his dominion have developed equally. Progress and technology don't just happen in your world, Cassie. They happen in ours as well. That sulphur pit is now the biggest city to ever exist."

Hush pulled Cassie along by the hand, pointing. Xeke said, "Here's the Pass. Just walk a few more steps . . ."

Cassie walked out ahead of them now, her flipflops crunching over the trail's carpet of twigs and fallen leaves. But as she progressed, she felt something strange, something that could only be described as variants of pressure and temperature. Vertical layers of hot and cold, an annoying strain in her ears. Then came a sensation like dragging her hand through dry beach sand, only the sensation encompassed her entire body, through her clothes right to her skin.

For a moment, all she saw was utter blackness.

Then—

"My God," she muttered, looking out.

That's all it took. One more step.

Now Cassie stood at the foot of another world.

Overhead the sky churned in gradients of scarlet. An exotic, sweet-smelling heat caressed her. A sickle-shaped moon hung in the horizon: a moon that was black and whose black light impossibly lit her face. Indeed, a scrub, smoking wasteland extended from her feet over what had to be the next fifty or even a hundred miles. She could see everything, every detail in a crisp macrovision. And beyond this intricate wasteland stood the Mephistopolis.

The scape of the city—with its buildings, skyscrapers, and towers—seemed forged against the scarlet horizon. It truly was immense. When Cassie looked to the left, the city's face extended farther than she could see, and the same to the right.

Smoke—more like black mist—rose from the city into the sky, and so did myriad spears of multicolored lights, which she could only equate to spotlights. Birds—or winged *things*—could be seen sailing away in the distance.

The sight of it all stole her breath.

The others had stepped through the threshold and now stood behind her. They seemed to marvel at Cassie's speechless awe.

"Pretty cool, huh?" Via bid.

"Kind of makes Chicago look like a pup tent."

"I couldn't believe it, either, the first time I saw it. Couldn't believe it's where I'd be spending eternity."

Finally Cassie was able to speak. She glanced again to the left and right. "It . . . never ends."

"Actually it does," Xeke explained. "Ever read the Book of Revelation? In Chapter Twenty-One, St. John reveals the actual physical dimensions of Heaven, so Lucifer deliberately used the same dimensions when he produced the original blueprints for Hell. Twelve thousand furlongs square.

That's, like, 1500 miles long and 1500 miles deep—the surface area is over two million square miles. If you took every
major city on Earth and put them together . . . *this* is still
bigger."

Cassie couldn't really even envision these dimensions. "So,
since Lucifer fell from God's grace, he's been building this
city?"

"That's right. Or, we should say his *minions* have. Most
entrants into Hell become part of the workforce in some
way. And in a sense, the Mephistopolis is just like any other
city. It's got stores and parks and office buildings, transportation systems and police and hospitals, taverns, concert
halls, apartment complexes where people live, courthouses
where criminals are tried for crimes, government buildings
where politicians rule. Just like any city, er, well . . . almost."

Via explained further. "In the Mephistopolis, people
aren't born—they arrive. And they live forever. And where
the social order on Earth is the pursuit of peace and har-
mony amongst the inhabitants—"

"The social order in Hell is chaos," Xeke informed.

"You have Democracy, we have *Demon*ocracy. You have
physics and science, we have black magic. You have charity
and good will, we have systematized horror. That's the difference here. Lucifer's social design must function to exist
in a complete opposite of God's. Lucifer has built all of this
to offend the entity that banished him here."

"So . . . it's not underground like in the legends?" Cassie
asked. "It's not on Earth someplace?"

"It's on a *different* Earth that occupies the same space,"
Xeke informed her. "It's just on another plane of existence
that God created. So is Heaven."

"So," Cassie began, "when you die—"

"You either go to Heaven, or you come here. Just like it
says in the Holy Bible. Just like it says in most religious

systems." Xeke cocked a brow. "Not really much of a surprise when you think about it."

As Cassie continued to stare at the distant cityscape, her mind turned over a thousand questions. How could she ask them all?

"Let's just go," Via said, as if deciphering her thoughts. "Your questions will all be answered."

Eventually, they were.

Cassie dreamed of it now—a year later. Not in the confines of a normal bed but on little more than a cot in the precaution ward of a private mental hospital. Indeed, she entered the Mephistopolis with Via, Hush, and Xeke, all for the purpose of finding Lissa. All Cassie wanted in the world was to be able to tell Lissa she was sorry for what happened, and her new-found powers as an Etheress would enable her to do that—or so she thought. Down a hundred different alleys and a hundred different smoking streets, through one district and prefecture after the next, wielding spells, hexes, and the most arcane charms, Cassie and her friends had invaded Hell time and time again, harassing the authorities, striking down Lucifer's agents, destroying power plants, Constabulary stations, and evil tabernacles like a squad of guerilla fighters. During these visits, she thought it best to maximize her time: while her search for Lissa was perpetual, Cassie and her friends felt it only appropriate to wreak a little havoc along the way—terrorism, by any other name. Once, they'd scaled the Industrial Zone's hundred-foot iron walls and managed to shut down the Central Power Plant by closing a pressure-relief valve at the exact same time the furnace was being stoked. It hadn't taken the outflow gases long to skyrocket, and the Plant's exterior structure—the size of a football stadium—to spectacularly explode. The detonation rocked the entirety of the district, flattened the

Foundry, and toppled all the Bone-Grinding Stations, all during peak hours. Lastly, the explosion had triggered a seismic shift which caused an impressive hellquake, opening a thousand-foot long fissure across the Zone. Not bad for three girls barely out of their teens. Last fall, Cassie had entered the Mephistopolis alone—she'd been bored and her CD player was broken—and she'd cast an Enchantment Spell on an entire garrison of Constabularies—Satan's police. She'd ordered them one by one into Boniface Square's Flesh-Processing Terminal where they'd each calmly and willingly lie down on the primary conveyor belts. The terminal's sweatshop of thousands of workers didn't bat an eye as the Constabs were submitted to "processing"; they were fileted alive, muscles promptly shorn off bone, organs removed, skin flensed—all to be tossed into the constant parade of rolling hoppers. It was in these terminals that most of the city's food came from; Cassie liked the idea of demons unknowingly feasting on police officers. She wondered if they tasted like chicken. Time and time again, either with her friends or without, Cassie had returned to that primeval city, racing through its crimson alleys, blasting any demon, Usher, or Golem with a mere thought, offending Lucifer at any opportunity, using her powers as an Etheress to simply do her part. But even as her powers accelerated, so did those of her adversaries. Hell's resistance movement—the Satan Park Contumacy—had been her greatest ally in the early days—an entire army of anti-satanic terrorists—but they'd all been wiped out by a single Faith Plague engineered by Lucifer's Biowizards and Arch-Locks at the College of Spells and Discantations. Millions strong, the Contumacy was destroyed overnight, each and every member succumbing to one of Lucifer's favorite afflictions: Karyolysis, Hell's equivalent to flesh-eating disease. The pus and putrefactive slime from all those Contumacy members rotting to death at once had actually formed a lake in the middle of Satan Park. Lucifer had immediately inducted the lake as a national landmark, and often ordered convicts and vagrants to be publically executed in it, via drowning.

But every time Lucifer and his agents struck, Cassie struck back. Since she'd been granted these Ethereal Powers, she knew that it was her obligation to use them, against the very entity that imprisoned her sister. Via and Hush were gone now, either destroyed or captured, and Xeke had turned out to be a traitor. Cassie was alone but she wouldn't let that fact stop her.

Instead, something else did. The reason she was in this mental hospital in the first place. Little more than a month ago, unknown envoys of Lucifer had burned down her house and killed her father. The fire had destroyed the Deadpass. Now, understanding more than she ever had about the true nature of Hell and her powers as an Etheress, Cassie had never been more helpless. She wanted to go back, to *keep* going back, until she found Lissa in that endless city of the damned.

But she couldn't go back now, could she?

She woke up, sweating on her cot, hemmed in by the padded canvas walls of her room.

Even if she found a way to get out of this locked psychiatric ward, the Deadpass was destroyed, her only doorway back to the Mephistopolis closed.

I'll never get back there, she realized.

Then a voice seemed to answer her regret.

The voice said: "Yes, you will."

Cassie's eyes widened in the dark. So now she was hearing voices? *Makes sense,* she thought. *People in psych wards hear voices, don't they? Crazy people . . . hear voices . . .*

"But you're not crazy, Cassie," the voice returned. It was

44

light and feminine; it even sounded kind of perky. The voice was in her ears, as anyone's voice would be, anyone else who might be in the room, which presented a problem, of course, because there *was* no one else in the room. At least, though, she knew it wasn't a voice in her head, like a hallucination, and Cassie knew this too: she wasn't talking to herself. What she was hearing was clearly not her own voice.

"Get up."

"What?" Cassie dared answer.

"Go on, get up. Don't be afraid. Go to your sink and turn on the water."

Now Cassie chuckled at herself. "I guess it's settled. I *am* crazy. Some girl just told me to go to the sink and turn on the water. What does she want me to do? Wash my face? Brush my teeth?" But all she did was shrug. If she was crazy, what did it matter?

She got up and went to the little sink beside the toilet. She turned on the water.

"This'll sound a little weird but now I'm going to transfer my image to you."

"You're right," Cassie said. "That sounds a little weird."

"Cup your hands under the water."

Why not? Maybe it was just a dream. She was an Ethcress, she'd literally been to Hell and back. Plus all the psych drugs she'd had to take during her teen years? *I'm entitled to have weird dreams. That's all this is.*

"It's not a dream."

Cassie cupped her hands under the running water, whistling "Living Dead Girl," by Rob Zombie.

"Keep the water in your hands and step away."

Cassie did so.

The voice seemed pleased. "Now. Look in the water. Do it from an angle, don't look down into the water directly.

Make it so you don't see your own reflection."

Boy, Cassie thought, *I can't wait to tell R.J. and Dr. Morse about this. They'll love it.* Nevertheless, Cassie did as instructed. She looked at the water in her cupped hands as some of it dribbled through her fingers.

Cassie stood very still. There was a reflection in the water: a face. Not her face but the face of a pretty girl with long, flowing snow-white hair. The hair looked as though it were submerged in water itself, floating around the girl's head as though she were lying back in a bathtub or pool. Cassie could make out this face with an alarming detail; she could even see the girl's eyes, so beautiful yet so strange. The irises of her eyes were beige, surrounded by the thinnest rim of bright violet.

Yeah, Cassie told herself. *This is a dream, that's all.*

"Hi, Cassie," the face said, smiling softly. "My name is Angelese."

Cassie's lips trembled before she could respond. "Yeah? Well . . . that's fine but . . ."

"What am I doing in the water in your hands?"

"Well, yeah. For starters."

"It's just a basic Transference Charm. All you need is a medium that's pure—snow, prism light, running water. You could even do this."

"I don't think so," Cassie said, still not believing she was having a conversation with a reflection.

"Sure, you could. You're an Etheress."

Cassie could hear her heart thudding. What should she ask next? *When someone else's reflection is talking to you—in a psych ward, no less—what exactly do you say?*

"I'm a Caliginaut, Cassie," the reflection—Angelese—said next. "I know you don't know what that is, and I don't have much time. The charm only lasts a minute or so. So I'll make it quick. I'm from an Order of the Seraphim, a very special order. Those from my order willingly descend from the Rapture."

"*Seraphim,*" Cassie repeated the word. "You're a—"

"I'm an angel," Angelese said, and suddenly her face began to stress as if in pain. "I've been sent here to help you."

"Help me do what?" Cassie asked, eyes blooming.

"I'm here to help you find the other Deadpass. I'm here to take you back into Hell—"

The water in her hands had turned to blood, and Angelese's words barely registered when suddenly Cassie was deafened by a high, shrill noise that filled the padded room like a fire alarm. Cassie thudded to the floor as if knocked down. The blood in her hand flew away and spattered the canvas walls, and that's when she realized that the sound that was piercing her eardrums—that high, shrill, alarm-like noise—was actually Angelese screaming.

Chapter Three

(I)

"Heydon, I think," Officer Cooper said behind the wheel of Dannelleton PD Mobile Unit 208. "Cassie Heydon, er, Cassandra or something."

They'd just passed the little-talked-about Dannelleton Clinic, where said Cassandra or something was currently undergoing psychiatric evaluation on a pre-trial order for an arson charge. And here were two Dannelleton cops speeding back to town on a suspicious fire call that was starting to sound a lot like arson. Correction, they weren't speeding anymore; Cooper, who had a penchant for pegging the speedometer at any reasonable opportunity had by now slowed down to ten miles per hour due to the sudden limited visibility.

Ryan poked his head out the shotgun window. "Jesus, you're right. It's not fog, it's smoke, and—" He tensed at a sudden fit of coughing. "And that stink? It's ten times worse now."

Cooper could smell it too; he could even taste it as his face wrinkled up. It was a smell like meat cooking, but not good meat. Rotten meat. Like the time when he was a kid back in Brackard's Point and they'd set that dead-for-four-days German shepherd they'd found at the dump on fire.

The most atrocious stench . . .

"Dispatcher said west end, right?" Ryan was peering out, seeing essentially nothing now.

"Yeah, and we're almost there . . . I think." Cooper had had to decelerate to a crawl by now. The smoke had thickened to the point that it was like driving through pea soup. Ryan keyed the radio mike again. "Still dead," he said. "When was the last time that happened? Sure, the fuckin' phones go out every now and then, but when was the last time the radio went out?"

"Never," Cooper muttered, then stomped the brakes and shouted "Fuck!" when a sudden rapid thumping began to beat on the windshield. Both cops fumbled for their guns until they noted the old man leaning over at the open driver's window.

"What the blamed hail's goin' on?" his cratchety voice asked them.

"Sir, do you know where the fire is?" Cooper asked.

"Hail no, but there sure as shit's a fire somewhere." The old man stood in pajamas, his dentures were out, which lengthened his lined face. "Where's the blamed fire department? How come there ain't no phone service? I can't even get the local news 'cos the blammed *television* ain't workin'."

"Hey, pappy, pipe down a minute and let me ask you something," Ryan said next, squinting over. Now the smoke was even seeping into the car, tendrils of a sickly greenish-gray. "Our dispatcher told us that there were complaints of people screaming out here. You hear anyone screaming?"

The old man needn't answer. In the distance, like foghorns sounding across the bay, they could hear it: a uniphon of moans, muttering, and screams.

Cooper said: "This is four shades of fucked up."

"It's coming from the town square near as I can tell," the old man offered.

Ryan checked the cylinder of his service piece, then checked his speed-loaders. "Wait here, keep trying the dispatcher," he said to Cooper. "I'm gonna check this out."

Cooper just gulped and nodded.

Ryan got out. "Come on, pappy. Show me what the fuck's going on," and from there the two men ventured forward into the souplike smoke. Ryan could see through periodic breaks, and his suspicions were validated when he first heard the crackling and then spotted the shifting. Bright blossoms of what could only be fire.

"See that there, sonny?" The old man pointed.

"Yeah, I see it," Ryan grated back. It was hard to even talk now, from the malodorous soot that seemed to be lining the inside of his mouth. But, yes, he could see it: a line of well-appointed rowhouses, divided by intermittent shops along Main Street, all aflame. Some of the fires had spread across the roofs leaving frameworks of radiant, crackling orange, while other buildings poured flame from their blown-out windows. Ryan wasn't sure—in fact, he convinced himself that it was just an optical illusion—but in one of the windows he thought he saw people running about in horror, dressed in sheets of flame.

"Must've been an earthquake or something," Ryan speculated, "or some big-ass gas-line rupture," forgetting that Dannelleton was all electric and had no natural gas service. "And now that we've established that there's a fire, where in the *fuck* is the fire department?" Hence, the next disturbing observation. Main Street was being devoured by fires yet he heard no sirens, detected no evidence of an emergency-service response. The only thing that he *did* continue to hear were the screams, some low, some high, some tortured and barely human anymore in their rubato-like trait that grimly made Ryan think of people being burned alive.

"There!" The old man pointed again. "Ain't that a bitch!"

It was a bitch. Now Ryan squinted through more stinking murk to actually see the fire department. Flames trailed around the sign on the front wall—DANNELLETON FIRE UNIT 1—and the great plate glass windows near the entrance had blown out, vomiting more fire. When the entrance door did in fact burst open, a man staggered out, wailing. There seemed to be some clumplike thing on his back, something that moved, but how could that be? It must be just an air-pack, or responder supplies in a backpack. The man, continuing to wail, disappeared into smoke. Ryan couldn't help but think, however: *What was that . . . thing on his back?*

The station's three open bays belched flame too, and the town's three proud fire trucks were easily seen burning. The entire building was engulfed now, and that slight but definite irregularity did enforce itself into Ryan's mind, given his own state of distress at the moment.

The entire building was made of brick. Brick didn't burn, or at least it wasn't supposed to as far as Ryan understood.

This is all fucked up, the cop cogitated. *What am I gonna do?* What *could* he do? He and Cooper were just two cops who had no communications, no fire-fighting gear, and, obviously, no fire department. Meanwhile, it looked like the entirety of beautiful downtown Dannelleton was burning up.

And still, the screams persisted, but they were fading.

Ryan turned back to the old man—"Hey, pappy, you got a—"

The old man lay convulsing at Ryan's feet. His toothless mouth gasped, opening and closing like the mouth on a fish dying on a pier. His bony fingers felt around at his abdominal area, and that was a big problem.

His abdominal area had been shorn open.

He'd been disemboweled in only the few moments that Ryan had been looking toward the town square. His fingers were desperately feeling around inside the evacuated cavity, feeling for innards that were no longer there.

"We'll get a fortune for these at the gut-diviner's," a sifting voice proclaimed with some enthusiasm. The voice was replied to: "You bet! Fresh guts!"

Ryan wasn't sure. He was *hoping,* in fact, that he'd inhaled too much smoke and the reaction was causing hallucinations. Nonetheless, he wasn't sure but he thought he observed two things: One, the voices he'd just heard were not human; and, Two, several squat figures had just shuffled off together in the smoke. The figures seemed to be carrying piles of something ropy and wet in their clawed hands, and the figures seemed to have horns.

Not trumpets or bugles. No, not those kinds of horns.

Horns coming out of their foreheads.

When Ryan got back to Dannelleton PD Mobile Unit 208, his partner's previous words echoed in his head: *Yeah, this is four shades of fucked up,* and the impression was trebled when he actually got a good look at his partner, who remained behind the wheel of the cruiser.

What Ryan saw was a big problem. Cooper was quietly shuddering in place, stooped over. His skin seemed wizened now, as though something vampiric had drained a good deal of his bodily fluids. But it was no vampire that had attached itself, via its hooklike mouth, at the back of Cooper's neck. It was a species of parasite known not in this world but in another as *Democephalus exsanguinius,* referred to less technically as a Caco-Tick. Cannulas slid out of its mandibular cavity to pierce the back of Cooper's neck and slip up into the skull through the carotid inlets and then drain all of the victim's spinal fluid. Once digested, the cannulas then moved on to the *corpus callosum* where they would spend the next few hours leisurely sucking all of Cooper's blood out through his brain. By now the Caco-Tick had swollen nicely, to something about the size of a pineapple. The parasite's vein-lined blood reservoir quivered as it continued to fill.

Officer Ryan himself didn't have time to get back into the cruiser—provided he would even *want* to get back into the cruiser when one considered what was also present. Someone tapped him on the shoulder, and when he turned to see who it was...

... he was presented with a big problem. It was Cooper. Standing next to him. Hence, the problem. It didn't matter that Cooper was wild-eyed and buck-naked and grinning deliriously. The problem was much more direct: How could Cooper be standing right next to Ryan when Ryan had, seconds ago, seen Cooper sidled over in the squad car with the giant tick on his neck?

"Hey, buddy!" Cooper cracked, "how about we go grab ourselves some ring-a-ding?"

Ryan stepped back. *Why are there two Coopers?* he plainly asked himself. Then he stepped back some more.

From nowhere Cooper seemed to produce a meat cleaver of impressive proportions, and he wasted no time in lunging toward his partner, swiping the cleaver back and forth so fast the blade was a blur. "Gotta cut me some pig!"

When Ryan emptied his revolver into Cooper's chest,

Cooper just keep coming. Odd what was coming out of the catastrophic chest wound, though. Not blood as anyone would expect but some bizarre organic puree, like loose ground meat. It didn't . . . smell good. Now Cooper was chasing Ryan around the patrol car, the cleaver swiping madly, but when enough of that puree had emptied from his chest, he began to falter and then he collapsed. The thing that had chased Ryan about the car clearly wasn't the real Cooper but instead some sack of animated meat that *looked* like Cooper. By now, of course, after all he'd witnessed out here, Ryan was insensible, and he'd never be able to conceive of the explanation anyway: that the evil Cooper lookalike was something known as a Hex-Clone.

Ryan wasn't sure what it was that eventually got him, or what it could even have been, but he did know this: One moment he'd been standing there physically intact, the next moment he was paralyzed on the ground, similar to the old man, clutching his abdomen. Squat figures bustled around him. Something had riven his belly open, and now those same figures were greedily hauling his intestines out of the wound, bickering. "Give me the spleen, give me the spleen!" one insisted. "I got dibs on the stomach," another proclaimed. More evil voices fluttered about as Ryan merely shuddered in place. They evacuated him with glee, mining their human ore, like voracious cotton-pickers. Two were fighting over what must've been his small-intestinal tract: "Let go, let go! It's mine!" and "No, it's not! Give me it, you Troll bastard!" It was a tug-of-war. "Hey, buddy?" yet another less-than-human voice whispered to him. "We're gonna sell your guts to an Anthropomancer. They pay *good scratch* for human guts. They use 'em to read the future, then send messengers to report the results to Lucifer. Thanks for your guts, pal . . ."

Incomprehension notwithstanding, that was pretty much

it for Officer Ryan. Eviscerated now, he lay dying, blood seeping freely from his calamitous wound. Were mites roving in the blood? Everything had happened so fast, his mind couldn't even attempt to calculate any of it. A clawed hand pulled the wad of cash from his pocket—the crack money he'd gotten from Dutch—but then he heard a guttural sputter. "These ain't Hellnotes! Fuck! What am I gonna do with this shit? Wipe my ass?" Footsteps plodded off.

Next, Ryan was being dragged away by someone—er, well, someone wasn't exactly accurate. It was actually a female Ghoul, sleek in her nutmeg-colored skin, lissome and even voluptuous, pert breasts like hard fruit on the slat-ribbed chest. She looked back at him with sparkling, billiard-ball-sized tourmaline eyes, then frowned. "I'd eat you myself but I'll get more money for your meat at a Pulping Station."

Ryan still didn't understand. In the real world and in this hideous nightmare as well, it seemed that nobody cared about anything but money.

Wind gusted off the bay, blowing vast holes in the noxious smoke, and the last visual image to register in Ryan's mind was a glimpse of downtown Dannelleton: the town square, the city hall, the quaint cafes and bistros and the shell shop and the German bar where he'd slammed down many a stein of Bitburger draft. It was all smoldering now, and behind it stood the grim gray skyscrapers which seemed to lean this way and that at the oddest angles.

This was a big problem.

There *were* no skyscrapers in downtown Dannelleton.

(II)

Walter popped the small almond-brown pills. No, he wasn't committing suicide—he'd bought the shotgun for that, a beautiful brand-new Remington 870 pump. The pills were ferrous fumarate—a commonplace iron supplement—because Walter, according to the doctor that Colin had made him see, was slightly anemic. You could tell that just by looking at him. His red hair and already fair complexion seemed to drastically accentuate his stereotypical college-geek egghead never-get-out-in-the-sun-even-though-you-live-in-fucking-Florida pallor. Eighteen years old and gaunt as Ichabod Crane. Freckles. And no self-esteem. It didn't matter that he had the highest I.Q. of anyone—including the senior professors—at the University of Southern Florida. His love was all that mattered, and that's why he was about to kill himself.

Walter Grey didn't have to live in the dorm room at Morakis Hall; his brother, Colin, would've put him up at a luxury condo right on the water if he'd wanted that, but Walter knew he had to adjust better socially. He wanted to meet people, be part of the "scene," make friends and hang out. None of that had worked at first; Walter was a geek in every sense of the word and, hence, the object of every practical joke that college kids could conceive of. Dogshit in his sneakers, anole lizards on his cheeseburgers at the dining hall, Sudden Death hot sauce in his gym-class jock strap, water balloons full of molasses dropped on his head from the dorm windows when he was coming back from class. One night some of the guys on his floor had Krazy-Glued his physics books closed, just when Colin had walked in to see how things were going. Colin looked like a geek in the same way that Walter looked like a geek, but Colin didn't give a shit. When you were a multi-millionaire, you didn't have to. "Hey, ass-bags," Colin had said to the perpetrators of Walter's torment that night. "Anybody who fucks with my brother gets his ass kicked." One of the students had challenged back at Colin's frail physique: "Oh, yeah? By who? You?"

"No, not by me," Colin informed him. "By these guys." Then Colin's hand gestured to the other gentlemen who'd just entered the dorm room after him: four very psychotic-looking bikers with a local motorcycle gang called The St. Pete Decapitators. One of them promptly punched a hole in the wall, as if on cue. Then another snapped open a ten-inch angel-blade. Did the knife's edge have rust on it, or dried blood?

"Walter's our friend," he told the wiseacre student in a voice scorched by years of PCP-toking. "If you ever give him a hard time," the biker grinned through black teeth, "I'll cut your cock off and make your mama suck it."

No one ever bothered Walter again. See, Colin merely hired the bikers to make his point—paying them quite well—and he'd hire them again if more severe services were ever needed. They never were.

But by the time that Walter realized he wasn't likely to be socially accepted by anyone, he met Candice.

The girl of all my time-held dreams, he thought yearningly now, love in his heart and a 12-gauge pumpkin-ball in his hand.

Yes. Candice.

Adriatic-blue eyes, long blond hair down past her waist, five-foot-ten and a half. Beautiful as one of those bikini models in a hot rod mag. Candice was a general studies major and at age twenty-six could boast of being the oldest sophomore currently enrolled. Her parents were putting her through school—to help her find her true aptitudes, and to keep her shenanigans—and her physical body—out of their North Hampton, New York, beach mansion. In truth, though, her aptitudes were more oral than academic, as just about any male athlete at the school could attest, and damn near every male instructor. She knew, in fact, that if she really made the effort, she could probably fellate her way to a quicker graduation, but her view was: *What's the hurry?* Even though Candice existed as the embodiment of every sexist cliche, she was quite happy with that lot. She loved it.

And Walter loved *her.* He truly believed in love at first sight because what else could these feelings be but love? He knew he loved her the instant he'd first seen her at the student lounge watching *Hollywood Squares* reruns instead of doing her homework. Walter had been having a Mountain Dew and whizzing through the day's chapter on the molecular possession of cesium and its relation to low-ionization energy fields. It was a piece of cake. When he'd looked up, though, the most beautiful girl he'd ever seen in his eighteen-year-old life was sitting at the same table, right across from him. She smiled at him—it was a distressed smile but a smile just the same—and then she pushed some of that shimmering blond hair back off her brow and said: "Hi."

Walter nearly had a *grand mal* seizure when she'd said that single, simple word to him. Instantly he was sweating, shaking even, and when he opened his mouth to respond to her greeting, what came out sounded like, "Huh-huh-huh-huh—"

"My name's Candice," she told him next. "What's yours?"

"Wuh-wuh-wuh-wuh—" Then he finally got it out. "Walter."

She scratched her head, and pulled out a spiral notebook. "Damn, I got this take-home quiz, it's due next period, and I just can't remember! Isn't math a bitch?"

"It's-it's-it's the only quantitative philosophy," Walter spewed. "Math is the meaning of life."

She giggled. It was the cutest giggle he'd ever heard. "Do you know a lot about math, Walter?"

"Yuh-yuh-yuh—"

"I just can never remember, damn it. The difference between Number Theory and Set Theory."

Here was Walter's chance to prove to this blond goddess that he was something more than a babbling putz. He could help her, couldn't he? Her query grounded him; something snapped in his head like a switch. "Number Theory is the science of integers and how natural numbers relate to one another. Set Theory is the science of the interrelation of collections of numbers as basic number-systems."

Another smile that made Walter want to melt. "You're so smart! Could you say that a little slower so I can write it down?"

Instant confidence. They were relating to each other, via a common interest! Walter reached over and took her pad, and began to write down the needed definitions, and *that* was just the beginning.

The beginning, that is, of an all-too-typical form of exploitation: the age-old Case of the Buxom Blond Using the Egghead. For the rest of the next semester, Candice exploited poor Walter for what he had far more of than she: brains. Walter did her math homework and coached her for exams he'd already aced. In return, Candice would go out with him—to places where she likely wouldn't be seen by anyone she knew—and hold his hand. She loved County & Western; Walter would take her to concerts in one of Colin's limos, and she loved big thick bloody steaks, so he'd take her to the best steak houses in Tampa. Afterwards, she's always whisper sweet nothings to him. She had him hooked at once, and poor Walter was too naive to even suspect that he was being used. No, it couldn't be that! Candice loved him! She'd told him so!

Even Colin warned him: "Buddy-bro, she's a hosebag, she's a ditz. The only reason she's in college at all is because her parents told her unless she got a degree she'd lose the trust fund. She's using you to do her fuckin' class assignments."

"She is not! She loves me!" Walter exploded back, outraged at such a cynical insulation. "You're just jealous because it's not *you* she's going out with."

Colin lit a cigarette and dismissively waved a hand. "I could shit care less about that floozy air-head. She's a jock-girl, Walter. She's not into eggheads like you. She goes out with the football team—the *entire fucking football team*."

"She does not! Shut up!"

"Walter, don't be a dickhead. Don't let her pull the wool over your eyes. She's not the kind of girl to fall in love with. I mean, if you're getting it on with her, great. Be realistic and look at it that way—she's fucking you in exchange for you doing her math."

By now Walter's face nearly matched the vibrant red of his hair. "That is NOT what's going on! She's my GIRL-FRIEND! Or, at least, she will be soon. We're kind of . . . casual now, but that'll change any day." Now Walter grinned, which looked ludicrous with his beet-red face. "She said she loves me."

Colin just rolled his eyes, astounded by his brother's ineptitude. "She's duping you, Brother-bro. Girls like her do this to guys like you all the time. She knows that without you she'll flunk her math class. She's jacking you around." Colin sputtered frustrated smoke into the air. "Well, she is a brick shit-house, I can't deny that, and at least you're getting it on with her. I mean . . . right? Please don't tell me you're doing all that work for her and you're not even getting laid."

"Of *course,* I'm getting laid," Walter lied. "What do you think I am, a moron?" In truth, there'd been a few times when Candice had plowed a few too many Bud Lights and had actually taken Walter back to her dorm for some whoopie. A charity fuck; Walter *had* done a lot for her, and what was another roll in the hay, especially after the entire football, basketball, lacrosse, and soccer teams, plus the wrestling squad—all weight classes? Candice could be *very charitable* when she was drunk enough. But wouldn't you know it?

Walter couldn't get it up.

Not even at the virile age of eighteen and being straddled by the living summation of female beauty. Walter's crane would not rise. She'd of course sweetly consoled him with comforting words like, "Oh, honey, don't worry, it happens sometimes" or "You're just nervous, that's all." Stuff like that. Walter, indeed, was very nervous. This was his first time, blast it all. If there really was a God, He was having a big laugh. Walter wanted to lose his male virginity just like any male virgin wanted to, and to lose it with the girl of his dreams would've been even better. But, alas, all that he would lose on these nights was sleep.

"So," Colin chided on. "You're *not* getting laid."

"Shut up!" Walter yelled back

"You're doing all that work for her, and she's not even hauling your ashes."

"Be quiet!"

What was the use? Colin didn't understand anything about love. He had all the women he wanted, and all of them were dancers at the local strip joint. Colin was just as nerdy looking as Walter, but the only difference between them was that it had been Colin, not Walter, who'd won the hundred million dollars in the state lottery.

Meantime, his love for her grew, as did the time he spent doing her assignments and prepping her for exams. Walter, in his eighteen-year-old romantic idealism, believed that he was in a budding relationship. And those guys he kept seeing her with? The jocks, the guys in letterman jackets, the football players who looked bigger than most compact cars?

They were just friends of hers. Sure, girls had male friends. Nothing wrong with that. Just because they were opposite sexes didn't mean something was going on. Right?

Just as Walter knew that an anomalus range of 2.5 to 8 electron volts was necessary to achieve plasmotic self-ionization, he knew that Candice loved him and would one day be his wife.

But back to that conversation he'd been having with his brother. Colin said: "Hey, did you hear the one about Candice robbing a bank? She tied up the safe and blew the guard!"

"Shut up!" Walter yelled while tapping out a quick paper on small energy loss during elastic collisions of electrons in magnetic fields.

"She doesn't love you," Colin reiterated.

"I'll have you know that I have a date with her. Tonight."

Colin smiled. "Oh, so she's got another math assignment for you to do, huh?"

"No, she doesn't. The date's at her dorm, smart guy. She invited me over."

"She's got another math assignment for you to do..."

He'll eat crow when Candice and I get married. Walter couldn't wait. He looked at his watch. "See ya, Colin. I've got to be over there in ten minutes," and then Walter headed for the door. As he left, Colin was just shaking his head, assuring his inept brother, "She won't be there..."

Candice wasn't there. Walter had the girl at the dorm desk call up to Candice's room ten times. "Walter," the girl said, getting annoyed after the eighth or ninth time, "she's not there."

Walter considered every possibility. Of course, she was there—she said she'd be, she invited him over. There was no way that a girl as considerate as Candice would stand him up. *Impossible*... She took a nap and forgot to set her alarm. She had a late class. She lost track of time at the library. "Could you ring her room again, please?" Walter asked. "She was probably just taking a shower." By now the desk girl was irate: "Walter, Jesus Christ. Candice has not been taking a shower for the last TWO HOURS!"

"Please?"

"All right, look. I'll call one more time, and if she doesn't answer, you'll leave, right?"

"Okay," Walter agreed because he knew in his heart that Candice would never treat him like this. *She was just taking a long shower,* he felt convinced. *She's there.*

"Tenth ring," the girl informed. "She's not there. Now— go home!"

Walter was crushed and, as promised, he turned and left. He would've been even more crushed if he'd overheard what the desk girl said in the phone right after the door closed behind him. She said, "Thank God, he's finally gone. Tell Bucky I said hi, Candice."

Eventually, Walter's dejection transformed into more denial. *She was probably just real tired, from her classes. She'll call tomorrow and apologize. Of course she will! She loves me!* He meandered across campus, as night fell. Two jocks in letterman jackets passed without even noticing him. "You put the blocks to Candice yet?" one asked, and the other responded, after chuckling, "Couple nights ago after the finals mixer— shit. I didn't just fuck her, I stuffed her like a turkey."

"What a woman!"

"She's like a machine you can't turn off. Just fill her with beer and let 'er rip!"

Walter scowled at this rough talk, and certainly they weren't talking about Candice—not *his* Candice. Some other girl named Candice, some jock tramp. When Walter turned the corner at Campus Drive, heading back to his own dorm, he spotted red and white lights flashing stroboscopically. *Ambulance,* he quickly realized. Then he saw cops and several tow trucks. Someone in a gold Dodge Colt had run the red light at the circle. Walter peered closer, then thought, *Oh no . . .*

A pedestrian had been hit in the crosswalk, a philosophy student, no doubt. Spiral notebooks lay flapping in the street, along with copies of Sartre's *No Exit* and Soren Kierkegaard's *The Concept of Dread.* A guy with glasses and a trimmed beard lay on an ambulance gurney, his neck obviously broken. *Dead,* Walter saw. He noticed the odd tattoo on the guy's left arm: NARRATION IS MY ENEMY. *No,* Walter thought. *Reckless drivers are.* The two EMTs by his side didn't even bother with CPR. The Colt had front-ended the flag pole in the center of the circle, a campus cop handcuffing the fat, inebriated driver. "Fuckin' pedestrians, Jesus Christ, the guy just walked out in the middle of the street."

"Yeah, because he had a walk light, asshole," the cop said. "Thank God for the new drunk driving laws. Five years, no parole, on any DWI/vehicular manslaughter charge."

As the EMTs scribbled on clipboards, Walter just kept staring at the dead guy on the gurney. His eyes were crossed, tongue hanging from an agape mouth. He wore a white t-shirt that read PIL: THIS IS WHAT YOU WANT, THIS IS WHAT YOU GET.

"Fuck, the shitface is gettin' froggy with the cop," one of the EMTs observed.

Walter looked over. The fat guy who'd been driving the car only had one wrist cuffed; now he was swinging at the cop with his other hand, shouting, "All I had was a couple of beers! I ain't going to prison for five fuckin' years!" and—SMACK!—the loose cuff hit the cop right in the face.

"Kid! Hold this for me!" the EMT said and slapped the clipboard into Walter's chest. Walter took it, startled, as the two EMTs rushed the fat guy and aided the cop. The scuffle didn't last long, but Walter, for a reason he couldn't identify, couldn't focus. He wasn't watching the ruckus, he was looking at the dead man on the gurney.

The dead man was leaning up now, on one hand behind him. His other hand grasped the back of his own head by the hair, angling the broken neck. A few vertebrae crunched as he did this. The dead man was holding his head so to look right at Walter.

Walter's bladder emptied.

"Sartre was wrong," the dead man said. "Hell *isn't* other people."

"Huh?" Walter managed to respond.

Then the dead man said, "The showerhead knows more about us than we know about ourselves."

Walter gaped. "*What?*"

Then: "Hell is a place, a city. A *big* city."

Walter spun toward the EMTs, shouted, "Excuse me! This guy over here! He's not dead," but after a moment of dumbfoundedness, he stood still, blinking. When he'd shouted the words, no actual sound came out of his mouth.

"I'll see you there soon," the dead man continued. Now he grinned insanely, holding his neck straight.

"See me . . . where?" Walter stammered.

"In the city."

Walter stared down, quivering.

"Your destiny awaits," the man whispered, but now his voice sounded like sandpaper rubbing together.

"What?"

"Embrace your destiny."

The dead man's eyes crossed again, and he collapsed back onto the gurney. Walter dropped the clipboard and ran away.

He wouldn't shoot himself in the head until tomorrow.

Chapter Four

(I)

The Halman Map Library
Laurel, Maryland

Penelope's orgasm struck with the sign-in clock—at midnight. For a moment it felt like the entire building was shaking, but she knew it was just her, all her desires unlocked yet again. Gary always spent himself quickly—like in a minute or two—which in itself would've been aggravating as hell, but he never failed to fulfill the rest of the obligation mechanically, i.e., with certain devices known as "marital aids." Didn't matter that they weren't married, and, Penelope, in truth, preferred this. It got right down to business. Gary had a considerable cache of such battery-driven implements, and tonight, as Penelope lay spread-legged and flattened on the guard room desk—wearing nothing but blue socks—Gary slowly withdrew one of the "toys" he'd brought along, an eight-inch, bump-riddled vibrator molded from translucent-orange rubber which Penelope fondly referred to as "Mr. Bumpy." She gasped once, in a final blissful hitch, as the device was extracted from her thrumming privates.

"There," Gary said. "That should simmer ya down some." He hauled up his Levi's and loped shirtless to the coffee pot, looking around.

Good God, Penelope thought. *I just came like a freight train.* And at that moment she felt like she'd just been run down by one. When she tried to get up off the desk, she quit in the middle of the process, still too exhausted from the explosive release of her ecstasy.

Gary lived in a boarding house, so they could never do it at his place, and Penelope lived with her infirm mother, so her place was equally out of the question. The two of them had been dating for about a year . . . or, well, perhaps "dating" wasn't the word. A different transitive verb—one that started with an F—might be a better designation. Penelope's workplace was about the only spot they could do it, save for rare occasions when either of them might have an extra forty bucks for a night at one of the fleabag motels near the Army base. Gary was unemployed most of the time, having recently gotten out of the Army himself. He'd actually been released short of the finish of his hitch, for urinating in the battalion commander's coffee pot. The accusation was hard to refute at his court martial, when the JAG prosecutor had shown the court the actual security video of Gary smiling as he completed the act. Thirty days in the stockade and a bad conduct discharge. His only consolation was the fact that the battalion commander had drunk from that pot all day before the crime was reported. As for Penelope, the employment office had gotten her this job when her welfare ran out. She was the night-shift security guard.

Now Gary was poking around with a cup of coffee. He looked down the hall, then looked out the window into the night. "This sure is a weird place you're working at," he commented.

He'd said that before, but Penelope never knew what he meant. The small brick building at the end of Soil Conservation Road—the Halman Map Library—was a Maryland Department of the Interior facility, quite unassuming. It occupied the top of a modest hill on an isolated tract of land just off the Baltimore-Washington Parkway. Most of this land comprised a protected nature and wildlife preserve, which Penelope never understood, because there was no wildlife that she could see, and no forests, just open, rolling hills. Penelope could scarcely believe they needed security at all in such a place—who would want to steal maps?—but she needed the job.

At last, she was able to sit up on the desk, still blissfully exhausted. "What's weird?" she asked, eyeing his butt in the tight jeans. However, it wasn't necessarily his butt she was most interested in. It was the bumpy orange vibrator sticking out of the back pocket. "It's just a job, just some place the state needs security."

"A friggin' *map* library?" he questioned. "What kind'a shit is that? I never heard of a map library."

"They store maps here," she said. "For the state government. Land grids, maps of sewer lines and gas lines, stuff like that."

Gary was still perturbed. "Sounds like bullshit to me. That kind'a thing is all computerized these days. And who's gonna try to steal a bunch of maps anyway? And even if someone did, what are you gonna do? You don't even have a gun."

This was true. The company for which she worked was not licensed to arm their guards. She'd never felt threatened here, though. Nothing ever happened, but she saw his point. What if something *did*? Then she answered, "The other guards have guns."

"What other guards?"

"The one's who work downstairs, in the basement."

"But I thought your security company didn't issue gun permits."

"The guards downstairs work for a different company," Penelope explained.

"A different company? You mean a different security company?" More puzzlement tinted Gary's already skeptical face. He had a mustache and short, spiky black hair, pocks on his face from acne wars as a teenager. "This is a *state* building, right?"

Penelope nodded, still just sitting there openly naked. She didn't really want to talk about her job right now, or maps. She wanted to talk about . . . maybe a little more action with Mr. Bumpy.

"Why don't they have *state* guards?"

She simply couldn't figure his inquisitiveness. "Gary, I don't know . . ."

"And, Christ, if those guys come up here and see me, you'll get fired."

"They lock themselves downstairs for their whole shift. There's four of them, and they never come up here except for shift-change. That's not till eight a.m. I'm pretty sure all they really do down there is sleep."

Gary noticed the lockers on the side wall, and he immediately opened one.

"Gary! Stay out of there!"

"I'm just takin' a look." Shirts, a gym bag, some books. The shirts had sleeve patches that read AHRENS SECU-

RITY. He frowned hard at some of the books: *Inside the Vatican*, and *Revealing Opus Dei and Other Roman Catholic Secret Societies*. "The fuck is this?" he immediately objected. "Church books? Security guards don't read church books, they read *Hustler* and *Penthouse Forum*!"

Penelope didn't know what he was talking about. Was there anything she could do to get his mind off the other guards in the building?

"Honey?" she called. When he turned to face her, she raised her foot, sliding it up the inside of his thigh. Slowly. "I don't know what you're all uptight about." Now her foot was openly rubbing his crotch. "Let's have some more fun."

The distraction was sufficient; he didn't bother looking at the book on the bottom of the pile: *Catholic Thesis on Exorcism and Demonology*. Instead, he grinned down at her, eyes roving her bare breasts. "Want some more whoopie, huh?"

"Yeah."

He held up the vibrator. "Want some more Mr. Bumpy, huh?"

"Yeah . . ."

He leaned over and kissed her, a big, wanton, sloppy kiss, all the while his hand straying over her breasts. The sensation left a tingly after-trail across her skin which immediately hardened her nipples. In another moment, there was a soft humming sound: the vibrator was on, and then he brought it gently up the cleft of her sex. Penelope moaned. *Jesus, they ought to give the Nobel Prize to whoever invented vibrators.* Just one touch relit all her nerves at once; she was sizzling on the desk top. Gary was kissing her neck as he whispered, "Yeah, I know what you want, baby, and I'll give it to you . . ." Then he roughly turned her aside so that her legs were hanging off the edge of the desk. He knelt on the floor, easing the vibrator inside her while simultaneously licking around her sex. Penelope was cringing. *God, I love it when he does that,* she thought between pulses of pleasure. Soon his efforts became more intent, more precise.

He looked up from between her tensing legs and whispered, "Yeah, I'll give ya what you want, so how about you givin' me what I want?"

Penelope's tongue was nearly hanging out of her mouth when she panted, "I'll do anything you want . . ." And she would, no matter how crude or debauched. Anything. Anything for more Mr. Bumpy. "Just tell me. Tell me what you want . . ."

"I want you to show me the basement, where they keep these maps you were talking about."

What the— She was aghast. "Gary, I can't do that!"

"What's the big deal?" He eased Mr. Bumpy out an inch. "You just got done sayin' you'd do anything I wanted."

"I don't have access to the storage lock-up," she almost whined but she wanted to yell at him: *Don't stop! Put it back in!* "I only have one punch station in the basement, in the power room. Everything else downstairs, the other guards worry about."

"Why?" Out another inch. "That don't make sense."

"Gary, I don't know why. I don't *care!* Those are my instructions! I couldn't take you to the storage area even if I wanted to, 'cos I don't have a key to the gate. It's locked from their side."

"What gate?"

Now she wished she *had* a gun, so she could point it at him and say *Shut up and get back to business!* "There's a security gate downstairs just past the power room, like a chain-link thing. That's where my jurisdiction ends."

"Then show me that."

"No! It's too risky!"

Gary shrugged, pulled the vibrator all the way out, and stood up. "Guess I'll be headin' home now. But don't worry, I'll leave Mr. Bumpy. You can party with him by yourself."

No no no! her thoughts screamed. She could use a vibrator on herself all night long but unless Gary's tongue came along with it, it wasn't the same. *Don't you fuckin' walk out on me, you prick! Don't you leave me like this!* But evidently he was prepared to do that. He had the vibrator on low now, and he stood right next to her, running the humming orange tip from her bellybutton to her right breast. He ran it slowly around the bottom of the breast, then up to delicately encircle the nipple. His other hand caressed her pubis. Penelope was cringing.

"Come on, honey. Just take me down there."

She could barely concentrate now on what she was saying as the divine sensations coursed through her. Her heart raced. "Why, Gary? What do you care about a bunch of maps?"

Now the vibrator's tip trailed back down, to her clitoris. "I'm just curious. It sounds like bullshit to me. I don't think there *are* any maps down there. I think this place is a front."

A front? "What are you talking about?"

"I just wanna see for myself is all, gotta see if I'm right." The fingers of one hand teased her nipples, while Mr. Bumpy slowly slid back and forth over the groove of her sex. Penelope was panting, practically cross-eyed now in her need.

"Just take me down there, just for five minutes. Then we'll come back here and I'll light ya up like a pinball machine," he whispered. "Oh, and look what else I brought—your favorites." From another pocket, he dangled something else, like dual pendulums right before her eyes. "The electric ben-wa balls."

That was it for Penelope—the summation of all her ecstasy right there in his hands. "All right, goddamn it!" She hopped off the desk, hauled her uniform and boots back on. "Come on!"

"That's my girl," Gary chuckled.

He followed her out as she grabbed her punch clock. The main hall was dark, sterile. Out the front window, Gary spied a great white full moon. But Penelope's aggravation still percolated. "This is a big pain in the ass, Gary. I don't know why you're making me do it."

"You know me, once my curiosity gets rollin', it won't let go."

"Shit, one of the other guards could see us. Then I'll be in big trouble."

"They ain't gonna see us."

She pressed the DOWN button on the elevator at the end of the dark hall. The doors hummed—which only reminded her of the vibrator—and then yawned open. "And I don't know what the hell you're talking about—this place being some kind of *front.*"

"You gotta admit, this whole thing is pretty damn fishy."

"No it's *not.* Jesus. It's just a damn map library."

"Yeah, a map library, something I ain't never heard of—and instead of having state security guards like any other friggin' state facility, they've got not one but two different private guard companies working here, and never mind that it's a place that doesn't need guards to begin with. Libraries and shit like that have alarm systems. And that other outfit? Ahrens Security? I ain't never heard of them."

"So what!"

"When I got my walking papers from Uncle Fuckin' Sam, I applied to every single security company in the phone book, and guess which one wasn't listed?"

The clash of her desires and frustration was infuriating Penelope. He was being ridiculous—like all men. "So what are you saying? That it's a fake company? Is *that* what you're saying?"

"I'm saying this joint is a front. I was a SECMAT MP in the Army for over three years. Whenever we'd have to transport sensitive material, or guard something off-post, we'd wear fake civilian security uniforms so no one would know it was military stuff we were guarding."

That took some spark out of Penelope. She looked oddly over at him. "Really?"

"Really. And I think the same thing's going in this place. We got four different Army security installations in a ten-mile radius. Fort Meade, Aberdeen, Edgewood Arsenal, and Fort Detrick."

Penelope maintained the odd look. "Really?"

"Yeah."

"So you think—"

"They could be storing anything down here, stuff they don't want to keep on a known military base. Documents, classified databanks, stuff like that. Or worse, material they want to keep away from government or foreign inspectors."

"What . . . materials?"

Gary splayed his hand. "Stuff we agreed to get rid of by treaty. VX gas, biological weapons formulas, ABM blueprints, neutron bombs. Stuff like that."

Stuff, Penelope thought and gulped, *like that.* Was that really what was going on here? Was she unknowingly guarding some secret military vault full of nerve gas cannisters?

"Just 'cos we signed a treaty saying we'd destroy all our neutron bomb warheads doesn't mean we really did it. That's just an example. Could be anything, but I'll bet my next paycheck—if I ever *get* a next paycheck—that one thing they *ain't* guarding here is a bunch of maps."

The elevator stopped; the door sprung open, showing

74

them another dark hall. But Penelope was really thinking now. All of a sudden, everything Gary was saying made a lot of sense.

"Don't say anything," she whispered. "Stay here till I wave you in."

Gary remained in the elevator, keeping the doors open with his hand. Penelope walked normally to a door several yards down, unlocked it, then looked quickly behind her. Gary couldn't see what she was looking at, but he guessed it was another hall that branched off from this one.

Penelope waved him over. He slipped out of the elevator and strode quickly into the room she'd unlocked. In the door was a long narrow chicken-wire window, over which a sign read CIRCUIT BREAKERS. Penelope hurriedly closed the door and turned on a single desk lamp. In another corner a silver key hung from a chain. Penelope turned the key in her punch clock, which logged the time of her round on a tape inside.

Gary looked around. There was the desk, a radio, a little refrigerator, mops and buckets. Several posters adorned the walls: the Redskinettes doing splits, last year's Playmate of the Year, and Jennifer Lopez embellished by computer-generated nudity. Penelope turned Gary away. "You don't need to be looking at that."

"Uh . . . oh . . ."

"The janitor uses this for his break room but he's off-duty at five p.m."

A single dented file cabinet sat in the other corner, next to multiple fuse panels and power switches. Gary went immediately to the cabinet and began to root through the drawers.

Penelope just shook her head. She remained flushed and sweaty from his teasing upstairs, and frustrated. But her confusion was distracting her desires, which she was brimming with now. "Gary, come on, let's go back upstairs," she urged, coming up behind him, sliding her hands about his waist. Then her hands slipped lower. *He's definitely interested,* she thought, feeling the evidence. "I showed you downstairs, now let's go."

"In a minute," he grumbled, rummaging through more files.

She could easily see Mr. Bumpy sticking out of his back pocket, and the shape of the ben-wa balls in the other pocket. Her lust was making her dizzy. In truth, she didn't really care that much about him, only what he could do for her with his toys. It made her feel selfish and greedy, but she didn't particularly care about that either. He started all of this, so he would damn well finish.

"Look at this," he said. He'd pulled out a sheet of paper, which she looked at but didn't really see. She was still kneading his crotch with her hand, trying to divert him.

"What is it?"

"It's a property tax assessment waiver. They don't have to pay any property tax for the land this place sits on."

Penelope didn't care, coming to the simplest conclusion. "Of course they don't. The state doesn't make *itself* pay land tax. State of Maryland *owns* this land."

"No, they sure as shit don't," he said, indicating the sheet of paper. "This right here says that the Halman Map Library sits on one and a half acres of land that are owned by the Catholic Diocese of Washington, D.C."

The Catholic— "Huh?" Penelope said. Then she inspected the paper more thoroughly and saw that it was true.

"Things just keep gettin' fishier and fishier," Gary said. He closed the file cabinet and turned to the door. Now he was looking out the chicken-wire window down the hall. He could see the chain-link gate. "What's behind that?" he asked.

"The storage area, and the other guard room, where the Ahrens guards work—I told you," she whined more frustration. "I'm not authorized to go past the gate, and even if I was, I couldn't because I don't have a key to the padlock on it."

"I'm checkin' it out—"

"Gary, are you dense? It's *locked*."

"Quit yackin' and open your eyes."

Penelope frowned, squinting through the little window. She didn't frown long. The padlock on the gate was unlocked.

"That's some top-notch bunch'a guards they got down here, huh?"

"They must've forgotten to relock the gate when their shift started."

"Come on—"

"Gary, *no!* They could come out any minute!"

"Yeah, and if they do all you gotta say is 'Hey, fellas, I'm just showin' my boyfriend around, oh, and by the way, you left your gate unlocked but don't worry, I won't tell the boss.' That's what you say if any of 'em come out." Gary could not be dissuaded; he was opening the door and walking out. Penelope fumed but at this point all she could do was go along with it.

He quietly opened the gate. They both stepped through. At the furthest end of the hall stood a door that read MAP ROOM. Next to it was a door that read GUARD ROOM. Beside Gary and Penelope stood another windowed door that read BOILER ROOM. She and Gary slipped into it.

"Boiler room, huh?" he said now as the next weirdness of the night presented itself. Penelope looked around in dismay. There were no boilers in evidence.

But there was a gun locker.

Four black rifles stood in the steel rack, secured by a

chain threaded through their trigger guards. On the floor, also chained and locked, were ten olive-drab metal boxes, which each read in stenciled letters: 200 CARTRIDGES, MSC LOT 1-M62-4, 5.56MM.

More sarcasm from Gary: "Yeah, I'd say that Ahrens is definitely an armed guard company. Four top of the line automatic assault rifles and two thousand rounds of ammo. You know, to guard against all the folks who wanna bust in here to steal *maps*."

This *was* weird. Now Penelope's raging lust was sufficiently diverted. She'd seen the other guards with sidearms a few times, but what could explain the need for automatic weapons down here? In a *map* library?

"Like I was sayin' before, same as when I was in the Army," Gary went on. "Fake door signs, fake civvie security guards. They want people to think this is a map library so no one'll bother breaking in. It's cover, it's a front. There ain't no maps down here. It's gotta be something military."

"So they're really Army MPs posing as civilian security guards?" Penelope asked.

"Not Army, not with weapons like that," he said, pointing to the gun rack. "Those are SA-80s. If these guards were U.S. Army they'd have M-16s. Only people I know of who use SA-80s as general issue are the Brits and the Swiss Guards, and—" Gary stalled, his eyes widening. On the black polycarbonate stock of one of the rifles, he noticed tiny letters: PROPERTY OF 2/37th COMPANY VICTOR, SWISS GUARDS.

"These guys *are* Swiss guards, and that's about the most fucked-up thing I ever heard."

"Gary, who are the Swiss Guards?" Penelope nearly shouted over the mounting confusion.

"It's a special military detachment of the Vatican."

"And we just found out that the library sits on land owned by—"

"The Catholic church," Gary finished.

Yeah, Penelope finally agreed. But what really *was* going on down here? What was really being kept in this place?

Penelope would never discern an answer, but that was scarcely the point. The room began to vibrate, then the cement walls began to crack. Suddenly the floor was shaking so violently, Penelope could barely stand. Ceiling tiles fell on them as Gary shouted, "Earthquake! Get out!"

They stumbled frantically back out into the main hall, then were retching when they found it full of the most evil-smelling smoke. The smoke seemed green in the overheard emergency lights, and though she wasn't sure, Penelope thought she saw figures in the smoke. Squat figures, like things huddled down. Then she heard shouts, small-arms fire, and a long steady noise that could only be described as cackling.

"The elevator won't work!" Gary shouted, holding her hand. "Where's the stairs?"

Penelope turned, yanked him toward the direction she believed the stairs to be in, then—

SWACK!

She'd run right into a wall, face-first, then fell back flat on her back. Gary groped through smoke to help her up. All Penelope knew was that the wall she'd run into... hadn't been there earlier. It seemed to angle out of the main corridor, leaning forward, and after she regained her senses, she looked at it, ran her hand against it. It seemed composed of chunky cement, only the cement was discolored and—

"What is—" she began.

"What the fuck is this?" Gary shouted, the foul smoke gusting from his mouth. He'd noticed it too. "This wall wasn't here five minutes ago!"

"It must be some kind of fire wall," Penelope could only guess.

Gary winced. "This ain't no fire wall. It's cement, and it's got..." He stalled again, touching the rough surface. By now, Penelope could see it too. Mixed into the "cement" were chunks of bones—joints, ribs, fingertips, all human. Lots of teeth too, some glittery with gold and silver fillings. She looked farther down the wall, then, and screamed.

"Holy *shit!*" Gary yelled.

A man's head and shoulders hung out of the strange wall, as if he'd been fused into it. He convulsed, still alive, his face twisted in agony. He seemed to be muttering something in Latin or Italian. Then he screamed himself and began to vomit up blood. There was nothing they could do to help him. The last thing Penelope noticed, though, was the shirt he wore, a blue tunic with epaulets, and an embroidered patch that read AHRENS SECURITY.

More cackling issued from the thickening smoke, along with more gunshots. She could see brief white muzzle-flashes in the distance, and some of the squat shapes she'd seen seemed to fall down after the shots. She caught glimpses of larger figures too, but could they possibly be human? Humans, with bloodred eyes the size of tennis balls. Humans with fangs like broken glass? With horns sprouting from their heads?

Two of the Ahrens guards ran out of the boiler room, each wielding a locked and loaded rifle. More *things* seemed to be encroaching down the hall, and when the guards determinedly opened fire, the things seemed to mewl. Misshapen heads flew to pieces, clawed hands flew up, plumes of blood sprayed this way and that, only the blood wasn't red. Some was black. Some was pea-green. The sound of the machine-gun fire deafened Penelope to the point that she couldn't even hear her own screams. She shrieked harder and grabbed on to Gary when something the size of an eagle whizzed by just over her head. The smoke churned in the creature's wake; when it flew over one of the Ahrens guards, the thing's claws lowered, and took off the guard's head. Penelope only had a split-second to look more closely. It was no eagle—not that an eagle could even find its way down here. It was something more like an immense bat.

The second guard smacked another mag into his rifle and resumed firing. Hot brass flew out of the bolt in a steady stream. Gary pulled Penelope aside but not before she saw who or what the guard was firing at: a tall perfectly still figure in a white cloak and drooping hood. This would be one of the higher echelon Warlocks from the College of Spells and Discantations, not that Penelope could ever be aware of that. The bullets that spewed toward the white figure seemed to slow down and dissolve in mid-air. Two other similar figures—but these cloaked in black—were burning the first guard's severed head over an ornate agate bowl full of red-hot coals. They watched intently, examining the shapes of the smoke that eddied from the dead guard's eye sockets and open mouth. These two figures were Hierarchs in Lucifer's Synod of Smoke-Diviners.

Gary was nearly paralyzed now by all he'd seen. "We-we-we . . . gotta get out'a here," was all he could stammer.

Some trick of reason alighted in Penelope. "This way! The door to the exit stairs is this way."

As she led him away, strange things seemed to crunch beneath Penelope's shoes . . . and she didn't want to know what they were. The smoke cleared a bit further down the hall; she thought she saw a rat scurry by, only this rat was the size of a house cat, and its pink feet looked too much like the hands of a human infant. The thing squealed when Gary kicked it out of the way.

"The door!" she yelled. "I don't see the door!"

"We'll find it." Gary was determined. He was feeling along the wall, then shouted, "Over here! I found it!"

Penelope looked over at him, and gasped. He had his hand on the wrought-iron latch of a heavy wooden door set into an arched doorframe made from bloodstained granite bricks. The keystone on the transom was an oblong skull with horns branching from the forehead long and sharp as a bull's.

"Come on!" Gary yelled, waving her over.

Penelope shuddered. "Gary, that's not. The door. To the stairs."

But he didn't hear her; he'd already opened the door, was preparing to go in.

He didn't go in. Instead, something came out.

A Tentaculus was a more recent hybridization from the Academy of Teratology, a lower-grade segmented demon also known as a *Mephistius Annelida*. It stood upright on two thin legs, sported two equally thin arms and an elongated abdomen, all the color and enslimed texture of an earthworm, only it stood six feet tall. Instead of a head on its shoulders, though, it bore an additional three-foot trunk. The end of the trunk was a mouth rimmed by hooklike teeth, and it was this mouth that immediately attached itself to Gary's mouth. Unable to scream, he shuddered in place as the trunk expeditiously sucked all of his internal organs out, then transferred them into its own gut. Penelope watched in revulsion; the thing's own abdomen suddenly swelled with its new, fresh meal. Gary collapsed, significantly lighter than he had been moments before. The Tentaculus burped, then the door slammed shut.

Penelope ran, screams wheeling behind her. She didn't really know where she might be running; it was simply that running seemed the only logical reaction. Even through the stinking smoke, she could see that the basement had changed, and she suspected that the entire building had, as if parts of it had merged with something else, something evil. Behind her, the machine-gun fire ceased, replaced by more screams. Penelope instinctively took a final glance behind her, saw that the remaining guard was being mauled by misshapen Trolls. She didn't hang around to watch his death in detail, but she did notice something else. The imposing white-cloaked figure was advancing down the hall while another taller figure appeared behind him: a man, the most handsome man she'd ever seen in her life. Lean, muscular but graceful, this man seemed to drift forward, a mist of light—a halo—encircling his head. More light flowed from his piercing eyes. He was fully naked, and for the briefest moment he glanced at Penelope through the smoke and smiled—the most stunning smile she could ever imagine.

"Hello, Penelope," he said to her, but his voice was more like light than sound.

Penelope stared, riveted.

"My name is Zeihl."

Penelope couldn't take her eyes off the magnificent man.

"Tonight you will see something that has never before occurred in history," the light-voice shone on. "Tonight you will witness the death of an Immortal. To my master, I sacrifice myself for his glory. Consider yourself privileged . . ."

More of the smoke cleared, revealing large, heavily shelled insects scurrying about on the floor but they were like no insects she'd ever seen on earth. The library's main storage room had been ruptured open, revealing something within that looked like a bank vault. The huge, multi-bolted steel door had been melted down by an expertly incantated Heat Spell. A high-tech vault like that in a place like this?

Penelope knew now beyond all doubt that Gary had been correct. This whole place *was* a front. They didn't need a vault like that to store *maps* in. So what *were* they really storing here?

Penelope would never know. Fear and partial insanity compelled her to run. She disappeared into another gust of smoke which stank worse than the putrefactive gas of a mass grave. But perhaps luck was on her side now: she collided with a door, and when she looked up bloody-nosed, she noticed the sign that would save her life. EXIT STAIRS. *Thank God!* She yanked open the door and shot up the steps.

Then screamed.

A green-faced demon-boy sat on the first landing; he grinned down at her through decayed fangs, quivering as he inserted a long hypodermic needle into a nostril. He was a Zap addict, Hell's version of a junkie. Once he'd worked the needle up into his brain, he depressed the plunger, sighed, and collapsed in bliss. Zap was the drug of choice in the Mephistopolis, an occult heroin made from infernal herbs boiled in Grand Duke urine, after which it was cooked down to paste at the Distillation Vats.

Her gut clenching, Penelope stepped over the boy, was about to dash up the rest of the steps, but screamed at the top of her lungs when she saw what was coming down the stairwell. The Fecaman was aptly named; it was a man-shaped creature composed of bewitched demonic waste. Two lidless eyes were set in the mush-brown face; two shit hands groped forward. Clumsy as it appeared, it grabbed her with surprising spryness, embracing her at once and pulling its face of excrement to hers. "Kiss-kiss," it gurgled at her, "Kiss-kiss..." She didn't have time to throw up before the thing's hole for a mouth opened over hers. Convulsing, she seamed her lips but that didn't matter. The tongue—a tumid turd—worked its way into her mouth, wriggling. Penelope gagged, almost mindless in her revulsion. The basest instinct caused her to clack her teeth shut, severing the fecal tongue, whereupon she spat it out and bellowed another scream. The Fecaman screamed along with her, bug-eyed, and she skirted around the abomination, and flew the rest of the way up the steps.

Upstairs, she fell into the lobby. There was much less smoke up here, and she could see more evidence of the impossible change that had occurred, the lobby's familiar appearance mutated into something else. Strange walls seemed blended with the lobby's normal walls. Segments of the polished tile floor had been overrun by something that almost looked like a street gutter, only the gutter was befouled with body parts and nameless waste. She even noticed a storm drain in this otherworldly gutter; sulphurous flames licked out between the grates, and . . . did she see a face down there, agonized and peering out? Heart racing, she turned toward the front glass doors, but they were all blown out. She dashed through them, out into the night, expecting to see the library's parking lot, and the long grassy hill which extended down from it, but that's not quite what she saw. She saw the parking lot, all right, and her little GMC Metro parked in her usual spot, but the parking lot was *upheaved*, as if some seismic plate had thrust up through the asphalt. Other things had thrust up, too—impossible things: huge brick and iron buildings, oddly windowed skyscrapers that spired so high she couldn't see their end. Living gargoyles traversed the overhead ledges, looking down. A city street surrounded the library, but it was a street from another world. She even saw a street sign leaning over at one corner. The sign read DAHMER BLVD.

Her feet carried her mindlessly down the street. She saw her manic reflection in the various shop windows as she ran. MEATS one window read. SPECIALS TODAY: GHOUL, TROLL. The word HUMAN was also there but it had an X through it. Fried demon heads hung upside-down from hooks in the window. Inside, a man with one half of his face sliced off calmly cranked a sausage grinder, his butcher's apron soiled by off-colored blood. The next window read RAPE CLINIC, which Penelope assumed was some sort of crisis center; the assumption only lasted for a moment after she looked in and spied demons in nice suits standing in line as a chained She-Imp was raped *en masse* on the floor by an array of slavering, hunch-backed creatures. More signs could be seen along the smoking block, the windows lit with the strangest lights: HEX-CLONES, LICENSED ALOMANCER SERVICES, BLOOD AL-CHEMIST. The last window on the corner read SKIN-CUTTERS but Penelope didn't look in.

She still didn't know where she was running to but she ran just the same. Her mind didn't ever bother trying to calculate what had squashed this evil place into the same space that the map library occupied. Yet the question kept occurring to her: *Where does it end?* When she turned the next corner, her answer awaited.

Another smoking city street stretched forward but only for half a block. Then it ended very abruptly. Past its limits she could see the quiet moonlit hill that descended away from the library. She was about to run out but—

"Help me," a voice beseeched her. "Please . . ."

Fuck that, Penelope decided. The only person she was going to help right now was herself—by getting out of this hellish place. But there was something about the voice. It was a woman's, and it—

She looked into the narrow alley from which the plea had issued. A heavy-metal poster flapped on the brick wall: THE BURNING BABIES, ONE SHOW ONLY! LIVE

AT THE BLOOD-SUCKERS BALLROOM. Across from it, someone had scrawled in chalk: GOD, PLEASE TAKE ME BACK, then someone else had written: DON'T HOLD YOUR BREATH!

The alley, like everything else, stank. Even in her horror, Penelope felt compelled to stop.

Was there something familiar about the voice?

"Help me," the voice repeated. "I was raped and beaten by a Grand Duke."

Penelope took one step into the alley. Yes, the voice *was* familiar. A naked woman sat huddled in the corner, reaching out.

"Who are you?" Penelope asked, voice quavering. "Are you one of the other guards?"

A giggle—a *familiar* giggle—and then the woman lurched up and grabbed Penelope, and all at once she realized just how familiar the voice really was.

It was her own voice that had been speaking to her.

And Penelope was now being attacked . . . by herself.

The naked woman that looked exactly like Penelope grinned. Well, she didn't look *exactly* like Penelope, because Penelope didn't have fangs, nor were the whites of Penelope's eyes bright crimson with white irises. Penelope didn't have four joints per finger, either, and she didn't have talons in place of fingernails. There was one other thing Penelope didn't have that this evil replica did: a penis.

Penelope screamed as she was dragged down. Perfect facsimiles of her own breasts swayed before her dread-distorted face, and her imposter's penis— more demonic than human in that it was gray as birch bark, with the same texture, and had an inverted glans, more like a plunger-head than a dome—throbbed against her stomach as she was molested. "I'm gonna stick it in hard, sweetie," the clone assured her in her own voice. "Say hello to *my* Mr. Bumpy."

The clone's hips shimmied between Penelope's legs. Penelope just kicked and screamed some more—useless reactions. Then hook-nailed hands began to pull at her pants . . .

SLLLLLLLLLLLLLLLLLL-UCK!

Penelope had closed her eyes against the horror but opened them again when her attacker seemed to fall limp. Another Tentaculus was leaning over the scene on its long, wormlike legs, having forced the end of its trunk into the clone's mouth. Penelope was able to crawl away as the creature's digestive process began to suck, the extended trunk pulsating. It made Penelope think of a vacuum-cleaner hose, only this vacuum wasn't sucking up dust, it was sucking out her macabre replica's internal organs, or so Penelope would've thought until the creature stalled, then retracted its trunk. The sound it made—clearly a sound of objection—pierced her ears like the whine of a dentist's drill. What Penelope couldn't have understood was that the Hex-Clone of herself didn't possess internal organs, just rotten reanimated goulash and vexed blood—not the meal that the Tentaculus expected. The creature jerked back, raised its trunk as an elephant would, and quickly expelled everything it had just ingested, spewing it all out in a shower of grue.

Penelope resumed her terror-tear down the alley. The sight of the moon—her moon, not a moon from another world—beckoned her. Finally she was there, and nearly collapsed when she took in her first breath of clean night air. She could hear crickets chirping, could see the plush, green grass sloping down the hill that the map library had been built on. All there was left to do now was keep running, just keep running away and get as far away from this place, or this nightmare, as possible.

"Adieu, Penelope," a voice reverberated in her ears, that

voice she'd heard from the man in the basement—the voice that was more like light. "Relish your life while you have it, because you've just borne witness to the home of your hereafter . . ."

Penelope stopped and turned. She couldn't help it.

She looked back into the alley.

It was the man, the magnificent man named Zeihl, standing at the front steps of the Halman Map Library amid all of the evil buildings that seemed to have grown around it. Zeihl's halo coruscated, and so did his quiet smile. Then came the sound:

Sssssssssssssssss-ONK!

It popped in the air. Penelope felt her ears pop too, like an airplane descending, and next came a flash of throbbing green light. The flash seemed to grow into a stagnant, shuddering blob a few yards from the library's front doors. The blob grew, painting everything on the infernal street an eerie luminescent green.

What—what IS that? Penelope wondered.

The Warlock in the white cloak and hood drifted out of the library, with something like a small suitcase under his arm. And the green blob, by now, had throbbed and shivered like living neon until it had changed into a shape that resembled an open aperture, a rimmed hole in the air but a hole made of the green light. A hole, yes, or a doorway . . .

The white-garbed figure drifted past Zeihl without a word or a gesture . . . and then stepped into that doorway.

The doorway began to shrink.

Zeihl cast Penelope a final smile. He knelt down and kissed the ground, and as he did so, Penelope noticed the charred arrangement of bones that seemed folded up into the middle of his back.

Wings, Penelope realized.

"Run, Penelope," the voice shined. "You will see this

place again, but this is the last time you'll see me . . ."

The earth began to tremble. All the strange buildings and spiring black skyscrapers around the library began to fade, and the bizarre green doorway vanished.

Zeihl stood back up.

Now, in his hand, he held a knife with a long curved silver blade and he looked up with that beautiful smile, closed his eyes, and slit his own throat.

The blood that flowed from the wound glowed bright as magma. Penelope was helpless to do anything but look on.

The Fallen Angel had told her to relish her life, but what he hadn't told her was that her life would end a second later—

—when Zeihl's body exploded into a mushroom cloud of blinding white light that vaulted a hundred feet into the air, incinerating everything in a quarter-mile radius.

Including Penelope.

Chapter Five

(I)

Cassie slept fitfully, sweating through nightmares of the Mephistopolis, of Dentata-Peds and Tentaculi, of Nectoports and City Mutilation Squads. She dreamed of taking the train from Tiberius Depot into Pogrom Park where destitute amputee demons bummed change and outdoor fountains gushed blood. She dreamed of the immense J.P. Kennedy Ghettoblocks—a slum district the size of the entire state of Texas. She dreamed of the Mephisto Building—666 floors high—and the one time she'd actually seen Lucifer looking out of one of its narrow windows.

At least her nightmares had changed. In the past, she'd always been tormented by nightmares of her sister's suicide. Now she was merely tormented by nightmares of Hell.

But she'd had one more dream, too, hadn't she?

Angelese, she recalled, sitting up now in the ward bed.

She rubbed sleep from her eyes and chuckled to herself. *The girl with snow-white hair.* An angel. But why would Cassie dream of something so strange? And had it really been a dream? *I'm from an Order of the Seraphim,* the image in the water had told her, *a very special order. Those from my order willingly descend from the Rapture.*

With all that had happened to her over the last year, Cassie had long-since stopped fretting over which impressions in her life were real and which were dreams. She couldn't trust her senses anymore. Since learning she was an Etheress? Since visiting Hell? She wished it could all be a dream but she knew it wasn't.

She wished she really was insane—as the people in this clinic thought. At least then she wouldn't have to worry about anything.

I should have asked her, though, she thought now, *dream or not. I should have asked Angelese why any angel would willingly leave heaven.*

"Because it's our job," a voice replied from no particular place in the room. "It's our duty."

Cassie rubbed her face. *Here we go again.* "Your duty to what?"

"Our duty to God. We're his spies." A chuckle. "We're, like, his commandos."

Cassie got up off the bed. She generally only slept in bra and panties, and she immodestly slipped them off and put them in the small laundry hamper they'd given her.

"Nice tattoo," the voice said.

Cassie frowned at the inanity of the situation. *A disembodied voice just told me I have a nice tattoo.* She looked down at it, as if she even doubted the tattoo's existence. It was a tiny half-rainbow that encircled her navel. She'd gotten it at a Goth parlor in D.C. with Lissa; they'd agreed to both get tattoos the same day.

"My sister has one too," Cassie responded. "It's—

"A garland of barbed wire around her navel," Angelese answered. "You should see *my* tattoos."

"Oh, angels have tattoos?"

"Sure, but mine are special. They're devotional."

Cassie smirked. Angelese never seemed to speak in anything but puzzles. "How did you know that my sister has a barbed wire tattoo around her navel?" she asked next.

"I've seen her a few times."

The comment locked Cassie in place, unmindful of her nakedness. "You've *seen* my sister?"

"Um-hmm."

"Where is she?"

"You know where she is. She's in the Mephistopolis."

Cassie was trembling. "Yes, but *where* in the Mephistopolis?"

"I'm not sure right now."

"But you just said you saw her!"

"I saw her a few times, but I don't know exactly where she was. We're waiting for more intelligence reports about her. I trance-channel into Hell all the time, all the Caliginauts do."

"What? You trance—"

"Think of it as an out-of-body experience, that sort of thing. Some humans can do it, and the same goes for angels. That's one of the first things they teach us how to do when we're inducted into the Order. We channel our spirits out of our physical bodies, can go anywhere, including Hell."

"Why?" Cassie demanded. "Why would angels go to Hell?"

"Scouting missions," she was simply answered.

Cassie pulled on her robe, knowing that someone would be by soon to escort her to the showers. Now she was intrigued in spite of her aggravation. "Your *spirit* has been to Hell?"

"My soul, yes."

"But not your body?"

"No."

"Why not? Why doesn't God just send all his angels down there and depose Lucifer?"

"I can't tell you."

Cassie looked around the room, trying to decide where the voice had come from. *This is probably all bullshit. There's probably a little speaker hidden in the room, and some prick's having a real laugh right now.*

But if that were the case, what had she seen last night? If someone was trying to trick her, or make her think she was insane, how could they have made her see the reflection last night in the water in her hands?

"You know I'm not a dream, Cassie, and you know I'm not a trick," Angelese's faceless voice said next. "You know that, right? You know that you really are an Etheress, right?"

"Yes," Cassie finally had to admit.

"Good, 'cos if you didn't know that, then we'd have a long road ahead of us, and there isn't time."

"Time for what—" Cassie shook her head in an abrupt frustration. "Look, this is really freaking me out. It just bugs me."

"What?"

"What? Talking to a disembodied voice, that's what. Maybe I'm weird but when I'm talking to someone, I'm kind of used to seeing that person's *face* along with the conversation. Can we do that thing we did last night? What did you call it?"

"A Transference Charm," Angelese reminded her. "Let's just wait a minute and we'll be able to do a better one."

"Where?"

"In the shower. He's coming now."

More frustration. "How do you know—"

Three solid raps sounded on the door. "Hey, Cassie, it's me, R.J. Lemme know when it's okay to come in."

Cassie's brow creased; she sashed her robe. "You can come in now."

The lock rattled as the door was unlocked. R.J. entered, smiling, his Notre Dame hat pushed up on his head. "Time for the good ole Personal Hygiene block."

"Yeah, I know, and then Sustenance Block, right?" Cassie asked a bit sarcastically. "Why can't you psych guys just call it breakfast?"

"Because Sustenance Block sounds much more therapeutic on the billing invoices."

Cassie followed him out, her flip-flops flopping. One of her dead father's life-insurance policies covered the bills here, overseen by his executors—a bunch of attorneys back in D.C.

"How are you feeling?" R.J. asked. He was tall, broad shouldered, and his shadow seemed massive as she walked behind him.

"How do I feel?" Cassie replied. More sarcasm was in order. "Like a perfectly sane girl being kept against her will in a private psychiatric clinic only because the bills are paid on time."

"That's the spirit," R.J. chuckled. "Did you get a good night's sleep?"

"No."

"More nightmares?"

"Yeah."

"Of your sister's suicide?"

"Nope."

The amiable psych tech looked over his shoulder. "You know, I am a qualified psychologist."

"Really? Not just a Notre Dame fan?"

"I'm a Cincinnati Reds fan too. But you should still want your father's executors to get their money's worth. I might be able to help you interpret your nightmares. Then you can reflect on those interpretations. It's called psychotherapy."

"You really want to know what my nightmares were about?"

"Sure."

"I dreamed of the time I took the sulphur-powered train from the Outer Sector at Tiberius Station to Pogrom Park. It's near the Riverwalk section of the Mephistopolis. On the train, I saw a girl give birth to a mongrel baby that had fangs and horns coming out of its head. When its head was all the way out, it looked at me and barked, like a dog. I ran back to my cabin when the baby came all the way out and started nursing."

"And you believe that," R.J. said, not asked.

"Yep. I was there. I saw it. There's nothing to disbelieve."

"You know, Cassie, I *believe* that you believe that."

Cassie just nodded with the same derision she'd known since they'd brought her here. "Yeah, I know, Dr. Freud. You believe that I believe the delusion."

R.J. stopped and turned, touched her arm to elicit her attention. "It's not quite that at all, is it? Your case is much more complex."

"Because I'm passing all your damn polygraphs, right?"

"That's part of it but I'm sure there's a lot more. We're going to find out. We really do want to help you, you know." Then he smiled again. "Oh, and I'm not a Freudian. Freud was an erotopathic coke-head who was totally full of shit."

Cassie laughed. *Thank God somebody in this joint's got a sense of humor.* She passed a couple of closed doors with stenciled letters on chicken-wire windows. NARCO-ANALYSIS, one read. OCCUPATIONAL THERAPY, DISPENSARY, SLEEP-DISORDER LAB, read some others. A last one read ECT. She saw Dr. Morse sitting at a desk beyond the glass.

"Hey, R.J.? What's ECT?"

"Electro-Convulsant Therapy."

"You mean shock treatment?"

"Um-hmm. It's not like in the movies, Cassie. It's painless, and it's still very useful in treating serious depression." He looked back at her again. "But you're not depressed, so you don't have to worry about it, right?"

"You say so. So what *is* my diagnosis, doc?"

"Clinically?"

"Yeah."

"You're messed up in the head, that's all. Everybody is."

Another laugh. Cassie liked R.J. Dr. Morse was another story. She couldn't say that she *dis*liked him, but he was definitely a stick in the mud. Aside from those two, though, she really hadn't met anyone else. The med nurse, the "chaperon," the janitor. They were just bodies here doing a job.

"R.J.'s got the hots for you," Angelese's voice suddenly resumed.

"He does not," Cassie blurted.

R.J. turned back around, a cocked brow. "*Who* does not?"

Shit! Cassie thought.

"Be careful," Angelese recommended. "*You* can hear me, *he* can't."

I wonder why, Cassie thought.

"Because you're an Etheress," Angelese reminded.

"Oh, yeah," then Cassie bit her lip again. When R.J.

looked back this time, Cassie just said, "Don't ask."

"Don't worry, I talk to myself sometimes too. Everybody does."

Yeah, but everybody does NOT talk to bodiless angels from the Order of the Caliginauts.

"You got that right," Angelese said and laughed.

When they got to the small office closest to the showers, R.J. looked around and said, "Sadie must be at an examination. I've got an admissions interview right now, so I'll see you at the chow hall when you're done."

"Chow hall?" Cassie tried to joke. "Don't you mean Sustenance Facility?"

"You've had the food here. It's chow. For what we charge per week for an in-patient, you'd think we'd have better food, huh?"

The food *was* pretty bad. "Then change to an obesity clinic."

R.J. held a finger up. "Not a bad idea. See ya in a little while."

Cassie was taken aback. "Hey. You mean you're gonna leave me alone here? As in . . . by myself?"

"Sure."

"Aren't you afraid I'll try to escape?"

"Nope. But, just so you know, we don't call it 'escape' here. We call it 'resident elopement.' " Then he pointed to a sign on the wall: DO NOT LEAVE ELOPEMENT RISKS UNATTENDED.

"Maybe I will escape," Cassie goaded. "Then you'll get fired."

R.J. shrugged. "I hear they're hiring at Wendy's." Then he walked away.

Probably just some behavioral psychologist's trick, Cassie considered. *Wants me to think he trusts me, then I'll trust him.*

"That's not it," Angelese said, unseen as always. "He just likes you. And you like him."

"I do not!" Cassie insisted. "Jesus, he's old. He's like, thirty-five."

Faceless chuckles fluttered about the small room. "How old do you think I am? You saw my face in the water."

"I don't know. Eighteen, nineteen."

"Try five thousand."

Jeez.

She was waiting for Sadie, the ward chaperon, but the woman wasn't to be found. A television on the desk was on, the volume all the way down. There was also a copy of the *St. Petersburg Times*. Cassie immediately caught herself eyeing the front page.

ARMY SAYS MD EXPLOSION NOT TERRORIST BOMB, the top headline blared. *What the hell is that all about?* Cassie wondered. She picked up the paper but quickly noticed a more local headline lower on the page. MASS HYSTERIA IN DANNELLETON?

Dannelleton? she realized. *That's where this clinic is!*

"Um-hmm," Angelese answered her thought.

Cassie addressed the faceless voice. "You sound like you know something about it."

"Um-hmm . . . Turn the TV up."

CNN was on; Cassie hiked the volume. A newswoman who looked more like an E-Channel hostess was reporting, ". . . strange and devastating explosion which completely destroyed the obscure library in Laurel, Maryland, last night. The bodies of five security guards and an unnamed civilian were recovered by local fire-department crews. Nearby witnesses reported seeing a small mushroom cloud expanding over the site at the time of the mishap, and rumors quickly spread that the facility had been the target of a terrorist bomb. But federal officials from the Army and Nuclear

Regulatory Commission quickly dispelled such rumors, stating that no radiation was detected at the site, nor does the site display any characteristics of a terrorist attack. Later, county and state officials explained that the unfortunate accident was the result of a natural gas line rupture . . ."

"I don't think so," Angelese sniped.

"What are you talking about?" Cassie asked. She was getting annoyed.

"Turn on the local news now."

Oh, well. Cassie did so. This time a newsman who seemed to have forgotten to comb his hair was saying, ". . . the small but exclusive downtown area of Dannelleton ravaged by fire last night, amid reports of earth tremors, power failures including battery-powered police radio communication failure and cell phone failure, foul-smelling fog, and mass screaming—" The newscaster cracked a smile. "Pinellas County public health officials attribute these observations to a case of simple mass-hysteria which often occurs at night, during times of limited visibility, and during traumatic public crises. Meanwhile, the fire marshal and his team of investigators explained that the fires were caused by gas line rupture . . ."

"And if you believe that," Angelese said, "I've got a bridge I can sell you."

Cassie turned the TV back down. "You're saying it's not true?" she asked, even though she had to admit, the coincidence seemed a bit far-fetched. "What do you know about it?"

"I can't tell you."

"Why?"

The voice in the air paused, almost as if fearful. "Because I don't have the courage. But I'll tell you soon. I won't just tell you, I'll show you. There are certain things I'm not

100

allowed to tell you. If I do . . . I'm punished, and believe me, the punishment hurts."

"I still don't know what you're talking about," Cassie said, her frustrations mounting.

"Just be patient."

"Patience isn't one of my best traits."

Sadie walked in, one brow raised. *Probably heard me talking to Angelese,* Cassie deduced. *But so what, she already thinks I'm crazy.* "Hello, Cassie," the squat, husky woman said. Her blond perm looked like a large order of curly fries sitting on her head, and her conservative business dress would've looked nice on just about anyone else but on her it didn't work at all. *No matter what she wears, she'll always look like a guard at a women's prison,* Cassie thought. Sadie, as the ward's chaperon, was charged with the duty of being present whenever a female in-patient was undergoing a physical exam or taking a shower.

"If she's a lesbian," Angelese said, "she sure landed the right job."

Cassie had to bite her lip not to laugh. She followed the rotund woman to the long shower stalls. Sadie was polite enough at least to keep her eyes averted when Cassie took off her robe and stepped in. The warm spray hissed down, revitalizing Cassie.

"Okay, now what were you—" but then Cassie bit her lip again.

"I told you to be careful," Angelese reminded.

"Cassie?" It was Sadie. She peeked around the shower wall and looked in. "Is there someone in there with you?"

Cassie turned with a frown, faced the woman totally naked and spread her hands. "Does it look like anyone's in here with me?"

Sadie's eyes narrowed. "I could've sworn I heard you talking to someone."

"I talk to myself sometimes." Then she laughed. "Just ask R.J."

"Well. Okay. I'll be out here."

"Don't worry, Sadie. I know you people think I'm a suicide risk but be real. How can I kill myself with a bar of soap?"

A final, worried pause, then Sadie went back out.

"Just listen," Angelese said, "and if you have to talk, whisper, so Boxcar Bertha out there doesn't hear you."

Cassie nodded, the shower spray tickling her.

"There are some things I can tell you," the angel's voice began, "and some things I can't. It's one of the Rules. Just like there are Rules in the Mephistopolis, I have Rules, too. If I break them, I pay."

"How?" Cassie whispered.

"In pain. In torture. Remember last night, when we did the Transference with the water cupped in your hands?"

"Yeah."

"What happened right before my image disappeared?"

The memory blared. "You screamed, and for a minute the water turned red, like blood."

"Because it *was* blood. My blood. I was being slashed because I broke one of the Rules. I told you something I wasn't allowed to tell you. Do you remember? I told you that I would help you get back to the Mephistopolis, that I'd help you find the other Deadpass."

A long pause.

"For that I was punished," the angel continued. "I was punished by a thing called an Umbra-Specter. It's a kind of demon that can live in your shadow, and it can become real for a few seconds, anytime you break a Rule."

Cassie had never heard of such a thing during her previous trips to the Mephistopolis. It sounded like a sword of

Damocles, that could swoop down and cut you without warning. "But . . . only for a few seconds?"

"A few seconds is enough." Angelese's voice grew solemn. "You'll see. Step back, out of the water . . ."

Cassie did so. The spray hissed out of the shower head. Then her eyes began to slowly widen.

The image was grained, like a pointillistic painting, but after a second Cassie could see the image of a short slender young woman standing under the shower spray. She thought of a television picture with bad reception.

"You can see me, right?"

Cassie nodded, speechless.

More of Angelese's image began to form, to the point that she nearly looked like a normal woman standing in the shower. Long snow-white hair hung in wet tendrils. She was very petite, fine-boned, and then she turned her head gracefully to look at Cassie and smile. The overlarge eyes sparkled, stunning with their violet-rimmed beige irises. The simple white gown she wore—low cut over a modest bosom—stuck to her skin in the water. Its hem went all the way down to her ankles.

"Hi," the angel said.

"Um," Cassie stalled. She stood aside, dripping. "Hi."

Bright fluorescent light tubes blared overhead. Angelese looked down at the floor slightly to one side. "See? See my shadow?"

Cassie could see it moving just off of Angelese's bare feet. There was nothing extraordinary about it, no demons seen hiding. "Looks just like a normal shadow to me."

Angelese just smiled. "Ask R.J. if you can move to the room at the very end of the hall, on the left."

"Why?"

"Because that's where I am. It will be easier for us to talk, face to face. This water thing is a pain in the ass."

Cassie couldn't believe she'd just heard an angel use the word ass. But she didn't understand, and Angelese could sense that.

"I use up a lot of my energy projecting my voice through the walls, and the Transference Charm makes me real tired afterward."

Did I get that right? Cassie needed clarification. "You mean you're staying in one of rooms on the ward? I thought you were an angel. Now you're telling me you're a patient?"

Angelese laughed. "No, no, I'm just occupying the room. I couldn't select it, it selected me. Any recruit in the Order of the Caliginauts can only physically occupy Death-Points in the Living World. We're attracted to darkness—it's part of our habitat."

Angels, Cassie contemplated the contradiction, *attracted to darkness.* "So what's the big deal about the room at the end of the hall?"

"Over the years, several dozen patients have committed suicide in it. When this sanatorium originally opened in the early 1900s, some of the patients were actually murdered by staff in that room, then they told the authorities it was suicide. Relatives often paid the staff to do this, to get the patients out of their hair, or claim their inheritance."

"How upbeat."

"Anyway, that's where I am. If you could get moved into the room directly across from me, it would be easier to talk."

"R.J.'s not gonna assign me a new room for no reason. What am I going to say? Will you please move me down the hall so I can talk to the angel? You know, the Caliginaut who's attracted to darkness? He and Morse'd have me on enough Thorazine to drop the Jolly Green Giant."

"Just tell him you want it for the view of the garden outside."

Can't hurt to try, Cassie thought. She squinted now at something catching her eye, a pendant around Angelese's neck. "What's that? Some kind of stone?"

From the end of the silver cord dangled a dark-purple stone shaped like an upside-down V. "It's a Tetramite—an Obscurity Stone," the angel explained. "It conceals my aura when I'm in the Living World. Humans can't see my physical body, but they'd be able to see my aura. All angels have auras, or haloes. And since you're an Etheress, whenever you're in Hell—"

"I know, I have an aura, too," Cassie said. During previous trips to the Mephistopolis, she'd always wear her onyx ring, to dampen the light of her lifeforce. Otherwise, she'd be recognized at once by the Constabularies or any other denizens of Hell.

Angelese took the pendant off and immediately the shower room filled with sparkling lime-green light that started at a blazing ring over her head.

"Wow!" Cassie exclaimed.

"Wow, what? Who are you talking to?" the stern voice cracked. It was Sadie, the chaperon. "Have you got a boy in here?" The woman's broad face peered right at Cassie.

"A boy?" She looked at Angelese. "Not quite. Look, I told you, I talk to myself sometimes, that's all."

Sadie didn't seem convinced. She glowered up and down the long room. "Well, hurry it up, will you?" A deeper frown. "And it helps to actually stand in the water when you're taking a shower," she sniped and then huffed off.

"She's delightful," Angelese joked, turning to look at the woman. But while she'd been looking, Cassie noticed something on the angel's back, on either side of her spine. Rough bumps of some kind.

"Is—is something wrong with your back?" she asked.

"Oh, my attentor joints," the angel replied. "I'm a terrestrial angel, that means we have to have our wings amputated. It's part of the investiture of my order."

Just the word—amputated—made Cassie grit her teeth. "You had to *cut* your wings off?"

Angelese shrugged with complacency. "Yeah, it's a prerequisite for my class of Seraphim—any terrestrial order. Some angels have three pairs of wings, some two, some one, other orders have prehensile wings that fold up in the middle of their back, and some orders have discorporate wings that can be rendered invisible by certain Obscurity Stones, Veiling Balms, and Imperceptiblity Spells. And some angels—Ornataphrim and Magitors—have no wings at all."

"Can any angel come to earth?"

"Some, not all. Most Fallen Angels can incarnate themselves into the Living World, but it requires a lot of cabalistic energy—as well as permission—and they can never go to Heaven, of course. Lucifer appears on earth regularly. The latest rumor is that he's been amusing himself by going back in time, to revisit periods of great tragedy and horror. That's what he does when he's bored."

"How can he go back in time?"

"Because of something he stole from God a long time ago. The process is called Astral Retrogation. It's kind of like a Merge, in that it only lasts for a short period of time. Beyond that, I can't discuss it."

"But if he can go back in time, can he go forward? Into the future?"

"I can't tell you."

More questions popped up, unbidden. "Are angels born or created?"

"I can't tell you."

"What about God? Is He an angel, too?"

Angelese smiled through the spray. "I can't say."

Hmm, interesting. But now came another concern. Cassie

felt embarrassed by Sadie's appearance. The woman would no doubt tell R.J., who'd only wind up thinking she was getting crazier. That wasn't the impression she wanted him to have. She continued to look, though, at the angel in the water. There was something enchanting about the softly hissing image.

Water ran down her bare arms; the long gown she wore stuck to her legs. Beneath the sheer fabric, Cassie thought she saw darker streaks of some sort, and then she remembered.

"Didn't you say you had tattoos?"

"You want to see them?" Angelese asked.

"Sure."

A strange tilt of the head. "Do you *really* want to see them?"

"Yeah."

"Okay . . ."

Angelese pulled down the shoulder straps, let the gown slide damply down to her ankles. Suddenly she was nude.

Cassie's breath froze in her chest.

"I guess I should have told you, they're not really tattoos . . ."

No, they clearly weren't. Crosshatchlike lines in groups of four scored the angel's white skin from her ankles to her bosom. Some of the lines were faintly pink, others a much darker red. Most of her body was a webwork of them.

Cassie's voice roughened. "They're scars, aren't they?"

Angelese nodded. She turned around, displaying the even worse sets of scars going up and down her back. "They're claw marks."

Cassie was close to shivering at what she saw. Angelese's skin provided a tapestry for the wounds.

"See these?" Now the angel ran a finger up her abdomen to her small but erect breasts: four fresh claw marks filled with scabbed-up blood. "I got these last night, when I told you that there was another Deadpass. This was the punishment, for breaking the Rule."

"That thing did it," Cassie knew. "The—"

"Umbra-Specter." Angelese looked down at the compressed shadow which seemed huddled around her feet. "It's an evil son of a bitch but it's part of the way it works. All Caliginauts have them whenever they walk the earth. It's the toll you have to pay." She tensed, gently touching the cuts. "It hurts so much when he does it. You wouldn't understand. Angels have heightened senses. We feel everything in much more detail and intensity—especially pain."

Cassie couldn't imagine. Even the undersides of Angelese's breasts were wounded, almost as though she were wearing a bra of scars. "It only happens when you say something you're not allowed to say?"

"Yeah," Angelese replied. "Or do something I'm not allowed to do."

Cassie recalled that in the Mephistopolis, Fallen Angels were immortal. "Can you die?"

"Not in Heaven, and not in Hell. But here?" Angelese smiled coyly. "Yeah, I can die. When angels kick the bucket in the Living World, they go out with a bang. And that's what I need to tell you about."

When she said that, something happened. Cassie wasn't sure, but the pressure in the room seemed to change. Even though she was wet from the shower, tiny hairs seemed to stand up on her neck. Then she noticed the shadow at Angelese's feet.

It was elongating, unfolding on the floor like black ink being spilled.

"Here it comes," Angelese calmly said. "It already knows what I'm going to say."

Now the shadow was rising. It looked like a craggy black figure standing up.

The angel began: "Remember what we heard on the news?"

"The fires in downtown Dannelleton?" Cassie referenced.

"I'll tell you about that too but I mean the other thing—"

"The explosion they blamed on a gas line rupture," Cassie said. "Some library or something, in Maryland."

"It was no explosion, it was Lucifer's best friend, a Fallen Angel named Zeihl—"

The room darkened as the shadow—this Umbra-Specter—grew larger. It was a solid black mass with no details save for its shape, and now its hands were opening, revealing awl-sharp claws that were each inches long. The darkest, guttural sound could be heard, barely audible, but a sound nonetheless. Cassie knew what it was: it was the thing chuckling.

"Don't say anything else," Cassie warned.

"I have to."

"That thing'll torture you. Don't do it."

"I have to," Angelese repeated. "That's what I'm here for," and then she continued, speaking in panicked bursts of words: "Zeihl, the Fallen Angel, he incarnated himself and then committed suicide, that's what the explosion was, an angel killing himself, sacrificing himself because if an angel sacrifices himself, material things can be exchanged, the place wasn't really a library, Lucifer wanted something there so Zeihl sacrificed himself in order to get it, and they succeeded by performing a Spatial Merge, it's an occult technology that Satan had never perfected until now but it's a way of bringing a small part of Hell to earth for a short period of time, just a couple of blocks but a couple of blocks is enough, because during the Merge that little part of Hell will share the same space with a little part of the Living

World simultaneously, so that's what happened, they Merged with that library to steal something and whatever it was they stole, they took it back to Hell, I know this is what happened because that's the only reason Zeihl would've committed suicide, it's one of the Rules, the only way you can take something out of the Living World and bring it to Hell is through a Power Exchange, and an angelic sacrifice would've generated that kind of power—"

But by then it was too late. The Umbra-Specter had fully solidified, its black form real as flesh, and now it had pressed Angelese against the tiled shower wall, and it slowly was dragging its claws up her thighs. Angelese was shuddering, still speaking through the catastrophic pain, her big beige-and-violet eyes even bigger now as they widened in horror. "—so that's what they did, that's the only thing it could've been, a Power Exchange during a Spatial Merge, when an angel dies in the Living World it's almost like a nuke going off—"

"Stop!" Cassie shouted, watching helpless as the shadow freely indulged in its torture. "Don't say anything else! Don't tell me any more!"

Angelese told her more, shrieking now through her unearthly pain, desperate to get it all out as quickly as possible: "—and that other story we heard on the news, the stuff about fires and screaming in downtown Dannelleton, that was a Merge too. It was a practice run, and I know what they're practicing for—"

All at once, the angel's shriek amplified tenfold; Cassie had to cover her ears for a moment. The Umbra-Specter was shivving Angelese, slowly drawing its claws in and out of her ribs. Blood poured from the wounds, luminous, like liquid red neon light, swirling down the shower drain.

Cassie wasn't sure but she thought she heard the shadow-thing say: "Please keep talking, keep betraying your oath. I

110

love torturing you," in the most corroded voice.

Angelese panted out more words through the agony. "They know I'm trying to get you to the other Deadpass, they don't want you in Hell on your own because they know you're too powerful, that's why they're doing these Merges—"

"I don't understand," Cassie sobbed.

"They want to Merge with this clinic, if they can successfully do that, they can capture you. Lucifer wants to abduct you and use your Ethereal Powers for something that's more diabolical than anything that's ever been done before, so that's why I have to get you out of here. That's what all of this is about, Cassie—it's you! They're coming for you!"

The Umbra-Specter reveled in its task, flaying Angelese with its claws. Cassie didn't know what to do, she could only think impulsively. Without light, could the shadow retain its form? She ran naked to the other end of the room, leaving glowing red footprints. *Light switch! Where's the light switch?* but she couldn't find it. Angelese was still screaming, unable to speak at all anymore as the claws gleefully molested her. Cassie grabbed a mop out of the closet, ran back, and then began to break all the fluorescent tubes with the handle. In blocks, the room fell into darkness. The shadow howled, glaring at her over its ebon shoulder. When Cassie shattered the last overhead tube, the thing began to dissipate.

So did the bleeding squirming image of Angelese.

Chapter Six

(I)

Why would Walter dream such a thing, such an *awful* thing?

He was standing on a street corner in a city, but it was unlike any city he could have ever imagined. The midnight sky was ruby-red, the low sickle moon was black. He could only see these features, though, by looking straight up because the buildings lining the street must've been hundreds and hundreds of floors high, skyscrapers unlike any he'd seen. He got dizzy just looking up. *Do they even make buildings that high?* he questioned himself.

"They do here," a little girl said.

She was skipping down the street, smiling at him. Walter almost fell over. Her pigtails flipped as she skipped. She wore black-strapped shoes and little white socks, a bright red-and-white checkered dress. Deep lines ran down her gray, wizened face—the girl was mummified.

She was playing hop-scotch but the squares weren't formed by chalk, they were formed by long, odd bones. She couldn't have been more than seven or eight. "You're in the Mephistopolis, you're in Hell," she told him. "This is Pogrom Park, and you're having a dream."

Dream, he thought. Somehow, the information comforted him. It told him that this weird place didn't really exist. Overhead, something flew by. A city pigeon was his first guess but then he looked closer at it and saw that it was some kind of a winged rodent. Was that a severed human penis it clasped between its teeth as it flew away?

The little mummy girl skipped along, the hop-scotch squares extending all the way down the street. "Bye, Walter. Your destiny awaits."

The comment pricked his distraction. "What?" he called after her. "What did you say?"

"Embrace your destiny . . ." She skipped away and disappeared around the corner.

He saw a sign, letters on smudgy glass: NEWCOMERS' INFORMATION POINT. WELCOME TO THE POGROM PARK DISTRICT GALLERY. Walter meandered in—what else did he have to do? The long empty room walled by glossy photo-murals reminded him of a tourist center, displaying pictures of local attractions. Frame by frame, then, he looked at photographs of Hell's greatest landmarks.

The Industrial Zone and its hundred-foot walls of iron girders. Inside this vast complex lay the city's Central Power Plant, the Foundry and Slag Furnace, the Flesh-Processors and Bone-Grinding Stations. One shot showed thousands of destitute workers cutting the flesh off of corpses. Endless conveyor belts then delivered the cuttings to the Pulping Plants, for further food processing; more conveyors delivered the bones to be ground up for bricks and concrete. In the Fuel Depot, wheeled hoppers delivered large chunks of raw sulphur by the tons, to be manually chopped into smaller chunks by stooped laborers—the city's endless fuel supply.

De Rais University extended over countless acres and appeared almost campus-like in its layout. Here, the finest Warlocks in the land taught their pupils in the blackest arts: divination, psychic torture, spatial transposition, and the latest in vexation.

The Rockefeller Mint provided the city with all its currency: brass and tin coinage featuring the embossed faces of all the Anti-Popes, and Hellnotes printed on processed demon skin.

Osiris Heights stood proud and posh, the residential district for upper-Hierarchals who lived an eternity of privilege in pristine highrises. A typical suite boasted the latest conveniences: harlot cages, skull-presses, iron-maidens, and neat personal-sized crematoriums. Television, too, powered not by electricity but by psychical theta-waves, offered up all the best torture channels.

Boniface Square encompassed whole city blocks in its leisure services. From the finest restaurants specializing in the best demonian cuisine to the most common street vendors pushing carts of flame-broiled meat skewers. Opulent nightclubs to rowdy hole-in-the-wall bars. From strip joints, bordellos, and peepshow parlors to the opulent Frederick the Great Opera House, all manner of abyssal entertainment could be found in the Square.

The J. Edgar Hoover Building existed in the Living World as well as in Lucifer's; here, though, the immense Gothic edifice housed the million-occupant Central Jail, the Drug Perpetuation Agency, the Commandant of the Mancer Divisions (headed by an articulate gentleman named

U. S. Grant), the Tamerlane Emergency Response Battalion, and, of course, Satan's official police department—the Agency of the Constabulary.

Other landmarks included Tojo Memorial Hospital, the John Dee Library and Infernal Archives, St. Iscariot Abbey, and the infamous Office of Transfiguration and Teratologic Research.

And wealthier Hierarchals who enjoyed beach-combing could always open their cabanas along the beautiful blood-filled Sea of Cagliostro.

"Terrific place, huh?" said a man with horns all over his face. He had three eyes, each the size of an apple, and he stood inside a little info booth.

"Yes, uh," Walter stammered. "Terrific. So this really is Hell?"

"You bet'cha."

"I don't even know if I believe in this place."

"Believe it." All three eyes scrutinized Walter. "You're not a Resident, are you? You don't have the look."

"What's the look?"

"Damned."

"I feel damned," Walter said. He walked back out to the street.

The air smelled like smoke, a bitter eggy smoke like burning sulphur; he could even *see* the smoke sifting up through cracks in the street. Suddenly bells clanged, and a siren sounded. *A fire,* Walter guessed, but it was the strangest fire truck that appeared moments later. It looked more like a flat-bed truck from the 1920s, spoked wheels, open cab, but there was a boiler where the engine should be and a smokestack gusted steam. A riveted water tank occupied the back deck.

"Out of the way, buddy!" the helmeted driver shouted at Walter. "We've got a fire!" The driver was a demon with pitted yellow skin and red eyes. Walter stepped back onto the sidewalk, thinking *Fire? I don't see anything on fire.* Did he mean the smoke coming out from the cracks in the street?

The fire truck clattered to a stop, and out jumped several more helmeted, raincoated demons, unreeling a long hose. They hurriedly approached the front of one of the buildings where a transom read TROLL MIDDLE SCHOOL. Through the window, Walter could see all the little misshapen demon children sitting at desks in a classroom. The firemen barged in with their hose, the nozzle was opened, and then the screams poured forth amid the instant crackling. It wasn't water that sprayed from the nozzle, it was flame. The middle school was engulfed. Walter ran away, trying to out-distance the shrieks of the burning demon children.

"You can't outrun the future," someone else said when he huffed around the corner. In the middle of the street, two Griffins the size of Dobermans greedily picked scraps of flesh off a corpse. The corpse was still moving.

"And it won't die, not really," he was told. "That's a Human. A human's Spirit Body only dies when it's completely destroyed. Then his Soul will transfer to something else, a demon, a bug, a worm."

Who was telling him this? Walter looked around in utter confusion, then noticed the stunning woman standing in the little brick cubby between two buildings. "Who are you?" he asked but then the importance of the question faded as he looked more closely at her.

The glossy blue-vinyl overcoat made her look like some kind of pop baroness. A black velvet choker girded her throat. Her hair hung perfectly cropped in a straight line, cut at the same level as the choker; it was lank and shiny as black silk. The burning phosphorus of a street light diced her face into a puzzle of hard, pretty angles. Her eyes were so big and bright they dominated her face almost surrealistically.

"I'm No-name," she said.

"No-name?" Walter almost laughed. "That's some name."

"I'm not allowed to say a name, Walter."

"How do you know *my* name?"

"Because I'm a soothsayer." She seemed to hug back into the shadows of the cubby. Her arms pressed together at her sides made her breasts push out. *God, she's pretty,* Walter took time to think.

"I was a Dactyl-class sorceress for the court of King Mursil the First," she continued, whispering. "I was executed for heresy—I deliberately spoke a false prophecy to the king—so I went to Hell. I've been here for a *long* time." Another nudge back into the shadows.

This only distracted Walter more. "What are you— Are you hiding in there? You seem—"

"Yes, I'm hiding. I'm only safe in the Netherspheres. When I sneak into the Mephistopolis, I'm considered a fugitive."

"Why?"

"Because I refuse to work for Lucifer's Diviners. I'm considered an offense against public law. The Golems are looking for me, probably as we speak."

Golems? Walter wondered. "Well, why come here? Why not stay where it's safe?"

"Because it's not in my future. *You* are."

"Huh?"

"This is a dream, Walter."

"So I've been told."

"I'm a presage..."

117

Walter frowned. "If you can tell the future, tell me mine."

"The future isn't mutable, Walter. If it was, then I could change it, couldn't I? I could change it by giving you options. But that's not possible, so what point is there in telling you?"

Even as smart as Walter was, that one went right over his head. A distracted glance into the street showed him that the Griffins had gone, leaving the corpse stripped to the bone. Then the bones got up and falteringly walked away.

"You want to kill yourself, don't you, Walter?"

The question shook him. He bowed his head. "Yes."

"Because of a girl?"

"Yes."

"You love her but she doesn't love you?"

What could he say?

"Don't despair," No-name told him. "Rejoice in your life."

Without Candice, I don't have one. This was pathetic. *I'M pathetic,* he thought. He looked back at No-name. "Well? Tell me. What difference does it make? Will Candice ever love me?"

"That prospect is . . . unlikely," No-name said.

Unlikely. A polite way of saying no. But he'd always known that, hadn't he? He was only eighteen years old, had virtually no experience whatsoever with women, but he *knew* this, and even though he knew it, hearing it from No-name felt like a wall had fallen down on him. "Should I do it then?" he asked now. "Should I kill myself?"

"I can't advise you."

Was it a rumbling he heard? Some weird noise that seemed to be coming from behind No-name.

She spoke more heatedly now. "No, the future isn't mutable, Walter. Whether you like it or not, you're going to have to embrace your destiny."

Embrace your destiny, he repeated the arcane words. Everyone was telling him that. But as far as he could reason, his destiny involved nothing more than blowing his head off in his dorm room tonight.

No-name's eyes widened, and she smiled very brightly at him. "They got me."

"What?"

"I'll see you soon," and then the old brown bricks of the cubby broke apart from behind; several of the bricks almost hit Walter in the head. He jumped back, his heart lurching. The wall had been broken apart from behind and now two very tall *thing*s had grabbed No-name. She didn't scream; in fact, she barely reacted at all. The two man-shaped things that grabbed her looked almost ten feet tall, with just leaning lumps for heads and stout crudely featured hands, like dolls made of clay by a child. The closer Walter looked, however, the more he guessed that the things *were* made of clay. They were drab brownish-gray and smelled of a riverbed at low spate. One held No-name securely upright by wrapping its fat arms around her shoulders. The other one twisted her head round and round on her neck, until—

crunch

—it came off.

The head was dropped into a garbage can, and No-name's body was heaved into the middle of the street where it was descended upon at once by a gaggle of Griffins. The Griffins squawked merrily, and stripped No-name's corpse clean in just moments.

The two Golems looked at Walter with totally blank faces. Then they lumbered off.

I'll see you soon, Walter remembered the girl's last words to him. He looked at her bones in the street. "I don't think

so," he muttered and jogged away. Only then did he fully
see the crested street sign at the corner: CHYME RESER-
VOIR AVENUE.

(II)

Bordeaux, 1348 A.D.

He was called many things, and his name bore many con-
tradictions. Lucifer, for instance, meant "The Light of the
Morning"; hence, he was sometimes called the Morning
Star. He was called Eosphoros, Iblis, the aduw Allah. But
he was lately and more popularly referred to as Satan. Once,
in eons past, he'd been the bringer of light. Now he was
the bringer of darkness.

He very much liked the darkness.

"Good, good," he whispered to himself. He was looking
out at the village street, peeking from behind the teetering
todesfall. From within the crude building's plank-wood
walls, he could hear moaning. *They don't even wait for them
to die before throwing them in,* the Light of the Morning
thought. He relished the notion. Every village had many
todesfalls—in these times? Sometimes they were simply
pits, or fenced-in wastelands of death. The more sophisticated townships erected roofed buildings for the purpose,
and Bordeaux, by now, had erected many such buildings.
The stench wafting through the wood slats was beyond
most human imagination, even in this filthy age. The ba-
cillus pestis and pneumonitis had brought a beautiful black
wave of death over Europe. He hoped the stench of rotting
flesh would rise up high enough to offend God.

"Good, good," he whispered again. He was looking out
in glee, a child peeking around the stairs at the Christmas
tree. Men in hoods and masks carted more bodies to the
todesfall, where they flopped over like long white sacks.

The only sound was the incessant buzzing of flies amid their feast.

An Oni stood beside him, for protection, he presumed, not that the aduw Allah needed protection; his generals had insisted. "You could be blemished, my lord," one, named Sherman, had told him. But Satan was immortal.

"From plague?" he asked.

"Villagers could set upon you," Sherman reminded. Immortality was one thing, disfigurement was sorely another. Why was it that he, one of the wisest beings of history, hadn't thought of that? In an earlier time, he would've destroyed Sherman for suggesting something so offensive but over ages, he'd matured as well. Satan had become a sensible monarch. "Let me go with you, my lord—at the very least," Sherman entreated, "or several of my best-trained Flamma-Troopers."

"No, there isn't sufficient power."

"The sorcery is so new. At least test it first, on someone else. On me, anyone. I implore you, lord."

"No." Lucifer smiled at this disheveled general who had slaughtered thousands without compunction. "The Capnomancers at the Synod have assured my safety." But for a moment, he felt neutered. All his power, and the limitlessness of his kingdom—and he had to worry about energy constraints. It didn't seem fair. "Dear general, there's husbandry in Heaven," Lucifer took the line from Shakespeare, "and here too." At least he was good-natured enough now to admit that his power wasn't absolute.

He'd agreed to the Oni. It was indestructible—and smarter than a Golem—forged of black granite carved out of Hell's deepest and most cursed quarry, and made malleable by the most ingenious Animation Spells. No one would be "disfiguring" the Morning Star while the Oni was present.

It stared at him—with no face—as he continued his secret vigil. The dead were piling up now, in human drifts. *Good, good,* he just kept thinking, *good, good . . .*

A little girl staggered down the dirt road, sucking her thumb and in rags. Her face was a pie of bubos. A masked man raced up, hit the girl in the head with an iron bar, and threw her onto the next death-cart. In the distance, the todesfalls that had been filled to capacity were set ablaze. Lucifer could smell it.

An astonished voice surprised him.

"Who . . . are you?"

Another man, another death-carrier. Fleas churned in his black hood, and the cloth covering his mouth billowed as he spoke.

Satan looked at the man and smiled warmly. "I am the light of each morning that you will see, for the rest of your life."

"How many more such morns will there be for me?"

Iblis extended his hand to the great morning sun. "Just this one, my friend."

"You are a soothsayer?"

Eosphoros' voice suddenly bloomed into white light. "I am an angel."

"Will you save me?"

"No. I can't. You can only save yourself. You wonderful pitiful people will just never understand that, will you?"

The man trembled in his black garb. "Will I die hastily?"

"You will die a slow death. You will die in utter agony. Then you'll come to me."

"Christ, have mercy—"

"He *won't.*"

The Oni walked around behind the man, somehow without making a sound. It picked him up, threw him into the todesfall, and closed the door.

Christ didn't save me. Why should he save you?

"Halt."

It was someone else, a knight, in chain mail and a white tunic emblazoned with a cross and the crest of the Council of Lyons.

"I'm not moving, am I?" Lucifer asked.

"Who are you?"

"Like you, I'm a Crusader."

"Your voice is strange." The knight unsheathed his broadsword. "You're no knight of God."

"Well, let's just say that I used to be."

"Are you a priest?"

"In a sense."

"I have no time for riddles. Evil is upon the land. There is a scourge."

"Yes. And what do you do about it?"

"I save souls. I end the misery of the children of God after hearing their confession."

"You think that saves them?"

"I know it does. The Holy Father says it does, and the Holy Father is infallible." The knight's smudged face looked suddenly confused. "You needn't fear me. My sword will save your soul."

"You're a little late for that."

"Have you been touched by the pestilence?"

"I *am* the pestilence," Satan said.

"You're an acolyte of the Devil. Let me hear your confession and I will save your soul. The Lord God forgives everyone."

Lucifer's voice turned so soft it could barely be heard. "Are you certain of that?"

The knight stared. He was shaking. "I'm looking right at you, yet . . . yet I can't see your face."

"My visage is too perfect to be looked upon. You are incapable of reckoning my perfection . . ."

The shadow loomed as the Oni stepped out from behind the todesfall.

"God in Heaven," the knight croaked.

This is so petty, Lucifer thought, *but it's so much fun . . .* Then he spoke words in a language unknown to this world. His breath flowed out as luminous mist. It was a simple Possession Invocation, child's play, but it seemed appropriate. With the arcane words, the knight's will was polluted by a hundred insanities.

"Crusader of Lyons. There are still some women and children alive in the village. They need to be raped. Do you hear me?"

"Yes . . ."

"They need to be dragged into the open street and raped as the others look on. Do you hear me?"

"Yes . . ."

"Every survivor in this town needs to *see* your red Crusader's cross as you are raping the women and children. Do you hear me?"

"Yes . . ."

"Then go."

The knight turned and headed for the village square.

All in a day's work. But was it possible for the First Fallen Angel to be queasy? Gastric distress? The Lord of Darkness' graceful hand came to his abdomen. When he frowned, a hedgerow of budding pink flowers died at once.

The White Stone, he realized. Of course. He chuckled aloud, and the sound rattled across the continent. *All that God in me right now. Of course it makes me sick . . .*

There'd been seven such stones, set into the Twelfth Gate of Heaven, the highest gate, so high that only a handful of Angels were allowed to pass through it. Seven stones to exist as the perfect number, and all white: the color of perfection.

Lucifer had pilfered three of the stones just before he'd been cast out.

A great shadow fluttered at the tree tops. Then he knew—it wasn't the stone in his belly that was making him sick, it was the sudden presence.

A blond angel—a Hermaphrim, part man, part woman—floated on great white wings above the trees, looking down. Its lambent face, at first, looked sad, then it glowered at Lucifer.

"You're a disgrace," the angel said, the voice a deafening hush.

"Not enough of one!" Lucifer blared back. "But soon I will be! Soon I'll show you disgrace!" The concussion of the Morning Star's words shook the birds out of every tree in the forest. The birds fell dead at once.

The angel maneuvered closer and cast a hateful glance at the Oni. Then came the strangest grinding sound. The Oni shuddered, and turned into black-flecked salt. A moment later, it collapsed to a pile of granules.

"Do that to me!" Lucifer yelled upward.

The angel just glowered back at him.

"You can't! It's because you *can't!*"

"Even if I could, I wouldn't. Better for you to fester in your infinity."

"I *adore* my infinity! You're *jealous* of it!"

A rabble rose aside. "An angel!" a voice cried out. "An angel's come to bless us!" and several villagers straggled out of their homes into the street. Two men hauling a death-cart stopped, looking up. They all stared up at the angel.

One woman held a dying child in her arms, her smudged face shiny with tears. "Help my daughter, I beg of thee," she wept up to the angel.

The angel smiled in spite of the distress on its incalculable face. "Your daughter will live to be a hundred," it said softly.

The child squirmed in the mother's arms, dropped to her feet, and scampered off, laughing, clean. The woman fell to her knees before the angel's great shadow. All the villagers in the street were staring up.

"It's God," someone whispered.

Lucifer gagged, ran out, pointing. "That *thing* is not God!" he roared. Houses shook. "I'm more of a god than *that!*" Lucifer's eyes brightened in their hatred, or was it really just despair kept hidden for millennia? He challenged the angel: "Heal them all! Make them all clean—all of them! Heal the *continent!*"

"Heal us, God—"

"Save us from the plague—"

"We believe in you . . ."

The angel's aura lost some of its luster. Was it crying? "I'm not allowed. But you will all be saved, through your faith in the Almighty Father . . ."

"Bullshit!" Lucifer raved, still pointing up. "That thing *can't* heal you! If God's so powerful, so benevolent, how is it that He even let this happen? Answer me that!" Then Lucifer rushed forward—"Watch me!"—and approached the death-cart. He looked at it and shouted, "Get up!" and the dying were restored and the dead came back to life. He looked at the crowd, and at the many more pouring out onto the street, and he shouted at them, "You're ALL HEALED!" and their festering bubos all disappeared, their infections were cleansed, their eyes cleared of hemorrhage.

"Worship me," Lucifer beseeched them. They all circled around him and fell to their knees. He held out his hands of light. "This entire town is healed . . ."

"Deceiver. Light of the Morning, you're weakest in your

darkness," the angel spoke. "I can't wait to watch you burn for a thousand years."

Lucifer smiled up at the entity, yes, a smile just like Christ's as He prepared to begin his Sermon on the Mount. "Fuck you," Lucifer said.

The angel was flying away.

He should feel victorious, shouldn't he? Lucifer felt crushed. With the angel gone, his pride felt useless. There was no one to show off for. He pushed through the throng of his new followers, ignoring their praise, not even seeing them, and he staggered to the pile of salt that had once been the Oni. *The stone,* he thought, *the stone.* He mustn't forget the stone. He dug through the salt and found it at the bottom. It was tiny, smaller than a marble, and pure white, perfect white. From the pouch on his belt he withdrew a pinch of Enguerraud Dust—a cosmic emetic agent—and placed it on his tongue. In a moment, he vomited into his hand, and the instant the second White Stone was out of his belly, Lucifer opened his eyes—

Take me back . . .

—and found himself standing in the great Scarlet Hall, before the open balcony at the 666th floor of the Mephisto Building in the heart of downtown Hell.

"Welcome back, my lord."

Sherman, with his elongated cranial transfigurations and implanted horns, stood timidly in black hexated armor. His pinkened face seemed to burn above the same beard he'd stroked while watching his troops, upon his order, rape and kill everything that moved in a city called Atlanta. "We were concerned."

Lucifer didn't hear him, didn't care what he had to say. He sat down on the throne of pure quartz, looked out into the crimson sky. "Lord of Darkness, what a joke," he sputtered and sighed. A lack of self-esteem was not his element. He felt puny and weak.

"Did you say something, my lord?"

Lucifer stared. *I don't want to be the Lord of Darkness. I want to be the Living Lord of the World.* A mile in the distance and down, he could see the ill-colored surface of the Lake of Great Mistakes, where he'd scored his greatest victory against an army of anti-luciferic insurgents, reducing them all to putrefaction with one viral spell. It was not water which filled the lake, but pus. Gazing out now at this achievement, the man in the crystal throne should've felt contentment.

But he didn't.

"My lord," Sherman said, "you're disconsolate. What can I do to allay your despair?"

"Go down and out and have yourself quartered in the Square, where I can see."

Sherman turned to leave.

"Stop." Lucifer put his head in his hand. *Can't anybody take a joke? They do anything I say because I have willed them to do so. Is that really power?*

No.

"Shall I order 50,000 Imps to be summarily drowned in the lake, my lord? Perhaps that would improve your spirits."

The idea sounded tantalizing but even the monarch of all of Hell had to be sensible. "We need them for the Atrocidome—for the next Merge."

"Of course."

He handed Sherman the two White Stones, whereupon the general gave them to an underling demon dressed in a cloak of flensed skin. The stones were then locked up in a Psychic Vault. Lucifer looked at Sherman, almost as one would look to a friend—even though Satan had no friends.

"I want power, General. I want what I've deserved for eons."

"You shall have it, my lord. Soon. And I have good news."

Lucifer's eyes widened in black light.

"While you were away, the Unholy Bearers arrived, just moments ago."

Was it hope that flared in the First Fallen Angel's heart? "The Merge is done?"

"Yes."

"Was it successful?"

"As your Mancers swore, my lord. It was more than a success. It was a triumph."

Lucifer was shaking. "And Zeihl is—"

"Dead by his own hand, Lord Lucifer, as he too swore."

Cloaked and hooded Levitators advanced into the room at Sherman's beckoning. They'd cut off their own feet upon their own ordinations from the Conditioning Academy. They floated across the onyx tile, a scuffed container like a small suitcase floating behind them. Red lights blinked on the edge of the suitcase, an electronic lock.

"Such technology," Lucifer remarked.

A Fourth Level Biowizard garbed in white stepped forward. "Open it," Sherman ordered. The Sorcerer merely looked at the case's sophisticated lock mechanism. The light went out. The case opened.

Please, please, Lucifer pleaded.

"Zeihl is a hero to history," Sherman uttered. "He's made the ultimate sacrifice, for your glory, my lord . . ."

Yes. And better him than me, the Morning Star thought. He'd promised his most loyal Fallen Angel that he'd never forget him, and with that promise, now, Lucifer would forget him forever.

Lucifer rose, levitating himself in his bridled joy, when he looked into the case . . .

(III)

Walter awoke about 10 p.m. He felt shellacked in sweat, and exhausted from the evil dream. He'd slept all day, hadn't he? After seeing that man get killed by the drunk driver yesterday, and the continuously grim revelations about Candice, his mind and body had shut down. He'd missed some classes but didn't care. *I'll be dead tomorrow so what's the big deal?* By now, yes, he was certain. Without Candice, there was no reason to go on living.

But he at least had hoped that the long sleep would leave him feeling better, if only topically. Instead, he felt devitalized, drained. He struggled out of bed and took his iron pill, but they never really made him feel better either. He thought that eating something might help but he knew that if he did he'd just throw up.

An accidental glance in the mirror showed him a skinny, dorky eighteen-year-old, with dark circles under his eyes and clown-orange hair sticking up. Skin pale as vanilla ice cream. Slack Fruit of the Looms hanging off his bony hips.

"Yeah, you're a real prize," he said to the reflection.

The message light was blinking on his answering machine. Not really caring, he pushed the PLAY button.

"Hey, Walter, it's me, Colin. Haven't heard from you in a while so I thought I'd give a call. Just wanna make sure my Buddy-bro is okay—"

Please, Walter begged the fates, *please don't say anything about Candice—*

"Hope you're not still boo-hooing over that pea-brained hose-bag jock-fucking blond bitch. Forget about her, man. Shit, I just saw her blowing some guy behind the bleachers at the baseball game. Gimme a call, Buddy-bro."

BEEP

The next message: A voice he didn't recognize, some guy's voice. "Hey, geek, listen to this, I recorded it last time I was giving it to her," and then he heard a switch pop, someone no doubt pushing the play button on a tape recorder. First the faintest hiss, then a steadily rising crescendo of moans and shrieks. It was clearly a woman in the throes of orgasmic bliss.

Walter knew at once that it was Candice.

Must have been one of the jocks, Walter reasoned. *Why would somebody do that, something that cruel?* he wanted to ask himself. But he didn't bother. *People* were cruel, that's why. Candice was cruel. Reality had set its teeth now. He *knew*. All Candice cared about was having sex with as many empty-headed college sports stars as possible. Never mind how *he* felt. Never mind that Walter was the only one who truly loved her.

His despair was growing vibrant, it made the hairs on his arms shiver, like static. He eyed the shotgun in the corner, then eyed the framed picture of Candice which he'd propped up on his study desk. There was also a picture of Colin on the wall and he supposed a good thing to do would be to see his brother one last time before he did the deed, but he couldn't contemplate that. He didn't want to see his brother ever again because there'd just be more wisecracks about Candice. Next he spied one of his textbooks lying opened on the bed, *Measurements of Sheer Viscosity: Principles of Fluid Dynamics*. Quite unlike him to be impulsive and disrespectful, Walter peed hard on the open book. What did it matter?

His appetite remained non-existent yet he left the dorm anyway, and headed for the Student Union snack bar. A last meal seemed appropriate, even conventional, and Walter was certainly a young man devoted to convention. It was late now, the mixer parties could be heard from afar. Parties

131

that Walter never had been and never would be invited to. He trudged on through the night, along the curving sidewalk lit on one side by the lights from the undergrad library, dark on the other. Walter took intermittent glances over into the dark side . . . and swore he saw things. Shapes. Figures that seemed to be following him, that seemed to be smiling, drifting along, but when he strained his eyes he saw no figures.

The snack bar raved in fluorescent light; Walter shielded his eyes. Why would he not like the light all of a sudden? Given his mood, perhaps, and the foreknowledge of what he'd be doing to himself in a little while, darkness seemed more fitting. He'd have to remind himself to turn off all the lights in his dorm, later, when he put the barrel of the Remington to his forehead. Yes, the darkness seemed more fitting. The darkness would comfort him.

"What do you want?" the heavyset, hair-netted woman behind the counter asked testily.

I want Candice, he thought.

"Come on, kid, do I look like I got all night?" she sniped.

She seemed in a hurry but when Walter looked behind him he saw that no one else was in line. Why was she being mean to him? Suddenly he wanted to drown her in the vat of steaming chili sauce, just dunk her head in and hold it down. He wanted to stick up for himself for once, at least snap back with a retort, like: "Grow a dick and blow yourself, Aunt Beau," or "Why don't you bend over and pound those chili dogs up your fat ass?" But all Walter said in response was, "Sorry, miss. I'd like one chili dog please, and a Mountain Dew."

She smirked and sloppily prepared his order which he then paid for and took to a table. The snack bar's seating area was empty save for one couple, a guy and a girl, obviously late-night studiers. Walter looked wide-eyed at them as they smiled happily at each other and began kissing.

Walter looked back down at his dog; it was the only company *he* was due tonight. "The last meal of the doomed man," he droned to himself. At least the chili dogs were pretty good here. He picked it up—some sauce dribbled off the sides—prepared to take the first bite. Walter didn't notice that the shadow pooled around his feet was moving independently but why, after all, would he notice that?

The first two bites were good. On the third bite, however, his eyes flicked to the plate-glass window that formed the front wall of the snack bar and he saw two people walking by, a guy and a girl. They were holding hands.

Then they stopped.

They were kissing.

The third bite fell out of Walter's mouth.

It was Candice and some football player in a letterman jacket.

Walter was tempted to curse God. Was there no peace? Not even in the last moments of his life? Why couldn't fate leave him alone in this waning hour? Why was God grabbing him by the back of the hair to give his face one last rub in the pile of sad crap that was his life?

She was wearing a lavender tank top that only accentuated her 38DD bosom. Also a short, tight denim skirt from which her long tan Brooke Burke legs emerged to end on stiletto heels. Her waist-long blond hair shimmered as she and the letterman kissed more ravenously, clenching. Walter watched through the dark pane, to behold the guy's hand plow up under the back-side of her skirt. Candice's hand was occupied as well, foraging around the guy's crotch. *Yeah, I need to see this,* Walter thought. If he had the shotgun now—right now—what would he do?

Kill them too?

Hmm . . .

The notion suddenly excited him but, alas, he knew it was just a fleeting fantasy. *I don't have the guts,* he knew all too well. It would be all he could do just to blow his head off all alone.

Candice and the boy sauntered off. Had they seen him through the window? Was she giggling? Now that she'd aced her trig and algebra, what did she need Walter for? *Colin was right,* he knew. *She's a cruel blond bimbo, and I'm the sucker . . .*

He got up and raced for the bathroom, stomach convulsing. He banged through the door, stumbling, then toppled to his knees—quite conveniently in front of the toilet into which he vomited up those first two bites of chili dog. It wasn't much, just a quick projectile burst and then his stomach was empty again. But he felt as though he was throwing up more from his heart than from his stomach.

Dizzy, he stood up, wiped sweat off his brow with the short sleeve of his very nerdy parrot-green-and-white-striped shirt. He flushed the toilet, taking deep breaths. Did everyone on the brink of suicide suffer such preludes? Again, it didn't seem fair, *nothing* did. A boy's last night on earth should be tranquil, low-key, even a little transcendent.

He leaned against the wobbly wall of the toilet stall. Much graffiti besmirched the shiny gray paint, but this was a college so the more intellectually elevated scribblings did not surprise him. . . . FULL OF SOUND AND FURY . . . SIGNIFYING NOTHING, someone quoted Macbeth. IF FLUID FLOWS HORIZONTALLY, PRESSURE DECREASES WHILE VELOCITY INCREASES. *Bernoulli's Theorem!* Walter thought. He knew it at a glance. He stooped to read some other things some people had scrawled. *They're poems,* he realized. Then he stalled. *I hope they're nice poems,* he thought. On the last night of his life?

He'd be grateful for some nice, happy poems, like Carl Sandburg or Robert Frost . . .

> My blood sifts through ashes;
> all my muses are dead,
> and your smile puts Glock 17 to my head.

Walter blanched. He read the next one.

> There's no reason left to wonder,
> no reason left to care.
> Why don't you put your head in the noose
> and kick out the fuckin' chair?

Frost or Sandburg probably didn't write these! He staggered out of the stall. Some *nice* poems! His mind ticked like a bomb. *Just go back to the dorm and do it,* he advised himself. *Just do it. Don't be a pussy anymore. Do it.* For some reason, however, he thought back to the evil dream, the pretty girl named No-name. When he'd asked her if he should do it, she'd simply replied "I can't advise you." But she'd also said something else, hadn't she? *I'm a presage. The future isn't mutable.* Certainly she was nothing but a symbol of his sleeping, subconscious mind, yet it seemed that she already knew what would happen. Walter, now, thought he knew too.

"I'm going back to the dorm now," he said to the echoing bathroom, "and I'm going to do it."

"No," a voice told him, but it was more akin to a hiss than a voice. "Don't, Walter. Please don't do it."

"Why?" he answered the absurd voice.

"Because you'll offend your providence."

The voice was coming from the toilet. Walter merely shrugged, unalarmed. This seemed appropriate too: that he should lose his mind as his suicide approached. It was the same toilet he'd just flushed his vomit down in. *What have we here?* he wondered half-heartedly. He looked down.

There was a face in the toilet, looking up at him through the water. A woman. Had someone actually cut her head off and put it in there? No, it wasn't deep enough. The face lacked dimensionality; it was an image, like a reflection.

"Don't end your life, Walter," the face in the toilet told him.

Walter shrugged. What more proof did he need of insanity? This must be some pre-suicide stress syndrome. He was seeing things.

The woman's face was pretty—in a way. Pretty, that is, if you overlooked the pus-yellow skin, bloodred eyes, vampire fangs, and the horns jutting from her elegant forehead. She smiled, blinking at him.

"If you kill yourself, you'll be missing out," the devil-woman told him. "Aren't you tired of missing out on things? Aren't you tired of everyone else having the fun but never you?"

Hallucination or not, Walter had no choice but to answer, "Yes. I'm so tired of that . . ." More thoughts of Candice. *Everyone gets her but me . . .*

Walter spun around at the sound of the bathroom door opening. It opened slowly, on its own, like the automatic doors you sometimes saw at public restrooms for people in wheelchairs. Only this wasn't an automatic door.

It *drifted* open.

Then a girl walked in, a pretty girl college girl—not as pretty as Candice, of course, but . . . she wasn't bad. Shapely, brunet, tight blue jeans and a hackneyed FLORIDA IS FOR LOVERS t-shirt. But she seemed to be struggling against something, as though someone unseen were pulling her back as she tried to move forward. Or perhaps it was the other way around, someone unseen was pushing her forward as she tried to move back and get away. Walter had never seen her before.

"Who are you?" Walter asked.

Her face pinched up. She whipped her head back and forth, eyes squeezed shut, teeth grinding. Yes, she was struggling against some force that Walter couldn't see. But what?

"You-you can't-can't—kill yourself!" she blurted.

"Why?"

"They-they-they're making me say it!"

Just once, Walter thought, *why can't I have a normal day like everybody else?*

"I'm-I'm-I'm . . . being machinated by Convulsionary Satanic nuns!" she blurted next and then began to move forward more, still struggling against something. Eventually she pinned him into the corner. Walter could only stare back at her.

"Don't-don't kill yourself. Here-here-here you have no power, but-but, over thuh-thuh-there you'll have everything!"

"Everything? Like what?" he asked.

"Pow-pow-power!"

"I don't want power," Walter told her, having no idea what she was talking about.

"Ruh-ruh-riches untold!"

"I don't want riches."

"Luh-luh-love!"

Walter paused on that one.

"Yes, Walter," the voice from the toilet added. "Love. I know a place where love will finally find you. Love like you could never imagine. Have you ever had that, Walter?"

He thought of Candice. "No."

"Don't kill yourself and you can finally have what you

deserve. It's a place where no one will laugh at you."

More from the twitching girl in the Florida shirt: "Yuh-yuh-you won't be a duh-duh-dork anymore."

The Toilet Devil: "You will be truly loved."

What did it matter? *I'm having a conversation with hallucinations because I'm crazy.* But at least it was an *interesting* conversation. Walter liked the subject matter.

"Where?" he asked.

Florida Shirt continued to twitch against whatever force was manipulating her. "The Meff-meff-meff-issssssssssssssss ssss-topolis!"

"Trust us, Walter," the girl in the toilet added before he could question anything.

Trust? "Why? I trusted Candice and look what happened? She just used me. Girls just use me. I'm a nerd. That's the way it's always been."

"Do as we say and you'll be a king," the Toilet Devil said.

Florida Shirt shivered in front of him. Now Walter could actually detect a trace of that unseen entity that was manipulating her: a misshaped ghost standing right behind her, its fat hands upraised as surreal puppet strings descended down to the girl, to make her do or say whatever it wanted. "Yuh-yuh you could be the most powerful mmmmmman in hiss-hiss-history. But not if you kuh-kuh-kill yourself."

Then the ghost behind the girl vanished like smoke, and the girl collapsed to the floor. She looked up, shock in her eyes. "Where am I? What am I doing here!" She jumped up and ran away.

"Walter?" The Toilet Devil again. She had a soft, sexy voice.

"What?" Walter asked.

"Your destiny awaits."

Walter's own shadow began to lengthen across the floor

even as Walter remained perfectly still. The shapes of ink-blot arms extended, long black-ribbon fingers sliding up the wall which faced Walter.

One finger began to write a final graffiti, like black magic marker, only this wasn't ink, this was pure shadow.

The shadow wrote this on the wall:

ETHEREAN! EMBRACE YOUR DESTINY!

When Walter got back to his dorm room, it was close to midnight. He was surprisingly unconfused. Hallucinations were common among the mentally ill, and what else could explain his current condition? He was suicidal. He was pathologically depressed. It messed with your brain chemistry, made you see things that weren't really there, and hear words that weren't actually being spoken. *My brain's not working right,* he acknowledged. It was that simple.

But what should he do? Take the advice of a bunch of hallucinations? Or follow his heart?

The dorm seemed silent as a morgue. He could hear his heart beating, and it beat louder when he looked at the shotgun still propped barrel up in the corner. Something nagged his eye from across the room: a framed picture of Candice. He gazed back as if in a dream. *She's so gorgeous . . .*

But was she smiling at him, or laughing?

What have I got? he asked himself, plopping his butt down on the bed. *I've got a major suicidal compulsion, but I've also got hallucinations telling me not to kill myself, which means, one way or another, I've got a serious psychiatric problem. I've got a genius I.Q. but I've also got a dorky, pencil-neck geek body to go along with it, plus I've got no personality and no social acumen, and on top of all that, I've got the girl of my dreams who thinks I'm the biggest joke in the world.* He rubbed his hands together in the concession. *That's it. That's all I've got.*

Oh, plus one other thing. A brand-new shotgun.

Walter, as a bona fide genius in the field of multiple sciences, tended to be an objective thinker. Philosophy wasn't his bag, in other words, but math and the hard sciences were. He believed in good and evil, as concrete ideas, and he believed that people should strive to be good. He also believed that *he* had strived to be good during his eighteen-year life. But that's pretty much where his belief systems stopped. He didn't believe in God, nor in the Devil. He didn't believe there was a Heaven or Hell, and to him, the concept of sin was an abstraction founded in cultural mythology. It wasn't science, therefore it wasn't real.

He knew, though, that suicide was universally considered a sin, a grievous sin, and for some reason—perhaps a subconscious instinct of self-preservation—which was actually a biological, not a spiritual, activity—he wondered . . . He just wondered.

What if I'm wrong? What if I kill myself and I go to Hell?

Then his eyes drifted back up to Candice's picture and he realized, *I'm already there.*

Walter got up. He took his last iron supplement, and his multi-vitamin. He might as well have all his RDA's, right? He went to the radio, to switch on some music. There should be something in the background as he ended his frustrated, unfulfilled failure of a life. Being the smartest person on campus meant nothing. What good was knowledge when all it got him was exploitation?

The radio fizzed on. He didn't fiddle with the dial—anything would do . . . or so he thought. A pulsating drumbeat and a squawky voice. What was this?

The singer was saying, over and over again: "This is what you want, this is what you get . . ." Over and over again.

He must've accidently put on the campus alternative station. Walter frowned and sat back down on the bed. He wasn't even inspired enough—minutes from his death—to go back over and change it. It was easier to just complain.

"This is what you want, this is what you get," the singer warbled on.

What IS this? he thought. Didn't people listen to hip good music anymore? Walter typically grooved to Abba, Air Supply, and Neil Diamond—the truly classic examples of music as an art form. His favorite album, of all time, was the *Baywatch* soundtrack. But then he remembered, as the discordant voice and rhythms nagged on: "This is what you want, this is what you get..."

Weren't those same words on the guy's t-shirt? *The guy who got killed on the circle yesterday*... The dead man with the broken neck, who'd also said "Embrace your destiny"?

Walter uttered a very rare profanity: "This is fucked up."

I want to kill myself, but hallucinations and a dead guy don't...

Yes. It was fucked up.

Now he got up and walked to the corner. He picked up the shotgun. It was an attractive weapon—if weapons could *be* attractive—in its black anodized finish and shiny stock. But Walter knew plasma physics and mathematical theory, he didn't know shotguns. At least Florida was an easy state to buy guns in; it was as easy as buying a candy bar. He'd taken a cab into Tampa because they had the most gun shops in the phone book. And the tall handsome bearded guy in the shop had been all too happy to not only sell Walter a serviceable shotgun but he'd also explained everything Walter would need to know. Showed him how to load the magazine, how to rack a round into the chamber, how to deactivate the safety. What a nice man. But then a pertinent question was raised: "What kind of ammunition will you be needing?"

Walter had read in a novel once something about "pumpkin-balls" or "deer-slugs"—essentially just a single, large steel ball inside the cartridge. It just seemed the logical choice.

"Pumpkin-balls!" Walter cheerily replied.

The shop keeper popped a questioning brow, then chuckled: "Whatever turns you on, but about the only thing those are good for are shooting bears and committing suicide."

"Gimme a box!" Walter cheerily requested.

The shop keeper hefted the shotgun. "Yes sir, say a scumbag breaks into your place, you drop hammer on him with *this*—loaded with *pumpkin-balls*?"

"Yeah?" Walter asked.

"One round in the head and he won't *have* a head."

"I'll take it!" Walter cheerfully announced.

And here he was now, in his dorm room, at midnight, holding the self-same shotgun that the nice man in Tampa had sold him. Was he having some last-minute doubts? Walter wasn't sure. He was sure he didn't want to live any more, so at least he was sure of something. An inept geek? In love with a girl he had *nothing* in common with? A girl who would never love him? What would he have to look forward to if he chose to stay alive? It didn't matter how smart he was, or how much money he would one day make in the private sector. Without Candice, he would never be happy.

It was time to make up his mind . . .

The annoying song on the radio beat on: "This is what you want, this is what you get . . ."

Walter picked up the framed picture of Candice and looked at it—

"—this is what you want—"

Then he looked at the shotgun—

"—this is what you get—"

That said it all.

Walter sat back down with the gun. He jacked a round. He turned off the safety by pushing the pin from left to right through the housing behind the trigger. He placed the end of the barrel against his forehead, leaned over, and put his thumb against the trigger.

"—this is what you want—"

I love you, Candice . . .

"—this is what you get—"

BAM!

Chapter Seven

(I)

Cassie brushed strands of lemon hair off her forehead. She felt agitated but mostly uncomfortable, squirmy in the hard chair opposite R.J.'s office desk. His Notre Dame hat was pulled lower over his eyes, which gave him a stern cast.

"You know what you look like?" he finally said, arms crossed behind the desk.

"Like a crazy whacked-out Goth chick sitting in a psych ward?"

"No, like a mousy little girl sitting in the principal's office because she was bad at school."

She wished it were that simple. Take a note home to her parents and get grounded for a week. What could she say?

R.J. sighed now, leaning over the blotter on his desk. "All right. Why beat around the bush? I'll just ask and you can answer. Why did you break all the lights in the shower room?"

"I can't tell you."

"I'm your doctor. Why can't you tell me?"

" 'Cos you wouldn't believe it. You'd think I was crazy and put me on meds."

"Cassie, I might put you on meds anyway, given that outburst. Now why did you do it?"

"I . . . have a fear of fluorescent lights?"

"Funny. You scared Sadie half to death. She thought you were in there killing yourself."

"Don't worry, I won't kill myself," Cassie said, "at least not before the next Rob Zombie tour."

R.J. maintained the stern gaze.

"Jeez, it's a joke!" Cassie complained. "Can't anyone in this place take a joke?"

"It's no place for joking. We don't know what's wrong with you, Cassie, and that puts us in a very precarious situation. Your father's executors are paying us a lot of money to see to your well-being and to keep you away from the state prosecutor's office while they prepare for your trial."

"The trial doesn't mean squat. There's no evidence."

"No, there isn't, and so far your tests and your behavior have indicated a stable, social person who isn't capable of arson and murder. That's what I've been putting in your psychiatric profile. But you tell me. What am I supposed to think now? What am I supposed to put in the remarks column of your daily report today? After what you did in the shower room, how can I possibly continue to claim that there's nothing wrong with you?"

"Maybe there *is* nothing wrong with me."

R.J. opened his hands in a clear frustration. "Then help me out here. Why did you trash the shower room?"

For the briefest moment, she considered actually telling him; she considered saying, *An Umbra-Specter was torturing my guardian angel, so I broke all the lights because I thought less light would decrease the Specter's power. The reason she was being tortured is because she was divulging forbidden information to me, and whenever she does that, she gets punished.*

Instead, she lied: "I freaked out. I have weird dreams that freak me out and sometimes I get too high-strung. Plus I'm having my period. Plus, I'm a real bitch in the morning before I have my coffee."

R.J. betrayed a smile. "Really? You're not B.S.-ing me?"

"Nope."

"That was quite an outburst."

"Sure. You ever had one? Ever had a day when nothing's going right and you just want to bust stuff?"

"Yeah, everybody has days like that."

"It's normal, right?"

"Yes, I suppose it is, to an extent. You get mad, you get road rage in rush-hour, stuff like that, and sometimes, yeah, you just want to snap and bust stuff. You *want* to, but you don't actually do it."

"Hey, until you have PMS like I do, I don't think you can make a judgement like that."

Another smile. "Your point is taken. Sadie said she heard you talking to someone? Who? Are you hearing voices?"

"Just yours."

"So Sadie was lying?"

"I talk to myself sometimes! Big deal!" she almost shouted. "You want to pump me up with Thorazine and straitjacket me 'cos I got a case of PMS and I talk to myself?"

R.J. laxed back in his chair, pushed the visor of his hat up a little. "Finally! We're communicating. So let me ask you something else. A minute ago you said you're still having bad dreams. Are they dreams about your sister's suicide?"

"No, those stopped a while ago. Just nightmares."

"About what?"

"About Hell."

"You mean the place you talk about during your polygraphs and narco-analysis? This big city, in Hell. The Mephistopolis."

"Yeah. They're just dreams, screwed up dreams. Me being an Etheress and all that."

"So now you're telling me that you're not really an Etheress, that was just a dream?"

"Yeah. Take some of that—what is it? Sodium—"

"The hypnotic? Sodium amitol?"

"Yeah, take some of that stuff yourself, doc. See if it doesn't put a little bit of a whack on *you*. See if *you* don't spout some wild shit with an armful of that. I have weird dreams to begin with and that stuff makes them weirder, and, yeah, maybe I confused the dreams with reality for a little while. I'm still trying to get over my father's death and the fact that I'm stuck in this looney bin—no offense. You ever have weird dreams? You ever been confused, ever in your life?"

A sharper smile this time. "You always try to defend yourself by challenging me."

"Why shouldn't I? Sometimes I have screwy dreams. Everybody does. So how come *everybody* isn't in this joint?"

"Because *everybody* isn't being charged with arson and premeditated murder. Because *everybody* isn't suicidal, and *everybody* didn't break all the lights in the shower room."

"I'll pay for the friggin' lights."

"No, but your father's lawyers will," R.J. corrected. "Let me ask you something else."

Cassie was getting bored, bending her flip-flops under her heels. "Shoot."

"Who burned your house down with your father in it?"

"I don't know. I only know it wasn't me. I loved my father." She shot him a frown. "You already know I didn't do it. You don't believe for a minute that I did it."

"No, Cassie, I don't. But who did? Who do you *think* did it?"

"Probably some stoner from town, some redneck all jigged up on PCP or something."

"I like that answer. But I just keep getting this feeling that you're only *saying* it."

"What do you mean?"

"That you're saying what you think I want to hear."

"I never do that," Cassie countered. "You're my shrink, you should know that. And what does Dr. Morse think? Does he think I had a psycho outburst? Does he think I'm a head-case?"

"No, but he's very confused about your case. So am I."

"Hey, I'm just a bitchy Goth girl from D.C. There's not much to be confused about." She did feel a bit foolish now. "I'm sorry I busted your dumb shower lights. Does it help to say it won't happen again?"

"Probably."

Cassie looked at her watch. "I got my occupational therapy class in five minutes. Can I go now?"

"Yes."

She stood up from the chair, suddenly remembering. "Oh, can I ask a favor?"

R.J. looked sarcastically quizzical. "Maybe."

"Can I move to the room at the end of the hall, on the left?"

"Why?"

" 'Cos there's a view of the garden."

"Why should I give you privileges after what you did in the shower?"

"Because you're a cool guy."

"You think you can manipulate me with flattery?"

"You're also probably the best shrink I've ever had."

"That won't work—"

"And handsome."

R.J. smiled. "I'm disappointed, Cassie. I thought you were a lot more sophisticated than that. And the answer is no."

"I'm glad you said that." Cassie smiled a great big smile. She pointed to his Notre Dame hat. "They play University of Maryland tonight, don't they? Maryland's supposed to kick their butts bad?"

R.J. looked immediately enthused. "How do you know that? You're a college football fan?"

Cassie scoffed. "Jeez, no—football's for morons. Come on, a bunch of steroid-bloated idiots running back and forth with a leather bag full of air, makin' five million a year."

Now R.J. frowned. "Then how do you know that Notre Dame's slated to lose big to Maryland?"

"I just know."

"And your point?"

"Are you a betting man?"

R.J. shook his head, leaning back in the chair. "So that's it. You want to bet—for a new room assignment. Ain't gonna happen, Cassie. I'm a doctor. I can't make bets with patients."

"It's not really a bet. What would you say if I told you Maryland's gonna lose 22-0?"

"I'd laugh hard."

"You wouldn't believe it 'cos Notre Dame kind'a sucks, right?"

R.J. took an instant offense. "They don't *suck*. They're . . . having a rebuilding year."

"Fine. They suck. So that's the deal. If Maryland loses 22-0, you move me to the new room, okay?"

R.J. laughed. "Okay, Cassie, you've got a deal."

She could still hear him laughing by the time she got off the admin wing.

Later that night, R.J. moved Cassie into the new room.

"Thanks," she said.

He cast her the sharpest frown. "I don't know how you pulled that off. And don't tell me you're clairvoyant. I'm a behavioral psychiatrist, I don't believe in crap like that."

"Believe," Cassie intoned. She sat down on the stiff bed, bouncing her butt on it a few times. "You should be happy. Your team won."

"Yeah. 22-0. When every sportswriter in the country said they'd get their tails kicked. I should've called my bookie and bet my life savings."

"You behavioral psychiatrists are too skeptical."

He stood at the door, looking down at her as she sat on the edge of the bed. "You're a very interesting young woman, Cassie."

"Yeah. Interesting. But not crazy."

"You're probably right. Goodnight. See you at breakfast."

"Go, Fighting Irish!"

R.J. left, locked the door behind her. Immediately she got up and looked out the decoratively barred window. *Yep, there's a garden, all right.* A spotlight lit up the small fenced court but it wasn't much. This time of the year, in Florida? A couple of short palm trees and a couple of flowerbeds that were turning brown. *Better than nothing,* she conceded. But the garden wasn't the genuine reason she'd wanted this room.

"All right. So where are you?" she said to the air.

Angelese's voice wafted into the room like smoke. "Right

150

here . . . You just didn't see me." At this hour, only one emergency light remained on in the room, leaving three corners dark. From the darkness in one of those corners, Angelese emerged, like a lapse-dissolve in reverse.

"I'm glad you got the room," the angel said.

"It was easy. Thanks for the tip on the football game."

"Men really are easy to manipulate, aren't they?"

"Yeah, but I think he would've given it to me anyway eventually. He was just busting my chops a little about the business in the shower." Cassie peered more intently as the angel fully revealed herself. "So you've been there the whole time, in the dark?"

"Yeah. I told you. Caliginauts *like* the dark. We were bred to exist in it. Angels who go where devils go."

"So if R.J. walked back in right now," Cassie asked, "he wouldn't see you?"

"Nope."

"Why not?"

" 'Cos he's human."

"So am I," Cassie felt she needed to point out.

"You're more than that." Angelese's voice reverberated. "You're an Etheress."

I keep forgetting that, Cassie thought. "I was scared. After the shower thing, I didn't hear from you for hours. After what that thing did to you? I thought you were dead."

Angelese had never looked so real before. The sheer white gown nearly glowed, as did her equally white hair. She shimmered, but she was flesh this time, not a projection through some spell. She sat down on the bed. "Angels are immortal in the Netherplanes: Heaven, Hell, and some other places. But here in the Living World we can die. It takes a lot."

"You went *through* a lot." Cassie gulped, remembering how viciously the angel had been savaged by the Umbra-

Specter's talons and teeth. The blood had *poured* out of her, blood like red neon light.

"But an Umbra-Specter doesn't pull much weight," Angelese continued with her explanation. "It can't kill anybody—it's one of the Rules. An incantation is what gives it life, but it's not a powerful enough incantation to allow it to kill outside of its realm. All it can do is hurt." One of the angel's fingers unconsciously traced one of the scars that rose past the neckline of her gown. Cassie noted more scars around her ankles and arms.

"Angels are stronger than humans, physically and mentally. When we feel pleasure, it's ten times greater than the pleasure you'd feel."

"But the same goes for pain, too, I guess."

Angelese nodded, smiling. "But the scars heal pretty quickly. They never fully go away, but almost." She pulled the hem of her gown up to her knees. Cassie gulped again. The angel was a mural of varying degrees of wounds. Some were lines full of clotted blood, others like heavy tracks of flesh-colored wax, and beneath all that were the faintest threads, like spider webs.

"So this room is—what?" Cassie asked. "A Dead-Point?"

"A Death-Point. Don't confuse it with a Deadpass. A Dead-Point's just a place where tragedy accumulates—I told you what used to happen in this room a long time ago. Caliginauts thrive in Dead-Points, but certain other kinds of angels wouldn't be able to come near this room. That's why we get duty like this."

Duty, Cassie thought. "You're not here because you want to be, right. I mean, who could *want* to be tortured by that shadow thing? You're here to do a job. You were ordered to come here, right?"

"Right."

"By who?"

Angelese's smile peaked, and the room's dark corners seemed to brighten when she said: "God."

I'm not touching that one, Cassie thought. She was tired and not in a very good mood. She lay down on the cot. "I don't want to talk about this anymore."

"I think you do."

"No I *don't.* I'm going to sleep."

"You can go to sleep."

"What about you?" The sudden question nagged. *Damn, there's only one bed.* She hitched over. "You can sleep here too. You don't have to worry, I'm not a lesbian if that's what you think."

Angelese's laughter fluttered. "Oh, I know . . ." Now her arms were outspread; she was levitating facedown, floating up into the air. "And besides, angels don't sleep."

Tired as she was, Cassie's curiosity kicked back in. "Do angels . . . have sex?"

"There are many different kinds and orders of angels. Most have to deny their desires as a gesture of love toward God. There are some angels that can breed, and several other orders of angels who don't have any genitals, and a few others that have both."

The image threw Cassie's mind for a loop. "That's a little too much information, thank you!"

"And as for my order, we have to be celibate, like Jesus. It's easy."

Cassie frowned, hugging the pillow. *Easy!* "I'm twenty-three years old and I haven't even *had* sex. I think about it all the friggin' time. Anytime I meet a guy I like I wind up just saying to hell with it 'cos if I *did* have sex, I'd lose all my Etheric Powers. If I'm not a virgin, I can't be an Etheress, right?"

"Right. It's a supreme sacrifice that you're making for God."

Cassie ground her teeth. "You want me to be honest? I'm not even *making* it for God. I'm making it for me, I'm making it for my sister. I have to stay an Etheress or I'll never see my sister again. So how do you like that? It's not for God."

"Oh, yes it is. It's just very complex. You're not sophisticated enough to understand."

"Thanks a lot."

"No human being is."

Cassie felt flustered, huddled on the cot. "I just don't know how long I can keep this up. It pisses me off sometimes."

Angelese was floating off her feet, smiling down. "We all have our trials, Cassie. You face yours very well."

Crap on that, Cassie thought. "How can not ever having sex be *easy*? How can it be *easy* to deny all sexual desire?"

"It's very easy. I'm celibate because it's a sign of the Kingdom where all of our love will be universal as God is universal. I'm celibate in the imitation of Jesus, who elected to be bound to no one in *particular* so that he might be embraced by *all,* in an eternal covenant of living sacrifice."

That's some answer! Cassie thought.

"Let me put it this way," Angelese added. "All you'd have to do is see Heaven just one time and you'd know . . ."

Cassie had no comeback for that. "Lissa should be in Heaven."

"She should be, but she's not. She committed suicide."

"She wasn't sinful, she was a good person."

"I know, but it's one of the Rules."

"Then the Rules *suck!*" Cassie blurted, frustrated. "She'll never see Heaven, and it's my fault. She's condemned to Hell because of me."

"She's condemned to Hell because of human error. It's got nothing to do with you. We are each our own keeper."

The smile again. It always seemed sort of mocking. "I thought you were tired. I thought you didn't want to talk any more."

I don't, she thought, but more questions kept swooping down, as well as things she needed clarified. She stuck to the basics; it wasn't as scary. "You came here to—"

"To get you out. To guide you to another Deadpass, to get you back into the Mephistopolis."

"Before Lucifer's people can abduct me." Cassie hoped she'd gotten it straight.

"My job is to slip you out of here before he can. And I've already told you, he's going to try."

"Why?"

"Lucifer needs you, but so does God."

Wow, Cassie thought. *It's so nice to be wanted.* "And that's what those merge things were about, what we heard on the news?"

"Yeah," Angelese said. "Spatial Merging—Satan's latest necromantic art. Lucifer's Warlocks have devised a way to allow a district in Hell to share the same space with a part of the Living World. It only lasts for a few minutes but that's all it takes. They do it by killing millions of inhabitants at the same instant."

"Huh?"

"It's at a place in the Panzuzu District, called the Atrocidome."

"Huh?" Cassie repeated.

Angelese explained further, hands clasped calmly in her lap: "In Hell, sorcery replaces science. For a thousand years, Satan has been trying to find a way, through sorcery, to harness energy for use in the Black Arts. That's why he built the Atrocidome. Think of it as a football stadium, only a hundred times bigger. It's a virtual coliseum designed solely for the purpose of transferring lifeforce energy into another medium. To effect a Spatial Merge, it takes a *massive* amount of energy. And we know they've been doing it, they've been succeeding. The fires downtown the other night, and that place in Maryland? Those were Merge sites. It won't be long before Lucifer orders a Merge here, and that's when he'll make his move."

"I still don't know why he wants me. He had Succubi burn down my father's house—the Deadpass—because he wanted to keep me *out* of the Mephistopolis. Now he wants to abduct me to bring me back in?"

"Yes. He only wants you back in during conditions he can control. You're too dangerous on your own. He wants you for your power, he wants to *use* you for some aspect of your power. What aspect, I don't know. Or maybe he just wants you for a trophy. In the Living World, you're just another girl, but in Hell, you're the most powerful Human to ever set foot there."

This sounded impressive—and ultimately terrifying. "I just want to find my sister, that's the only reason I'd ever want to go back there. I just want to find her and talk to her and tell her I'm sorry about what happened to her. Then that's it. After that, I'll never go back."

Angelese's smile seemed to float before her face. "Yes, you will."

"Shit on that noise," Cassie said. "I don't care if you think I'm selfish or scared—"

"Everybody's scared, Cassie. You want to know something? Even *God* is scared. You'll meet your sister again. I'll see to it. If I have to sacrifice myself and a thousand more of my order, I'll do it. But you have to help us too."

Cassie wasn't the sort who appreciated being told what she must do. "The only thing I *have* to do is stay Goth and die."

"It's providential, Cassie. You'd say no to God?"

Cassie chuckled. "Until God does something for me, why should I do anything for Him?"

"He's saving you from being imprisoned by Satan."

"That's what *you* say. And it sounds to me like it's a pretty even deck. You haven't even told me exactly why Lucifer wants me. Why's he want my power? What's he going to do with it?"

"Something diabolical, something monstrous. Beyond that, we don't know. That's why I was sent here. I'm going to escort you back to Hell to find out."

"That's great, that tells me a lot." Cassie felt steeped in sarcasm now. "I should be jumping up and down to go on this trip, huh?"

Angelese just smiled. "You'll see."

Cassie's eyes shot to the blot of shadow at the angel's feet. "And how come that thing's not doing a number on you? I thought any time you broke the Rules, any time you told me something secret, you'd get punished."

"I can't be re-tortured for elaborating on information I've already revealed. I've got plenty more to tell you, and when I do"—her eyes flicked down on the shadow—"that thing's gonna rake me over the coals."

"Then don't!" Cassie exclaimed. "Don't do it. Don't tell me anything and you won't be hurt."

The angel's voice went coarse. "I *exist* to be hurt. I am God's unworthy servant forever."

"I don't want to watch you get torn up by that thing again!" Cassie insisted.

"Whoever said life has anything to do with what we want or don't want? Life's a gift, Cassie. Sometimes we have to give something back. You will see me tortured again before our plight is finished." Angelese didn't seem the least bit daunted by the prospect. She casually crossed her legs, diddling with the pendant around her neck, the strange gem she'd called an Obscurity Stone.

"Why can't God just *know*?" Cassie countered next. "He's omnipotent, right? He's all-knowing. Why can't He just *know* what Lucifer's planning and then stop it?"

"It's doesn't work that way. The same reason he doesn't just put His hand down and stop wars, stop disease, stop poverty. And all that. He gave humans the world as their own. It's up to them, it's up to *their* free will. Yours too, Cassie."

Cassie slowly paced the room. She didn't like guilt trips, and usually they didn't work on her anyway. But now she didn't know how she should feel. Was she being selfish? It was easier to cop out, to change the subject. "I don't understand about this Merge thing, this Atrocidome. How's it work?"

"Like I said, it's an immense coliseum. They put a million inhabitants out on the field at once. They can't escape 'cos they close all the gates. Hovering over the 'dome is an iron plate that weighs hundreds of thousands of tons. It's able to hover because a regiment of specially trained Biowizards put a Levitation Spell on it. More incantations and spells are needed, too, of course, to direct the Merge, but when everything's ready, Biowizards terminate the Levitation Spell and the giant iron plate falls, squashes everybody in the 'dome field at the same time. Like dropping a cinderblock on an ant hill, only here the ants are living inhabitants of Hell. They'll use anyone they can round up, Trolls, Broodren, Imps, any class of demon, but it's mostly damned humans 'cos they have souls. More juice. You know all about how that works—when the Spirit Body of a damned human is destroyed, the soul descends into a lower life form, but there's a lot of necrotic energy that's released during that transfer. All those lives ending at once creates a massive energy flux, and then Lucifer's engineers tap that energy. It's the power that's used for the Merge. It allows a district of the Mephistopolis to exist in the same space with a chunk of the Living World, and it just goes to show you what lengths Satan will go to to get what he wants. Kill all those people just for a magic trick, just to keep offending God."

Cassie tried to picture the macabre event in her mind, but really couldn't; even with all the impossibilities she'd previously seen in the Mephistopolis, she couldn't quite fathom such a spectacle. But her biggest question—Why? What did Lucifer plan to do if he was able to kidnap Cassie?—was beyond even Angelese. Without thinking, Cassie asked: "When is the next Spatial Merge going to occur? Do you know?"

The Umbra-Specter instantly elongated on the floor, its black arms and claws gleefully outspread. *Damn, I forgot about that thing!* Cassie's mind raced. "Forget it, don't tell me!"

But Angelese just sighed, a strangely casual resignation.

A voice, like the etchings of two insect appendages abrading, seemed to say, "Please, please! Tell her! Let me tear your pretty body up . . ."

"We know," Angelese began, "that it's going to happen within the next few days," and then the shadow's claws lengthened and reached forward, slowly sliding up the angel's white legs but leaving luminous-red thread-thin slashes. The thing moaned in some demented ecstasy. Angelese just shuddered, braving the pain.

"—yes, within the next few days, and when that happens I'll be ready to get you out of here and show you to the other Deadpass, there aren't many Deadpasses beyond the nearest Migration Point in this area but I know where one is"—she flashed a triumphant grin through the rising agony—"I know because the Archangel Gabriel told me!" and

159

now she screamed, shuddering on the bed. The Umbra-Specter's vitality and physical form grew nourished by what was being said. Its ink black configuration slid forward and up to embrace Angelese and haul her linen gown up over her hips, the ebon awl-sharp points of its claws rending slow, delicious grooves up and down the inside of her thighs. Blood poured freely as water from a faucet.

Cassie sat down in the corner, in tears, pleading, "Stop stop stop!"

Angelese was panting, though, laughing as she defied the Specter's meticulous torment. "There's something else, too, Lucifer's backup plan—"

"DON'T TELL ME!" Cassie shrieked.

"Lucifer knows that he might fail in abducting you, so he'd need another Etheress but there isn't one. You're the only one in history—"

Now the shadow's black hands were up Angelese's chest, racking line after bloody line across her breasts. The talons began to dig just under the sternum, clawing a hole until the claw disappeared. The Specter whispered, "Sweet little angelic bitch, let me play with your immortal heart, let me tickle it with cuts—"

"But there's something else coming too," the angel gasped out, "It's called an Etherean—"

"What's that?" Cassie cried.

"The male version of you—" and that was all Angelese could stand as the shadow's claw hand molested her beating heart. The scream exploded from her throat and she collapsed flat on her back on the floor, liquid red light spraying from her wounds. The Umbra-Specter chuckled like someone who'd just had a greedy orgasm, and its form retreated back into the shadow which outlined Angelese's very still body.

Cassie's mind was swimming, her cheeks wet and teeth

chattering from the spectacle of atrocity. Bright red blood glowed all over the walls and formed a shallow pool on the floor.

The words replayed in her mind like a whisper in a dream: *Etherean, Etherean . . . The male version of you . . .*

Cassie fainted dead away.

Part II
Suicide

Chapter Eight

(I)

"Straight 4.0 student with a 170 I.Q. He's never taken a test in his life that he hasn't aced. Eighteen years old and he's already in grad school, but, look. Look how dumb he really is. How can somebody so smart be this stupid?"

Each word seemed like the bite of a shovel digging down into Walter's grave and grudgingly unearthing him. But Walter didn't want to be unearthed, did he? What was happening?

He'd just blown his head off with a Remington 870 that had a 12-gauge deer-slug in the chamber.

"What an asshole. What a shit-for-brains blithering moron."

The person berating him was his twin brother Colin who sat next to Walter's bed, reading *MAD* magazine. Colin's kinky tumble of fire-orange hair—identical to Walter's—

glowed around the shape of his head from the lamp beside his chair.

Where am I? Walter thought.

"You're in the hospital, Brain-child, in case you haven't figured it out," Colin told him. "And, no, you didn't die. Jesus Christ in a hot-dog stand, Walter. Where'd you get that shotgun?"

"What difference does it make?" Walter finally spoke through a throat drier than beach sand. He'd failed. He'd survived his own suicide—the ultimate humiliation. But how could that be? He leaned up in the raised, side-railed hospital bed, on his elbows, cringing at a twinge of head-ache, and looked at Colin. "How could I possibly survive the impact of a 12-gauge pumpkin-ball to the head? The cranial trauma would've been absolute. The man at the gun store said there'd be no head left on my shoulders."

"Walter, you are a prime *ass*," Colin replied. "I was at the dorm when the ambulance came. You should've seen yourself, you looked ridiculous."

"What?"

"You looked like Moe in the episode about the organ grinder's monkey. You didn't shoot yourself in the head, Walter. You weren't holding the shotgun right, it must've slipped up when you pulled the trigger. The pumpkin-ball just grazed the top of your head, dickbrain. All you did with that pumpkin-ball was part your hair."

Walter felt the top of his head. He had a hat of bandages. Then he fell back in the bed, almost in tears. *I can't do anything right . . .*

"You should've called me," Colin continued to berate. He got up, went across the room, and was turning a wheelchair around the side of the bed. "I had no idea you were suicidal. It's my fault. You almost fucked *everything* up."

Walter didn't get the meaning of Colin's last statement,

Join the Leisure Horror Book Club and
GET 2 FREE BOOKS NOW—
An $11.98 value!

— Yes! I want to subscribe to — the Leisure Horror Book Club.

Please send me my **2 FREE BOOKS**. I have enclosed $2.00 for shipping/handling. Each month I'll receive the two newest Leisure Horror selections to preview for 10 days. If I decide to keep them, I will pay the Special Members Only discounted price of just $4.25 each, a total of $8.50, plus $2.00 shipping/handling. This is a **SAVINGS OF AT LEAST $3.48** off the bookstore price. There is no minimum number of books I must buy and I may cancel the program at any time. In any case, the **2 FREE BOOKS** are mine to keep.

— Not available in Canada. —

NAME: _____

ADDRESS: _____

CITY: _____ **STATE:** _____

COUNTRY: _____ **ZIP:** _____

TELEPHONE: _____

E-MAIL: _____

SIGNATURE: _____

The Best in Horror!
Get Two Books Totally FREE!

An $11.98 Value! FREE!

PLEASE RUSH MY TWO FREE BOOKS TO ME RIGHT AWAY!

Enclose this card with $2.00 in an envelope and send to:

Leisure Horror Book Club
20 Academy Street
Norwalk, CT 06850-4032

not that he was paying much attention. He'd tried to kill himself because of Candice, and look what happened.

"Come on, Buddy-bro. It's time for Walter to leave the building."

Walter looked at the wheelchair, duped. "I can't leave yet, can I? Will the doctors let me leave this soon?"

"Sure." The strangest smile. "I've already talked to the doctor. I checked you out."

This didn't sound right, but who was Walter to argue? It just seemed odd that they'd let him out without even a final checkout. He'd just attempted suicide. Wouldn't they want him to see a counselor or something?

"Get your ass in the chair. The limo's waiting. You'll probably have one motherfucker of a headache for the next few days so..." Colin gave him a pill and cup of water. "Take one of these."

Walter didn't argue. His head did ache, which was understandable. After he swallowed the pill, he clumsily let Colin help him into the chair.

He felt woozy at once, light-headed. Suddenly he just wanted to sleep. As Colin wheeled him out into the hospital's main corridor, Walter groggily said, "Hey, Colin? Are you sure the doctor said it was all right for me to leave the hospital this early?"

"Sure, Buddy-bro. It's all taken care of."

"But . . . aren't there release forms to sign, and health-care forms?"

A pat on the shoulder. "All taken care of. You just relax and let me get you out of here. We have a lot to talk about."

"Mmmm," Walter said. That painkiller was making him nod out. "What . . . what do we have to talk about, Colin?"

"Your destiny," Colin said back.

The words shocked Walter's eyes open but only for a moment. The drug was dragging him down into a sweet lulling unconsciousness. He was almost asleep again before he could see anything of consequence in the hall but when the evidence snagged his vision, he saw that it was a considerable consequence, indeed.

Splotches of red shined on the clean white walls. Walter let his head roll to one side, and on the floor . . .

I must be hallucinating, he thought. *From the painkillers.*

Still, what he was seeing as his brother dutifully pushed the wheelchair down the hall was . . .

Lots of dead people?

Everyone on this wing of the hospital was dead . . . or at least that's what Walter, in his dimming vision, was seeing. Everyone. Every doctor, nurse, patient. Every janitor and every security guard. Everyone in the waiting room, too, lay sidled over, dead.

There was blood everywhere, as if the walls had been deliberately painted with it, and also the floor—it shined beneath a fresh wet shellac of crimson.

"I'm hallucinating, Colin." Walter even chuckled at the impossible imagery. "The painkiller's really whacking me out."

The wheelchair rolled steadily onward. It was soothing, comforting. "What do you see, Buddy-bro?"

"It looks like everyone here is dead."

"It doesn't *look* like it, Walter. It *is.* Everyone here *is* dead."

Walter's lips bumbled as his wobbly faculties tried to cogitate the information. "But that-that-that's not possible . . . Is it?"

"Sure is. I didn't want to fuck around, you know? I need to get you out of here without any hassles. Easiest way was to just kill everyone here."

More bumbling. "Huh-huh-how did you—"

"I did it by burning a thurible full of baby's blood while

reading an incantation from the forbidden book called the *Fourth Testament of Albigerius*. He was a Carthaginian sorcerer who could have out-of-body experiences in Hell and bargain with the Devil to give him secrets and spells. I recited one of his unholy rites. It's called an Exsanguination Spell, Walter. It made everybody's blood come out of their bodies at the same time."

Walter chuckled at the ludicrousness, though the chuckle lost some of its tenor when the automatic doors to the front lobby opened and Walter saw a lot more blood and a lot more dead people.

"Oh, no, this can't possibly be real." Walter felt sure, eyeballing the gore. The atrocity was, somehow, stunning. It looked as though the walls had been washed down with a fire hose, only the fire hose expelled blood instead of water.

Two more automatic doors slid open. Walter was rolled out into a warm, starry night which felt utterly serene, yet his confusion kept snapping his sleepy eyelids back open. The lights around the hospital glittered; everything seemed perfectly still and quiet. Down the front entrance walk to the circular court where patients were dropped off. One of Colin's long black brand-new limos sat waiting. He'd bought a bunch of fancy cars since hitting the state lottery but lately he seemed to prefer being driven around in this. The driver's door popped open and out stepped the driver: a tall dark-haired woman with voluptuous curves. She wore knee-high black boots, black-leather slacks, black vest over a white long-sleeve satin shirt, and a cute little black driver's cap. Colin liked flamboyance. The woman said nothing as the wheelchair approached. She smiled slyly, dark eyes like cut gems.

"Walter, meet Augustina. She doesn't say much, she just

looks good and drives my ass around. Pretty hot stuff, huh?"

Walter groggily nodded. In all that had happened, though, he really wasn't concentrating on the girl.

"Her name isn't really Augustina. I named her that when she came over."

"Came over?" Walter managed.

"I thought it would be kind of nifty to name her after the saint who cut his cock off because he thought sex was a perpetration of evil."

Walter drifted further away. The words sounded like echoes in his head now. When Augustina opened the back limo door, an automatic lift lowered out. Her vested bosom bloomed before his face when she leaned over and eased the wheelchair onto the lift. In another second, Walter was being drawn into the car.

A few more moments of perplexion. Walter could barely talk anymore. "This-this-this doesn't feel right, Colin. What-what-what's happening?"

The door gently thunked closed. The car's motor could barely be heard when they drove off into the night.

"Cool stuff, Buddy-bro. That's what's happening. All *kinds* of cool stuff. And you're part of it. In fact, you're the key player."

Walter could make nothing of what his brother had said. Something else kept bothering him and it was hard to focus on what it was, but eventually he snagged it as his mind and senses faded further from the drugs.

"Colin? Did you say something earlier? Did you say we have a lot to talk about?"

A cork popped. Colin had just opened a bottle of Kluge champagne. "Uh-hmm," was his response to the question. He took a sip of the champagne, then spat it out the window. "What is the big deal with champagne? Tastes like rotten club soda—Jesus!" Aggravated, he lobbed the bottle out of the car.

There's something else, there's something else . . . Walter remembered the man who'd been killed by the drunk driver, and he remembered what he'd seen and heard in the snack bar rest room last night.

"Did you say something about destiny?"

"Your destiny awaits, Buddy-bro." Outside, the stars swam by in the window. "It's time for you to embrace your destiny . . ."

(II)

Colin owned the entire top floor of the Strauss Building in downtown St. Petersburg, overlooking Tampa Bay. That's what Walter's eyes opened to when he began to regain consciousness—the low moon glowing over the bay. A gentle breeze off the water revived him. He winced; his head ached.

It took several moments to re-sort all that had happened. He wasn't sure what was real and what was imagined. He was still in the wheelchair—someone had put him out here on the balcony to look at the bay—but when he tried to stand up, he couldn't, still too shaky from the painkillers.

"Buddy-bro!" Colin's voice called from behind. "I see you moving out there. How you feeling?"

"I've been better," Walter grumbled under his voice. His arms felt weak as he grabbed the wheels and began to turn the chair.

"Augustina? Give him a hand, will ya?"

The buxom shadow slipped outside. The loveliest scents drifted off the tall woman's hair. But when Walter's eyes adjusted, as she came around to the other side of the wheelchair, her form seemed ghostlike and white. That's when he discerned that she was naked now.

Walter shuddered when her hands smoothed up his chest, then over his cheeks. A cooing sound faintly drifted around his head, like a caress itself, and then he was turned around and wheeled slowly back into the suite.

Walter squinted; the expansive room off the balcony was done up in dark wood paneling and large, ornately framed paintings. Maroon carpet hushed the chair's wheels. The entire room seemed to flicker darkly, tiny shadows licking up the wood-grain walls. There were no electric lights here, just dozens of tall black candles.

Colin was standing knee deep in a churning hot tub. "Want some of this?" He held up another bottle of champagne: Perrier-Jouet. "It's six hundred bucks a bottle. Can you believe that? *Six hundred bucks* for a bottle of hooch?"

"Colin," Walter reminded, "we're not even old enough to drink."

"When you win a hundred million in the lottery, Buddy-bro, you're old enough to do any fuckin' thing you want." He took a slug off the bottle, winced, then spat it out in a bubbly spray. "Jesus Christ, that's worse than the other shit I was drinking." He winged the bottle, like a bowling pin, out the open sliding doors where it sailed over the balcony and disappeared.

Walter just looked at him. "Colin. What's going on?"

"Lotta cool shit, brother. And I'm gonna tell you all about it right now. Everyone has their destiny, you know?"

Walter, by now, was starting to get scared by that word.

"Some people have a modest destiny, some people have a great destiny. But *your* destiny . . . is monumental."

"I don't know what you're talking about."

"Relax. We've still got a little time to screw around, I guess. Till midnight, I mean. Kind of hokey if you ask me, but midnight really is the Witching Hour. It's all about faith, Walter. Belief in myth is just another form of faith." Candlelight flickered over Colin's face. He smiled sharply. "And faith is power." He hitched up his baggy swim trunks. "Entities of power reward the faithful—with *more* power."

I guess my brother's gone off the deep end, Walter thought. *Give an eighteen-year-old kid a hundred million dollars and look what happens.* But at least Colin had gotten his dream. Walter hadn't, had he? Colin got his riches, but Walter never got Candice.

"Augustina, hon? Grab that caviar, will ya?"

Walter hadn't even noticed that the tall nude woman had left the room. *How could I have missed that?* he wondered. It was as if she'd vanished, and here she was now, coming out of the kitchen, holding something. Walter's eyes bugged. He wasn't looking at what she was holding, he was looking at her. The visual image of her embellished nudity struck him like a punch in the eye.

"Oh, the tatts," Colin realized. "You've never seen them."

Walter saw them now, and perhaps that revealed a lot. Augustina slunk into the room, still totally nude, and with a body curvaceous and lusty as a Penthouse Pet. The straight black hair shimmered, dancing at her shoulders, and her perfect breasts jutted. But even the impeccable body wasn't what Walter was staring at. The flawless white skin looked almost checkerboarded with raven-black tattoos from the tops of her feet to her throat. The tattoos weren't squares, though. They were upside-down crosses.

"Slick, huh?" Colin remarked.

"What?" Walter finally spoke up. "She's a Satanist?"

"No, no, Buddy-bro. Augustina's not a Satanist, she's just a little toy that I was given, a little doll to play with. *I'm* the Satanist."

173

Colin grinned further. The woman smiled too, right at Walter, her eyes dark as volcanic glass.

"I want an explanation," Walter began, still unable to get up from the wheelchair.

"What's the rush?" Colin glanced at a ticking pendulum clock with a moon-face. Elaborate hands ticked toward eleven-thirty. "We still got a half hour, so let's chow down on this fancy grub."

Augustina ran the tip of her tongue over her top lip as she opened a hockey-puck-sized tin of caviar on a plate. "Try some, Walter," Colin offered.

"No, thanks."

"Oh, well. This stuff cost five grand. It's from Iran, supposed to be the best." Colin ignored tiny platinum caviar spoons, electing instead to dip two fingers into the mass of shiny black eggs. He sucked the caviar into his mouth, winced, then spat it out. "That shit tastes awful! Boy, am I a sucker." He lobbed the can through the open doors, over the balcony. "I guess you can't buy class, huh?"

"Colin, what's going on?"

Augustina stepped into the hot tub; she stood behind Colin and rubbed his shoulders but she was looking right at Walter. "No, you can't buy class, which I guess means you can't always have what you want. You have to maximize what you *do* have, though, right? You have to take advantage of it. Everybody's born with something. Augustina, for instance. She uses her beauty for her own gain. And you, Walter, you've got the brains, and you were well on your way to using them to your best advantage. But me? What have I got? I'll tell you. I've got ambition."

Walter couldn't figure out what his brother was getting at.

"That's it. Ain't got looks, ain't got smarts, ain't got charisma, and I sure as shit ain't got class. So I gotta go with what I've got."

"Colin, this is a really weird scene . . ."

Colin and Augustina both stepped out of the hot tub at the same time, coming around toward Walter from opposite sides.

"But sometimes we fuck up, don't we?" Colin continued. "Like those fuckin' Enron assholes, for instance. They had it all but now they're in jail. And another example—you. All that potential, all those brains, and you almost blew 'em all over the dorm room, and why? Because of a girl. Well, I'm not gonna fuck up, not me . . ."

Augustina came around and stood behind the wheelchair, while Colin stood in front of Walter in his ludicrous swim trunks. Did the candlelight in the room actually darken? Colin's voice seemed to darken with it. "You almost queered *everything*, and you don't even know it; it wasn't supposed to happen this soon. I made a deal—how do you think I won all that money?"

"What?"

"You and I both have a destiny. *My* destiny is to see to it that you fulfill *yours*."

"This is really creeping me out, Colin! What are you talking about!"

"I'm talking about infinity, Buddy-bro. I'm talking about immortality and things that never end. There are secrets not of this world. I know all about them. I found a way to read some of the secrets."

Before Walter could object further, he was being wheeled into another spacious, plushly paneled and carpeted room. More candles guttered, an entire wall of them. It was in here that Walter saw the strangest scene.

"What . . . *is* this?" he asked, peering.

Long tables were arranged about the room and sitting at

the tables were a dozen naked women. The women weren't robust and attractive, though, not like Augustina. They all looked emaciated and straggly, dirty hair hanging before wan faces as they leaned over the tables. They were all writing very intently, almost frantic as they scribbled on yellow legal pads. The sound of their etching filled Walter's ears like locusts.

"Welcome to my Scriptorium. Meet my holographers, my Unholy Transcribers." Something smelled funny in the room, something burning.

Then Walter saw the burner in front of the tables, a crucible sort of thing sitting on top of it, and a large tank marked FLAMMABLE.

"Bones," Colin said. "We're burning bones, which takes a very high temperature, by the way. The girls inhale the smoke, and it puts them in a Conveyance Trance; it's kind of like catalepsy, only they can move. Think of it as a phone line to that other world."

Walter just kept looking at the row of girls as they sat scribbling away. They were all so skinny and slat-ribbed, their hands and fingers bony under parchment-white skin. Their eyes looked dead.

"Only the bones of murderers, rapists, and child molesters work, but in Florida?" Colin let out a modest laugh. "They were pretty easy to find. The girls are all junkies and crack whores from Tampa and St. Pete. The drugs corrupt their willpower. Weak-willed people are the easiest to turn over. They all work for me, or I should say for a greater glory. They'll write till they die."

At that, one girl on the end flopped over onto the floor, her tongue out, eyes opened staring at nothing. That's when Walter noticed several other dead girls who'd been shoved out of the way under the tables.

"They're pretty much done," Colin continued. "They're

hooked up to someone downstairs, if you know what I mean, and they're transcribing the *Evocations of Lucifuge* in their entirety, the first book to ever be published in Hell. Not the kind of thing you can pick up at Barnes & Noble, you know. That's why I'm having it transcribed by the girls. It contains something very important, something that you'll need to read right away—a chapter called 'The Unsacred Edicts of Hellspace.' It's like a rule book. *Hell For Dummies.*" Colin chuckled again. "And there's a sub-chapter, Walter. Please read it. It's called 'Etheresses and Ethereans.'"

The incessant scribbling was sidetracking Walter's ability to properly process the information. *He's crazy,* came the eventual deduction. *He's crazier than I am. All I wanted to do was kill myself...* Another girl toppled over. She twitched a few times on the carpet, urinated weakly, and died.

"I made a deal," Colin said. "A you-scratch-my-back-I'll-scratch-yours kind of deal. I got the hundred mil, and I've gotten to live like a king. But it's over now. Something even better awaits."

"You're not making any sense at all," Walter said.

"You'll read the whole scoop later, but I'll give you the short version. We're a rarity, Buddy-bro. For one thing, we were born on May 18th. You probably don't know this, but May 18th is a balls-to-the-the-wall occult celebration day."

Walter frowned. *Occult celebration?* "What's the big deal with May 18th?"

"On May 18th, 636 A.D., Pope Honorius the First sold his soul to the Devil. That was a *big* feather in Satan's cap. Occult holidays are very important in the jazz you'll read about later. And there are other things that make us important, too."

"Like what?"

"We're both identical twins, and we're suicidal."

177

"You're not suicidal." Walter felt sure. "You've always been the most confident, level-headed guy I've ever known."

Colin laughed heartily. "Every motherfuckin' *day,* man. I wake up, take one gander at the dork looking back at me in the mirror, and I just wanna blow my head right the fuck off. People are shit, they're schmucks, they're liars who only care about themselves and they'll walk on anybody, trash anybody, hurt anybody, just to get one more nickel out of life. They pretend to be your friend but shit all over you the minute your back's turned. They write you off like you're chalk on a fuckin' blackboard. The whole world is full of 'em, Walter, full of phony backstabbing assholes who need people like you and me just to keep their self-esteem up. I'd had a belly full for *years.* I *hate* people, they all *suck.* They lead you on, lie to you, set you up, and tear you down. Why? Because they *can.* Because it's *fun.* It's the beautiful over the ugly, the powerful over the powerless, it's the nice guys getting mowed down by the Black Hats simply because we're standing there and can be mowed. It's their power, Walter, and guys like me and you are their ego fodder. We're the meat they eat for breakfast every day, and there's nothing we can do about it. I guess the only reason I never really *did* blow my head off is because I was afraid some chump would curse my nerd corpse for making too much noise."

Walter sat mortified. He was in utter shock by the revelation. "I . . . never knew. You were always the one I looked up to when I was depressed. You never seemed depressed. You never seemed suicidal. You never seemed—"

"Things are *never* as they seem," Colin cut in. "People are *never* as they seem. That's why I joined the club, that's why I went over to a belief system that knows what I'm all about. I'm an outcast, Walter, and I always have been. And who was the first person to *ever* be cast out? Ever?"

The silence chilled Walter to the bone.

"There's one other thing, the most important thing that makes us special," Colin continued. "We're both virgins."

Walter raised a brow, looked back at the sultry, grinning, and still very nude Augustina. "You're telling me that you never—"

"Virgins in the Biblical sense, Walter. Hands and mouths don't count, if you catch my drift. Augustina is very well-practiced. She kept me happy without breaking any of the Rules. And you haven't broken the Rules, either, have you? I know you haven't, I *saw* to it."

Again, Walter said, "What are you talking about?"

Colin winked to Augustina, who then leaned over behind Walter and began to brazenly rub his crotch. Walter squirmed. Soon her hand slipped down into his pants . . .

"Nothin', huh?" Colin said with the same grin. "No life south of the belt, ain't that right?"

It was true, as it had been for some time now. Even the few times he'd gotten a chance to be intimate with Candice, Walter's erection had failed utterly. This he could only attribute to nervousness and performance anxiety.

"Those iron pills weren't iron pills," Colin informed.

"What?"

"And you're not anemic."

"But the doctor said I was!"

"The doctor said you were because I paid him to say that. The pills are something called cholaxinol tartrate. It's something the courts make sex-offenders take. Makes it impossible to get hard."

Walter was instantly enraged. "I'm gonna kick your ass!" he shrieked, but it was more like a girl's shriek, his voice cracking. He tried to push himself out of the chair but he was still too weak and light-headed.

"Relax. It had to be done. If you'd lost your virginity,

179

everything would've been ruined. I couldn't let that happen, Walter. I couldn't let that blond bimbo jock-chasing tramp wreck my whole gig. Just one roll in the hay with her, and everything would've been lost. That's one of the Rules. You have to stay a virgin, and so do I."

I've been sabotaged! By my own brother! Walter had never been so mad in his life, nor so confused. Why would Colin do such a thing? He knew how Walter felt about Candice!

"Your destiny is a million times more important than your jones for Candice." Colin seemed to answer the thought. "So I fucked it all up for you. Sorry, but it had to be done."

"When I get out of this chair, I'm gonna—"

"Save it. And listen." Colin whipped his finger at Augustina, and then she was wheeling Walter back out to the big room off the balcony. The pendulum clock ticked on. It was a few minutes till midnight. "Not much time now. Faith is everything. Belief is the bedrock. You've got to give everything to your faith because our gods protect the faithful. They empower us. Do you believe that, Buddy-bro?"

"I'll believe that you're crazy!" Walter warbled back. "You're some kind of crazy devil-worshiper!"

"Augustina?" Colin beckoned. "Show my brother the power of your faith."

The nude woman traipsed around the chair, walked elegantly as a runway model out to the balcony, then jumped over the rail in total silence.

"See?" Colin said.

Walter gulped.

"It has to be you, it can't be me." Colin grabbed a can of Milwaukee's Best from the bar fridge, popped it open, and swigged. "Ah, now *that* I can drink. But where was I? Oh, yeah. I'll get my own reward, so don't worry about me. Shit, I wish it *could* be me, but that's not how the cards fell. That's why I shit a brick when the college called me and said you'd tried to kill yourself. Walter, it's very important that you understand something. *You* can't be the one who kills himself. *You're* the one who is destined to be the Etherean." More candlelight flickered on Colin's face. "The Prince of Lies wants you, brother. I'm just the pawn. We all play our little part." He chugged the last of his beer, shot a glance to the clock, and then said, "It's almost time."

"Time for what, Colin?"

"First, your present!" Colin presented Walter with an fancy, intricately carved mahogany box. "Open it, brother."

Walter did—and screamed till the whites of his eyes turned red. Looking back up at him from the box was Candice's severed head. "What did you do!"

"I killed the hose-bag," Colin said. "I never liked her anyway, but the reason I killed her is to motivate you. Look in the box. There's a page from her diary . . ."

Walter was close to having a hemorrhagic stroke when he fumbled out the piece of paper. It was lined, pretty paper, the softest pink. It smelled like Candice's perfume, and sure enough, it was filled with her familiar florid script. The last entry on the page, dated yesterday, read:

I know it's just a phase with these other guys anyway, and that phase of my life is finished. It's time to get serious. Those moron jocks don't love me, Walter loves me. And I love him. And tomorrow I'm going to tell him . . .

Walter shrieked again, this time so hard it felt like razors were tearing his throat up from the inside out. Nothing mattered now, did it? Questions didn't matter, explanations could no longer serve any purpose. Walter threw himself out of the chair. He was still too dizzy to walk but he could sure as hell crawl.

He began to crawl toward the open sliding doors. There was no doubt. Once he got out to the balcony, he'd drag himself up the rail and throw himself off.

Colin chuckled coyly. "Where are you going?" A switch clicked and the doors slid closed on their own. "Can't have you doing that either. You didn't let me finish what I was saying. I was saying that I killed Candice to motivate you." He held up her severed head by a rope of long blond hair. "She's dead in this world, sure. But she's alive and well in another. She's waiting for you, Walter. And she loves you. You can go and see her, and you'll know how once you read all those papers in the other room."

Walter scarcely heard him. He bawled like a baby on the floor, his puny fists clenched in the carpet.

"Now I gotta fulfill my part of the deal," Colin went on. He tossed Candice's head into the hot tub where it bobbed around in bubbles.

The pendulum clock began to chime, signaling midnight.

"My glory awaits, and so does yours . . ." Colin's voice grew darker and darker, as most of the candles in the room began to sputter out. Walter craned his neck to look up. Did his brother's barely visible shadow have horns sprouting from its head? "I know it all sounds crazy, but, believe me, Lucifer's plan is totally sane. You can't be the one who commits suicide. It's got to be me." Colin looked down. "We're both geeks, Walter. But in the place we're going, we'll be kings. Your destiny awaits. Embrace your destiny."

Walter's eyes felt pulled open by fingers as he watched. He didn't want to watch but something seemed to be making him.

From behind the bar, Colin grabbed the Remington shotgun and racked a round one-handed into the chamber, a slick move like Linda Hamilton in *T2*:

CLACK!

"Now *this,* Buddy-bro, is how you kill yourself with a pumpkin-ball!" He put the end of the barrel into his mouth, at an upward angle, and instantly pulled the trigger.

The room shook with the weapon's deafening report. Colin's head essentially vaporized as the single 12-gauge slug blew through his skull.

A second later, red mist and tiny bits of bone floated down, dotting Walter's face and the white bandage wrapped around his head. He moaned on the floor. The sound of the shot had been the loudest thing he'd ever heard in his life; he trembled in the after-shock.

He sensed figures around him, but he didn't look up. He didn't want to open his eyes because if he did he'd see his twin brother's headless corpse lying somewhere near him. Urgent, callused hands were on him: several of the girls from the other room. They were picking Walter up.

They put him back in the chair and were wheeling him back into the room with the tables.

The smoke from the crucible had gone out. On the tables lay several of the yellow pads, neatly stacked. Walter still couldn't think very concretely; he was still getting over the shock of 1) seeing his brother kill himself and 2) finding Candice's head in a box. Madness reigned supreme now, which seemed logical.

The girls—the naked drug-addicts—all stood in a line now before Walter, like an Army squad awaiting inspection, and Walter was the drill sergeant. He looked at the rail-thin creatures, their soulless eyes and deadpan faces. Malnutrition had sucked them down to stick-figures; in most cases their breasts were but flaps of skin, and nests of needlemarks could be seen at the insides of their elbows. The girl on the end broke the queer formation and approached Walter, her hair the color of dirty dishwater and the texture of straw.

"We're done now," she peeped to him.

Walter didn't know what to say in response.

"We'd like to go now. Can we?"

Walter nodded.

The girls who remained standing in the line were all holding knives. They just looked straight ahead as they all raised their knives to their throats and began to cut. None of them uttered a sound. Blood sprayed. They all collapsed to a twitching pile at once.

The straw-haired one offered a knife to Walter. "Would you kill me please? It would be the holiest honor."

"If you give me that knife, I'll kill *myself*," Walter managed.

"Don't do that. If you do that, then you'll lose all your power. You want to have your power, don't you? When you go to reclaim your Candice?"

Candice, Walter thought. Her head was in the hot tub. Here she was dead, but Colin had implied that she was alive, in some other place.

Madness not withstanding, Walter knew that he had to go to that other place.

"Tell me," he asked the girl.

"It's all here." She grunted as she turned his wheelchair toward the table. Her scabbed, bony hand touched a stack of the notepads. "Read this and you'll know everything."

Walter looked at the pads. Could such secrets really exist in them?

She handed him a slip of paper on which someone had written an intersection address that appeared to be in the south side of the city. There was also something else: a thin piece of black stone, the size of a dime. Onyx, Walter felt sure.

"It's from your brother," she said, her voice husky from years of crack and crystal-meth fumes.

"What is it?"

"You'll know later." And for the faintest moment, the soiled, naked street urchin looked vibrant, an impossibly dark radiance glittering around the outline of her body, her eyes alight.

She smiled in ecstasy, and whispered: "Etherean . . ."

Very slowly Walter asked, "What does that word mean?"

Her light was out. She was back to her ruined self, skin the color of curdled milk and pasty in junkie sweat. Her shaking hand patted the stack of notepads.

She raised her hands as if to solicit the stars. She leaned her head back and moaned: "Hail, Etherean . . . Hail . . ."

Then she cut her throat and collapsed, sullied blood pumping over the corpse-pile like cherry syrup over a pallid-white dessert.

The candles flickered. For some reason the presiding silence seemed very comforting, along with the shifting, dark room.

Walter turned the wheelchair back around.

He slid the first notepad over and began to read.

Chapter Nine

(I)

"I want to see it. I'd ... *love* to see it ..."

His name was Ernst Rohm. In life he'd organized a private army in Bavaria called the Strumabteilung which existed to beat, terrorize, rape, and murder Jews. It was Rohm, too, who'd propagandized that German Jews secretly supported local communist fronts, which wasn't true at all, but the perpetuation of that belief won Rohm the popular support he needed to keep killing Jews. Rohm himself liked to rape young boys and would often shoot them when he was done, "for posterity," he'd laugh to his peers. His barbaric deeds eventually brainwashed enough voters into believing that the Jews sought to destroy Germany, and it was this sentiment that helped install as Chancellor a man named Adolf Hitler.

That was Rohm in life. In death, he was a Chancellor

himself, of Occult Energy Operations. His ultimate superior considered him a very important man.

He and his aide, a former Roman castrator and standard-bearer named Flarius, watched from the observation post atop the immense Atrocidome.

"We'll see it soon," Flarius assured him in a less-than-enthused tone. He had four arms, two added surgically by the Holy Transfigurists, to make him able to do more things at once. He adjusted some knobs on a panel made of mica. "One-point-three million," he said. "That was the final count. I can't believe we got that many into the dome."

"Nothing is impossible," Rohm enlightened, still looking out over the crowded field. "Not to me. And there are lots of children this time. Demon or human, it doesn't matter. The younger they are, the more innocent. Innocence is just more raw power we can suck."

Flarius was too busy to listen to his taskmaster's pompous words. It was his job to calibrate the various fluxes of Deathforce from the Killing Plate at the precise time. One misjudgment would throw the stream off and send it down somewhere into the city. That wouldn't bode well for Flarius's immortal career, no. Destroying an entire district in Hell? He'd be grilled over phosphor coals for time immemorial.

It was a high-stress job to say the least.

Rohm's Reclamation Squads were working non-stop now that the system had been perfected. They'd achieved two successful Merges already, but tonight's would be the most crucial. The Squads had hand-picked over a million inhabitants and packed them all into the 'dome where they now stood shoulder to shoulder, entranced and staring up at the Killing Plate.

"I can't wait to see them all die in the same half-second," Rohm whispered.

Shut up, Flarius thought. He could feel the dead static all around them, he could even hear it crackling on the skin of his four arms. The Stasis Trance kept everyone on the field perfectly still and perfectly silent, and he could see the glowing black auras burning off the heads of the Archlocks as they tensed to keep the Killing Plate levitating over the field. The Archlocks were a particularized class of Biowizard—and an honored class. Their mental conditioning encompassed hundreds of years; physical training was required as well, including physical alterations. They were blinded and deafened, for instance, and their bodies were covered with anaesthetic balms. Shutting down their major senses only heightened their powers as mystics. Six hundred and sixty-six of them stood around the 'dome's upper rim tonight, staring blindly upward and focusing the power of their conditioned minds on the Killing Plate.

Below, the oval field extended like a small sea, only this sea was filled with people, not water. Smoke of different colors eddied from thuribles, from different Incantation Posts, as prayers, intercessions, and spells were chanted. Below, at the Ingress Gates, still more residents were forced onto the field by battalions of horned Constabularies and Reclamation troops. Chancellor Rohm smiled down upon it all.

"What have you heard, my dear Flarius?" he asked.

"Heard about what, sir?"

"About the Merge."

"Nothing, sir," the underling replied, when actually he'd heard plenty. He'd heard, for instance, that the Merge would take place tonight, and he'd heard that the Anthropomancers and Extipicists had seen very positive readings in their most recent divinations. And he'd heard that other occult sciences had been perfected recently, sciences that could change everything.

Flarius had heard a lot of things.

"Our lot is merely to serve, though, isn't it?" Rohm asked. He was fat, bulbous, and he looked stuffed in his scarlet tunic and armor. Rohm still lived in his Spirit-Body but he hoped that soon his master would Transfigure him into a Grand Duke—the ultimate reward in the Mephistopolis. And if this next Spatial Merge succeeded, perhaps that would happen sooner than he thought. "We ask no questions, we simply serve."

"Yes, sir."

Rohm's cheesy yellow eyes returned to the field below. *Soon,* he thought. *Please, Lord Lucifer, let it be soon . . .*

(II)

Where was she? Ranks of Gargoyles gazed down at her from levels of stone ledges which seemed to never end. Black tongues licked steel-sharp beaks. Then one of the hideous things jumped from the lowest ledge, landing just ten feet away from where Cassie stood on the street. It lunged, extending talons, but Cassie merely looked at it and thought, *Incinerate,* and the Gargoyle exploded into flames. A ball of black smoke unfurled. It was dead before it could even shriek, and a second later even the flames were out, leaving only ashes.

Green fog rolled down the narrow street. Through it she saw headlights, and then a steam-car clattered by, its side door reading CONSTABULARY FLENSING UNIT. From chains fixed to the vehicle's rear hitches, two naked Humans and a naked Troll were being dragged. They'd be let go once the coarse sandstone bricks of the street had abraded off most of their skin. In a doorway, two little gray-skinned Broodren chuckled as they cut off strips of their skin with a rusty straight razor; the sign over the doorway's transom read EPIDEROMOMANCER: WE BUY SKIN HERE.

Cassie moved on, the fog parting around her legs as she walked. She'd been here before but she hadn't seen the entire street as she was now. She knew this was a dream but she also knew that as an Etheress, her dreams of the Mephistopolis would blend with reality, part dream, part psychic channel. A Bapho-Rat ran across the street; she could see the wave it made beneath the fog, and she thought: *Squish.*

Next came the expected wet squishing sound, and the fog-wave stopped, brownish blood flying up in a loop. *Clear,* she thought next, looking at the street. *Fog go away.* In an instant, the fog was sucked off the street as if by a sudden blast of wind, but there was no wind at all. It was just the force of her mind, her Power as an Etheress.

More Broodren played near a garbage can filled with body parts; they had a length of intestine and were jumping rope. A curvy Lycanymph tried to turn tricks at the next corner, her champagne-blond fur shining. "Come on, lover," she cooed to a stout, runnel-faced Imp. "Fifty Hellnotes for a half and half."

"Hell, no!" the Imp asserted. "You'll eat me when you're done! Crazy Werewolf bitches!"

In a window, a man covered with Leeches groaned in relief as he used a back-scratcher on his back. *Oh, nice,* Cassie thought, wincing. The back-scratcher was a severed hand tied to a stick.

"Man-Burgers?" a Troll asked when she passed his vending stand. Pale patties sizzled on a foul-smelling grill. Each time the heat evicted a parasitic worm, the vendor drove it back into the meat with his dirty finger. "Stay in there, ya little buggers. You're the best part." His eyes looked like a hard-boiled egg cut in half. "How about some Ghoul-Spleen

Hash? It's really great, tastes just like scrambled eggs."

"I'm a vegetarian!" Cassie yelled back and strutted away.

But what was she doing here? Oh, that's right—she wasn't *really* here, she was just channeling through a dream. But even in her dream, she didn't forget her purpose. She was not an Etheress by choice; it was a power given to her against her will, initiated by her sister's suicide. That was the only reason Cassie wanted to return to the Mephistopolis.

I have to find Lissa . . .

But all she'd found instead was just more horror, more exploitation, sadism, and cruelty. Next she passed a brick church with an inverted cross at its steeple. Its stained-glass windows depicted pastoral landscapes in which screaming pregnant women disbirthed demons as smiling peasants looked on. At the doorway stood a bowl on a stand as would be found in a church for holy water but this one was filled with vexed blood. A peek through the arched door showed Cassie a sacrifice taking place on the altar as chants fluttered through the air.

"If I cut off my foot, would you buy it?" a tiny voice peeped. Cassie looked into an alley crevice and saw a young demon girl in rags sitting there. She was wasted, one eye socket empty, both of her horns and one pointed ear already cut off. "You can sell it to a diviner," the girl said with hope in her voice. Then she looked forlorn and held up a syringe. Her hand was missing some digits. "I'm down to my last bang of Zap."

"I'm sorry," Cassie said sadly. "I don't have any money and even if I did, I couldn't let you cut off your foot."

A tear glistened in the demon-girl's good eye. She began to stick the syringe needle into her nostril, but then Cassie said: "Hot. Real hot," and the girl dropped the syringe. It turned red-hot on the pavement, then poofed into flame.

191

"Why did you do that!" the girl sobbed. "That was my last slam! I sold my *finger* for that!"

Cassie stared down at her. *You don't need it anymore. You're cured* . . .

The demon-girl shivered as if suddenly chilled. Her good eye and her socket opened wide. "Thank you, thank you, thank you!" she rejoiced, jumped up, and ran away with her hands upraised.

Cassie, over time, had honed her Etheric Powers, but she knew this was just a parlor trick, and what did it matter anyway? She knew a Re-Tox Unit would pick the girl up shortly and re-addict her to the drug. *But at least she'll be free for a little while. At least she'll get to know what it's like to be free* . . .

Cassie wasn't free, though, was she? The notion put her at odds. Most would say she'd been given great gifts but she'd never wanted that in the first place. She just wanted to live her little life and mind her own business, and that only intensified the crux. Cassie didn't *have* to use her Etheric Powers, she didn't *have* to come into the Mephistopolis. She very well could live her life and mind her own business. But if she did that . . .

I'd never see Lissa again, she realized.

Yes, a curse, fueled by her own guilt. And though this was just a dream-channel, she had Angelese back in her room telling her that she knew where another Deadpass was, an opportunity ro re-enter Hell in the flesh and search for Lissa. *But everybody wants something,* came the regret. *Nothing's free. There's always a catch* . . .

On the street, she felt something like static, then everything fell silent and still. Bats and Ghor-Birds lifted off from leaning building ledges and the malformed trees in the park. By now she knew what was coming—she'd learned to sense it—and before she could even take cover—

Sssssssssssssssss-ONK!

In the center of the street, the green blob of light wavered, then grew, then delineated into a moving oval shape. The street shimmered in eerie green light. *A Nectoport,* Cassie recognized at once. Lucifer's intra-district transport system powered by diabolical energy and Warlock spells. Cassie stood unflinching before the opening oval, this arcane doorway, expecting a Mutilation Squad to charge out, or some manner of Monster. She wasn't afraid, though. She was ready because here her thoughts were weapons more savage than any Usher's claws or Constabulary's scythe-blade. *Come and get it, you ugly assholes,* she thought, but it never happened.

A voice. It was Angelese: "No Mutilation Squad this time, Cassie. No raging demons. It's just me. We stole Lucifer's Nectoport technology a while ago. It's great, isn't it?"

"Yeah, I . . . guess."

"We've also learned how to manipulate convergences in Spectral-Wave Emissions—same way magnetic fields can be manipulated in the Living World. We can fly these things around like planes, and keep the Egress open all the time."

It was too much information too soon. Cassie didn't know what was going on, much less why Angelese was here in her dream-channel. She'd always thought that a Nectoport was just an occult transportation device that brought two distant points together in a few seconds, like the transporter on *Star Trek.* But now it was something much more versatile, a magic carpet, a magic doorway.

She stood warily, until Angelese, her white gown and hair tinted green by the light, leaned out of the Port's opening. She held out her hand. "Come on, let me take you someplace. Your REM sleep's almost over and you'll wake up soon, so come on!"

Cassie didn't move. She'd learned not to trust any entity

in this place. "You could be a Blood Mirage. You could be a Hex-Clone..."

"It's good that you don't trust me here," Angelese smiled. "But it's me, angels can't lie."

"Demons can."

"Sure, but you're just dream-channeling, so even if I am a Clone, you can't really be hurt. Come on, I want to show you something. You've done a lot for me so I want to do something for you."

Cassie still didn't know what to think. But it *was* just a dream-channel. And she was a very adventurous girl by nature.

"All right..."

She got into the Nectoport with Angelese and—

Ssssssssssssssss-ONK!

—they were off.

Angelese kept the Egress open as they soared through the smoke-streaked sky. In no time they were miles up but when Cassie peered down, she gasped. The glowing city below extended seemingly without physical limit. It was a terrifying vision on its own but the motive was even more unnerving: that Lucifer had built this city—a city bigger than every city on earth put together—just to serve as an abode for every conceivable corruption, a city that existed solely to revile God.

Cassie's bright yellow-and-red hair danced in the wind. She could not avert her eyes from the intricate sprawl below. "It looks...endless."

"It pretty much is, Cassie. Satan's been very busy for a long time."

Even this high up, the soaring air stank. She focused now, noticing something as the rim of the Nectoport rose higher. The jammed-together districts of the Mephistopolis formed patchwork-like designs—an endless urban mural that glowed. The districts formed pentagram-shapes, triangles, demonic faces, and inverted crosses. It was diabolical art.

Angelese could tell that Cassie was noticing this, so she took the Nectoport even higher.

The shapes and diagrams below were all integrated, collectively forming a much larger mural. Cassie couldn't see it all, even at this altitude, but she could see enough. *Lucifer is his own patron of the arts* ... The pattern criss-crossed into a configuration that seemed to show an outspread arm below an immense wing. *An angel's wing,* Cassie realized. But she was grateful that she couldn't see the rest. She never wanted to see the face ...

They soared further, and Cassie noticed a strange black edifice. "Is that a—"

"A pyramid? Not exactly."

"It looks like black glass, but, this far away? It must be huge."

"It's the Bastille of Otherwise Souls," Angelese explained. "It's the vessel that holds the soul of every person who committed suicide, souls that otherwise would've gone to Heaven."

Cassie gulped. "Is ... my sister's soul trapped there?"

"I'm not allowed to say."

Cassie smirked. Next she noticed one district that seemed uniform in color, a brick-red. "What's that?"

"The Panzuzu District," Angelese told her. "Every single building there is painted with blood. It just happens to be the place I'm taking you to. I want you to see it with your own eyes."

The port began to lower again, like a fighter plane taking a dive. Cassie's belly did flip-flops. *This sure beats Busch Gardens* ...

"Look ..."

Cassie could see it, the thing that Angelese had previously

described as something like a colossal football stadium.

"The Atrocidome."

Jeez, that thing must cover an entire square mile. She squinted then. An immense circular black blot. She could see the outline of the place, she could even see the grandstands, like those that would surround a sports field. But . . . where was the field?

"We can't see every detail," Angelese said, "we're too far away, and I don't want to get close enough to be spotted by observers. The black circle is the Killing Plate. It's hovering over the field as we speak, that's why you can't see the field itself. Archlocks are keeping it levitated until they can pack as many people in as they can."

"And when they do—"

"The Archlocks release the Levitation Spell, and the plate falls. It crushes everybody on the field at the same instant. All that Deathforce surges at once, and Satan's Biowizards use more Necromancy to contain and manipulate the energy—through those Energy Converters—" She pointed toward the farthest edge of the dome, where black skeletal towers at least a mile high pitched in the wind. "It's all that energy that allows them to cause the Spatial Merge."

Cassie couldn't imagine it. Who could even think of it? Who could devise such a thing, even in a world where wizardry functioned as science?

"Originally Lucifer built the 'dome to serve as an entertainment field for the demonic elite. His version of gladiators. But eventually his Wizards found a better use for it." Angelese made the Nectoport veer off sharply. It whizzed across the sky, across the shape of the black sickle moon.

"Where are we going now?" Cassie asked, gripping the rim for all she was worth.

"The Satan Park Zoo," Angelese said.

Zoo? Great. A zoo in Hell. "Why are we going there?"

Angelese didn't answer. Instead, she looked out at the evil spectacle that was the city. Her snow-white hair danced around her head, the wind pressing the fabric of her gown against her breasts. Through the thin material Cassie could see the webwork scars. At one point, the angel's pendant—the Obscurity Stone—blew back behind her neck, and while it was no longer in contact with her skin, her aura raged. The emanation of intense, lime-green light projected from the Nectoport's dimensionless rim. "Damn it!" she exclaimed and pulled the stone back to her bosom. "That was *real* smart."

"What's wrong? Your aura's beautiful."

"Here it's deadly. If Spotters see it, they'll report it to the Agency of the Constabulary."

"But we don't have anything to worry about," Cassie reminded. "Like you said back on the street. We're just dream-channeling. We can't be hurt or captured because our physical bodies aren't really here."

"That's right, but if someone saw us, that would tip the Constabulary off. Lucifer would know that someone's getting ready to fuck with him."

Cassie's jaw dropped. "Angelese! You're an angel! You can't talk like that."

The angel grinned. "That's just a misconception. Angels can talk any fuckin' way they want."

Cassie was *shocked*.

Then: "Damn it!" Angelese yelled.

Before Cassie could ask what was wrong, she saw it. Four Griffins, like a squad of attack planes, could be seen soaring up toward them through wisps of ill-colored clouds. Cassie had never seen Griffins so large—with twenty-foot wingspans. Their wings moved too fast to be seen.

"Do something!" Angelese shouted.

Cassie was dumbfounded but then she thought, *Oh!*

That's right, I'm an Etheress... Below, the flock disbanded into different directions; several disappeared into clouds. They flew so quickly it was hard for her to focus. *Come on, come on,* she sputtered to herself. Then she saw one, much closer, and thought: *Decapitate...*

The Griffin didn't even have time to shriek. Its beaked, scale-plated head flew off mid-flight at a perfect line along its neck. Cassie didn't even see any blood. When another of the beasts turned out of a cloud and approached the mouth of the Nectoport, Cassie thought, *No feathers,* and suddenly the thing was plummeting helplessly. Its cover of scaled feathers fell off its twisted body, dispersing in a confetti-like cloud. The Griffin was gone.

Angelese was taking the Nectoport lower. "Where are the other ones?" she asked with some concern. Then she was screaming. Two Great-Dane-sized heads shot over the Port's rim. One beak swiped at Angelese's face, missed, but got a length of her white hair. It was trying to pull her out.

The other Griffin was climbing into the Nectoport.

"Help!" the angel shrieked.

"No beak," Cassie said to the creature that was attacking her friend. The beak fell off, leaving a black-pink tongue roving within an agape hole. It raised a talon, but then Cassie said, "No claws." They fell off. Suddenly the thing was foundering on the rim; without claws it couldn't maintain its grasp. It fell off.

"Jesus!" Angelese exclaimed in relief.

The last Griffin made a sound like a jammed gearbox when Cassie thought, *Inside-out.* Suddenly its body inverted, organs hanging off its exterior, its small brain smeared like pudding around the prolapsed skull. Everything that was inside now hung outside. It shuddered uselessly.

"Out," Cassie said, and the Ethereal force behind the word jettisoned the thing out of the Port's mouth.

"That's some skill you have." Even Angelese was impressed, breathing deep in the aftermath.

"It doesn't work on everything here," Cassie said. She watched the heap-like Griffin turn end over end as it fell fast. "Lower species, mainly. The more evolved the demon, the less effect I have. Can't touch a higher-echelon Warlock or Necromancer." She grinned. "But it can be fun."

"You're evolving so well, it's amazing." Angelese narrowed her pretty beige eyes. "I'll bet you could give an entire Mutilation Squad a run for their money, and I'll bet you could give a Grand Duke a serious headache."

"I try." Cassie peered further ahead and down. They were much lower now, skimming the tops of corroded buildings, shooting through smoke. "Isn't it dangerous being this low?"

"A little. The smoke will give us cover." The angel pointed. "Look. The Mephisto Building. See it?"

"How could I miss that?" Cassie said. Through occasional breaks in the smoke, Cassie spotted the tallest building ever constructed. *666 floors high,* she thought in awe. Monolithic, the building spired high, looking out on the city with hundreds of thousands of gun-slit windows. Gargoyles could be seen prowling the stone ledges of each level; Caco-Bats nested in the iron trestle that crossed to form the structure's fastigiated antenna-mast. Even from this distance, it made Cassie dizzy just to look at. "That's where Lucifer lives," she muttered.

"It's the heart of Hell. Rumor is he hasn't left the building in a thousand years."

"Have you ever seen him?"

"Once. A long time ago."

"What's he look like?"

"He looks just like ..." Something severed the angel's

answer, as her Umbra Specter began to rear. "Just . . . bright light," she said instead.

At the base of the impossible edifice, Cassie could see the strange pinkish heaps, like intestines. They looked like organic masses of something that rose several floors up. They glistened, throbbing. These were the Flesh Warrens; the only way into the Mephisto Building was through these organic channels. It was the ultimate security system. The Flesh Warrens possessed their own immune-system.

"We have to go there, Cassie," Angelese began.

"What? You're crazy! It's impenetrable. The Flesh Warrens *eat* anything that enters."

"We'll find a way. Not now, later. There's something going on there. Our spies have told us that Lucifer has left the top floor."

"Why?"

"We don't know. We gotta find out what he's doing up there. Here, take these and look."

Angelese handed Cassie a pair of what she thought were binoculars, and they were . . . in a sense. Cassie yelped. The odd black object hummed faintly in her hands, brimming with some occult energy. Jutting from the two forward lenses were a pair of huge, blood-shot eyes. *Binoculars, my ass!* Cassie thought.

"You can see miles with those things. It's an Ophitte Viewer, the eyes of a Gargoyle charged by a Blood Spell. Gargoyles are Satan's sentinels; that's why he's got them crawling all over the Mephisto Building, to watch for possible trespassers. They have very good vision."

The fascinating meld of technology and the occult didn't particularly impress Cassie. Every so often, the binoculars blinked. She hesitantly brought them to her own eyes and looked out, now surveying the very top of the Mephisto Building. *She's right, something's going on up there . . .* She could see demons working, like a construction crew. They seemed to be building something around the ramparts of the roof, cranes droning to set in place rows of what appeared to be shiny greenish pillars.

"What are those pillars?"

"Plinths made of jasper. Any gem that exists in the Four Gates of Heaven has an opposite power here. In case you didn't know—and haven't read *The Revelation of John the Divine,* the outer wall of Heaven is made of jasper. In Hell, symbols have power the same way that an electric generator has power in the Living World. The symbol of something holy in Heaven—such as jasper—can be used sacrilegiously in Hell. The holy becomes *un*holy. Get it?"

"No," Cassie said, still looking at the macabre rooftop construction.

"Lucifer's got a bunch of plans brewing. The Merges, you, the Transposition that took place at that library in Maryland the other night. And now this, the jasper dolmens. They can be very dangerous Power Relics."

Cassie didn't understand and didn't think she wanted to. She put down the hideous, blinking binoculars. "I don't care if he's got a Tupperware Party going on up there—we're *not* going to the Mephisto Building."

"No, not now. But later . . ."

"Have fun," Cassie huffed. "I'm not up for it."

"Calm down. The only place we're going right now is the zoo." Angelese's white hair churned around her head almost like an aura itself. "But there aren't any giraffes and koala bears in *this* zoo."

More confusion whipped around Cassie, with the wind blowing in. The Port slowed, cruising lower. Hell was full of abominable odors, but the odors here took the cake. Rot, offal, spoiling meat, and sweat on bodies that hadn't been washed in centuries. A winding lane was lined with cages;

Cassie saw upscale Demons, humans, and other elite Mephistopolites meandering from cage to cage. The Nectoport raced along over the lane too quickly for Cassie to make out details of the creatures in the cages, and she supposed she was grateful for that. At one cage, several well-dressed Broodren cawed as they poked sharp sticks through the bars. Each jab was responded to by a thunderous roar.

"They're coming up," Angelese said, looking down more intently now.

"What?"

"The Oubliettes."

"The—" Over the next curve in the lane, the facility's structure changed. Now all the infernal spectators, instead of looking up into the cages at either side, were looking down.

Into pits.

They were like cement cells forged into the ground, each covered by a locked frame of iron bars. And in each cell, cowering in a corner, or looking up in rage or horror, was an "exhibition." Most were fugitives of one species or another—many Human. This place wasn't as much a zoo as it was a display emporium for political heretics and convicts. Some had been torsoed, some skinned or mutilated, some infected with diseases specifically designed to increase the shock-value of their appearance. But not all of those condemned here were criminals. It was a business, after all, and visual outrage was the market. Other of the cell's occupants were accidents from the Teratology Institutes and experiments gone awry from the Academy of Transfiguration: hexological mutations and transplantees. *It's like a circus freak show,* Cassie realized, getting sick just looking, *only they're manufacturing their own two-headed cows* ... Spectators openly spat and urinated into the cells below, an encouraged debasement (she caught a glimpse of a sign: DO

NOT FEED THE ANIMALS, BUT FEEL FREE TO
EXCRETE ON THEM). She also caught half-second
glimpses of what seemed to be pipe-exits on either side of
each cell . . .

"Are those *pipes?*" Cassie inquired, a bend in her voice.

"Twice a day, they open the domestic sewer lines from
the district—through every cell in the Oubliette Reserva-
tion," Angelese informed. "Keeps the cells neck-deep in
waste during off hours. It's for the city's most exclusive
prisoners. Instead of putting them on the Gacy Detention
Archipelago, or locking them away forever in the City
Prison or one of the Emaciation Camps—they put them
here. They put them on display to the public. For money,
of course. In Hell, everything is for money, just like in your
world."

It was mortifying. Cassie looked away, she couldn't witness any more of this, but that's when the pertinent question
finally struck her:

"Angelese? Why did you bring me here?"

The question gave her so much focus that she hadn't
noticed the Nectoport had stopped, its one-dimensional aperture hovering at the end of the Oubliette section.

"We don't have much time," the angel said.

"Answer the question!"

"Look. Look down."

"I'm not looking at that place anymore!"

Angelese's voice softened. "Look down, Cassie . . ."

Cassie did, preparing herself for some new vision of disgust and degradation, but what she actually saw was worse
than she ever could've imagined.

"Cassie?" a voice shrieked upward. "Cassie, is that you?"

Cassie screamed. Looking up at her from the demented,
sewage-smeared cell, was her twin sister, Lissa.

"Cassie, for the love of God help me!" The plea shot up

through the bars like arrows. "Get me out of here!"

Cassie trembled, choking. She tried to speak, tried to say something assuring to her dead sister but all that croaked out was: "Lissa . . ."

"We have to go," Angelese said. "We'll be spotted."

"No!" Cassie shot back, and all the emotion behind the response shoved the angel back. "We're going down there and getting her!"

"We can't. We're channeling. We're not corporeal. If we got her out, we couldn't take her with us. She'd be recaptured immediately." The Nectoport was sailing away fast as a missile.

"Cassie! No!" Lissa screamed. "Please don't leave me here! How can you leave me here?"

Cassie was on her knees, sobbing. "Why? Why did you do that?"

"I promised you you'd see your sister again."

"Yeah, great! She's in a hole in the ground in a fuckin' *zoo!* You show me that but won't do anything about it? What kind of a damn angel are you?"

"A smart one. We'll go back and get her, Cassie, but we have to be *incurare* to do it—we have to be in the flesh. I just wanted to prove to you that I knew where she was. We'll rescue her when we go back."

"I want to get her out of there now!"

"That would ruin everything. If a sentinel or even a spectator saw us, they'd report it to the Constabs. Then Lucifer would know we've discovered Lissa's location, and he'd move her. He'd put her someplace where we'd never find her."

"When, then?" Cassie insisted. "I want to get my sister *out* of that place!"

"Soon, Cassie." Angelese was standing at the Port's rim, looking out at the macabre sky. She picked up the Ophitte

Viewer and trained its living demonic eyes toward something in the distance. "Yeah. *Real* soon. Maybe tonight, if we're lucky."

Cassie was still gulping back sobs in the aftermath. "What are you . . . looking at?"

The deranged binoculars were handed to her. "Look there, back at the Panzuzu District."

Cassie wiped the tears off with her hands and looked. Four bright hyacinth-colored bolts of light, each the size of a tornado, seemed to be pulsing up into the night sky from a distance. When Cassie edged the binoculars down, she saw their source: *The Atrocidome. . . .*

"We have to wake up now, Cassie," Angelese said. "They're getting ready to begin the Spatial Merge . . ."

Chapter Ten

Sarajevo, 1993

The snipers were both clinical sociopaths; many of Milosevic's special operations and paramilitary soldiers were, in
fact. It was brilliant. They'd checked in wearing business
suits, not battle dress, with meticulous credentials that iden-
tified them as ethnic Albanian textile merchants. The "spot-
ter" set up his observation post in the old hotel across the
street from the target perimeter. First thing he did was
measure the room's current air temperature. Why? Varia-
tions in propellant temperature affected projectile trajectory.
These two men knew their job. Ironically, the weapons that
had been hidden for them by Serb undercover agents were
both American-made—an M-40A1 long-range sniper rifle
and an M-79 grenade launcher—traded to the Serbian Materials Command for Russian ACRID air-to-air missile

blueprints as hand-me-downs from the Afghan War in the early '80s. Some of the managers of this trade would later become members of a political group known as the Taliban.

Sniper One loaded the rifle's integral magazine with five special 7.62 × 51 millimeter rounds that were filled with a lower-than-standard amount of propellent, this to reduce initial muzzle velocity to something slightly lower than the speed of sound and resultantly produce a soundless report through the chambered M11-SD sound-suppressor, which was screwed onto the end of the barrel. The Unertl 10x scope had already been calibrated specifically to Sniper One's eye at a military range in the Vogvodina Flats west of Belgrade.

"I'm ready," he said very softly.

"I'm not," Sniper Two replied. He unwrapped four 40mm projectiles for the M-79. Two were incendiary, full of white phosphorous, the other two were APERS, which stood for anti-personnel. In parlance, the latter were referred to as "flechette"; it was a cannister packed with metal barbs that were deliberately rusted and infected with exotoxins.

"You won't have time to fire all four," Sniper One instructed. "Just two."

"I know. I'm not sure which to choose but I like willy-pete," Sniper Two replied, hefting a white phosphorous round. "They've been burning our children for five hundred years. I like to burn theirs."

"Amen."

Sniper Two would only be firing two rounds, and One five. They had to engage their targets and be out in fifteen seconds. They'd done this five times before, together, and had succeeded spectacularly.

And six is their lucky number. The imperfect number, Lucifer thought. The Morning Star and an Oni stood behind them, both unseen on this latest Astral Retrogation. The Oni held a Hand of Glory, each fingertip flittering with flame, like candle ends. Freshly severed and properly incantated, the Hand of Glory would provide them with total invisibility, while an Utterance Spell would render Lucifer's voice soundless; anything he said would be osmosed into the snipers' minds as thoughts of their own.

"Christ, I hope we survive," Sniper Two chatted, raising the grenade launcher's pop-up deflection sight. "I want to go back to the Love City."

"Oh, we'll get there. I feel it. I had ten last time, in two days, young things, too, lookers."

Satan smiled at the axiom. In Dachau and Belsen the SS had coined them Joy Divisions, here they called them Love Cities. Rape camps. Rape was a component field protocol for all of Milosevic's Security troops and SOG personnel. Fenced compounds with tents for barracks housed abducted girls and women, some even children—through which troops were cycled for sexual release. Once impregnated, the women were often released back into their provinces where they became social outcasts. Muslim women pregnant by non-Muslim men became instant anathema. Just one woman in such a camp could be raped by a hundred soldiers in one day. Sometimes the exploits were videotaped and sold to European and American underground pornography markets.

Sniper One sighted his scope down the street, toward the market. "This is beautiful," he whispered.

"What is?"

"How accurate the S-3's are with their intelligence. An open street market less than fifty meters from a day care center."

"Yes." Sniper Two closed and locked the receiver of the M-79. He was about to say *Let's do this,* but then Lucifer leaned over and whispered into his ear. "You're using the wrong ammunition. The incendiary grenades will kill the children. Use the APERS grenades. It will wound them all horribly. Make your enemy expend his medical supplies, exhaust his care personnel, and crowd his hospitals."

Sniper Two blinked. Then changed grenades.

"I thought you were using willy-pete."

"Flechette's better. Poison their blood, blind them."

Sniper One nodded. "Let's acquire targets." He opened the window and sighted the market again through the Unertl scope. In the scope, he saw a young woman in a green government services uniform. *Perfect,* he thought of his first target. The first one always had to be perfect. He put his crosshairs on the woman's head.

Lucifer frowned. "Drop your firing line, aim for the lower abdomen. Paralyze her and rupture her kidneys. Make it so she never walks again and spends the rest of her life on dialysis. You'll expend far more of your enemy's resources by doing this. Putting her in a grave costs them nothing. Plus she's got a husband and three children. If you paralyze her, you'll crush them all."

Sniper One lowered his sight-line to the woman's lower abdomen. "On my mark," he whispered, "after three."

"I'm green," said Sniper Two. His target range was so close he'd be able to fire his flechette grenades straight through the day care center's front glass.

Sniper One took a deep breath, let half of it out, and counted to three. He squeezed his rifle's trigger. The only sound the first report made was a light metallic *pop!* and then a *clink!* when he ejected the spent casing. The woman fell, face ballooned in agony. The next two shots dropped a young male construction worker and a nine-year-old boy holding a toy airplane while waiting for his mother to buy tomatoes.

Then came the familiar ear-concussing *PLUNK!* when Sniper Two put his first APERS grenade into the day care center. The front glass crashed inward, then—

BAM!

Consternation ensued. A wave of screams rowed down the street. Several dozen children who were still ambulatory staggered out of the center, in shock, along with several teachers. Blood dripped from all their ears; the first grenade going off had ruptured their eardrums.

BAM! came Sniper Two's second discharge.

Everyone immediately in front of the center fell down at once, mostly children. They squirmed, all hooked with flechettes. Most wouldn't die but would instead drain local hospital resources for months. Sniper Two dropped his weapon and was heading for the motel room's door along with Sniper One, whose last two shots paralyzed a utility foreman and a Bosnian soldier on leave. Total time of engagement: eleven and a half seconds.

Lucifer stood back and watched, radiant eyes gleaming.

Before the snipers could exit, the door was kicked open. Both men froze. *No Love City tonight, boys,* Lucifer chuckled.

"Halt!" the voice banged into the room.

Two uniformed Bosnian military police had barged in, 9mm CZ-75 pistols cocked and aimed at the snipers' heads. One was a sergeant, one a corporal.

Just before the sergeant would order "Kill them," Lucifer whispered into his ear:

"Don't kill them. I know you want to, for what they've just done to your citizens but be practical. They have valuable intelligence information . . ."

"Which one do you want, Sarge?" the corporal asked.

"Hold your fire," the sergeant ordered calmly.

"Bullshit! I'm killing these butchers!"

"No . . ."

The sergeant stepped forward, strangely sedate. Both snipers stood, gritting their teeth, with their hands raised.

"No, we won't kill these two monsters . . ."

BAM! BAM!

The sergeant shot both men in the hips. Then—

BAM! BAM!

—shot them each in a knee. Both snipers howled on the floor. Eventually one passed out from the pain, while the other, the grenadier, shuddered, his face puffed and almost purple.

"The City Defense Corp will be very happy to have them. They'll torture them in ways you could never imagine, and get every bit of information they have, and when there's no more to give, they'll torture them some more. For days. They'll take snapshots of them being tortured and send them to their families . . ."

Good, good, Lucifer thought. There was a tear of joy in his eye. While the young corporal shot each sniper in the ankle and scrotum, then radioed for a military ambulance, the Light of the Morning looked out the window onto the street below. The blood and horror and heartbreak and terror all seemed to congeal there in a human tableau. *So beautiful, so beautiful . . .*

"Throw it up," he ordered the Oni, holding out his perfect hand. The massive creature of stone leaned over at once and drily vomited the White Stone into Lucifer's palm. Instantly the thing disappeared.

"Revel in your hatred," Lucifer silently told the men in the room. "Hold your hatred sweet to your heart. Believe me, love doesn't work. It's hatred that makes the world go round."

He put a few flecks of Enguerraud Dust on his tongue, winced, and vomited wet light into his hand. Amid the luminous slime sat the other White Stone, and next thing he knew he was standing before Sherman and a Warlock in the Scarlet Hall.

"My lord. I can discern by your aura that you're in better spirits than the last time you returned from a Retrogation."

Lucifer smiled at his thoughtful attendant. "Indeed I am, general. It was wonderful. And the Utterance Spell that the Hexologists prepared worked beautifully. I want them all elevated in grade and rewarded. Give them an all-day shopping spree at Baalzephon Mall and a night with the Succubi."

"Consider it done, my lord."

Off the great stone veranda, he looked out into the maroon sky of his kingdom. Sherman walked up from behind. "And they're raising the Killing Plate as we speak, my lord. Can you see it?"

The next Merge . . . In his bliss, it had slipped his mind. Even from so many many miles away, his angelic eyes could see the immense plate incrementally rising over the lit Atrocidome.

"We got one and a half million, this time, my lord. The charge of all that Deathforce will be the greatest ever attained. The Dean of the De Rais Academy predicts a Merge this time with a duration of more than twenty minutes in the Living World."

Twenty minutes, the thought seemed to sign in the Morning Star's mind. *An infinity* . . . But a doubt soured his joy. "Any word from our Houngan engineers at the Department of Voudou Research? We still don't even know if it'll work."

Sherman was a man who *never* smiled, yet he did so now.

"General, why are you smiling?" Lucifer asked without looking at the general. "That's unlike you, and it unnerves me."

Sherman's beard drew up as the smile grew more intense. "I cannot constrain my joy—"

Lucifer spun around, his long silken hair drifting in fetid wind. "What is it?"

"The engineers are ahead of schedule."

Lucifer began to shake minutely. It was his nature to always hope for good things, and by now, after all these thousands of years, he was used to disappointment.

"It worked, my lord. It is my greatest honor to tell you that."

No, no, no, the Lord of Darkness droned in his head as he walked numbly back out to the shining atrium. Then he fell to his knees, clenched his fists about his perfect face. "Show me . . ."

Sherman glanced at the Warlock and said, "Bring it in."

(II)

"Say you take a snapshot of this clinic, then you take a snapshot of a city block in the Mephistopolis, you get them made into color slides, then you put one slide on top of the other and hold them up to the light and look at it. That's a Spatial Merge. Two pieces of two different worlds overlap," Angelese was saying.

When Cassie opened her eyes, back at the ward in her bed, the white-haired angel was the first thing she saw. She was leaning over the bed, talking. She seemed jittery, wired. Cassie felt thoroughly confused, but then her senses began to refit. They'd been Dream-Channeling in Hell. *The Panzuzu District,* she remembered. *The Atrocidome . . .* Angelese had taken her to some kind of zoo, in a Nectoport, and . . .

Lissa was there . . .

Too much was happening too fast. A weird pressure

seemed to be pushing against her head, almost like hands gripping her scalp.

"Can't you hear me? Wake up! Wake up!"

Cassie's vision finally focused. Angelese was pacing back and forth in the room, wringing her hands. "First the static, then the smell, then we'll begin to hear it."

"Angelese! What's wrong? Why are you so high-strung?"

"I've been telling you, I've been telling you—the Merge! I think it's happening right now. We have to be ready!"

How do you get ready for something like that? Cassie thought glumly. She dragged herself from the bed to her feet. The pressure around her head increased, and— *Did she say something about static?*

When Cassie took an erring glance into the mirror, strands of her bright-yellow hair were sticking up. A neon-purple electric arc crackled between her fingers.

"Ooow!"

"And you can smell it too, right?" the pent-up angel asked.

"Would you relax? Jeez, you're more freaked out about this than I am." Then Cassie's nose twitched. A faint but awful smell slowly insinuated itself into the room.

"They've already dropped the Killing Plate," Angelese said. "The Deathwave is already coming."

"What do we do?"

"Wait. In a minute there should be a—" and that was all Angelese had time to say before the entire building jolted. Then came a deafening sound like a massive water-fall.

"It's happening," Angelese whispered. "It's happening now." Her eyes were growing luminous in a faint silver light. Her lower lip trembled. "My God, I've known this was going to happen for ages. I've been preparing for it—

for ages! And now that it's happening, I don't know what to do, Cassie!"

"Calm down!" Cassie shouted even as the room was changing—merging—around her. The angel's panic didn't exactly inspire confidence in Cassie. She didn't know what to do either.

Then the lights blinked off.

"Oh, that's just fantastic!" she yelled. Eventually, a dim battery-powered emergency light came on, and Cassie was grateful for that dimness; it was easier to disbelieve what she was seeing. The plain white wall seemed to be shifting—something seemed to be growing over it: part of another wall, but there was a window in the wall.

A dark-orange glow rose into the room as the window itself rose. It was as if this other oddly angled window were being thrust up into the dorm unit from the ground up.

Cassie looked into the window—

—and staggered backward at what she saw. A sign read: MUNICIPAL PULPING STATION NO. 727,368. An obese Troll with wet carbuncles on his face was *smack-smack-smacking* a gore-smeared meat cleaver into the rib cage of a naked female Imp/Human Hybrid. The cross-bred woman's banana-yellow eyes hemorrhaged red at the first series of whacks. Her spotted arms and legs flailed on the metal butcher table. When she shrieked—a noise like brakes squealing—the Troll frowned, then quickly jammed a paring knife down into her larynx and jiggled it around until the shriek wore down to a gargle. She was still quivering when the butcher began to remove her innards and feed them into a grinder. Then he snapped on the grinder's power switch and watched the meat disappear into the chute.

The aproned monster paused. His great ridged forehead creased as if sensing something. Then, with a grunt, he jerked his gaze right at the window, right at Cassie.

Cassie shuddered. "Angelese!"

The Troll was opening the window now, the cleaver in his knuckly fist.

More of the room was metamorphosing around them. The hot stench of rotten meat blew in when the butcher had raised the window all the way. "I'm coming for ya, cutie. Gonna make a meat loaf out'a ya . . ."

"I think you better do something," Angelese said. "Now might be a good time."

"What do you want me to do? Spit on him? My powers don't work in the Living World! Only in Hell!"

"Cassie," Angelese pointed out. "Right now you're standing in the middle of a Merge between your world and a sector of the Mephistopolis. As far as your powers are concerned, this *is* Hell."

Cassie, in the avalanche of her terror, hadn't even thought of that. She let her fear turn to rage and shot a glare at the Troll. The stout creature howled, lurched backward as if shoved, staggering. In her mind, Cassie pictured two big hands grabbing the Troll's head. She focused the thought more sharply, thinking, *The grinder. Put him in the grinder,* and then the Etheric hands hauled the Troll back into the butcher shop and shoved his head into the grinder. The motor's metallic whine degraded to a sputter for a moment, as the blades bit into its new chore. The Troll convulsed, disappearing inch by inch as the invisible hands fed him into the machine.

"Good," Angelese said. "Now let's get out of here."

"Not through there!" Cassie insisted, pointing to the hellish window. She turned to the dorm unit's door. The door was locked from the outside but she knew she could knock it down simply by projecting a thought. However . . .

"Any time now," Angelese said.

"Who knows what's on the other side of it—"

"Sure, but we can't stay here. Don't you understand anything I've told you? The sole purpose of this Merge is to capture you. So use your powers and open that—" The angel's shoulders slumped. "Too late . . ."

Cassie looked at the door again. The gap around the frame seemed to blur—then it disappeared. The door and the frame were now one piece. "What the hell happened?" she asked.

"A Psychic Weld. So you can't escape. When the Merge peaks, they'll send a Nectoport in here to get you. Come on, this way!"

The angel was climbing into the butcher's window. *I do NOT want to do this,* Cassie thought, but what choice did she have? She climbed into the window, holding her breath against the stench.

"What about you?" she asked, coming up behind. A young Imp paid them no mind as they passed. He was cracking bones on a table, scooping out the marrow. "You're an angel. What about *your* powers?"

"Mine are all Masochistilated."

Cassie frowned. "What?"

"They take too much time to initiate."

"What about *your* Nectoport? When we were Dream-Channeling, you had one. Couldn't we use it to get out of here?"

"It's too limited a perimeter. We don't have the power to energize a Nectoport during a Merge, but they do. Just trust me, and do what I say."

This, too, was not encouraging. *Wooo!* she thought when her flip-flops touched the edge of something. She looked and saw what she'd almost fallen into a bottomless pit in the floor with a sign that read: DROP ALL ORGANIC

WASTE HERE. *Great* . . . Angelese's hand grabbed her and pulled her away. "This way!"

A wall made of horned skulls set into black mortar stood before them, and in it was another window. Behind them, though, three more Troll butchers were racing after them, all bearing boning knives and cleavers. *Chop each other up,* Cassie hurled the thought at them. Suddenly the Trolls were skirmishing amongst themselves, sinking blades into each other, cutting chunks out. "This is too easy," she said. She couldn't believe how effectively her powers had developed. How hard could it be to get safely away from the clinic when her thoughts could achieve such feats?

"Who are you?" someone shouted when they climbed through the next window. A family of Imps—mother, father, and small son—sat on a couch before an oval, grainy-pictured television. On the screen was what appeared to be a sitcom: giggling children machine-gunning parents at a PTA meeting.

"Sorry to intrude!" Cassie exclaimed.

When Angelese opened the front door to the family's house, she sighed. They stepped out into the in-patient corridor of the clinic. It was very dark, and much of it had transformed via the Merge, but from here they'd at least be able to find their way out.

"Get down!" Angelese whispered. She pulled Cassie behind a desk in front of the med station. They ducked.

"What is it?"

"A Flamma-Trooper . . ."

Cassie peeked around and saw it. This particular species of Terrademon was hybridized exclusively for special operations, usually in Extermination Squads. It had three legs but no arms, and had a humanoid head sprouting horns through an asbestos helm. It wore a shiny slate-gray uniform whose breastplate was crisscrossed by heavy black straps. On either side, hooked to the straps, were metal tanks, like scuba tanks, and tubes from the tanks led up under the thing's jaw. The organic igniter in its mouth was what lit the pressurized napalm.

Flamma-Troopers vomited fire.

Its jack-booted third foot kicked down each patient door, then it leaned its head in and belched a crackling orb of fire the size of a beachball. Screams resounded from inside each room.

It's coming our way, Cassie realized. She shot upright, shouted, "Hey, fireface!"

The Flamma-Trooper glared at her. It adjusted a knob on one of its tanks, then inhaled in preparation for the next heave of flame.

"Get tiny!" Cassie yelled next.

Just as the Trooper would incinerate them, it . . . shrank.

"Oh, that's great!" Angelese celebrated, springing up next to her.

The Flamma-Trooper was now three inches high. Cassie picked up a telephone book off the desk and dropped it—
splat . . .

A minuscule puff of smoke drifted up from the book.

The act gratified Cassie, but then she looked up at another, more resonant sound—

Sssssssssssssssss-ONK!

—as a familiar blob of green light suddenly appeared at the end of the hall. Cassie knew it at once: the egression orb of a Nectoport. The green light darkened; the orb floated, growing, then it began to widen forming a fluctuating aperture in mid-air.

When the Egress finally solidified, a dozen Ushers stormed out onto the corridor's floor, raising axes and spiked bludgeons. Their slug-brown skin shined in slimy sweat. Once in place, they fell silent for a moment, looking at Cassie and Angelese through chisel-slit eyes. Then their fanged mouths all opened at once and they howled, charging.

By now Cassie wasn't even afraid. Why should she be? She repeated her fun with the Flamma-Trooper, and yelled, "Get tiny, you ugly bastards!" and that was all it took. The Etheric Power behind her command shrank the entire Mutilation Squad down to doll-size. They scampered around on the floor in disarray. Then Cassie and Angelese proceeded to stomp on them all.

"God, this is fun!" Cassie announced, squishing.

"Yeah?" Angelese countered. "See how much fun you have dealing with *that* . . ."

The floor vibrated. A nine-foot-tall Golem trudged toward them, its stout three-fingered hands of clay opening and closing in some mindless anticipation.

"Get tiny!" Cassie shouted.

Nothing happened.

"Shrink, damn you!"

It wasn't working.

"We're screwed!" she shouted to the angel.

"Air, fire, earth, and water," Angelese said. "Only those elements will work against a Golem, because it's not really a living thing."

Oh. Cassie shifted through ideas. *A Golem's made of clay. Heat bakes clay, and fire produces heat . . .*

She closed her eyes and thought solely of heat. A wave of intense, searing heat.

As the Golem walked through the wave, its movements began to retard. It was baking, like a giant clay mannequin in a kiln. When it stopped completely, smoke floated off its features. Then it fell over and shattered like porcelain on the floor.

"Maybe we can get out through this window," Angelese suggested.

They ducked into the office beside the med station. Cassie was relieved when she looked out the window. The Merge hadn't progressed much past the clinic's grounds. Outside she could see the garden and courtyard, and beyond that, the road into town.

"Come on!"

"Wait," Cassie said. She saw the property locker, yanked it open and rooted around in the small boxes until she found the one with her name.

"What are you doing?" Angelese griped.

"I want my locket. Lissa gave it to me." Finally! She found her box and tore off the lid.

"Cassie, we've got *Hell* coming down on our asses, and you're fucking around looking for a locket?"

Cassie's smirk drew lines in her face. "I can't *believe* that angels are allowed to cuss like that."

In the box was her locket, her watch, and her onyx ring. She scooped them all up, then said, " "All right, I'm ready—"

"Too late . . ."

More rumbling, like an earthquake. More shards of Hell grew up the walls around them, and outside—

"Holy shit," Angelese muttered.

Cassie's eyes were glued to the window. Outside, through ember-like light, fog like green steam floated by, but through it she could see the face of a building. It seemed to be made of lusterless black metal, with gash-like windows. Things barely discernable seemed to scamper back and forth on narrow ledges, and some of the ledges sprouted iron spikes on which severed heads had been planted. The face of the building extended further than she could see, and when she looked up—

It was Cassie's turn to mutter, "Holy shit."

The building must've spired a mile into the air.

"I can't believe it," Angelese said, incredulous. "They Merged the Mephisto Building..."

"What does this mean?" Cassie asked.

"It means we're not going out that way," the angel answered and shoved Cassie away from the window. They ran out of the office, were about to turn back down the hall...

The phone on the desk was ringing.

They both looked at each other. Given the circumstances, the logical reaction would be to FORGET about the phone, but...

Both Cassie and Angelese got the vibe at the same time.

"I guess you better answer it," Angelese said.

Cassie picked up the phone, paused a moment, then put it to her ear.

"Hello, Cassie," greeted the voice at the other end. The simile was impossible but the voice sounded like light. "Do you know who this is?"

"I...think so."

"Look at the end of the hall."

Cassie's eyes flicked up. *Oh, no* ... Sadie, the clinic chaperon, quivered with eyes wide as coasters. A thin, pale-white forearm braced across her neck; standing behind the heavyset woman stood a gaunt, waxen figure in a scarlet cloak and hood. Within the hood came suggestions of a face: sunken eyes, skin so sheer she could see veins. But the figure's mouth was sealed shut by rivets.

"That's one of my Mutatos," the voice on the line seemed to sift. "He's from an imperial class of stewards that starve themselves for centuries to prove their service to me. And they don't talk, as you can see, so they can't tell anybody what they see in my abode. I want you to go with him. If you do, he'll let the woman go. If you don't, he'll dig a hole in her head with that tool, and swizzle it around in her brain."

Now she noticed the flat-metal implement in the Mutato's bone-thin hand, something like a screwdriver with a large grinding-burr on the end, which he held against Sadie's temple.

"Whatever he's telling you," Angelese advised, "don't do it. Don't listen to him."

"Plus, I'll guarantee your safety and the safety of your little angelic friend. I just want to talk, that's all."

The voice was radiant. It was the most trusting voice she'd ever heard.

"I want to make you a deal," the caller went on. "If you don't like the deal, you can go back to your precious Living World and do whatever you want to do."

"Nnnnnno," Cassie managed.

"And there's someone here who wants to talk to you—"

The pause switched. Then another voice came on.

"Cassie? It's me, it's Lissa . . ."

"Lissa!"

"Don't let them put me back in that zoo . . ."

"Cassie, hang up," Angelese said. "We have to get out of here."

"But it's my sister!"

"We can't do anything for her here. Hang up."

Cassie's eyes gestured down the hall. "And he'll kill Sadie if I don't go talk to him. He said he just wants to talk."

The Mutato pressed the burr harder against Sadie's temple. Sadie began to scream.

"Cassie, what's going on? This is crazy," another voice said, from behind. Phone still in hand, Cassie turned around.

223

It was Sadie. Not at the end of the hall but standing behind the desk. Sadie was speechless, then, when she too looked down the hall and saw *herself* with the Mutato.

"Cassie, it's a Hex-Clone!" Angelese informed. "Kill it, and kill that thing!"

"Burst," Cassie whispered, looking at the counterfeit Sadie. The manufactured woman began to swell, then it *popped,* splattering hexated meat against the wall. After the burst, the Clone's skin lay on the floor.

"And you," she said to the Mutato, "stick that thing in your *own* head."

It didn't take long. The stick-like figure quivered in place as the burr ground through the skull and into the brain. He flopped over.

The real Sadie, uncomprehending, ran away in the opposite direction.

"Oh, Cassie," the voice regretted over the line. "I'm so tired of this. I just don't understand what's wrong with people. Now I'm going to have to—"

Angelese took the phone and slammed it down. "Cassie, you're wasting your time talking to him. I told you before, we'll find your sister on our terms, not his. Everything he says is a lie."

Cassie stood dazed. The catastrophic reality of what was going on around her finally got the strange, hypnotic voice out of her head. Yes, she knew who she'd been talking to, and he wasn't far away. He was in the impossible black skyscraper that had just materialized outside the clinic. The putrid fog was oozing into the hallway now, half-shrouding the new, atrocious features that the Merge was incorporating into the clinic. Past the hall, by what used to be the nurse's station, was the door to the office wing, partially Merged with a statue of a split-faced demon on which fanged pigeons with worms in place of feathers squatted.

But there was enough left intact of the door for them to get through. "There's our way out," Cassie said.

She took off, expecting Angelese to follow, but she immediately sensed something wrong. Through the fog, she looked back. Angelese was standing there. Each time she moved forward, something invisible pushed her back.

"What's wrong?" Cassie shouted.

"Damn it," the angel muttered. Nothing looked amiss, but when she took her necklace off—her Obscurity Stone—the aura from her halo lit her up like spotlights.

In the light, Cassie could see a webwork of wires surrounding Angelese.

"Just go!" Angelese shouted back. "Somebody's put a Warding Spell on me, and it'll take me a little while to unhex."

"We don't have a little while!"

"Just go! I'll meet you outside!"

Cassie didn't like it, though she had no choice but to obey. Her own powers hadn't developed enough to combat advanced sorcery. Gagging in the fog, she ran down the rest of the hall, squeezed through the next door, and continued running down the office wing. A spider web, with threads thick as spaghetti, spread across her face; she screamed when she saw the attendant spider, something about the size of a gerbil, but with a beak like a parrot. The beak clipped at her face as she edged away, but when she turned she was screaming again, and ducking at a silver blur in the air.

Swoosh!

A Conscript, faceless save for the eyes glaring through the black helm, swiped at her with a long double-edged dirk. His black armor had veins pulsing through it, and an emblem on the breastplate depicted saints being boiled in oil—the emblem of the Asmodeus Legion. Behind him on the floor lay a freshly cleaved corpse: Dr. Morse, the psychiatric chief of the clinic.

Cassie tried to project a violent thought at him but it never got out of her eyes. Only anger charged her powers, fear inhibited them, and at this moment she was brimming with fear. A second swipe of the shining dirk nicked her arm, and she toppled. Tendrils of the sickly green fog turned in the air. Above her, the Conscript raised the dirk again. A final scream exploded from her throat.

Then the Conscript collapsed. The dirk clanged against the smoky floor.

R.J. lunged forward and yanked her up. "Are you all right?" he yelled.

Cassie pressed her hand to the wound on her arm, blood leaking between her fingers. "I think so—" Then she looked down at the Conscript, who was twitching on the floor. A hypodermic needle jutted from his throat. "What did you do?"

"I shot him up with a enough Stelazine to kill ten men—" Next he pulled her into an exam room, slammed the door, terrified. "Cassie, what is happening here?"

"You wouldn't believe me if I told you . . ."

More otherwordly features merged into the room. The floor became a brick-laned street, only the bricks were composed of crushed bone matter and teeth. There was a gutter clogged with blood and nameless waste, a sewer grate spewing smoke, an iron man-hole cover; imprinted in the metal were the words SALOME COUNTY PUBLIC WORKS-WASTE & SEWAGE REFLUX DEPT. R.J. had never appeared more disconcerted, which was understandable. "Cassie, at this point, there is *nothing* I won't believe."

"There's no time, we have to get out of here—I'll explain later—" Her words seared off with the sudden pain; she yelped. R.J. was applying an antiseptic wipe against her wound. "At first I thought it was an earthquake but," he talked as he worked. "But—shit!" Now a tree slowly merged into the room, half embedded in the wall. Red snakes coiled about its twisted branches.

"This is no earthquake," R.J. said. "Are you seeing that?"

"Yes."

"Then I don't know what this could be. Chemical leak, or something. Maybe somebody put psychedelics in the water. We all seem to be having the same hallucinations—"

"Ow!" Cassie yelled next.

"I have to disinfect," he said. "God knows what was on that knife—if there really *was* a knife." He sprayed rubbing alcohol on next, and after that—

clack-clack-clack

He closed the cut with a surgical stapler.

"Jeez! That hurts like shit!"

It was clear by the expression on his face that the doctor/scientist in him was being thoroughly challenged; the denial of what he was seeing stacked against simple observation. "The smartest thing for us to do is just stay right here—"

"We can't do that!"

"—and wait for this hallucinosis or whatever it is, to pass. Then we'll get tox screens and see what turns up in our blood. This has *got* to be a hallucination, Cassie. There's no other explanation."

Oh yes there is . . .

"Now let me get a bandage over these stitches," but he frowned, noticing that the supply cabinet now appeared to be merged into a brick wall on which a service sign had been mounted: PLEASE RECYCLE ROTTEN BLOOD. He managed to pry the cabinet door open, and retrieved a bandage. "Let me get this on you, then I'm going to call poison control."

"No! We have to get out! I'll tell you what's going on once we're out of here—"

A familiar weird pressure rose, and a chill. She squinted at R.J., saw him rubbing something between his fingers. A dried leaf.

"What's that you're . . . ," she began. She stopped, noticing something else now. In the fracas, R.J.'s medical tunic had come open a few buttons. She could see his bare chest but something else too.

A pendant around his neck, from which dangled a dark-purple stone shaped like an upside-down V.

An Obscurity Stone, she realized very grimly. *Just like the one Angelese has . . .*

He'd seen by her eyes that she'd noticed, and he touched the small odd stone. "Shit. Looks like you made me pretty fast. Doesn't matter now, anyway. There's only one way Angelese can break the Warding Spell, and believe me, she doesn't have the fortitude to do it."

His voice had shifted down as he spoke, octaves blended with other octaves that clearly weren't human. He continued to touch the stone, as a woman might unconsciously diddle with a necklace she was fond of. "You wanna see? Oh, hell, why not?"

He took off the pendant.

It would be impossible to describe the color of the light that poured off of R.J.'s head, except to say that it was bright and dark at the same time: the halo of a Fallen Angel. Without the Obscurity Stone, his wings bloomed into full view, angled high and spanning some twenty feet, all bones, though, not feathered at all. The feathers had all burned off during his plummet from grace so long ago. The webwork of bones were charred black and etched with glyphs and numerals and the oddest letters of some para-human language, the same way people have names signed to casts on their arms.

Cassie stared up into the light of this terrible being.

"God sends *His* agents, we send *ours*," R.J. said. He was still crushing the leafy substance in his fingers, letting flecks fall to the floor. "And here comes our cab."

The pressure in the room rose steadily, and then came the sound she was *very* familiar with:

Sssssssssssssssss-ONK!

The phosphorescent-green orb, like a blob of light, appeared in a snap and hovered in the room. *A Nectoport,* Cassie realized with the lowest feeling in her gut.

R.J. showed her what he'd gotten out of the supply cabinet, four small sterilized packages of something but she knew they weren't really bandages.

"They're pre-packaged tourniquets," he told her, "for emergency amputation cases."

And now he was holding something else: a bone saw. "I'm not allowed to kill you—even though I'd like to very much," his corroded voice flowed on. "I'd like to drink your Etheric blood, I'd like to cut your skin off and hang it off my wings as decoration, and suck the meat off your bones. But I can't. My mission is to take you into custody, and when that Nectoport opens, that's just what I'm going to do."

The hovering orb was growing, spreading out to a squirming, oval shape that would soon form its entrance.

Don't be afraid, don't be afraid, don't be afraid, Cassie thought over and over again. She must lose her fear and turn it into rage; only then could she harness her powers. *Hate, hate, hate, hate . . .*

"But I can't have you carrying on," the Fallen Angel continued, "can't risk letting you escape—you've been very cunning and elusive in the past. You won't be escaping to anywhere—not without your arms and legs, hmm?" He ran his finger along the bone saw. "Don't worry, you won't die. The tourniquets will stop you from bleeding to death."

An impulse goaded her to try to flee but she knew that such an instinct would only reinforce her fear. Fear was her enemy now, she knew she must banish it to survive. She must stand here and fight him . . .

Then he spoke words from an unknown language—his native language perhaps: "Eòñw nalde fl°avelaaiz me staadpa stilluadte," and Cassie collapsed.

She'd fallen flat on her back. She couldn't move.

"Pretty good Paresis Incantation, huh? Fallen Angels know their shit. We've had a long time to practice."

Don't be afraid, don't be afraid, don't be afraid, her thoughts raced. True, she couldn't move, but she could still think, and it was with her mind that she would summon her powers.

He picked her up, his wings constricting, and placed her limp body on the counter. "You know, I just thought of something. After I dismember you, I guess I should bring your arms and legs back to Hell too. I'm sure the Son of the Morning would love to have them as souvenirs. The arms and legs of an Etheress! He'd put them on his mantle, or put 'em on display in the Grendel Corrupted Arts Gallery."

She focused on his deception, on his lies, his conceit, and his falseness. She focused on what he stood for and what he represented. *Hate, hate, hate, hate!* she kept thinking.

His face hovered over her. So did the bone saw. "*Better* idea. I'll take your leg and beat your pretty little sister to a pulp with it, just beat her head right in, break all her bones with it. Wouldn't that be ironic?"

That last comment did it. Cassie's fear disappeared, burning away and replaced entirely by her rage, and then she looked at him and thought: *Burn* . . .

The air stilled.

She stared right at him.

"Burn!" she whispered.

The smile spread monstrous across his face, and when he laughed, bricks shook loose from the wall.

"Cassie, I'm a *Fallen Angel*. Your jive doesn't work on me . . ."

Then he opened the first tourniquet and deliberated over which arm or leg to cut off first.

(III)

Angelese strained against the unbreakable wires of the Warding Spell. She was trapped in a radiating cage of negative energy. Every arcane counter-measure she knew she'd used, every Reverse Hex and Repulsion Charm. Nothing worked.

I can't get out, came the futile thought. *I was sent by God to protect Cassie . . . and I've failed. I've totally, utterly, failed . . .*

In all the thousands of years that she had lived, she'd never felt so useless.

Despairing, she looked down at her feet. The shadow of her body extended a yard or so from her feet.

Wait a second . . .

She took a step sideways. The corridor lights from the clinic had long-since failed, all electricity severed by the Merge. But there was still sufficient light coming from a fire that sputtered out from a hellish wall to her left. It was that fire-light that projected her shadow.

She back-stepped, a little closer to the flame. It lengthened her shadow another two yards.

Now her shadow extended well past the outer boundary of the Warding strictures.

I don't know if this will work, but it can't hurt to try . . . She chuckled to herself. *Well, I guess it really can hurt to try . . .*

She began to speak. She began to give voice to the most crucial secret she'd ever been told, the most important utterance of knowledge in living history. She began to say aloud: "And on the twelfth day, God created—"

—and when she spoke the rest of it, her Umbra-Specter came alive in a rage, the shadows of its foot-long talons rising off the floor.

The evil glee percolated in its voice: "Thank you!" it rejoiced. "Now I get to tear you up . . ."

(IV)

"You're . . . very pretty," the Fallen Angel observed. He'd already applied the pre-packaged tourniquets to her arms and legs, which were now going numb. His hand smoothed over her belly, then up to her cheek. Cassie couldn't even flinch in the spell of paralysis he'd put on her. Her disgust and her hatred boiled over in her mind but she remained powerless against this obviously higher being.

Behind them, still hovering, the mouth of the Nectoport had opened fully. Through it, Cassie knew, he would take her to a secure location in the Mephistopolis, where the monarch of the city, and his lieges, would do what they would with her, expropriating her powers with their occult science, for some unknown design. She would never see Lissa again. She would never see anything again.

God help me, she prayed, but what good would praying do now? Cassie knew there was a God, but why should

232

God do anything for her? *I never did anything for Him,* she regretted.

And a darker notion: Perhaps God *couldn't* do anything for her, even if He wanted to. Maybe God really was losing his battles.

"He is, Cassie," R.J. said, usurping her thoughts. "He's losing so bad it's funny. And He deserves it. Let's just say he's not keen on democracy. We deserved as much as He, but he threw us out."

"You turned your back on Him first, didn't you?" Cassie managed.

The Fallen Angel glared at her, teeth grinding.

"Isn't that how it happened? He gave you something but you turned your back on Him anyway?"

Veins stood out on R.J.'s forehead.

"Sounds to me like God gave you a great gift and instead of saying thank you, you gave Him the finger. Instead of being grateful, you said 'Fuck you, God. I want more.' "

The Fallen Angel's hands quivered in rage as they closed around Cassie's throat. His face had turned beet-red.

Cassie smiled—a weak smile but a smile nonetheless. "I'm glad He threw you out," she whispered. "I hope your anguish and your misery and your pain lasts for a million years."

His hands continued to shake on her throat, but then they came away. "Nothing you can say will make me violate my oath. You have no conception. You want me to kill you but I will not. Instead, I will take you to him, as I promised. When he's done with you, when he's changed the Living World to what it should've been all along, and when you are drained and depleted and useless, perhaps he'll give you to me . . . or I should say, your torso."

He brought the bone saw to her leg, just under the tourniquet. "I will relish this," he said, about to cut.

Suddenly his scalp was sizzling. It sounded like a raw steak dropped on a red-hot grill. He jerked back, howling, as his scalp peeled off as though he were wearing a beret and someone just slipped it off his head from behind.

The *someone* was Angelese.

Cassie looked but still couldn't move. Angelese's face glowed in streaks from a grievous wound. Four deep slashmarks. But she smiled calmly, then knelt before R.J. who shuddered on the floor. "No, her jive doesn't work on you, but mine does. So you like to dismember people?" She grabbed R.J.'s upper arm, and her hand burned through the flesh and bone. The arm fell off, cauterized. His screams shook the building's foundation as she did the same to his other arm, and then his legs. The flesh continued to sizzle as smoke rose.

"There," Angelese said very quietly.

The head on R.J.'s torso looked at her, beseeching. "We're going to win. You know that, don't you?"

"Not *you*, brother. You *lose*."

"Just kill me. Burn out my heart."

"That's too easy. That's too merciful, and not all angels are merciful. No, I won't kill you. I'll send you back to your piss-ant master—a total failure. What will he do to you, your Son of the Morning? What will he do to you for letting him down?" and with that, Angelese picked up the Fallen Angel's living torso—

"NOOOOOOOOOOOOOOOOOO!"

—and heaved it into the Nectoport.

" 'Bye," Angelese said.

The Nectoport's maw snapped shut, then it disappeared.

Angelese sighed, sat up on the desk. "Are you all right?" she asked Cassie.

"I'm friggin' paralyzed!"

"Oh, what'd he do, lay a Paresis Spell on you? It'll wear off in a minute now that he's gone."

Actually, Cassie could feel the effects dulling already. She leaned up on the counter as much as she could. "Thanks . . . What was that all about? Your touch burns?"

"I'm blessed, he isn't. I can kill any lower-grade Fallen Angel just by placing my hands on him."

Nifty, Cassie thought. And her good fortune. Then she peered around, alarmed. "I'm all right, but you definitely aren't. What happened to your face? And how did you get out of that Warding Hex?"

"I told a *big* secret, so my Umbra-Specter came alive and slashed my face. It also slashed the Warding lines in the process."

Cassie gaped at the straight gouge-like wounds. "It must've hurt like . . ."

"Like a motherfucker," the angel said.

Cassie winced. Her paralysis continued to lift, and she noticed that the strange charge in the air was weakening.

"The Merge'll be over in another few minutes," Angelese informed.

But Cassie was astonished at what she was seeing now: the angel had reached into the desk and removed a cigarette. She was lighting it.

"Angels *smoke?*" she asked.

"I've had a tough day, and so have you. Let's get out of here."

She helped Cassie to her feet, then led her out of the Merged exam room. Yes, the charge in the air was definitely losing its vitality, but they were still in a meld of Hellspace. *We're not out of the woods yet,* Cassie realized. In this wing of the clinic, there was an exit door at the end, but when they turned the corner—

"Oh, gimme a break," Angelese muttered.

At the end of the hall stood a black-garbed Grand Duke, oxen-headed, eight feet tall, overly muscled shoulders spanning a meter at least. Its eyes smoldered, and the horns jutting from its rippled forehead were longer and sharper than those of a mature bull.

Behind the monster stood a platoon of slavering Ushers, some armed with bloody halberds, some with broadswords, some with spiked cudgels, yet all with newly honed talons, mouths full of teeth like long shards of glass.

The voice resonated. "Etheress. I am Grand Duke Lescoriere of the First Infernal Brigade. I am charged with the duty of escorting you to the Mephisto Building. The property owner would be honored to receive you as his welcome guest. He has much to discuss with you, and much to share. He has blessings of wonder to bestow—good things, all. And on my immortal soul, I guarantee your safety."

"Sit on your horns, dickhead," Angelese said

"If you come of your own accord—you, Etheress, and your confidante—you will be rewarded beyond all imagination."

Cassie grinned. "I'll go with you on one condition."

"Speak it, Etheress, and it will be done."

"Cut your head off," Cassie said.

The Grand Duke, unblinking, took a broadsword from one of the Ushers, held it straight out by the haft, and flicked his corded wrist. The blade blurred backward and popped the Grand Duke's head off his shoulders like a disconnected jack-in-the-box.

"You gotta be shitting me," Angelese whispered.

Cassie's jaw dropped. *Man, these guys are HARDCORE.*

The Grand Duke's monstrous body remained standing, fully poised. An Usher picked up the head and held it out by the horns.

"I've done as you have bid, Etheress," said the Grand Duke's head.

"I hate to tell you this," Cassie said, "but I was just kidding."

"As I've said, your humble host awaits you, and someone else too, someone who loves you and yearns to see you—"

"Yeah, I know, my sister. But I don't believe what devils say. I'm not that stupid, so why don't you do us all a favor? Why don't you and your goon squad hit the road?"

"Come with us of your own free will, or we will take you," the Grand Duke said, and behind him, several of his beasts were unfolding a barbed net.

"You can't take doodly-squat," Cassie began, and then she shouted, "because you're all BONELESS!"

The Grand Duke's head went limp as a rubber sack, dangling. His erect body collapsed on itself, then every Usher in the hall seemed to deflate as all their bones disappeared from within their flesh. In the time it had taken Cassie to merely say the word, the Grand Duke and his platoon were transformed into a quivering mass of flesh.

"That's so cool!" Angelese exclaimed.

But Cassie began to go weak-kneed. "God, I can barely move, I'm so tired all of a sudden."

"Every time you use your powers, you drain your physical vitality, and you've used a lot today. But we've still got to get out of here. The Merge is wearing off, but I don't know for sure how long it'll take to end completely."

Yes, Cassie thought, light-headed and squinting ahead. *Let's just leave.* She looked at the cinderblock hallway, and thought: *Fall down . . .*

The corridor toppled like something made of a child's blocks suddenly swept by an irate hand. Air gusted in their faces, dust billowed outward in waves, and where the walls had been was now just open night. The perimeter of the confines of the Merge dwindled before their eyes, hellish structures, streets, and features dissipating. Cassie had collapsed in psychic exhaustion. Angelese put her over her shoulder and began to run.

Part III
Fall

Chapter Eleven

(I)

Walter felt woozy, tunnel-visioned, as though he'd just stepped off a particularly vigorous roller coaster. *I'm in a city,* came the clipped thought. He tried to blink away some vertigo. *Just a big city, a run-down district, like southeast D.C. or maybe Detroit.* These thoughts were reactive, against the extreme disorientation. It would occur to him in a few moments, though, that neither southeast D.C. nor Detroit possessed a perpetual twilight of dark scarlet. The moon that overlooked D.C. and Detroit was not black, nor were the stars jaundice-yellow.

Walter staggered down the stinking alley. His head hurt, and with each throb of pain another dollop of memory returned. He put his hand to his head, felt the wrap of bandages, then remembered still more.

He'd tried to kill himself, but he'd failed. Colin, instead, had been the one to successfully complete the act.

He chuckled. *So . . . I'm an Etherean. Either that or this is a really bad dream.*

A cone of light from a leaning streetlamp bathed the end of the alley. There stood a pile of rubbish, as might be found in any city: an old metal barrel stuffed with junk. Amid empty cans and splintered furniture legs sat an oblong mirror webbed with cracks. Walter stared down at his image, watched himself unwrap the bandage from his head. His shoulders slumped at the geek reflection and the ludicrous wound. A shaved line of stitches parted his hair right down the middle. *Colin was right, I DO look like Moe in the episode about the organ grinder's monkey . . .* What difference did it make, though? If this wasn't a dream, then he was in Hell now, a Hell that had evolved over thousands of years into this endless metropolis full of skyscrapers. And he was unique in this place. In the Living World he'd been a nobody.

Here, he'd been informed, he had great power.

But where was the evidence of such power? He hadn't *transformed*. He didn't radiate blazing light from his eyes. He was the same Walter, just standing in a different place.

A different world, he reminded himself.

Back at Colin's penthouse, he'd read all of the pages that had been transcribed by the prostitutes, and if there was one thing about Walter it was that his genius I.Q. accommodated quite a capacity for reading as well as data retention. He'd read the entirety of the *Evocations of Lucifuge,* the first book to ever be published in Hell. He'd scrutinized the crucial chapters: "The Unsacred Edicts of Hellspace," and "Etheresses and Ethereans."

He knew everything now. He knew all the Rules.

But there was no description whatsoever of the actual powers of an Etherean. How did they manifest themselves?

If he was so powerful—the first Etherean in all of history—why wasn't anyone here to greet him? He expected to be carried off on a throne. Why weren't the minions of the underworld bowing at his feet?

Graffiti loomed on the urine-streaked alley wall: I WANNA FUCK SHIT UP! and HELL SUCKS. In the darkness, barely seen shapes that could only be rats chittered by, and drug vials cracked under his sneakers. Walter shook his head. "Maybe this *is* Detroit," he muttered. "I guess Lucifer's not into urban renewal." Then Walter peered at more graffiti—FREE MEATBALLS AND BLOODY FACES!—and shook his head again. A final scrawl stared back at him: CANDICE LOVES WALTER.

Morose, he walked off.

The city's true nature began to reveal itself. Out of the alley, he could indeed see the sky, like dark blood, and the black sickle moon that looked several times larger than the moon that orbited the Living World. Fires crackled beneath sewer grates, and strange faces clearly not human peered at him from dim windows. But Walter wasn't afraid. Why should he be?

I'm an Etherean.

The details of getting here began to resurface. That place in south St. Pete, The Mound, it was called, some local landmark. The prostitute at Colin's had given Walter the slip of paper with directions.

It was a Deadpass, and now that he'd read the transcriptions, he knew what that meant. He'd merely walked across The Mound. Everything went black for a moment, and he felt a queer pressure pushing, but after only a few steps, he was here.

Walking through the Deadpass had brought him from one world to another, and here he was. In the city. In the Mephistopolis.

In his pants pocket he kept the polished onyx stone, one of his dead brother's final instructions. It would debilitate his visible life force. He felt it growing warm in his beige Dockers, and though he didn't quite understand, he thought it best to do as he was told. He was here for a reason: to see Candice. He couldn't have her in the Living World, but as an Etherean he would have her here. They would spend eternity with each other, in love.

CANDICE LOVES WALTER . . .

Poor Walter . . .

Bizarre street signs wavered overhead: CRANIOPAGI AVENUE, HEMIHYPERTROBE ROAD, CHANCROID BLVD. *What? No Primrose Lane?* Out on the sidewalk now, the sulphurish streetlamps tinted the asphalt like yellow frost. He was passing another alley when he heard the faint but definite sound . . .

clip

clip

clip

clip

Walter stopped, peeked into the alley.

Some sort of humanoid mongrel, with horns surrounding his head like a crown, and a face stretched out round and tight as a black balloon, stood in the alley with his rotten trousers down. He was snipping warts off his elephantine penis with a pair of toenail clippers.

"Get out of here!" the thing grumbled. "Can't you see I'm busy!"

Walter got out of there and fast. Around the next corner he stumbled onto a street that seemed to be paved in cobblestones. At first it looked pretty, but when he examined the stones more closely he noticed that they were clear, like transparent bricks, each containing a demonic fetus. Up ahead, a Lycanymph leaned against a mailbox. The drop-door on the mailbox wouldn't close due to overfilling with body parts. But Walter had read about the Lycanymphs: sultry tramp werewolves that prostituted themselves. She was picking her vulpine nose, pulling out worms.

Man, this place is A LOT grosser than Detroit! Walter thought, aghast.

The streets seemed strangely devoid of activity, though. "Where is everybody?" he mumbled to himself. A city in Hell? It should be sprawling with damned souls and demons.

"Mutilation Squad came through a few hours ago," the pretty werewolf told him. Now she was extracting a worm at least a foot long from her nostril. "They hit us twice this week. That's never happened before."

Walter averted his eyes from her current activities when he asked, "What's a Mutilation Squad?"

"Usually a regiment of Ushers and Conscripts. They come in by surprise in Nectoports, kill everything on the street. Funny this time, though."

"Whuh-what?"

"The last two times they didn't kill anyone, just carried them all off in nets. Mancer Squads have been doing it too, and the Constabularies. Rumor is they're taking everyone in alive to use them in the Atrocidome. Some new hocus-pocus going on's what I heard from a trick a couple days ago. And it really pisses me off 'cos it's wiping out my business. I lost some of my best johns in their last grab." She winked at him with a long-lashed agate-like eye. "You wanna date, cutie?"

"Uh-uh, no thank you," Walter stammered. "I don't have any money."

She hissed, showing yellowed fangs. "Then get off my street, you useless dork!"

Walter didn't care for the comment. "You shouldn't talk

to me like that," he suggested. "If I weren't a nice guy, I'd use my powers on you."

"Powers? What powers?"

"I'm an Etherean," he told her.

The Lycanymph's eight pert fur-covered breasts jiggled as she laughed. "There's no such thing as an Etherean, asshole. It's a fable. It's like Santa Claus. And even if the Etherean legend is true, it could never be you."

"Why not?" Walter challenged.

"You're a dweeb, not a hero."

Walter rushed away, crushed. What she'd said couldn't be true, though, could it? He knew that he was alive, yet in Hell. Only Ethereans could do that. It was the only way a member of the Living World could enter this place.

He turned the next corner—

"Man-Burgers?" a Troll asked. He stood bloody-aproned and stout at his wheeled vending stand. His face could've been meatloaf. He skillfully spun a spatula over pallid meat patties cooking on the grill. "Or how about some of these?" he pitched, pointing to three sizzling things that looked like white bratwursts.

"What are those?" Walter inquired. "Sausages?"

"It's ghalestro pajata, grilled baby ghoul intestines, still filled with the mother's milk. It's great, tastes like salty pudding."

Walter's stomach clenched.

Next the vendor opened a metal box beside the grill; steam floated out. "This is even better, and it's only two Eichmann Quarters per order." Walter saw the ramekin-like containers, crusted around the rims and bubbling with something that could've been melted Muenster cheese. "This is Baked Meconium Imperial, my own mama's recipe."

Walter was choking but his curiosity wouldn't let up. "What—what's meconium—"

"Fetal bowel contents. In this case, a third-trimester Cacodemon fetus. Dee-lish!"

Walter staggered off and threw up on the sidewalk. His vomit glowed as if he'd thrown up on the lens of a floodlamp. The vendor was laughing, and he heard a scurrying. He leaned against a steam-car parked at the curb, catching his breath, but the scurrying got louder, and now he heard murmuring too.

Stomach still flinching, Walter looked aside. Several young Brooden—half-breed demon children—congregated with enthusiasm around, of all things, Walter's vomit.

Walter stared, revolted. *What on earth—*

But this *wasn't* earth, was it? The Brooden were all scooping up Walter's luminous vomit and racing away with it in their cupped hands, their faces alight. Several got into a fight over the remaining smears.

Then it made sense, and it was proof that he truly was an Etherean as the books had said. Any material object or substance from the Living World was of immense value in Hell. Including vomit. *Especially* an Etherean's vomit. It was as good as cash here.

You learn something new every day, he thought, dejected.

"There he is!" piped a nasally voice. Weird bumpy little faces peered at him—the remaining Broodren.

"Look!"

"Yeah, right there!"

"An ETHEREAN!"

This was not the welcome Walter imagined. When they began to give chase, Walter ran off down another alley. The little buggers followed him intently as a pack of rabid terriers, chortling, and Walter knew they were much faster than he. What would they do when they caught him? It wasn't hard to figure. If his vomit was worth money, wouldn't his body parts be worth even more? *Those little psychos'll tear me apart!*

Some Etherean. What a joke. He had no *power*. He hadn't even been in Hell ten minutes, and he was about to get killed.

His heart almost stopped when he looked to the end of the alley.

Something stood there still as a chess piece, in silhouette. Nine feet tall, wide-angled shoulders, and a head like a lump.

A Golem.

Walter had read about them, and all the inhabitants of this place. A Golem was akin to a brainless police officer. They were made of clay from the tidal beds of the River Styx, for the Agency of the Constabulary. They moved slowly but were nearly indestructible.

If Walter turned and ran in the other direction, the chattering Broodren would get him. He could only suspect that this thing in front of him would be much more efficient. Either way, Walter knew he would die, and it wasn't that terrible a prospect since he was already a suicidal basketcase.

His teeth chattered. "Please don't make it hurt much," he pleaded to the Golem.

The thing approached clumsily but steadily. It did not raise a mitten-like hand to Walter but instead looked down at him with the featureless lump of its face. Walter squeezed his eyes shut and prepared to die.

The thudding of its footsteps rumbled off. Then—

Squealing, screams, howls of terror.

Walter turned around and looked. Behind him the Golem was stomping the Broodren, crushing them, pulling them apart.

Walter ran.

Why did it save me? It could've killed me in a second but it didn't.

Then he remembered a little more, some of the last things Colin had told him before he'd redecorated the ceiling of his penthouse with his brains. *The Prince of Lies wants you, brother* . . . Walter had little confidence in the man's title but still—There was the implication. The power circles in the Mephistopolis *wanted* Walter and that was difficult for him to dismiss since he'd essentially lived his entire life *un*-wanted. There'd been promises of great things to come, of power like that of a king. That last straw-blond prostitute, too, had implied as much: that in Hell Walter would be something great, and would reclaim the woman he loved.

So he dreamed on.

He cleared his head and walked, found another smoking intersection. A steam-car, driven by an Imp in a Yankees cap, soared out of the low-hanging fog. A Griffin circled lazily overhead, appraising him, then was off. From distant, lit windows he heard laughter, moans, and shrieks.

The next street sign snagged his attention: CHYME RESERVOIR AVENUE. It rang a bell, then more pieces of memory kindled. *The dream,* he recalled. But it was just a dream, wasn't it? And he recalled the pretty girl in the punkish clothes who'd been beheaded by the Golems: Noname was her name. *A Dactyl-class sorceress for the court of King Mursil the First,* she'd told him, whatever that meant. And he remembered one more thing: in the dream, the Golems had thrown her head in a garbage can.

A garbage can stood right in front of him.

There better not be a severed head in this garbage can, Walter thought, looking in.

There was a severed head in the garbage can.

"Hello, Walter," the head greeted, tilted in the trash. A

249

flesh-colored bug crawled across her face as she aggravatedly twitched her nose to get it off.

"No-name," Walter whispered down.

Just that moment something occurred to him. No-name was essentially the only girl who'd ever been nice to him. *Just my luck,* he thought now. *She's a severed head.*

He picked her up by shimmering jet-black hair.

"It took you long enough."

"But you were only a dream—"

"You're an Etherean, Walter. In your dreams you can leave your physical body and come here, or anywhere in the Netherplanes."

"What exactly are the Netherplanes?"

"We don't have time to talk about it. Let's get out of here before another Mancer Squad pops up."

Walter, flummoxed, headed down the street, carrying No-name by the hair. "I feel . . . unsettled . . . carrying a severed head down the street. Especially . . . a *talking* severed head."

"Don't worry about it, Walter. You're in Hell. Heads talk. But you have to be strong. There's a lot we have to do."

"Like what?"

"Time . . . will tell."

Walter could've done with a more specific answer. "I know that Lucifer wants me. Are you going to tell me how to find him?"

"No, my purpose is to make you aware of things, to make sure you see what you're supposed to see. It's all about free will, Walter, and it's very important that you understand that. You're forgetting the details of my curse—my eternal damnation. I know the future but it's impossible for me to reveal it to anyone."

This flustered Walter. Women always did. "But what you

just said—your *purpose*. That indicates to me that you're here for a reason, and that reason corresponds to me somehow."

"Correct," the pretty severed head replied. "I was waiting for you. I was specifically sent here, to elucidate your options."

"Great. God sent you?"

"No."

"Who did then?"

The head sighed. "Intermediary agents representing an antithetical design."

"Ah, that," was Walter's best effort at sarcasm.

"You're hurting my scalp. Could you please put me under your arm?"

Walter obliged. He felt let down by the whole scene. Etherean? He was walking around with a head. "I thought I was supposed to have powers, like it said in the book."

"You have powers, Walter. It'll just take some time before you're evolved enough to use them. Or that may never happen—I can't tell you. You have to learn to control your emotions. Self-oriented emotions—like fear, and despair—impede your gift. You're in a new place that's strange to you. You have to get used to being here. You must overcome distractions, overcome all mental barricades. You must *de*-obstruct your senses."

Walter shook his head. "De-obstruct. Fantastic. Is that even a word?"

"If you want the truth, Walter, you're probably too messed up in the head to ever develop your powers."

"So I'm a powerless Etherean?"

"Yes."

Another rip-off. Another kick in the chops. It didn't matter which world he went to, he was a loser that nobody noticed. He turned another corner, sneakers scuffing. "Wait a minute, if I'm powerless, why does Lucifer want me?"

The head was getting more and more illusory. "You're Plan B, Walter. Plan A failed."

"I'm gonna put you back in the garbage can," he said, disgusted. He could make nothing of what she was saying; it seemed as though she was doing it on purpose, to confuse him, to frustrate him.

Now she sounded sad, or disappointed. "You don't even have the mettle for that, Walter. The more people hurt you, the less aggressively you defend yourself. You're a pushover. You're too nice a guy to make it, here or anywhere. I'm not telling you what you need to know—you *should* put me back in the garbage. But you don't have the capacity even for that."

Only the vaguest impulse flickered, to turn back around and throw her away. But she was right. He couldn't throw anyone away even though people had been throwing him away his whole life. No-name was his only friend. Granted, she wasn't much of one—but she was a friend nonetheless.

A metal sign on a brick wall read PDA MANDATORY ZONE. A male and female Imp strolled hand in hand down the lane. The female was holding a flower, and they both looked at each other with the deepest love in their eyes.

"Public displays of affection are mandatory?" Walter asked, miffed.

Suddenly the male Imp was howling over a wet *thwack-thwack-thwack!* sound; Walter was horrified at what he was seeing.

The female Imp was chopping into her mate's groin with a small hatchet. Green blood shot up as the male thrashed on the pavement. And, next:

thwack-thwack-thwack!

—she was hacking into his chest, right through his ribs.

More blood looped up. Her intent was clear: she was chopping out his heart.

"Not affection, Walter." No-name rolled her eyes. "Public displays of atrocity. Oh, and take a look over there. See her?"

A skinny Human girl wearing canvas rags for clothes lay spread-eagled and bug-eyed in a doorway across the street. She was pregnant yet her swollen belly seemed to deflate in abrupt stages, and out from under her ragged skirt things that looked like tadpoles—but the size of squirrels—scampered away on little hands and feet. The girl was birthing a litter of the creatures, and when Walter got a grim look at one he saw that it had suggestions of a face that mirrored the girl's own features.

Oh, lord! Walter thought, winded just by witnessing the scene.

"In Hell, Humans can't reproduce amongst each other," No-name explained from under his arm, "because they have souls. But Human women can get pregnant from interspecies sex. That girl's got it bad, probably got raped by a Troll. Those things coming out of her are called Pollihoppers, the product of the latest STD—*Condylomo Abhorrius*. The infection produces cervical tumors that suck up any semen that enters the vagina, then it mutates each sperm cell with its own DNA and releases it back into the womb."

"I'm gonna be sick, I'm gonna be sick!" Walter insisted.

"*Don't* be sick again, Walter. You already know, your Etherean vomit glows in the dark. It'll give you away."

Walter staggered onward in this hellish urban quagmire. He wanted to cry he was so disheartened. This place was so cruel and disgusting—how could it really exist? Here the psychological cruelties of the Living World were made flesh, the symbols and subtleties becoming physical and real.

All of this, created by one person to punish people for their sins?

"Let me tell you something, Walter," the head said next. "I understand your confusion, I understand how you feel. You don't know what purpose this place really serves—you're a scientist, an academic, and it seems illogical. But illogic is a logic of its own. Do you understand?"

"Not at all. Not one bit," Walter groaned.

"If you take the impulse behind the conscious desire to be good, and you take the impulse behind the conscious desire to be evil—if you put them both together and look at them very closely, you'll see . . . they're the same."

More esoteric gobbledygook. Walter just groaned some more, his despair rising. Each step seemed to double his confusion. "What did you mean when you said I was Plan B?"

"Plan A failed."

"You just told me that!" He was getting testy. "What does it mean?"

"Lucifer has a vast plan. He's kind of like you, actually—"

"Thanks."

"I mean in that all he wants is to be loved. But the one he wants to most be loved by cast him out. So now he exists for vengeance. You already know what an Etherean is. What about an Etheress?"

Finally, a linear conversation. "Yes, I read about them in the *Evocations of Lucifuge.* An Etheress is a female Etherean."

"Correct. And there's one living as we speak. She was Plan A. Lucifer needs either an Etheress or an Etherean, for his plan. He tried to capture the Etheress but she got away. Plan A failed. Which leaves Plan B. You are Plan B. Lucifer couldn't catch the Etheress, so now he's going to try to catch you. He wants to use *you.*"

Walter staggered on. *Lucifer wants to use me,* came the blandest thought. He didn't want to hear any more; he didn't want to even try to understand. He scuffed down the road as Caco-Rats chittered.

"Where are we going?" he asked. His voice sounded dead.

"To Candice's," No-name said.

(II)

The Mound lay south of the city. That's what it was called, simply The Mound. It was four hundred feet long and thirty high, just a long grass-covered rise. No one talked about it, but local historians knew exactly what it was: a mass grave for hundreds of Muskogean Indians who were slaughtered by adjutants of Andrew Jackson in the early 1800s. Rumors had it that The Mound was haunted. This rumor was true, but that was beside the point.

The Mound was a powerful Deadpass.

"I can feel it," Cassie said under her breath.

"Oh, yes," Angelese replied.

They crossed town on foot, slipping away through darkness from the wreckage of the clinic. After the Merge had ended, and all of Hell's components had spatially relocated themselves, the clinic and its property lay in shambles, smoldering. The news would report another catastrophic gas leak, but that was beside the point too.

The point was that the forces trying to abduct Cassie had failed in their efforts.

The part of town that surrounded The Mound seemed abandoned, run-down salt-boxes mostly, and dilapidated cars in sun-scorched yards. But as they approached, Cassie could feel something invisible crawl on her skin. Angelese paused as if sensing something.

"Someone's already been here, through the Deadpass," she whispered.

Cassie remembered what the angel had told her a few nights ago. "The Etherean," she guessed.

"Yes. He's already on the other side."

"Is that good or bad?"

"Bad," Angelese said.

Cassie couldn't fathom it. A sudden breeze broke the heat and humidity. As she stared at the top of The Mound, in total silence, she thought she could see something in between blinks.

Lights.

Lights in a very dark city.

A police car was turning down the street. It stopped, shined its spotlight on them.

"Let's give this guy something to talk about back at the station," Angelese said. She took Cassie's hand and led her to the top of The Mound. That's where they disappeared.

Something rough, something hot and cold at the same time, licked Cassie's skin. A moment ago the scope of her vision had been filled with stars spread across the night, but when she stepped through the Rive, everything went black. Her legs moved as though she were walking on air, she felt she might plummet. Static glittered in her hair, and then she was through.

Smoke and a stench burned her eyes. The black was gone, replaced by sickly yellow streetlight.

A sudden scream overhead froze her heart, then there was a loud crash off to one side. "JESUS!" Cassie shouted.

"Get out of the way," Angelese said and pulled her back. "Someone's throwing people off the top of the building."

Cassie looked up the side of a crooked skyscraper that

must've been a hundred stories. In the alley where they stood, a Human woman hauled herself out of the dumpster she'd just landed in. Her face was collapsed, most of her bones broken in the fall, yet she was alive. In Hell, the damned could never die. Another scream, then, and two more bodies hit the pavement just yards away—

SPLAT! SPLAT!

Cassie and Angelese ducked out, the angel perturbed. "Damn it! There's supposed to be one waiting for us . . ."

"One what?"

Angelese didn't answer. She was staring down the street. The ever-present mold-green fog was rising, and in it Cassie could see—

"Are those *faces?*"

Half-tangible shapes formed in the fog, suggestions of long-fingered hands, suggestions of eyes and malformed mouths full of teeth.

Suddenly the fog began to move forward very rapidly. Its twisted mouth-shapes began to bellow.

"Shit!" Angelese exclaimed. "Djinn!"

It was coming too fast to react. Two Constabularies brandishing pronged nightsticks stepped unaware into the street. When the fog swooshed over them, first their uniforms, then their skin eroded away.

Cassie tired to project a thought to counter the mass, but her fear was still cresting.

"Damn it!" Angelese spouted again. "Where *is* it?"

"Where is WHAT?"

Ssssssssssssssss-ONK!

The lit, throbbing orb of a Nectoport appeared just behind them. It shuddered and began to open.

"It's about fucking time," Angelese muttered. "Climb in! Hurry!"

The living fog moaned forward, abrading even the pavement, like a sand-blasting. The Nectoport hadn't fully matured but Cassie and the angel climbed in anyway, their hands slimed green. It was through some mode of enchanted telepathy which enabled Angelese to maneuver the Port; it shuddered and pitched, then took off and upward like a reckless kite. Below them, the swell of fog convulsed, howling its rage at them.

Cassie slumped against the inner wall of the port, her heart slowing. "I tried to stop it with a projection but I was too afraid. It happened so fast, I couldn't control my fear."

"You're going to *have* to control your fear," the angel said, settling down herself. She was peering down. "You're going to have throw it aside. We won't last long if you don't."

Cassie simmered now. "What about you? You're an angel. You're telling me you don't have *any* powers yourself?"

"In Heaven, I have great power, but in Hell? Just basic sorcery. Witch-stuff. I'm outclassed here. In the Mephistopolis, my only useful power is in the secrets I know."

"Oh, that's useful. Secrets you can't reveal without getting torn up by that shadow thingie."

"Umbra-Specter," the angel corrected. "But there are a lot of secrets I *don't* know, and we're going to start off by getting to the bottom of some things."

Cassie's hair blew around in a tumult from the wind blowing into the Nectoport. She looked over and saw Angelese peering out with the pair of Ophitte Viewers; the bloodshot eyes for its lenses blinked. "They're filling the Atrocidome again. I don't get it."

"I guess they're going to do another Merge," Cassie said.

"Yeah, but why? We know the Etherean's already here, and the Merge they initiated to try and capture you at the clinic failed. There's no reason for them to do another Merge, at least none that I can think of."

But Cassie's own thoughts began to interfere with the matters at hand. She couldn't stop thinking about Lissa. *Where is she now? What are they doing to her?* Was she still at the Mephisto Building? Did they put her back in that pit in the zoo? Guilt piled up upon guilt.

"We'll find her," Angelese assured. "They'll make it easy for us. Remember, she's the bait they're going to use to try and catch you."

This didn't comfort Cassie.

"But we've got a few other things to do first," Angelese added.

The Nectoport was descending again. "Step back. We're going inside."

Cassie didn't know what was happening. The orifice-like oval of the Nectoport began to suck shut, like a camera aperture. When it was shut completely Cassie could only see the angel in lines of dim green light. She sensed the port's variable solidity passing though objects, walls perhaps, as its occult technology impossibly shortened the distance between two points.

But where was their current point?

Sssssssssssssssss-ONK!

The aperture snapped open, hovering. *Good Lord,* Cassie thought, peering out past the gelatinous green light. They weren't in a building, they were in some sort of subterranean cavern.

"What is this place?" she asked.

"The Mater Sequestrum . . ." Angelese climbed out of the port, then helped Cassie down.

"The what?"

"It's a special place where the mothers of great people spend their eternal damnation."

"Great people?"

"Great in the sense of historical importance. They can be evil people or very benevolent people—it doesn't matter. Hitler's mother is here, for instance, and so is Herod's. This place is sort of like a trophy house for Lucifer."

Cassie followed her escort down a trail carved out of black pumice. It was hot and lined with torches set into crude sconces to either side. Occasionally she'd see a head pilloried in the rock, then she looked up and gasped. The cavern's ceiling seemed a hundred feet high and suspended overhead were more Human women in iron cages. "This part of the Sequestrum is kind of dull," Angelese was explaining. She was holding a shiny stone in her right hand, rubbing her thumb over it as she talked. "The very special mothers get very special treatment."

Cassie scuffed onward through the foul air. "But whose mother are we here to see?"

"Yours."

The response bolted Cassie. She and Lissa had never been very close to their mother, who'd divorced her father for another man a long time ago. *I'm the great person?* she wondered. It seemed inconceivable. But something much more obvious popped into her awareness. *If my mother's here, then she must've died and gone to Hell.* "How did she die?" she asked, her flip-flops smacking on the rough stone.

"Well, as I understand it, the guy she left your father for caught her with yet another man. So he shot her, shot the guy, and shot himself. You can't feel bad about every tragedy, Cassie, just because of a blood-bond. You want the truth, most people in the Living World aren't very cool. They're selfish and dishonest. You mother was just a gold-digger. She got what she had coming."

Cassie couldn't relate to that. A gnarled black tree twisted over their heads, and from a stout branch hung another woman by a noose around her neck. Her bare legs kicked in the air while her hands fisted around the noose. *Eternity,* Cassie realized. *She'll be like that for eternity* ... Did this woman get "what she had coming?" What could she have done to deserve this? What could *anybody* do?

Then a hitch caught in her chest and she nearly screamed. Elevated slightly before them, on a rock ledge, stood a rhinoceros-sized beast with multiple eyeclusters and a great depending belly the size of a small sports car. The belly squirmed from something alive inside, and Cassie grimly suspected that there were actually several Humans in the beast's gut. From its slavering, toothy maw a woman hung, her legs swallowed to the waist, but her arms, head, and bosom exposed. Her drool-slimed head hung upside-down as they passed, and she looked right at Cassie and said, "I hope you're sorry for your sins ..."

Then the woman was gnawed some more, her screams firing like rifle shots throughout the cavern.

"You can't help her, it's not allowed," Angelese urged and pulled her along.

"How can God let this happen to people?"

"He doesn't. It's the people themselves that do. And remember what she said."

I hope you're sorry for your sins, Cassie reflected. This cavern dizzied her, and she suspected far worse things to come. They must be going to the place Angelese just referred to, the place for *very special* treatment.

Some women stood waist-deep in little pools of lava, so used to eternal agony they didn't even bother screaming any more. Others were pitoned naked to the rock walls as Griffins and other, worse vulture-like birds picked at them with their beaks.

Angelese kept rubbing the small stone in her hand, seeming annoyed.

"Is that another Obscurity Stone?" Cassie asked.

"It's a Nephrilene. The best way to describe it to a Human is to say that it's been magically encoded with a tincture of your mother's spirit. It's like a direction-finder. It should lead us to her."

"It just did," a soft voice flowed from the dark.

The voice paralyzed Cassie. She hadn't heard it in so long but she recognized it at once. Angelese took down one of the torches and brought it around, for light. Its endless source of pitch-tar crackled and threw roving shapes of illumination forward.

A head looked at them, and at first, Cassie thought it was severed, but then she could see that her mother's body seemed to be embedded, to the neck, between two smooth rocks pressed together, each rock tall and wide as a refrigerator.

"Hello, Cassie," said the smiling face thrust up between the rocks. Short blondish hair with fashionable gray streaks, pearl-white teeth, bright aquamarine eyes. She was still pretty, even here.

"So, your father's dead? Believe it or not, I'm sorry about that. And Lissa's here, do you know that?" The woman's smile brightened. "It's your fault."

Cassie wilted.

"Shut up!" Angelese said. "Don't listen to her, Cassie."

The eyes flicked to Angelese. "Ah, a little broken angel, scarred and torn. You seem a bit used, don't you? Why didn't they send someone important? I'll tell you why. Because they already know in advance that you will fail, so they don't want to risk losing someone valuable."

"Fuck off," Angelese said.

"Such eloquent words from a sister of God." Now the eyes flicked back to Cassie. "I never loved you, and I never loved Lissa. I wanted to get an abortion but your father wouldn't allow it. I didn't want to rock the boat and risk being taken out of the will."

"I don't understand," Cassie wept. "Why are you being like this?"

"Because I'm a horrible person."

Angelese put her arm around Cassie. "You know the Rules. Any question I ask you in the presence of your daughter, you must answer."

"Oh, really?"

"Yeah. Really. Like why is the Constabulary filling up the Atrocidome again?"

Cassie's mother smiled. "I'm . . . not going to tell you."

The defiant smile seemed to float before them, but then it vanished. The woman's face began to puff, as if great pressure were being exerted on her body between the rocks. Instantly she looked nauseated.

"Fine," Angelese said, smiling cruelly. "Don't answer the question."

Cassie's mother's head drooped. "They're going to keep doing Merges. They're doing them non-stop."

"Why? Cassie escaped and the Etherean is already in the Mephistopolis. It doesn't make sense for them to keep doing Merges."

"They're going to Merge with every known Deadpass."

"Why?"

"To destroy them."

Angelese nodded as Cassie stared. "If they destroy every Deadpass," the angel informed her, "then you'll be trapped in the Mephistopolis. There'll be no way for you to get out because all the Rives will be gone." She turned her next question to the head between the rocks.

"Our intelligence has it that the Hexology Institutes, the Houngan Re-Animation Offices, and the entire Department of Voudou Research have all been moved out of the Industrial Sectors and relocated to the Mephisto Building. Is this true?"

"No," Cassie's mother defied.

"No?" Angelese turned the word.

More agony and nausea ballooned the woman's face. "Yes, God damn you! Yes, it's true!"

Cassie could scarcely watch any more of these ministrations. It didn't matter that her mother had never loved her—she couldn't stand witnessing this.

"One more question, then we'll be out of this literal hell-hole," the angel promised. "Several nights ago, there was a Merge in Maryland, some kind of a state document library. A Fallen Angel named Zeihl incarnated himself there, and then he committed suicide in order to effect a Power Exchange, so that a physical object in that library could be taken back to Hell. There's no other reason why a Fallen Angel would do that."

Lines of hatred drew deep into the woman's face. She hissed at Angelese, displaying a long thin tongue like a snake's. "I'll never tell. I don't care, but I'll never tell."

"Sure you won't change your mind?"

The woman's face was already going sick again. She began to gag. "Never. I'll never tell."

Angelese stepped back, urging Cassie with her. "So be it."

Eyes squeezed shut, face swelling, turning yellow, Cassie's mother violently whipped her head back and forth.

Then the pair of rocks she'd been embedded in . . . began to rise.

What in God's name? Cassie thought.

"Don't get too close," the Angel warned. "It's an Intestisaur . . ."

Like I know what that is, Cassie thought.

She'd see exactly what it was, in a moment.

The two smooth rocks weren't rocks. When they rose, they did so by two stout legs, each a dozen feet long, that had been folded beneath them. Cassie saw now that it was some demonic living thing that her mother was embedded in.

It stood up completely and turned around. It was massive, hairless, fleshy, with great slablike folds of skin hanging off its stunted physique. It had no arms, just the sumo-like legs it had been squatting on, a protuberant belly with multiple navels. No visible neck; instead the beachball-sized bald head grew out of its narrowed back, sitting on more folds, under which great flesh-satchels for breasts depended.

Cassie almost fell over when she looked up at its face in the firelight. Two inlets, like bolt-holes, for ears. No eyes, no nose. Just a big thick-lipped mouth. And now that it stood up, she discerned its true function. The two "rocks" from which her mother's head jutted were actually the thing's buttocks.

"It's considered a supreme punishment," Angelese said. "All the Intestisaur exists for is to eat. It's a lower-grade species of Cacodemon. The Teratologists at the Office of Transfiguration surgically implanted your mother's Spirit Body into its bowel. She is now *part* of its digestive system. Her mouth serves as its anus."

Cassie couldn't handle this, even with all she'd seen thus far during her ventures to the Mephistopolis.

"Your mother's a very strong woman. She's going to take it rather than answer my question—it's unbelievable." Even Angelese was queasy in what she anticipated. "We'll have to find out somewhere else. Let's get out of here. You don't want to see this . . ."

No, Cassie did not, but she'd put two and two together and that was enough. She couldn't even speak. Angelese led her back out of the heinous cavern as the Intestisaur, behind

265

them, began to massively excrete. Even a hundred yards away, they could hear the vocal blasts of Cassie's mother screaming intermittently between the monstrous voids of the demon's bowel.

When they were back in the Nectoport, and sailing away, Cassie lay nearly paralyzed against the curved wall. The Port's egress was crossed completely as they folded hellish space.

Angelese sat in contemplation. "It must have something to do with organic replication, or Hex-Clones."

Cassie looked at her through slitted eyes. "What?"

"Your mother confirmed our intelligence reports, that the Hexology Institutes were all recently moved out of the Industrial Sectors and relocated to the Mephisto Building. You know about those places, right?"

"Not really," Cassie answered, numbed. "I've heard of them, occult science stuff, I think."

"It's where they make Hex-Clones for the Constabulary. They've moved all those facilities to the Mephisto Building for a reason."

"What do you think the reason is?"

"Security, is my guess. All we know is that Lucifer's plan is something that, if it succeeds, could be the most devastating thing to happen to the Living World, but beyond that? We can only guess. He moved the Hex-Clone agencies to a place where they'd be safe from you, in the event that you weren't successfully captured."

"I don't get it."

"You're an Etheress. In theory, you're powerful enough to destroy those facilities."

Was she? The prospect daunted her. But at least Cassie felt she had a purpose now—anything to get her mind off what she'd witnessed in the caverns. "So that's why you want to get into the Mephisto Building? Well, I'm all for it. If I have the capability of destroying all the stuff—and wrecking his plan, whatever it is—then I'm game. But I don't think there's any way to get inside."

"There is one way."

Cassie perked up. "Really? What?"

"Trust me. But there's more we have to do first anyway." Angelese stood up and re-opened the Nectoport's threshold. They were very high up now, frighteningly so. The black sickle moon in its perpetual phase was close enough to re-veal surface details. The clouds up here looked like billows of mold.

"What do we have to do first?" Cassie asked, looking grimly out onto the scape of the city.

"We have to find out what your mother refused to tell us. We'll have a better idea exactly what Lucifer plans to do once we find out what was taken out of that library in Maryland."

"How do we find that out?"

"Hell is full of secrets, Cassie," the angel explained, her pure-white hair dancing in the wind. "But all those secrets must be written down—Satanic Public Law, Number One—and those secrets are kept in the most secret place in the Mephistopolis. It's a library, too, of sorts. The Infernal Archives."

"Hell's library," Cassie responded. Then she tried to joke, "I don't have a card."

Angelese didn't laugh. She seemed focused, preoccupied—and worried.

"So you know how to get to this place?" Cassie asked.

"Yeah."

"But you just got done telling me that it's the most secret place in the Mephistopolis. If its location is such a big secret, how can you possibly know where it is?"

"God told me," Angelese said.

Chapter Twelve

(I)

The purple neon sign out front read: KEDESHAH'S HOUSE OF SIN. This could've been Bourbon Street in New Orleans, but it was actually the Annwyn Avenue in Boniface Square, the city's entertainment hub. Saloons, live sex shows, massage parlors, and gambling joints.

And bordellos. Like this one.

"It's the biggest whorehouse in Hell," No-name said. "It's named after the first whore of the earth, who was actually a subcarnate fertility goddess."

Walter looked up at the enormous aircraft-carrier-sized building. Lights blinked hypnotically; neon burned. Walter, without knowing why, walked toward the closest entrance— a pillar-sided, jewel-studded door, guarded by spike-fisted Licentogres, heavily muscled hybrid sentries each with a line of black stitches where their genitals used to be.

"Why are we here?" Walter asked in a death-like drone. "Please don't tell me that Candice works in there."

"She doesn't," No-name began—

Relief overwhelmed him.

"Not inside," she continued. "Candice is just starting out, so she's working the streets, you know. A streetwalker."

Walter's relief died, as phony as just about everything else that had been told to him in his life. "So we're not going inside, I take it," he murmured.

"No. We'll just walk around the tenderloin until we find her. Just keep walking."

She's getting a little bossy, Walter reflected. Oh, well. A change of subject seemed in welcome order. "Tell me more about the Plan A, Plan B thing."

"Plan A failed," No-name repeated. "You're Plan B. It's something I'm surprised you're not thinking about."

"I just asked you about it!" Walter raised his voice, a rarity for him. "I must be thinking about it if I asked you about it."

"Calm down. I mean, you don't appear to be thinking about it in a transitive manner. Be deductive."

Women, Walter thought. *They're all nuts.*

"The Etheress was Plan A. Lucifer wanted her but he failed to get her—"

"Yes."

"And she's here now, in Hell."

"Yes. On her own conditions, and I can tell you that Satan and his agents aren't pleased about it."

"But I'm the male equivalent of her, and I'm here under my own conditions."

"Are you?"

"I don't know. I think so. I want to meet the Etheress. Can I?"

"I can't divulge that."

Walter frowned, something he'd been doing a lot lately. "Where is she?"

"I can't say."

"Is she alone?"

"No, that I can tell you because it doesn't involve a inference to the future. She's with an angel, a mid-order Seraphim. You can think of her as a tainted angel. She's a Caliginaut. They're all whacked out of their heads. Some are even insane."

The Etheress has an insane angel for an escort, Walter thought, *and I've got a talking head.* He wondered who was better off.

"The Caliginauts are like Heaven's commandos. They do deep cover, in Hell, in the Netherspheres, and on earth. They have to have their wings cut off to prove their faith. This one's a lot like me."

"You're not an angel," Walter asserted.

"No, I'm a damned soul, a mystic in Hell."

"Then what did you mean when you said the angel's a lot like you?"

"She can't reveal any Heavenly Secret, without suffering great pain. I can't reveal what I know about the future, without losing my spirit body—and as you can see, I don't have much of one left."

Walter made little sense of this. *An angel without wings, and a seer who can't tell what she sees.* He was tired of being confused, which seemed, by now, a perpetual mental state. "I don't know why you can't tell me what to do, or what's going to happen. Some soothsayer."

"I'm sorry, Walter, it's my curse."

"You know all these universal secrets but you can't tell them. What good does that do? What purpose does that serve?"

"They're not universal secrets, Walter. They're preternatural. They're abstruse."

Abstruse. Walter sputtered to himself. *Wonderful.*

"Remember one of the first things I told you," No-name continued from under his arm. "The future isn't mutable. It just *is.* I am part of it and so are you. We are both an integral component of what could happen, what might happen, or what might not. You're smart. Think about that."

"I'm not a philosopher. I'm a physicist and a mathematician."

"And an Etherean," the head reminded.

"Yeah, big deal. An Etherean with no power."

"Walter, I never said that you'll never harness your powers. I only suggested, without violating any *abstruse* codices, that you probably won't because you're not strong enough. You don't have the resolve, or the confidence."

Walter was walking aimlessly. He was just as depressed here as he was in the Living World, so what was the point? The only reason he didn't want to blow his head off *here* was because there was a chance of seeing Candice. And he'd already been told—by a friggin' Dactyl-class soothsayer for King Mursil the First—that Candice would never love him.

What's the point? What's the point in anything?

"Look," No-name said. "The Wall of Skin."

Now they were walking by a long section of the bordello that was composed not of bricks or board but of smooth sweating flesh. Yet in the flesh were lead-lined windows where various prostitutes sat for display to passersby. There were all manner of demonian species in the windows—Mongrel, City-Imp, Troll, Succubus, Hybrid, etc., along with some Humans—all naked and poised voluptuously. When ugly, butt-faced demons strolled by, the girls would enthusiastically raise their windows and whistle at them, urge them to come over, with corny lines like "Hey handsome, where you been all my eternity?" and "Take me, I'm yours." Others were much more direct: "Come on! Let's get it on!" and "I'm the best trick in Hell! What are you waiting for?"

Sadly, though, none of the girls so much as noticed Walter. A few of them even looked at him and laughed.

He trudged on, with the inexplicable head tucked under his arm.

"Are we getting close to where Candice works?"

"Maybe."

"Thanks for being so informative."

"Hey, Walter, that little-boy-hurt stuff doesn't work with me."

Walter just frowned and let it slide off. At least that was one thing he was getting good at. "Can I ask you something, No-name?"

"Yes, but only if it doesn't involve the revelation of an ethereal abstrusion."

"Are you my friend?"

"Yes," she said without pause.

"Then why do you give me crap all the time?"

"Because I'm your friend."

Walter could've laughed.

Sometimes it sounded like he was walking on something wet, and when he looked down he'd see periodic used condoms lying on the sidewalk, demonic seed leaking though their factory-made perforations. He'd also see occasional charred hands and feet, from low-end hookers who'd sold the parts to street-side smoke-diviners for drug money. Across the street, two horned pimps were mugging a john, and a block down, a pair of Imp prostitutes were stabbing each other. Golem police officers walked slowly by, unconcerned.

"Turn here," No-name said when they finally got to the end of the half-mile-long bordello block.

BOTTOM OF THE BARREL ALLEY a street sign read.

Denizens strolled out, hands in pockets. One bearded man was walking and he looked right at Walter and said, "I told you I'd see you here." His head sat on his shoulders at an angle, and the bloody shirt he wore read: PIL: THIS IS WHAT YOU WANT, THIS IS WHAT YOU GET. Walter watched him walk by, speechless.

Shouts could be heard from the distance. The left side of the alley remained the window-pocked Wall of Skin, but here the skin shined less lustrously and eventually grew infectious. Chancres throbbed, gonorrhea raged in folds of flesh, chlamydic discharge oozed from pocks. Some of the epidermal pocks squirmed from chiggers embedded beneath.

The women in these windows were all afflicted in one way or other: missing a limb, missing a scalp, burned, covered in demonic rashes, and the like. One girl sat dejectedly in one window, looking to one side. She appeared petite and attractive, until she turned to reveal the other side of her face, which had been scraped off to the bone. Another Human woman could've been a model, save for the fact that her breasts had been chewed off. Another, a She-Troll, looked out her window sightlessly, her eye sockets empty. A sign under her window read: ANY HOLE OF YOUR CHOICE: $5.

Walter felt petrified now. What would await him?

"Get ready, Walter," No-name consoled. "Remember, it's better to regret the things you have done than the things you haven't done."

"Meaning?"

"You're not going to like what you're about to see. But

273

you wanted to come here. You willingly came through that Deadpass to see Candice, and now you're going to see her. So. We're here. This is what you want..."

Another refrain. Walter stood still in the moment.

This is what you get, he thought.

The red-light district in Hell.

A muffled voice eddied out from the dark as a slinky figure approached, high heels clicking. "Half-and-half, ten Hellnotes, cutie pie. I'll give it to you like you never got it before."

Yellow light from the windows glared down, and it was into that light that the figure stepped.

Walter's heart pattered.

It was her. It was Candice.

Walter could only stand and stare, enamored.

Here she was as he'd always envisioned her: the Adriatic-blue eyes, the long blond hair down past her waist, five-foot-ten and a half, and taller on the stiletto heels.

Then those Adriatic-blue eyes widened.

"Walter?" she questioned.

Her voice sounded muffled, almost like someone talking through a mouthful of food. Walter didn't understand it . . . and didn't care.

Because she was here.

"Yes, it's me, Candice." His words sounded miles away. "I came here for you."

She stood in the light, but a shadow obscured part of her face. "So Colin wasn't bullshitting me. He killed me, to send me here. Then he killed himself."

"You know?" Walter was dismayed. "You know that I'm—"

"Yeah, I know all about it. You're an Etherean now, because Colin blew his head off before you could. You don't look very powerful to me."

Walter didn't feel it, either. He felt helplessly human, love radiating at his heart, his very mortal heart. He took a deep breath. He wanted to talk to her, about so many things, and about the future he could provide for her, even in this damned city . . .

But something wasn't right. Something was out of place. Her voice.

It sounded so muffled, so garbled. He didn't understand.

"Candice, what's wrong with your voice?"

"Try talking through this, asshole," came her next garble, and then she took another step closer and brought the rest of her face into the light.

The mouth of an infernal sea creature known as a Bapho-Octopoid had been surgically affixed, replacing Candice's human mouth. A tight, toothless o-ring of gray-white rubbery flesh. It was actually a not-so-rare surgical transfiguration for prostitutes, to embellish oral proficiencies. Around the rim of her new mouth, tiny tentacles squirmed, that reminded Walter of sauteed calamari.

"Still love me, Walter? Still wanna kiss me?"

"Yes," Walter said.

"This is all your fault, you geek piece of shit," came the next wet mumble. "Your goddamn brother killed me just so you'd come after me. I didn't have anything to do with that occult shit—I was used." She pointed to the tentacle-rimmed sucker mouth. "This is your fault."

Walter desperately shook his head. "I can fix all that, Candice. They have surgeons here, they have these Trans-figurists. They'll change you back to normal. Once I hook up with Lucifer, he'll do anything I ask."

Wet laughter fired from the mouth-hole. "You are such a gullible dweeb!"

"No, no," Walter was growing frantic. "I saw the page in your diary. I've come to rescue you. I'm an Etherean, I have great power and Satan will reward me if I agree to use my power for him. I'll make sure he rewards you too. I read your diary page, and I know now that you truly do love me."

The constricted ring of flesh twitched as she talked in a gargly whisper. "I hate you, I hate your guts."

"But-but, your diary page!"

"Colin made me write that bullshit with a gun to my head, you dickless asshole. I hate you, I hate you, I've always hated you. The only reason I was ever nice to you was because you did my homework for me."

"You-you-you'll change your mind—you're under an understandable amount of stress. I'm telling you, when I go over to Lucifer, he'll give me anything I want. I'll have him give you your regular face back. It'll be wonderful. We'll finally be together."

No-name rolled her eyes. "You poor sap."

"I'm serious, Candice," Walter babbled on, "we'll live in a big palace with servants and every luxury. Satan rewards the faithful."

Her mouth twitched some more. "Satan rewards only himself through the misery of others. Colin was faithful and look what he got as a reward."

She pointed across the alley, where a large Ghor-Hound-drawn carriage sat, the fanged Ghor-Hound itself bigger than the largest horse. The carriage was rocking on the springs over its great spoked wheels. Outside the carriage stood a line of at least a dozen fat, well-dressed Trolls, each holding Hellnotes in their stubby hands. And standing at the carriage door was somebody Walter remembered.

Her nude beauty was impeccable, her black hair shining like oil. It was Augustina, Colin's former limo driver in the Living World. Here she looked the same as she had on earth: the perfect hour-glass physique, the erect bosom, and the blazing white skin checkerboarded from ankles to throat with stark black inverted crosses. She was taking money from the Trolls standing in line.

She's . . . a pimp, Walter realized.

Then the carriage door opened, and out climbed a corpulent Troll, grinning in satisfaction as he hauled up his trousers.

"See, Walter?" No-name observed. "She's the pimp, and your brother's the 'ho."

Aghast, Walter watched as the next Troll gave Augustina a stack of bills and climbed into the carriage, unbuckling his pants. Before the carriage door was re-closed, Walter had time to catch a glimpse of his brother. Colin had not been transfigured into a Grand Duke as he'd anticipated. His head had been shaved, and he'd been tarred and feathered, save for his buttocks. His wrists were chained to the floor, and right now the Troll was bending him over the carriage seat. The door slammed shut. Walter turned away when Colin began to scream.

Augustina smiled at him, waved daintily.

"But that's nothing compared to what you'll get," Candice mumbled, trying to smile herself through the Octopoid mouth. "And you'll be getting it soon."

Walter felt as though his heart had been blown out.

"Let's go, Walter," No-name said.

Walter headed back toward the main drag. Augustina continued to wave after him, Colin continued to scream, and Candice continued to laugh.

I'm the biggest sucker in Hell, Walter thought.

No-name's head seemed to be contemplating something, her mouth opened in a pause. She seemed bothered. "Walter, I know you're sensitive, so don't take this too hard but—"

"But what?" he asked, looking down.

He'd been carrying her all this time under his arm. "You need a better deodorant. Consider my position. I'm practically living in your armpit right now."

Walter, again, thought about the possibility of dropping her into the nearest garbage can. The last thing he needed now was more shit from other people. "Well, I'm really sorry about that, No-name. I'm under a little stress here, if you don't mind. I'm an Etherean—I'm a living myth in Hell—and with all that, I come to find out that I have no powers anyway. And I just found out that the girl I love is one of Satan's hookers, and so is my brother. I've had a bad day."

"Oh, poor Walter, boo-hoo. Pity poor Walter. Poor Walter's under so much stress." The head glared at him. "What about *me*? *I'm* not under stress? *I* haven't had a bad day? I'm a severed head!"

"That's not my fault!"

"No, nothing's your fault, Walter. You're too afraid to ever take enough of a risk. You'd rather shuffle around with your stooped shoulders and mope. You wanna know why people think you're a geek, Walter? Because you act like one. You let yourself be the target of other people's cruelty because you *ask* for it. You're not man enough to change that. You're your own nerd, Walter, because you made yourself that way. If you don't like it, then do something about it."

Tears flowed down Walter's cheeks. He grabbed No-name by the hair and held her out, looking at her. "I don't know what to do."

"I can't tell you what to do. There's gotta come a time in your life when you make a positive decision on your own. Here, or back in the Living World. That time is now. Grow up. Stop acting like the wimp you're certain you are."

"Please stop being mean to me," he pleaded. "I can't hack it anymore."

"Then do something about it. Summon the courage within yourself."

"What? Throw you away?"

"If you like."

"But you're my friend! You just said so! Are you lying too?"

"No, Walter, I can never lie to you. And I am your friend. I rag on you to provoke you, because, very soon, you're going to need to make a very serious decision."

"The only decision I have to make is do I kill myself here or back in the Living World? You already know, but you won't tell me."

Now No-name looked equally disheartened. "I'll tell you this. There's another decision you're going to have to make first."

"What is it?" Walter's mind reeled. "Why don't you help me?"

"That's what I'm trying to do. You're not thinking clearly. I already told you. Be deductive. Be *smart*."

I am smart, he thought, angered. *What is she talking about now?*

"What do you know about your current situation, Walter?" the head asked next. "Be transitive, be—"

"Yeah, yeah, be deductive; I heard you the first time." Walter tried to let some of the fog clear from his head. Yes, he knew he was smart—that was about the only thing he was certain of—but he also knew that the shock and horror and despair of everything he'd just seen was sidetracking him.

He repeated No-name's question: *What do I know about my current situation?*

"One," he started, "I'm an Etherean, and right now I'm in Hell."

"Good," No-name said. "Go on. *Why* are you in Hell?"

"Because I came through the Deadpass."

The head frowned. "*Why* did you come though the Deadpass?"

Walter frowned back. "For the express purpose of getting here."

"Why? What were your motivations? Start again. Be deductive."

Walter let out a long sigh. "One, I'm an Etherean. Two, I'm in Hell. Three, I came to Hell willingly because I wanted to see Candice, to see if I had a chance with her because in her diary she said that she loved me. Four, it turns out that Candice doesn't love me, Colin just made her write that. Five, that's the reason that Colin killed her in the first place, to send her soul to Hell." Walter slowed, thinking. "That's about it, isn't it?"

"No!" No-name bellowed. She was getting mad. "I can't tell you! You have to figure it out for yourself!"

Now Walter stopped completely. He blinked. Then he whispered, "Holy shit. . . ."

"Yes?"

"I'm Plan B. Plan A failed. Lucifer wanted to capture the Etheress but he failed. Colin had Candice fake the diary page and then sent her to Hell because he knew that I would follow her here. Lucifer failed to capture the Etheress so now he wants to capture me. Candice was the bait he was using to lure me here."

"Yes," No-name affirmed. "And now? Deductively?"

"Candice was the trap." Walter blinked again. He finally got it. "And I just walked into it."

"Yes," No-name whispered. "And you're standing in the middle of that trap right now, right this instant."

When Walter looked up the street, he saw a regiment of armored demons standing there in total silence. Some of the demons had chains, others had nets. Then he turned around and saw a similar regiment behind him.

"We're trapped," No-name observed.

"And there's no way out," Walter added.

Two wedge-faced demons broke from their ranks and approached, armor clattering. One dragged a net, the other carried a mallet so large he needed both hands to hold it. The mallet's head was as large as a microwave oven.

No-name's head was grabbed from Walter and placed on the ground. "The head is an enemy of the state," the first demon proclaimed, and to the other he ordered, "Destroy it. I'll bring the Etherean in." The demon eyed Walter with amusement. "An Etherean with no power. It takes a man to be an Etherean. I see no man here."

The other demon—the one with the mallet—laughed. "Our lord's diviners were right. This boy is harmless."

No-name's head looked up at Walter from where it lay in the street. "Your test is upon you, Walter. Only faith can save you now."

"Faith in what?" Walter asked dismally. "In God?"

"No, in yourself. If you fail your test, you will be taken in chains to the Mephisto Building, and there they will drain all your blood—your *Ethereal* blood. In your blood there is a monumental power to be tapped. That power exists nowhere else. And Lucifer wants it. He doesn't want *you*, Walter. He just wants your blood. It will enable him to change the world. Whether you give it to him or not... well... that's all up to you."

"I don't understand."

"Choose. Now."

Walter looked absurdly at the two massive demons. "I can't fight these guys. And even if I could, there's a hundred more of them in front of me and behind me."

"Choose," No-name said. "Now."

"Send this soothsayer's spirit into the body of a worm," the first demon ordered. The second demon began to raise the mallet over No-name's head.

"Leave her alone!" Walter shouted.

The demon exploded. It sounded like a howitzer going off. In a split second, the demon flew away in black bits, in a tornado-like rise. Even the mallet exploded.

The same thing happened to the other demon, the instant it lunged and tried to throw the net over Walter. The street shook in another cannon-like bang.

What the hell? Walter thought. His knees wobbled, and his ears hurt from the sound. No-name, below, smiled up at him.

"Get ready," she whispered.

"Seize him!" a black voice barked, then a wave of rallying shouts rose. Walter peed in his pants when he saw both regiments of demons charge at him.

"Walter," No-name said. "They think *they're* bad? Show them what bad really is."

Walter put his hands over his eyes, and his voice cracked like a boy entering puberty when he shrieked. "Fuckin' DIE!"

Both ends of the street exploded in encroaching stages, as if carpet-bombed. The concussion knocked Walter down, and the buildings on either side trembled. The street broke apart into great chunks, like an instantaneous earthquake. The demons were engulfed by the rubble and ground up to pulp. Arms, legs, and heads, boots, helmets, and breastplates, flew up into the air and then rained back down, along with a torrent of demonic blood.

Then: total silence.

The only part of the street that hadn't been destroyed

was the immediate area of space that Walter and No-name's head occupied. Walter sat huddled over the head, teeth chattering, shell-shocked.

"You can get up now, Walter," No-name said.

Walter did so, shakily. Both sides of the street were now a massive pile of rubble and gore.

"Did I do that?" he peeped.

"Yes."

"Did I pass the test?"

"Like every other test you've ever taken in your life, Walter—you got a hundred. Congratulations. You're a walking meat-grinder."

He peered at the mounds of wreckage and carnage. Body parts twitched, while corpses lay crushed. Steam rose off the piles of rubble. *That's the secret,* he wondered. The secret to unlocking his Ethereal Powers. *Confidence.* In that last fragment of a second, he'd released his fears and terrors and believed in himself.

Walter, stupefied as he gazed at the destruction, considered this. "I could do some serious damage down here."

"Yes, you could. But is that really your destiny?"

"I guess not, since you put it that way."

"Destiny is like fate, Walter," No-name informed him next. "You don't have to go searching for it. It finds you."

Embrace your destiny, the words kept ringing in his head. With No-name safely tucked under his arm, Walter began to climb over the heaps of rubble and bodies, back toward the main road. From the windows of the surrounding buildings, citizens of Hell leaned out, hooting, whistling, applauding. "God be with you, Etherean!" a voice trumpeted.

Walter looked up, awed at the demons and Humans waving at him, wishing him well.

"Look at that, Walter," the head said. "You're a star."

Yeah . . . He waved back at them, then continued climbing over the rubble. "So I guess I don't even have to ask you where we're going next, huh?"

"Wherever it is we're supposed to go, it'll find us," No-name replied.

Chapter Thirteen

(I)

"They're hybrid Armilus," Angelese said. They'd closed the Nectoport, and were hiding behind the barbican a block away from the windowless limestone castle known as the Infernal Archives. The structure loomed, hundreds of feet tall, and occupied most of the largest block of Nero Square. Cassie and the angel were staking the place out.

"Hybrid . . . *what?*" Cassie squinted around the rampart edge.

"Armilus. Hybrid offspring of Lucifer, sort of like a genetic mutation where the base subject was one of Lucifer's sons. There's only two of them here, but they're very powerful. They guard the entrance to the Archives."

Cassie looked at the atrocious things, thinking of the most overdeveloped body-builders. Bulbs of muscles growing over more muscles, tree-trunk-stout legs bowed and tensed from all the muscle mass they had to bear. Veins like ropes beat beneath mottled caramel-brown skin that shined as if oiled. When they walked, their flat feet and the huge balls of their heels thumped on the brick pavement. Their bald, horned heads were divided by still more muscles, and their eyes, too, were barely visible through their facial bulges.

"You'd think that there'd be more of them," Cassie ventured. "If the Infernal Archives is such an important, sensitive place—how come there's only two of them?"

"They're so strong they can punch through stone walls," Angelese warned, "they can break iron bars and kick though iron plate. They can lift several hundred times their own weight, and they're impervious to fire. They don't need more than two of them to guard the Archives, because they're very, very powerful."

Cassie frowned at them, then shouted "Rigor Mortis!"

The two things jerked their attention toward Cassie. They began to thump forward but only for a few steps before their flexing unwieldy muscles began to spasm. Cassie's Etheric command caused the creatures' muscle fibers to expend all of their myofibrillar proteins at once.

Two great *THUMPS!* resounded when both Armilus flopped over onto the pavement. They convulsed a moment, then went stiff as statutes.

"They're not *that* powerful," Cassie complained.

Angelese smiled at Cassie's creativity. "Don't get overconfident. When you use too much of your energy too fast, you can deplete yourself."

Cassie remembered what had happened at the clinic. Her last command had caused her to lose consciousness, and the angel had had to carry her out. "I'll be careful," she tried to assure.

"Good, because you'll need a little more in a minute once we're in the Archives."

Cassie didn't understand. "But you just told me there were only two Armilus guarding the place."

"Guarding the *outside* of the place."

Cassie didn't feel particularly challenged by more Armilus. "You mean there's more inside?"

"No," the angel said. "Inside there's something worse."

Hmm, Cassie thought. *We'll see.*

They approached the front steps of the Archives, the pair of Armilus frozen on their meaty backs. Ahead, the Archives stood strangely as if in wait for them, like a citadel, a medieval fortress with garrets, turrets, and unscalable flat outer walls. "So this is like Hell's library?" Cassie asked.

"That's exactly what it is. And there's only one person inside running it. She's known as the Maémaè."

Cassie wasn't fearful. *How tough can a librarian be?*

"But to find her, we have to go through the Labyrinth. It's the only way to get to the Main Document Repository, and the Labyrinth is inhabited by two Necrotiks. They're already dead, so they can't be killed."

Cassie's confidence waned a bit. She didn't even like the name: *Necrotiks.* It sounded . . . disconcerting.

She thought of Greek mythology's Theseus and the Minotaur when they entered the Labyrinth: a series of narrow passageways. Irradiated moonstones were all that lit the corridors—Cassie could barely see at certain points, and it was around one such very dark corner that she bumped into something.

"What the—"

A hand that stank and felt skeletal opened over her face.

"Get back get back get back!" she shrieked. She and Angelese retreated.

"What was it?"

"Something . . ." was all Cassie got out.

"Did it stink? Like a rotten corpse?"

287

"Yes!"

Angelese took one of the moonstones down from its sconce and shined it forward like a flashlight.

"Jesus Christ!" Cassie complained.

A stick figure stood before them at the corner. A skeleton with a patchwork of corpse-skin grafted over its bones. No internal organs, no muscles or tendons, just buttermilk-white skin stretched over bone. The empty eye sockets were looking right at them, *seeing* them.

It just stood there, holding up one bony hand like a cop directing traffic.

"That's really bizarre," the angel observed.

"Yeah, a friggin' skeleton covered with dead skin? Bizarre is right!"

"No, I mean its actions. Necrotiks are animated by Enchantment Spells and are motivated by Satanic vengeance. It should be attacking us by now. Instead it's just standing there, blocking our way."

Fragments of language cracked from the rotten hole that was its mouth. It said, "Do not attempt to pass. Retrace your steps and leave. Please."

Cassie grabbed Angelese's arm. "Maybe we should do that. I mean, come on, it said please."

"We can't, Cassie. We're here for a reason. We have to find out what your mother refused to tell us. If we don't, we fail." Angelese peered queerly at her. "What happened to all that Etheric confidence? You act like you're afraid of the dark."

"I am!" Cassie exclaimed.

Up ahead, the second Necrotik appeared, standing at the other's side. It, too, held up its skin-tattered hand.

"I don't understand this," the angel went on. "They're acting like they're afraid, but they're not capable of feeling fear, just wrath. They're unkillable, and we're just two chicks. What the hell are they afraid of?"

"I don't know, and I don't want to know. This place creeps me out. There's gotta be another way in."

"There isn't."

"Let's go around to the other side of the building. I'll knock down a wall with a mental projection—we can get in that way."

"The walls are all protected by Indemnity Hexes. Not even the strongest Etheric thought can crack them. But I think I know what the Necrotiks are afraid of."

"What?"

"You. You're an entity of innocence in a place where no innocence exists. In their eternal death, they sense your living spirit. They've never seen anything like you before; you're not what they're used to."

Cassie winced. "Am I supposed to be, like, *encouraged* by that? I don't know what to do. Tell me what to do."

"Try something," Angelese threw out. "Project something at them."

All right, Cassie thought. *Think. If I were a reanimated corpse, what would I be afraid of?* Her thoughts paused. *I know . . .*

"Cremate!" she yelled down the corridor.

The verb turned into a wedge of hissing flame—white-blue hot—that bulled down the passageway and collided with the two figures. It hovered there, engulfing them, hissing, the heat so intense that a reactive wave swept back and burned Cassie's face. On either side of the passage, the black stone walls turned red like burners on a stove.

When the fire died, Cassie said, "Shit."

The Necrotiks remained unaffected, unscorched, their hands still upraised.

"Shit is right," Angelese said.

It worked before, maybe it'll work again, Cassie thought next, and yelled, "Boneless!" *Christ, that's practically all they are is bones.* She repeated it: "Boneless, boneless, boneless!"

Nothing happened.

"Armless! Legless! Now!"

No effect.

"You're trying to take away from them," Angelese suggested. "They're fleshless corpses; symbolically there's nothing you can take away..."

When the angel said that, the pair of Necrotiks rushed forward, howling like nails across slate.

You can't take away from them, Cassie thought, steeling herself, *so try adding TO them...*

"Obese! Fat! Adipose tissue!"

Their howls fluttered as their movements forward ground to a halt. When Cassie looked at them again, they were immobile in fat, the patchworks of dead skin stretched to such an extreme they appeared fit to burst. Hundreds of pounds of fatty tissue now filled the space between their skin and bones. The things could do nothing now but churn face-down on the stone floor, like quivering balloons.

"So much for them," Angelese remarked.

"Gross," Cassie added, looking down. The Necrotiks sloshed as they struggled, but it was clear: they weren't going anywhere. "Try Weight Watchers," she added, then she and Angelese climbed over the obese things and continued down the corridor.

The angel held the moonstone, both of their faces uplit in the musty darkness. "So where are we going now?" Cassie asked.

"The Main Repository. That's where Hell's greatest secrets are kept."

"And this person we're looking for, the—"

"The Maémaè," Angelese pronounced the arcane name.

"She's the Archivist. In life she was the curator of the Library of Alexandria, she maintained the royal files of the Ptolemies, the great kings of Egypt."

"Why is she in Hell?"

"She sold her soul to Lucifer in exchange for the love of Alexander the Great."

"He fell in love with her?"

"Yeah, and then he died a week later. The Maémaè wasn't happy; she sold her soul for nothing. But Lucifer's always had a thing for her so he let her keep her old job. In the Living World, she was known as the most beautiful woman in Alexandria. Now she's known as the most beautiful woman in Hell."

That's some tagline, Cassie thought.

The moonstone's light led them up winding stone steps that seemed to never end, but when they did, they were standing in a great vault of books. Shelves upon shelves, piles upon piles. Some books were huge, some tiny. The wan light from countless moonstones made the books look like uneven bricks forming an infinite edifice.

Cassie picked up one black-bound book. The title read *Terra Dementata,* but when she opened it, the pages were all blank. She picked up another one—*The Confession of Judas Iscariot*—and its pages, too, were blank. More books, then, with the strangest titles: *The Synod of the Aorists, The Recant of St. John the Divine, The Proclamation of the Red Sect* . . . All their pages were blank.

"A Sorcery Encryption," the angel explained. "It protects the secrets here, plus it serves the basic function of Hell. All the secrets of history are here, but you can't find out what they are. Lucifer won't allow it. Only he and the Maémaè know."

"So that's why we're here?" Cassie said. "To ask Maémaè?"

"In a sense. We're going to ask her for permission to read."

"But the books are all blank!"

"Not if she casts the Unbinding Spell."

Cassie was getting irate. "And why would she do that? She won't! We're wasting our time! There's no reason for this—this *Maémaè* to help us."

Angelese smiled faintly. "Maybe I can give her a reason."

Through one vault after the next they proceeded, through more veritable mountains of books.

They walked for hours.

Cassie felt wobbly, buzz-headed, like the one time she'd smoked pot. (She'd never smoked it after that because it made her eat like a pig.) Was the air thinner here, or was it something else?

"It's knowledge," the angel said, again sensing her questions. "There's so much buried knowledge here, unknown, unread, it sort of ferments and releases something into the air."

"It makes no sense for this place to exist," Cassie complained.

"Of course it doesn't, and that's precisely *why* it exists. And guess what? We're almost there."

Woozy, Cassie walked on. Off to the side she noticed one small cove indented against the wall. It contained one moonstone and a single teetering wooden bookshelf. A curiosity forced her to stop and look at the spines of the dozen or so books stored there. *The Gospel According to Mary*, *The Restituta of Sister Anastasia*, *The Book of Dictums*, *The Second Book of Exodus*, *The Epistle of Timothy to the Philippians IV*.

"What is *this* weird place?" Cassie asked.

"Lucifer's greatest achievement—the Cove of Expurgation."

"It's not very big."

"Doesn't have to be. These are all books that should've been in the Holy Bible, but Lucifer got them expunged."

Now the floor canted upward as they entered another vault whose ceiling was a hundred feet high. All the walls were lined all the way to the top with laden bookshelves, yet the floor of the vault lay empty save for a raised desk and platform at the very center, like a judge's bench. Cassie noticed the figure of a woman sitting in the high chair behind the desk. The woman looked interminably bored.

The clatters of their footsteps echoed loudly, and inch-thick dust on the floor puffed up as they approached.

A soft voice lifted above the echoes: "In our endless darkness we weep, but even our smiles we keep—at the beckoning of angels."

Cassie and Angelese stopped before the great risen desk, looking up.

The Maémaè looked down.

Surrounded by this massive open space, she appeared tiny, svelte. When she stood up from the desk to appraise them, she displayed the body of a Ford Agency model—long sleek perfect legs, tiny-waisted, a willowy merge of curves and flawless body lines—but Ford Agency models didn't have horns in their heads. A corset of human black leather compressed a further perfection of breasts that—even nearly spilling from the confines of the intricate brassiere—seemed buoyant and erect. Delicately carved black glass had been fashioned by some infernal artisan into spiked stiletto heels, and the panties beneath the garter straps were made from some kind of abyssal dark-maroon lace. The earthen-blond hair cut in a sassy bob seemed too human for this unfathomable creature, as did her skin when she stood at the right angle in the moonstone light. It was impeccable skin, poreless, a nut-brown tan, until she changed positions to reveal its next hue: a meld of chartreuse streaked with salmon-pink. The Maémaè's face was as beautiful as something painted by Raphael, and she had a smile full of wonders, not horrors. The whites of her eyes were cognac-red, the irises azure.

"What are a pair of angels doing in this place?" came the question. The Archivist's voice drifted like a breeze; it seemed to come from everywhere but her mouth.

"I'm not an angel," Cassie countered. "I'm an Etheress, and if you don't tell us what we need to know, I'll destroy you."

The smile drifted just like the voice. "You can't destroy anything here. The ill-will you bring from your world matches the ill-will here. I hope you will think about that."

Cassie kept looking up at the petite, fascinating woman.

"I can tell you nothing," the Maémaè added. "Both of you know that. This room is filled with all the knowledge of every world, but none of that knowledge can ever be revealed."

"It can be revealed by you," Angelese said. "You can let us read."

"I will never let you read. I will never let anyone read, ever. That is my eternal pledge. You know this, and what you pursue is futile." Then the Archivist's smile turned even brighter, like someone musing in ecstasy. The sleek, finely nailed hands opened to them. "But come up if you like. I long for guests, I long for those who seek."

Cassie and Angelese walked behind the risen desk and mounted some short wooden steps. Thousand-year-old wood creaked like a witch's titter. The Maémaè's golden hair seemed to flow even though there were no drafts in this windowless place, no breezes. Once up, Cassie could see more of the Archivist, more of her physical perfection in a world built upon error. When she moved, she drifted, like her voice, something like total elegance, total grace. The orbs of her breasts moved too, sliding minutely in the devilish brassiere, the outlines of her distended nipples betrayed by the sheer material. The fishnet stockings covering her coltish legs were not fabric but a meticulous lattice of preserved demonic veins and arteries. The Maémaè's hair continued to shift on its own, and so did the tint of her skin, which at the next moment appeared mulberry-dark, and the next white as frost and dusted by some crystalline mist. But there was nothing demonic about the She-Demon's scent; it was another opposite. From the shining, shifting, flaxen hair came an essence like the scent of a green field in the summer, after rain.

"These are pretty," the Maémaè whispered, running her slim finger up Angelese's arm, over the gridwork of scars etched by the Umbra-Specter. Then she drifted around to Cassie and ran the same finger gently down the center of her throat where it stopped on the silver locket containing Lissa's picture. "And so is this . . ."

"What would happen if you let us read?" Angelese interrupted.

"I would lose my position here at the Archives." The scarlet eyes flashed behind the impossible smile. "And I will never jeopardize that."

"What's the big deal? It doesn't look like much of a position," Cassie commented. "You get to sit here for eternity and guard a bunch of books that no one can ever read."

"I like complacency." The voice swirled around Cassie's head like a stream of moths. "Never take what you have for granted." Like the voice, now the woman herself was drifting around Cassie, her finger moving along with her, across Cassie's shoulders, her back, across the top of her bosom. "Yes, an angel . . ."

Cassie grew flustered, and off-guard. "I told you, I'm not an angel. I'm an Etheress."

Now the Archivist's elegant finger traced a line down Cassie's bare arm and played over her hand.

Please, Cassie thought, biting her lip, *please tell me that the librarian of Hell is NOT putting the make on me!*

"Providence, infinity, resplendence, and hatred," the Maémaè whispered next. Her hand came off of Cassie's. "It's all the same, in a way."

Cassie didn't understand, nor did Angelese, or if she did, it was clear she didn't care. But when Cassie thought about it a moment, she guessed that the woman meant people, and their aspirations, were the same everywhere.

Then she thought: *I wonder if they're the same in Heaven . . .*

"I have something to trade," Angelese told the librarian.

"You have nothing I want."

"Are you sure?"

"I should say, there's nothing I desire that you can give me."

The angel repeated: "Are you sure?"

When the Maémaè moved closer, her skin diverged again, to a brown-black, like a chameleon on dark tree bark. "Go back to Heaven, and be grateful."

"Don't you want to know?" the angel goaded.

I sure as hell do, Cassie thought, and then she remembered what Angelese had said earlier. When Cassie had implied that the Maémaè had no reason to help them, Anglese had answered with the strangest confidence, *Maybe I can give her a reason.*

"No, I'll just be disappointed," the Archivist said, her cryptic smile hanging in the air. "That's what my home thrives on, that's the blood of its heart. Disappointment."

Angelese looked right back into her eyes and said, "I have the power to revoke your Condemnation."

The words echoed for a long time.

Tiny tears, like diamond dust, glittered at the rims of the Maémaè's eyes. Her lips parted a few times, as if to speak, but she could summon no lilting words. Instead, a long dark tongue, like a monitor lizard's, slipped out between her lips and tasted the air. "I don't believe you," she eventually declared.

"Your home?" Angelese challenged. "What it really thrives on are lies, all the lies of history. My home thrives on truth."

"If you're trying to convince me that angels don't lie, I must take exception. I know an angel who's been lying quite effectively for five thousand years."

"I can release your Spirit to Purgatory," Angelese said. The silence bloomed before them.

"You put your trust in Lucifer," Angelese went on, "and look what you got. Try putting your trust in God. I'm one of His emissaries."

The Maémaè just stared, her fanged smile open in awe.

"You've got nothing to lose," Angelese finished.

On the desk lay a single, rather dully bound book. Gold leaf on the cover read APPENDICES. The Maémaè daintily picked up the book and handed it to Angelese, but when she opened it in the wan light, she frowned. "The pages are still blank. Don't fuck with me."

The Maémaè sighed like someone who'd just been embraced by a lost love. Her smile kept beaming, and then she closed her eyes, looking up, and raised her arms.

Suddenly the Repository was filled with the brightest sunlight.

Angelese looked at the book again, and croaked, "My God . . ."

But Cassie stood horrified. Her mind reeled, her thoughts like teeth grinding, and when she glared at the angel, it was with pure hatred. She hissed, "You bitch . . ."

Angelese gawked at her. "Cassie, what's wrong with you?"

"You BITCH!" Cassie shouted, and the words hit Angelese in the chest like a machine-gun blast, blowing her over the platform's railing and slamming her to the floor. The book flew away into bright light. When Cassie ran to the rail and glared down, a very dazed Angelese was trying to drag herself up.

"Let me HELP you up!" Cassie yelled, and then she pictured giant hands, and those hands grasped Angelese by the neck and lifted her twenty feet into the air. The angel squealed in terror, feet kicking, arms flailing. "What are you *doing*?" she gagged.

"I didn't know you could revoke condemnations!"

"I can," Angelese struggled, her face darkening from the invisible stranglehold. "I can, any angel in my order can. It's one of God's earliest codices. I can free one damned soul every thousand years . . ."

"Then free my *sister*! Send my *sister* to Purgatory!"

The hands clamped down harder.

"I can't," the angel choked. "If I could I would, but it's not possible."

"But you just said—"

"Your sister isn't eligible . . ."

"Why?"

"Because she committed suicide!"

Cassie's spirit plummeted, and Angelese almost did too when Cassie nearly lost the telekinetic grip. *What have I done, what have I done?* She let Angelese down as gently as possible, then she fell to her knees.

"I'm sorry," she begged. "I don't know what came over me."

Angelese took deep breaths, rubbing her throat. "It's all right."

"No! I'm really sorry!"

"Forget about it. You're human. Humans are fucked up."

Tell me about it, Cassie thought.

Angelese picked up the book of Appendices. Then she looked inside again.

The Maémaè had drifted down from the platform, standing off, her perfect body a sleek curvy line. Her smile burned into Cassie's eyes. In spite of the tiny fangs, it was a smile of good-will, not the opposite, not a smile born in Hell.

"Not all angels have wings," she said to Cassie. She closed her scarlet eyes again, and raised her arms.

"Cassie," Angelese said. "I have to keep my part of the bargain. Destroy her."

Cassie understood. She liked the Maémaè, so she tried to think of something painless.

"Please," the Maémaè whispered through the smile. "Send me out of here . . ."

"Smoke," Cassie said.

There was a faint *PUFF!* and the most beautiful woman in Hell dissipated into black dust. Within the dust, however, a glittering mist swirled, very faintly. It hovered, then rose.

Then disappeared.

The dust of the Maémaè's Spirit Body settled like soot to the wooden floor, leaving a ghostly, diaphanous outline, but within it the woman's features could still be deciphered, especially the tiny-fanged smile. The smile of bliss in the midst of misery.

The light which now filled the Repository was nearly blinding. Cassie shielded her eyes when she approached Angelese, who was reading the book with wide-open eyes. "I haven't seen this language in ages. Even the Archangels have forgotten how to speak it."

"What language?"

"It's called Zrætic, the first protodialect of the Tabernacle of God. This language predates the Enochian alphabet; it's what was spoken before Adam and Eve."

The text was stiffly handwritten. Had it been the Maé-maè who had written it? Cassie glimpsed the first incomprehensible lines:

Eeaan nesaaa sen fø Brud de Liaat . . .

The same strange language that R.J. had spoken in back at the clinic during the Merge: the Paresis Incantation he'd put on her. Was this the language that all angels once spoke in? It scarcely mattered, though. *I'm not an angel,* she thought. *I could never understand it.*

"God Almighty," Angelese whispered.

"What's it say?" Cassie asked.

The angel had never appeared more troubled. Her lips moved in silence as she continued to read.

"What!" Cassie snapped, twisted in suspense.

"Well, the first part is something that we already know, but it's not complete. It's something to do with Retrogations. Astral Retrogations."

"You told me about that," Cassie recalled. "Sorcery-based time-travel."

"Um-hmm. Lucifer's had the power to do that for a while, from something he stole from Heaven. He can go back into different time-segments, for very short periods of time."

"And whatever this big plan of his is, it's got something to do with that?"

"Evidently, but this entry isn't complete."

This miffed Cassie. They'd come all this way and gone to all this trouble, and they still wouldn't get the whole story? "I thought every secret in Hell was kept here?"

"*Complete* secrets. There must be a final part that they're working on that isn't complete yet, so that's why it's not here. And I think it has something to do with you."

"The reason that Lucifer wants me," Cassie guessed.

"Yes. He doesn't want *you,* he wants your *power,* for something else. Same reason he wants the Etherean I was telling you about earlier. Lucifer always likes options, and he's well-versed with failure. If he can't get you, he has a back-up."

"The Etherean?"

"Right. And that's probably who he's gunning for now, since we escaped the Merge at the clinic."

All this just frustrated Cassie more. She'd never been known for patience. "What else? What else is in the book?"

"The second entry is a summary of the Spatial Merge in Maryland, where—"

"I know, I know, you told me. A Fallen Angel named Zeihl committed suicide, at some . . . map library or something."

"Yes. And why?"

How could Cassie forget the angel's previous explanation—when the Umbra-Specter had tortured her with its talons for divulging it? "Zeihl incarnated himself during the Merge at the map library, then he committed suicide to generate a Power Exchange. It's because of a Rule. If an angel sacrifices himself, then material objects can be exchanged. Zeihl took something from that library in the Living World, and through his suicide had it transported back to Hell."

"Right."

"So what was the object that he exchanged from the library? Was it a book?"

"No, that place wasn't really a library. It was a front."

"You mean a place that they wanted people to *think* was a library, but it really wasn't?"

"Correct. They made it look as unassuming as possible."

Cassie thought about it. "Who are 'they?' "

"The Pope's security contingent."

"The . . . *Pope's?*"

"Yes. The Catholic Church has its Power Relics just like Lucifer does, and just like God."

"So they were protecting some kind of object in the fake library?"

"Yes."

"And Zeihl's suicide provided the necessary occult power to—"

"To transfer that object from the Living World to Hell," Angelese grimly affirmed. When she closed the book, the Repository, as well as the entirety of the Infernal Archives, snapped back into its former moonstone-lit darkness.

Cassie didn't like the vibe. "What was the object?"

Angelese stared a Cassie, eyes propped open in dread.

"What was the object?" Cassie repeated.

"The Shroud of Turin."

The . . . Then Cassie frowned. "The Shroud of Turin is at the Vatican, everybody knows that, and everybody knows it's fake. They tested it. It's phony as a three-dollar bill."

The angel's voice grated. "Not *that* Shroud of Turin, Cassie. The *real* Shroud of Turin."

Chapter Fourteen

(I)

"I wish you'd stayed in school, Walter," No-name's head remarked. "Get your doctorate by twenty-one. One day you might've won the Nobel Prize."

Walter considered the comment. No-name was a soothsayer. *Is she implying that might have happened, or will happen?* "I thought you weren't allowed to reveal the future."

"I'm not."

"So why did you just say that? Are you suggesting that if I abandon whatever it is we're doing here, I win a Nobel Prize someday?"

The head smirked. "Sorry. No. I was just daydreaming about your potential. You *do* have a lot of potential, you know."

Walter took it as a compliment. "You're the nicest severed head I've ever met."

"Oh, thanks a lot!"

But it was clear what she really meant. *I'll never win the Nobel Prize* . . . "So . . . does this mean I'll never get my doctorate, either?"

"Walter, you know I can't tell you that!" No-name almost seemed scolding. "Sometimes I think you deliberately try to make me slip up."

"Is that possible? Can a damned soothsayer accidently break her vow?"

"With me, it's not a vow. It's a curse. If I disrespect the curse, then I'm destroyed."

"What about the angel you were telling me about?"

"The guardian of the Etheress," the head recited. "What about her?"

"You said she was like you in a way. She can't reveal secrets either."

"No, she can't. But with her, it's a vow. With me—a curse." No-name smiled under Walter's arm. "The angel and I serve a similar function. She's the Etheress's guardian, and I'm *your* guardian. But at least I'm lower maintenance. I'm just a head."

Walter didn't quite connect with the levity. He just kept thinking. "I'm Plan B," he remembered. "I could really screw everything up, simply by leaving. I could go back to the Deadpass, go back to the Living World."

He waited for a response.

Nothing.

She'd said that everything was already mapped out, she'd said that the future wasn't mutable—it couldn't be changed. "With my brains? I could get a big job with a big research company, make millions."

"Yes, but—" No-name bit her lip. "Walter, it's not like you to be deceitful."

"What do you mean?"

"Stop trying to make me slip up! I'll admit, I'm easy to fool. I'm not as smart as you—it's not fair. Don't take advantage of me. It's not nice, and you're a nice person, so be nice."

Walter shrugged. *Can I help it that I want to know what's going on? I don't even know where I'm going but according to her that's how it's supposed to be. I won't find my destiny. My destiny will find me.*

"This is the district's Steamworks," No-name said. They were walking down what seemed to be a service lane paved with ground skulls, and to either side were factory-sized networks of pipes fifty feet wide. The giant pipes vibrated, hissing. They seemed endless.

"What's the function?"

"Heat regulation. Lucifer doesn't want any area of Hell to be cooler than another. He wants *everything* hot."

And hot it was, like Texas in August. "That's the dumbest thing I've ever heard," he remarked, gazing up at the ranks and ranks of pipes. "It's all useless. It's an affront to logic. With all these resources, and all that power? Lucifer could turn this place around in a heartbeat."

"Of course he could. But he doesn't. You know why?"

"No."

"Because he's vain. God's better than him and he knows it but he can't ever admit that. He can't ever admit that he's inferior because of his pride. So all these resources, and all his power, he uses to offend God. You're right, it's the dumbest thing, but Lucifer's very insecure. So he'll just keep doing what he's been doing."

Something snagged Walter's thoughts. "Wait. Did you just slip up?"

A pause.

"No, Walter, what are you talking about? I was being . . . conjectural."

305

Edward Lee

"Yeah. And I'll bet you were being *abstruse* too, huh?" Walter allowed himself the smile. "I think you just slipped up."

"Shut up, Walter. Just shut up and walk."

Walter walked. He was dehydrated and hungry, but when they passed another Man-Burger vendor, he declined the offerings. Every so often, a far-off scream could be heard; above them, a demonic worker would lose his footing on the giant pipes and fall. The scarlet sky shifted, like a mirage. Fanged rodents with wings sat perched on power lines, as crows would in the Living World.

Walter didn't know where he was going as he trudged further through steam and murk and awful odors. But for the first time since he'd arrived in the Mephistopolis, he felt content.

He'd never really felt content before.

A mile distant, something tinted the sky. At first he thought of swamp gas, an eerily glowing fog, but soon he saw that this was different. A diffuse silver light hovering in the sky in something akin to a pyramid shape.

He thought about what No-name had said, about the nature of destiny.

"That light. Is that where we're going?"

No-name didn't answer.

"That's where we're going," Walter said.

(II)

They hid, high in the air, within a reef of clouds the color of bile. Cassie's fear of heights was quickly being dealt with by default. A mile in the sky, what choice did she have but to get over it? She thought of the Nectoport as a flying carpet of sorts, or, better, a flying cave. She was starting to get used to this mode of transportation, she was even beginning to enjoy it.

What she knew she *wouldn't* enjoy, though, was their next endeavor.

"Look, your mother wasn't lying." Angelese lowered her Ophitte Viewer and pointed out the Egress, toward the Panzuzu District. Cassie could see the Atrocidome unaided. The huge Killing Plate that hovered over the dome suddenly dropped.

"Jesus," Cassie muttered.

"They're doing Spatial Merges constantly now, destroying every known Deadpass."

"So I can't get out of Hell."

"Um-hmm."

Cassie stepped back from the Egress. "And now we're going to the Mephisto Building? I still think you're out of your mind," she said.

"Of course I'm out of my mind," Angelese replied too easily. She was on her knees, peering down over the rim of the Port with the Ophitte Viewer. "I'm a Caliginaut, we're not a stable bunch."

"You don't know how secure that makes me feel." Butterflies fluttered in her belly when she looked down again. Through a break in the soiled clouds she could see the top of the Mephisto Building. Gargoyles lurked about its ledges, while horned sentries prowled the roof. The building's iron antenna mast swayed, draped by living bodies dangling on gibbets.

She wants to go inside, Cassie realized. *She IS crazy.* Getting in was impossible, everyone knew that. She squinted, barely able to see the intestine-like coils that snaked around the building's first level. *The Flesh Warrens,* she remembered. It was the Mephisto Building's security barrier. The only way in was through the Warrens, but if anyone entered, and immune-response was triggered, the Warren's antibodies would attack at once. "It's impossible so I don't know why you're even thinking about it. The Flesh Warrens are impenetrable."

"Not if you have the vaccine," the angel informed. "How do you think the other Fallen Angels and other authorized personnel get in?"

"A serum?" Cassie questioned.

"Sure, it's like an inoculation. It's very short-term, but if you've been injected with the vaccine, the Flesh Warren's immune system won't attack you."

This was an explosive revelation. "And you've got the vaccine!" Cassie nearly rejoiced.

"Well, no."

So much for explosive revelations. Cassie smirked at the outrageous let-down. "Then what are we doing here? We're wasting our time."

"You're wrong about that."

"Angelese! Read my lips. We CAN'T get in!"

The angel focused the strange binoculars. "At least not physically."

"And we can't Trance-Channel, either. The walls are all hexed, they're protected by every spell in the abyss."

"That's true, and you're right. *We* can't get in, but there's a way we can use somebody who's had access." The angel leaned back into the Nectoport and looked at the Ophitte Viewer and its living demonic eyes for lenses. Every time the eyes blinked, Cassie was unnerved.

"It's kind of a coincidence," Angelese said, looking at the viewer.

"What?"

"Eyes," the angel said.

"Eyes?"

"Seeing."

Cassie opened and closed her fists in sheer frustration. "Eyes? Seeing? As usual, I don't know what you're friggin' talking about."

She handed the viewer to Cassie. "See the guy hanging from the highest crossbeam of the antenna?"

Still unnerved, Cassie looked in the viewer, aimed down. A naked figure hung by the neck from the top of the mast. Naked, shuddering, wrists cuffed behind his back. *Gross,* Cassie thought. The figure's skin was blue-white, with dark-red veins showing through. He was bald, hornless, his face pinched in torment. "What kind of demon is that?"

"It's a Kathari-grade Diviner, the highest class of satanic visionary. Lucifer is very big on Diviners, and that one there has had access to Lucifer's Scarlet Hall."

"Why's he hanging by the neck? Is he being punished?"

"No, he hangs himself there willingly, as part of his Loyalty Gesticulation. Like monks who flagellate themselves as a gesture to God. That one down there hangs there whenever Lucifer isn't using him. Notice anything fucked up about his face?"

Cassie winced at the angelic expletive. She focused the viewer a few more notches. The Diviner's face was hideous as the rest of his body, the veins showing through livid skin. But then she saw what Angelese meant. *Oh, jeez . . .*

The Diviner only had one eye, large as a peach and centered in the middle of his face. It was squeezed shut now against the excruciation of being hanged.

Cassie's hair jumped up as the Nectoport suddenly lowered at an extreme velocity. It reminded her of a roller coaster dropping from its highest inclination.

Cassie didn't like roller coasters.

"What are we doing?"

"You'll see," Angelese answered. "Pun intended."

"What? You're going to go talk to that *thing* on the antenna?"

"We're not really going to talk to him . . ."

In a matter of seconds, the Nectoport had stopped and was hovering right in front of the hideous, naked Diviner.

"Hey!" Angelese shouted out. "Handsome!"

The single eye opened and looked at them. Black teeth showed through the gnash of agony; Cassie could see the noose digging into the thing's neck as it shuddered.

"Satan, save me," it croaked. "A Caliginaut." Then the huge eye shot to Cassie. "The . . . Etheress . . . Do what you will. I live to honor and serve the Son of the Morning." Then it squeezed the revolting eye shut again, in expectation.

"Don't worry," Angelese told him. "We're not going to kill you. Cassie, make him open his eye."

Cassie didn't get it but by now she'd learned the futility of asking too many questions. "Eye open," she uttered.

The eye snapped open again like a shutter. It was clear the Diviner was trying to keep it closed but was helpless to do so. Meanwhile, Angelese brandished what appeared to be a fork.

Cassie looked agape. "What's that?"

"A fork," the angel answered. "What's it look like?"

And that's what it was. Just a regular, everyday dinner fork. "What are you doing!" Cassie shrieked a second later.

The Diviner twitched vigorously on the end of the rope as Angelese calmly leaned forward and stuck the fork's tines into the massive eye. She turned it around a few times and eventually unseated the eye from its socket. All the while, the Diviner howled. "See ya!" Angelese said, and then took the Nectoport back up to the clouds.

"What did you do that for?" Cassie asked, aghast.

"We need it."

"His *eyeball*?"

"Yes. You'll see—er, sorry. Another pun."

When they were back hovering amid the soiled clouds, Angelese looked at Cassie forlornly. "Sorry, but your mental powers are greater than mine. So you're gonna have to be the one."

Cassie was horrified looking at the glistening eyeball on the end of the fork. An optic nerve hung off it like a tail. "Be the one *what*?"

Now Angelese smiled, quite wickedly. "The one who eats it."

"Oh, sure! That'll be happening!"

"Cassie, you have to. If someone with Etheric propensities consumes the eye of a visionary, she will see everything he has seen. We have to find out what's going on in that building. If we don't, we lose and Lucifer wins." She offered her the fork. "This is the only way."

"I'M NOT EATING A DEMON'S EYEBALL!"

The angel's voice was calm but stern. "You have to. Everything depends on it. If you don't, then everything we've been through is a waste."

"YOU NEVER SAID ANYTHING ABOUT EATING AN EYEBALL!"

Angelese smirked. "It's not that big a deal."

"THEN YOU EAT IT!"

"The effect will be better if you do it. You're an Etheress. The sooner we get this over with, the sooner we'll be able to focus on finding your sister."

More blackmail. Cassie thought she could throw up just looking at the veiny eyeball.

"Do you have any idea what kind of pain I subjected myself to when I told you those secrets?" Angelese asked next. "Do you have any idea what it feels like to be sliced up by an Umbra-Specter?"

Now guilt shrouded Cassie's rage and disgust. Maybe she was being selfish. And there was Lissa to consider. "But, but—" she began.

"Cassie, just shut up and eat the damn eye."

Cassie took the fork. *Oh, man. What am I doing?* So this was her Ethereal duty? *Good God . . . All right. Just pretend it's something else,* she told herself. *Yeah, yeah, a big candy apple on a stick.*

She took a bite.

It did not taste like a candy apple on a stick.

When her teeth broke the leather-tough sclerotic wall, the eyeball's vitreous humors filed her mouth like warm Spam jelly. With the wall so tough, she reasoned it best to suck all the humor out and then swallow the rest of the sclera whole, and this she did with an impressive resolve. Worse than all of that, though, was the optic nerve, which she sucked down like a noodle.

And collapsed, overwhelmed by nausea.

"Good girl!" Angelese celebrated. "What a trooper."

Cassie began to crawl for the opening of the Nectoport. "I think I'm going to . . ."

"Don't throw up! If you throw up, we'll have to find another eye!"

Not a chance. One demon eyeball a day is my limit. The very notion of having to do this again was motivation enough not to vomit.

"Just sit back, close your eyes," the angel instructed. "It'll start in a minute."

It didn't start in a minute, it started in a second. Suddenly the darkness behind Cassie's closed eyes began to glow in a tint of slate-blue, and then she saw visions like a steadicam on a movie set soaring down strange empty hallways. It was that vast *emptiness* that astounded her—a reflection, perhaps, of the owner's heart. She almost shrieked, then, when a figure breezed by, like a drifting chess piece. Within the figure's white hood there was just skin, no face.

"What?" Angelese's voice floated to her. "What are you seeing?"

"Empty halls. Some... thing in a white robe, drifting. No face."

"It's a Levitator. It means you're on the right floor—the penthouse. Look for a big red room with a high ceiling. The Scarlet Hall."

Several more Levitators slid by, plus a Grand Duke and several well-armored Conscripts. Perhaps Cassie's own thoughts were guiding her, for a moment later, the vision careened her into a room just like the one Angelese had described. High red walls, a floor of agate tile. The great room sparkled, and near an open veranda, she saw a throne of dark crystal. The throne was empty.

Cassie was an invisible eye in the air, seeing everything, her own personal volition somehow allowing her to turn about at will. She saw two more figures near the center of the hall. One, the tall one, stood with his back to her vision. The other, much shorter, in an odd, squirming cloak. His hood was down about the neck, and Cassie could see his facial features: skin as black as anthracite, pointed ears and curved horns, sunken eyes. At first she thought he was bald but then she noticed that he'd been scalped. He walked around the second figure as if in appraisement.

"I see two men. One's got black skin, black as coal."

"What's he wearing?"

"A cloak that—" Cassie squinted through the visionary's sight. Her stomach hitched when she noticed the true nature of the cloak. She noticed why it was squirming...

"Cassie, is the guy's cloak made of baby snakes?"

"Yes," she nearly gagged.

"He's a Hounganite, an upper-echelon Voudou Technician. It's all true. Lucifer really did move the Hexology Institutes and the Re-Animation Department into the Mephisto Building. But you said there were two figures in the room. Describe the second figure. Is it a demon?"

"No, Human." she could see from here. The man stood with his back to her. Tall, slim, naked, well-toned. Cassie wheeled the mystic vision around to see him from the front.

Long dark hair and beard. A face that seemed tranquilizing.

Cassie snapped out of the visionary trance, shuddering.

"What? Can you describe the second figure?" the angel asked, leaning over.

Cassie just sat shuddering as if in the middle of a devastating chill. Eventually she looked up at Angelese and said, "It was Jesus. It was Jesus Christ . . ."

Chapter Fifteen

(I)

The light was impossible to describe. Darkness that somehow glowed? If despair had a color, that was the hue of what radiated above the edifice that loomed before Walter and No-name. It was a pyramid, larger than that of Cheops, but made entirely of black quartz.

"Why are we here?" Walter droned, staring up at the huge creation.

"I can't answer your question."

"Did fate bring me here?"

No-name smiled.

Walter could never imagine such a structure; it was fascinating yet depressing to look at. It projected a certain feel that reminded him how he felt on the night he tried to kill himself. He couldn't escape his own immediate premonition: *This is it. This is my destiny, this place.* Walter's destiny no longer awaited him. It was here, before him, now. All that remained was to embrace it.

He couldn't take his eyes off the mass of black glass and its ghostly shroud of incalculable luminosity. "I don't know how to explain it but it looks . . . sad."

"It should."

"What is it? What is this place?"

"It's the Bastille of Otherwise Souls, Walter. It's a prison, for spirits. There are millions of souls held captive there."

"Every damned soul in Hell?"

"Oh, no. There are billions of damned souls in Hell. This place is just for the special ones."

"Special in what way?"

"Souls that really shouldn't be here. *Otherwise* souls."

Walter scratched his head in confusion, then winced at the pain from the pumpkin-ball stitches. "I don't get it."

"Think of it as a sepulcher, Walter. It contains the souls of people who *otherwise* would've gone to Heaven, had they not committed suicide."

Walter's eyes remained fixed on it.

"It's another of Lucifer's greatest achievements, his greatest slight to God. Being able to keep people here who really shouldn't be here."

"Then why am *I* here?"

No-name just smiled again. "I can't tell you. You know that. But what have I been telling you all along? Use your head. Use the smarts that God gave you. Be deductive."

Walter's powers of deduction weren't exactly feeling up to snuff tonight.

"You can go back to the living world if you like," No-name continued. "But I can't tell you if things will be any different or not."

"They won't be," Walter asserted himself. "I know they won't be. Maybe that's *my* fate. I know that I will never be accepted. I know that people will never like me, some might pretend to but it's all a veneer. Am I right?"

No-name just looked at him.

"If I go back to the Living World, I'm pretty sure I'd walk straight back to my dorm and blow my head off, only this time I'd do it right. And what happens then? My soul is damned for eternity and I get sent straight back here but this time with *no* powers. My soul would come to this place. Am I right?"

"Yes."

"So I could just stay here as an Etherean."

"And remain an enemy of the state. You could do great damage, but you wouldn't last."

"Wouldn't, or might not?"

"Might not."

She just slipped, Walter thought.

"Damn it," No-name muttered.

Walter smiled. "So it's all up to me. I can stay or I can go."

"Exactly. But you would never fit in here, Walter. You know why?"

"Because I'm a dork."

"No, because you're not evil. Even if you survived, you would never be content here. You've never been happy or content anywhere, in your life, have you?"

"No."

"Because you're not evil. Only the evil prosper here. Is that you? Could you change yourself that extensively, in your heart?"

Walter shook his head, listening but still staring up in miserable bliss.

"Of course you couldn't. And, Walter . . . you're not a dork. You're a pretty cool guy actually."

Walter released the greatest sigh of relief in his life. "Thank you."

"Now. You're a physicist and a mathematician. Be deductive."

Walter saw it at once. "Either way, I'm screwed."

"It's an abstrustion, but, yes, either way, you're screwed. Some people are victims of circumstance. Like you. And like me. That's just the way it is. It's unfair but nobody ever said that life was supposed to be fair. We're both screwed, Walter. I am. You are. You know what you can do, don't you?"

"What?"

"Go out in style."

Go out in style? Walter repeated in his mind.

"Think about it, Walter," No-name bid. "But think quick. There isn't much time left . . ."

(II)

Angelese looked stupefied as the Nectoport rose high into the air, seeking cover in the spoiled clouds. Cassie just sat there, numbed herself by what she'd seen. The thought kept replaying in her mind: *It was Christ, it was Christ . . .*

Angelese's voice was a depressed rattle. "Now it all makes sense; it's actually *easy* to see . . ."

Cassie was too staggered to perceive the implications. "Lucifer's plan . . . is what?"

"They stole the real Shroud of Turin from the Living World, Cassie. They used it to make that Hex-Clone of Christ. They will send it back in time through an Astral Retrogation. Lucifer's going to replace the real Christ with that thing."

"That's not possible. It'll never work." Cassie felt sure.

"That Hex-Clone is a *perfect* facsimile, Cassie. It looks

exactly like the real Savior. But what's the difference?"

"It's *not* Christ. It's just animated meat, an elaborate dummy. It can look and sound and act like the real Jesus, but nobody'll believe it."

Now the Nectoport assumed a static position in the clouds. When Cassie looked down, she saw that they were hovering a mile over the Mephisto Building.

"No," she repeated. "Nobody would believe it. It wouldn't work. It's not a man, and it's not the Son of God. It's a bag of meat that's alive only because of spells and incantations."

The angel's eyes looked terrified. "There's something you're forgetting, Cassie. The part of Lucifer's plan that involves you."

The comment stunned her. "Me?"

"The whole reason the Morning Star needs you —someone with Ethereal Powers. The reason he tried to capture you during the Merge at the clinic. Same reason he's trying to capture the Etherean. An Etheress or an Etherean. Either will do. And for all we know, he's already caught the Etherean and is preparing him."

"Preparing him for what?"

The inside of the Nectoport turned cold as a mausoleum. "Oh, no," Angelese sighed, looking behind her. The body of the Nectoport extended into darkness, like a tunnel. Even Cassie could feel it now.

They weren't alone here.

A sudden flash of light, bright as lightning, blinded Cassie. There was a rushing sound, clatter, movement she could sense but not see. "Angelese!" Cassie shrieked, "What's happening!" but the angel's only response was to shriek herself. Large, scaly hands grabbed Cassie, and then something was dragged over her. When her vision returned, she could see what it was: a net.

Edward Lee

Reeking of death and corded in muscles, a horned Usher held Cassie within the net, like a bundled package. She couldn't move. Foul breath gusted into her face as the slug-skinned servant of Lucifer gently traced a talon down her cheek. The knife-gash-like eyes glimmered. The grinning mouth was a hole full of broken glass.

A voice reverberated, like a hopeful minister's voice in an echoic cathedral: "Cassie. It's an honor to finally get so close to you—a true Etheress. In the flesh. And what stunning flesh it is."

Cassie looked right at his face . . . but could see nothing. His body looked angelic; he looked bathed in sunlight. She sensed a smile within the fog-like aura about his head. And as for his voice, she'd heard it before, on the phone at the clinic.

"You let your guard down"—now he was speaking to Angelese, who'd been similarly netted and seized by an Usher—"It wasn't difficult to locate the operating signature of an unauthorized Nectoport. I apologize for not knocking first."

More of the haze cleared from Cassie's eyes. A half-dozen more Ushers stood on watch in the Nectoport, and standing aside was a solemn figure in a black cloak and hood, which Cassie recognized at once as a high-ranking Biowizard. From black fingers, the wizard held a tiny green-glowing stone which swayed back an forth like a hypnotist's pendulum.

Then the man of light moved closer. "And I apologize, too, for not properly introducing myself." The voice fluttered like the wings of a flock of birds. "I am the Light of the Morning. Welcome to my domain of night." He knelt serenely before Angelese, and whispered, "I'm going to torture you for a hundred years, then I'll send you back to God, raped, pregnant, and ruined. It's only fitting. I owe

Him a gift or two." He stroked the angel's face, tenderly as a mother to a child. "I like this." Lucifer produced a long awl, long as a knitting needle but much sharper. "Let's start with this. Oh, how I love to hear angels scream," and then he gently inserted the awl into Angelese's chest and pushed it through her heart.

The angel bucked, firing a high-pitched bellow from her throat. Each time the awl was withdrawn and reinserted, she bucked within the net like someone holding a live wire.

"Stop it!" Cassie shouted through the most powerful surge of hatred in her life, but their unglimpsible host just smiled.

"I'm a Fallen Angel, Cassie," he explained. "Your Ethcrea has no effect on me. You know that."

"No, no, no!" Cassie shouted. Lucifer just kept reinserting the awl, with tender slowness, into Angelese's heart. "You can't die here, can you, Caliginaut? You're so brave to have ventured to my kingdom. I'll make sure God is apprized."

Angelese shuddered at the torture, her blood oozing in tiny, neon threads. Then she gasped, "Cassie, here's another Rule, another secret I must pay to reveal. If an Etheress dies in Hell, all that energy combusts. A human with Ethereal powers—in *Hell*—it's like matter and anti-matter. There's an explosion of tremendous magnitude," and then her screams quadrupled as the Umbra-Specter rose, its shadow-claws reaching up and swiping back down across the angel's chest. In doing so, as it had at the clinic, the Specter's claws slashed through the net and released her.

She jumped up, grabbed the Light of the Morning about the neck, angelic blood painting his face like red fox fire. She quickly blurted another secret—"It's not you he wants, it's just your blood! Your Ethereal blood! It can be used as a Power Transfer!"—and this time, when the Umbra-

Specter tried to claw her, Lucifer was in between its talons and Angelese. The result was—

A sound that had never been heard before: Satan screaming in pain.

The talons, aiming for Angelese's face slashed Lucifer's instead. The Nectoport rocked, the Morning Star's howl like a rock slide on a vast mountain range.

Several Ushers broke the angel's clench at once, pinning her to the Port's floor with long, iron-bladed pikes.

Eosphoros shivered, hands to his face. The blood that poured between his fingers was black as oil.

After several deep breaths, he recomposed himself and said, "Even bad guys have bad days, yes? Nothing will ruin the jubilation of my victory. Not a lackey angel, nor a useless Etheress."

Useless? The word spiked her senses—as Angelese remained spiked to the wall, quivering. *My powers won't work on him but they'll sure as hell work on those Ushers,* so she focused all her rage and shouted "Fall apart, you fuckers!"

There was no effect. The Ushers remained unharmed, twisting their pikes in Angelese's chest.

What's . . . wrong? Cassie wondered.

"See? Useless," the Morning Star reassured. "To all but me. Your bloody friend is right, Cassie. I don't need you, I just need your blood."

The words spun around her mind. She was trying to direct her thoughts, but she was thinking of the other things Angelese had said. If an Etheress dies in Hell, the result is a tremendous explosion. But did she really have the nerve to kill herself? It might destroy the Nectoport, but it would not destroy Lucifer, an immortal. And it wouldn't even necessarily foil his plan, which she still didn't understand. *My blood? For what?*

Then it hit her, so obvious. *He's going to use my blood to—*

"Excellent, Etheress," Iblis read her mind. *"That's* my plan. The Hex-Clone you stole a glance at is an exact physical duplicate. I will Retrogate back to Golgotha, to Christ's tomb, and replace your Savior's body with my Clone. And on the Third Day, it will rise again from the dead. But before that, I'm going to transfuse your blood into it, and it will have *your* powers. It will reappear to Mary, and kill her. It will reappear to the Apostles, and murder them. It will kill everything it comes into contact with for the entirety of the Retrogation. And what will that result in?"

Christianity will never exist, Cassie thought. *It will never be born . . .*

(III)

"I don't know what you mean," Walter said. "Go out in style?"

"One last ride before the end of it all," No-name muttered. Her eyes darted. "Oops. Looks like you get to have some more fun first."

Fun? Walter heard the clatter of armor himself. In a moment, the empty street wasn't empty anymore. They were blocked off again, on either side. Not Conscripts, Ushers, or Golems, this time—an entire regiment of Grand Dukes, their great horned heads throwing shadows down the street in a tapestry of sharp points.

They didn't look happy.

They began to march forward. Some, he saw, even had guns, crude ones—as in the Revolutionary War—but firearms nonetheless. Through the phalanx, their barrels aimed, then jerked as they fired. Plumes of sooty smoke poured forth.

"Miss me," Walter whispered, unshocked even by the potential, and the atrocious sound. They were clearly aiming low, for his legs, because they needed him alive. This he easily deduced, even though he still wasn't sure exactly what they needed him for.

The hand-poured, iron-ball bullets all missed. Those fired from the left cut down the first line of Grand Dukes on the right, and vice-versa. Walter was bored. The things were ten-feet tall, hundreds of them, and more terrifying than anything he'd seen here.

But he was purely and simply bored.

"Go away," he said to each phalanx. The words from his mouth plowed both regiments away until they could no longer be seen, as effectively as bulldozers against piles of autumn leaves. In only a second, the street was vacant again. Silent. Calm.

"That was a piece of cake, No-name," Walter said.

"Don't get cocky!"

She's right, he considered. *Something serious is going on here. I'm part of it. I better not let this Etherean stuff go to my head.*

"What now?" he asked.

Her head sighed under his arm and her eyes flicked up to the shining black edifice. "Look at the Bastille, Walter. I've told you what it is. If it's destroyed, then all the souls who've been condemned will be released."

Souls that otherwise wouldn't be here. Walter looked at the indestructible pyramid. "I can't destroy that."

"Are you sure there's not a way?"

"I don't know what you're talking about!"

"Be deductive. Be the mathematician. If an otherwise good person could destroy that place by a suicidal act, would that person's immortal soul be condemned to Hell?"

324

No, Walter deduced. *No. So what is it, exactly, that she's trying to tell me?*

Then he thought back to what she'd previously said, something about going out in style . . .

(IV)

The revelation was clear now: the plans he had for the Hex-Clone. Angelese remained staked to the floor by the pikes piercing her chest. And Cassie . . .

Cassie was, indeed, useless.

My powers don't work against the Ushers. She shot a thought of death at the Biowizard, too. Nothing. The net abraded her face, incising her frustration. *I can't do anything. And even if I had the courage to kill myself, what good would that do? And I CAN'T kill myself because I'm tied up in this friggin' net!*

"And look who we've brought to see you."

The Morning Star's voice was all over the Nectoport, his glee perhaps, in spite of the slashes across the unfathomable face.

"Look, look," he whispered.

Cassie screamed. Something was dragged forward by one of the Ushers. At first Cassie thought it was a sack drawn by a rope.

But it wasn't.

It was Lissa, or what was left of her, drawn by her hair. Her arms and legs had been removed, and in their place were just her hands and feet surgically reconnected at the shoulder and hip joints.

"This is how she will spend eternity. I'll see to it. She'll be on display like this at the zoo. And she'll drown in sewage every day, but won't die."

Lissa's head lolled on the floor. Her eyes beseeched her sister. "Please help me . . ."

More uselessness. Cassie sobbed against the net. That was all she could do.

"Ah," the aduw Allah intoned. "Such lovely regret. It's so sweet. But I guess it's time now, isn't it? Time to return to my mansion, and fill my Clone with your blood."

Angelese ground her teeth. Her violet eyes, rimmed by beige, were wide open on Cassie, when she said, "Cassie, look at the Biowizard . . ."

What? But she did as was told, and her own eyes swerved toward the squat cloaked figure standing just behind Lucifer. From his fingers, the pendant still dangled, the pendant with the tiny stone on the end of it, glowing like a green ember.

"Now look at your arm," Angelese said.

My . . . arm. Cassie turned her head in the net, still not understanding. Her arm. She could see the small line of stitches that R.J. had applied at the clinic when she'd been cut. The wound was swollen now, flecked with dried blood, and now she could see something else.

Something embedded in the wound, showing through the stitches.

Something glowing.

(V)

No-name's words echoed in Walter's: *If it's destroyed, then all the souls who've been condemned will be released.*

He looked at the arcane structure, shouted every idea of destruction he could think of at it, but nothing happened. "I can't destroy it! I can't even scratch it!"

"There. Is. A way," No-name stuttered. She sighed again,

326

wearied. She even sounded forlorn. "I have to go now, Walter. It's time for me to destroy myself."

"No! I don't want you to go!"

"It's my destiny. And it's no fun being a severed head."

Walter couldn't manage the idea. "If you're destroyed, what will happen to you?"

"This head is all that remains of my Spirit Body. If it's destroyed, my soul will be transferred to some other life form in Hell. It's potluck; I don't get to choose. I could be transferred to a demon's body, a Troll's, a Griffin's, a Caco-Tick, or even a Bapho-Flea that spends its entire existence living on a rat's ass. But it's a chance I have to take. I have to take the risk."

She's lying, Walter thought, so not to break her oath. *She already knows what will happen to her.*

"I understand," he said, teary eyed. *She's got to do what she's got to do. She knows the future.* He took her head out from under his arm, held it up and looked at her face. "Would you like me to destroy your head for you? I'll look for a mallet or a brick or something. Or I'll use my powers."

"Thank you, but that won't be necessary. There's a way for me to do it myself, and I'm going to do it now. But remember what I said earlier. Be deductive."

Walter nodded, wiped his eyes. He'd already figured it out.

"I've already told you, I'm cursed to never reveal a cabalistic secret. If I challenge the curse, I smolder to nothingness. Do you understand?"

"Yes."

"If an angel commits suicide in the Living World, the resultant flux of released etheric energy becomes fissionable. You know what fissionable means."

"Yes. But I'm not an angel, and this isn't the Living World."

Smoke was leaking from No-name's ears. "If an Etherean commits suicide in Hell . . . it's the same thing, the same result."

Walter's eyes went wide.

Now smoke was pouring off the head, the hair burning off. Smoke poured out of her mouth as she spoke her last words: "My name is a preternatural secret too, Walter. I can never reveal it without the consequences."

"I understand," Walter sobbed.

"Goodbye, Walter." No-name smiled through the crackling and smoke. "My name is Afet."

The head *hissed* away in his hands and disappeared as a stream of fine ash.

"Goodbye, Afet," Walter said, choking. *I'll miss you . . .*

His hands held nothing now. Walter was alone. But he understood everything now, everything she'd implied. Deduction came easily to geniuses.

He scratched his head. *Hmm.*

Down the street a lone Grand Duke staggered toward him. On a chain-mail belt was a crude pistol, which the Duke was drawing.

"You!" Walter shouted. "Don't shoot!"

The Grand Duke froze, his great horns poised.

Walter jogged up to the creature. It simply stared down at him, covering him with its broad shadow.

"Gimme that gun."

The Grand Duke handed it to him.

Walter looked at it, confused. It wasn't like a modern pistol, just a metal tube on a shaped piece of wood that served as a grip. There was a trigger, and on top, a hammer that vised a piece of flint.

"Is this thing loaded?" Walter asked.

The Grand Duke nodded.

"How does it work?"

The Duke took the pistol, cocked it, then returned it to Walter's hands.

I guess that's it. "Thanks," he said. "Now pretend you're on a pogo stick and pogo your ugly ass out of here."

The Grand Duke hopped away.

Walter wasn't afraid. Hefting the pistol, he walked leisurely into the obsidian doorway of the Bastille of Otherwise Souls.

(VI)

Something glowing, beneath the stitches. The same emerald-green.

"That's right," Lucifer confirmed. "Stealthy, yes? It was planted on you, by my confidant. It's a chip from the Rock of Boolya. Sorcery is science here, Etheress. What's in your flesh is the same as what hangs from my Wizard's pendant. It damps your powers."

"Cassie, get that chip out of your arm!" Angelese shouted, then groaned as the pikes were twisted deeper into her chest.

Eosphoros smiled. "Yes. Please do."

Cassie tried to drag her hand up against the net. She would tear the emerald chip from her flesh. But it was impossible. The Usher behind her was twisting the net so tightly, she was cocooned. She couldn't move.

I've got to get this son of a bitch OFF ME! she screamed at herself, but there was no way.

Then Angelese said, "Think. Remember."

Satan held his impossible-to-see grin. "Think what, Caliginaut? Remember what?"

"R.J.! At the clinic! It had to have been the same language we saw at the Archives!"

Cassie's eyes bloomed. *Yes, yes . . .* But how could she possibly remember that?

Think!

Lucifer's ungodly brow turned up. "What are you babbling about, angel?"

Then the Biowizard collapsed.

This caught them all by surprise. Iblis rushed to the fallen Wizard, shook him. "What the fuck is going on!"

The Biowizard's black eyes fluttered open. He was coming out of some sort of communicative trance. "My lord, I-I-I—"

"You WHAT?" Lucifer demanded.

The Wizard's voice sounded like rocks being crushed. "I must report intolerable news . . ."

"WHAT?"

Think! Cassie kept telling herself, using the distraction. *It's in your head somewhere. So find it!*

A droning pause, then the Wizard's lips parted and said, "The Etherean just committed suicide—"

"NO!" Satan exploded.

Think! Cassie kept repeating. *Think! Remember! What was it?*

"—at the Bastille of Otherwise Souls," the Wizard finished. "The Bastille is destroyed."

"NOOOOOOOOOOOOOOOOOOOOOOOOOOOOO!"

Lucifer rushed to the mouth of the Nectoport. He looked out, just as a distant light flashed. Even Cassie could see the light. A flash and a mushroom cloud.

Lucifer fell to his knees.

Then Cassie remembered, dragged the incomprehensible words from her mind, and said: "Eòñw nalde flåveaaiz me staadpa stilluadte."

Silence.

Angelese smiled, and froze.

The Usher holding Cassie's net stood immobile from the Paresis Invocation. The remaining Ushers, the Biowizard, and even Lucifer himself were totally paralyzed. Cassie managed to shrug out of the Usher's grasp now, and dragged off the net. Wincing, she dug her fingers into her wound and unseated the glowing green chip of stone. She flicked it out of the Nectoport. Then she turned to the Usher behind her and said, "Out." The Usher churned against its paralysis, lumbered toward the Nectoport's Egress, and jumped out. "Pull those out of her," she commanded the pair of Ushers who still held the pikes in Angelese, "and then jump out." They did, and then a final command, to the Biowizard and remaining Ushers, "All of you, out!"

One by one, they all jumped out of the Nectoport. More silence. Cassie's hair whipped around in the wind when she looked out. *The Bastille,* she thought. Angelese had mentioned it during their Trance-Channel from the clinic. *All those suicidal souls . . . released.*

Suicidal souls . . .

"Lissa?" Cassie jerked around, stared down at where her sister's disfigured body had been lying.

It was just dust now.

She could only hope what that meant. She returned her gaze out the Nectoport. In the distance, the glowing mushroom cloud was dissipating, drawing a shroud of dust over the entire district.

So that's what happens when an Etherean or an Etheress dies in Hell. But a further glance showed her the now-familiar Atrocidome, its huge Killing Plate dropping yet again in the next Merge. Another Deadpass destroyed.

"Uh, excuse me?" Angelese said. "If you're not too busy, I'd prefer not to spend eternity unable to move from a Paresis Spell."

"Sorry," Cassie said. "But what should I do with him?" Her eyes fell on the Morning Star, who remained paralyzed himself.

"Send him on a trip. The fucker will never die, but I'm sure a good long fall will at least muss his hair."

Cassie liked the idea.

"Don't," the First Fallen Angel said. "Join me. You'll be more powerful than any woman in history."

"Gimme a break!" His shoulders felt warm when she began to push.

"God damn you," came his crystalline whisper. Black sparkles seemed to hover in the wake of his words. Cassie pushed him out of the Nectoport. She didn't even bother watching his fall.

"How do I break the Paresis Spell?" she asked next.

Angelese rolled her eyes. "You're an Etheress. Why do you think all those Ushers jumped out when you told them to? They were under the Spell too."

My words break the Spell, she realized. She looked at Angelese and said, "You're not paralyzed."

Angelese got up, worse for wear. Her blood had dried on her gown and had turned it into some kind of hip tie-dye. The wounds were already beginning to heal.

"I'd ask you if you're all right but that would be a pretty dumb question, wouldn't it?"

"I've been treated worse," Angelese said.

"I'm trapped here, aren't I?"

"Yes. By the time you found a Deadpass, they'll all have been destroyed by the Merges."

Cassie leaned against the Port's slimy wall. "I don't know what to do now. I know what I *should* do, but I don't know if I can do it."

"What do you want more than anything?"

Cassie's fingers touched her locket. "I want to see my sister."

"She's gone now. But you know where she is, right?"

"Yes."

The angel grinned slyly. "Have you been a good girl?"

"I've never stolen, I've never hurt anyone, I try not to lie, I try to be cool to everyone." Her mind ticked. *Who knows?* "Jeez, I've never even been to third base!"

"Then don't worry."

Cassie's heart was thumping. "What about you?"

"I'll be fine."

Cassie put a hand to her belly and looked down again over the edge of the Egress. They were still hovering. Directly below her stood the massive Mephisto Building.

Oh, man.

"I guess I'll never hear Rob Zombie or Sisters of Mercy again," she murmured.

Angelese laughed. "Probably not. But there are better things to hear. Wondrous things."

Cassie turned one last time to the angel.

Angelese was smiling. She took off her Obscurity Stone, and at once, the Nectoport was radiant in light. But even through that light, the angel's smile could still be seen, and that's when Cassie jumped out of the Nectoport.

Epilogue

"This sucks. I'm gonna have to find some new digs."

Her name was Totty, a Human when she'd arrived here for a life of considerable indulgence, uncharitablility, and deceit. The appealing looks of her sultry Spirit Body quickly caught the eye of the Agency of the Constabulary, who'd just as quickly done the job on her, for the sake of commerce, of course. A simple Lycantropic Organic Vexation plus several Transfigurations had changed the attractive streetwalker from San Francisco's Mission District into an attractive *werewolf* streetwalker from the Mephistopolis's Eichmann District. Totty was now a full-fledged, to-the-max, turn-every-head-in-town, down-and-dirty Lycanymph.

"Shit, business is in the tubes," she complained to a half-melted woman at the carry-out café. "I've only had two tricks all night, and they were both bj's. Fuckin' chumps are such tightwads." She bought a hot cup of rusted water for a five cent McVeigh piece. Awful, but at least it helped get rid of the taste. The taste Humans left in her mouth was bad enough, but—yowzah!—Trolls and Zombies were the worst.

"I knuh-low," the attendant mumbled back. "The-the duh-duh-dlagnets."

Totty guessed she meant dragnets, and she was right. The Merge operations were cleaning the streets. No customers! Like she was telling that skinny kid the other night. What was a girl to do? Erotopathic Lycanymphs had bills to pay too, you know.

Her silken blond fur shimmered in the sulphur light. Her high-heels snapped on the bone-embedded pavement. Rings pierced all eight of her gorged nipples, glittering like tinsel. She'd really dolled herself up tonight, but why? The dragnets made the johns too scared to come out for some action.

Two lousy tricks, she complained. *Tap-tap-tap,* went her high-heels. *Shit, shit, shit,* went her thoughts. She passed some shops—GEIN'S CUTLERY (LESSONS AVAILABLE), WALLACE WHEELCHAIRS, MEHITOBEL'S ROTTEN HEAD BOUTIQUE—and at least noticed with some satisfaction that the dragnets were killing everyone's business, not just hers.

"Man-Burgers?" a voice inquired.

Aw, Christ. Totty hated to be tempted. The sizzling sound wafted wonderful aromas into her nostrils. She turned, stood arms crossed and hip cocked, tapping her foot. The Troll vendor's liverwurst face looked hopeful as her vulpine eyes appraised the sizzling patties. *I got ten bucks tonight! I can't blow my dough on food.*

"Gimme one burger and I'll give ya a knobjob, cutie. Lemme suck the chrome off that trailer-hitch."

The vendor crackled laughter.

Totty frowned. After all, she gave a *great* knobjob. "All

335

right, one burger for a half and half. And you can take all the time you want."

The vendor kept laughing.

"Hey, buddy, I've had your burgers before and lemme tell ya, they ain't all that great. What's so damn funny?"

"No, no, you don't understand!" the vendor chuckled back. "I'd love to take ya up on that deal, but I can't."

"Why not?"

"I got penecomied and gelded by the Constabs five hundred years ago." He pointed to the groinal area of his blood-splotched apron. "There ain't nothin' down there you can do a half and half *on!*"

Asshole. Totty strutted away. *Why does my eternal life have to be so fucked up?* Then she stopped. *That's why . . .*

She'd stopped mid-stride in the middle of the street. She was looking up.

In the bright phosphoric spotlights of Satan Park, the 666-floor Mephisto Building shined, the black sickle moon shimmering behind its obelisk form.

"*That's* why my life's all fucked up. Because of the asshole who lives *there . . .* " All right, so she hadn't been a model of good-will and altruism in the Living World, and, sure, she'd sinned her butt off.

But *this?* Did she really deserve *this?*

I gotta live in this gore-hole of a city for eternity, turning tricks as a fuckin' eight-titted werewolf, and for what?

The question seemed legitimate, or at least to an eight-titted werewolf prostitute in Hell. She pointed up at the impossibly high building, jabbing a finger like a knife. "You've got all the power, you schmuck. You could make things better for all of us. It doesn't have to be *this* bad, does it? No, but you *make* it this bad just 'cos you're an *asshole!*"

Totty huffed off, fuming, and either fantasizing or praying, *Yeah, man, one of these days I hope someone fucks you up but good—*

WWWWWWWWWWWWWWWWWWHAP!

"Whoa-boy! What was that?"

Ahead of her, twenty-foot-long cracks spiderwebbed the pavement, and a figure lay there. He'd obviously fallen from a tremendous height.

Jesus Christ! And he's getting up!

It was hard for Totty to make out any details of the figure. He seemed tall, slender but toned and whatever it was he wore was dappled with blood that looked black. He struggled to his feet. Obviously broken-boned but somehow still able to rise, and before he staggered away, he looked at her.

Totty's eyes narrowed. He was looking right at her but for some reason she couldn't see his face.

Then he hobbled away.

A Fallen Angel? she wondered. Only one of that crowd would be able to get up after a fall like that. Totty just shrugged. Big deal. Crazy shit happened here, and there were plenty of Fallen Angels bopping around. She sure didn't mind seeing one of them get his clock cleaned.

Just as she would stroll off again, though, she stiffened. Her fur began to stand up, like a cat in a room that had just been entered by a predatory animal. Totty had certain hyper-sensitivities now that she'd been transformed. Her hearing, for instance, was as perceptive as a wolf's.

Her ears pricked up; her gaze shot high.

It wasn't a scream she heard, was it? It was a wheeling, swirling shriek, yes, but it seemed gleeful, like someone on the fastest ride at the amusement park.

"Weeeeeeeeeeeeeeeeeeeeeeeeeeeeeeeeeeeeeeeeeeeeeeeeeeee!"

Then Totty's eyes spotted something, too. Way, way up. Just a speck falling in a straight line.

In a second, it was gone, and so was the shriek. Whatever that speck had been, it had fallen right onto the top of the Mephisto Building.

"What the hell was that?" she wondered aloud.

She'd never really know.

A split-second later, Totty was knocked to the pavement by the concussive blast that hit her hard as a sledge-hammer to the chest. Before she could even think what had happened, a white flash lit the sky. It was blinding.

Then came the roar.

Like the loudest thunder she had ever heard. The ground vibrated, then trembled, then it seemed that the entire district, if not the entire city itself, was shaking at its foundations.

A pillar of fire rose in the distance. Through the teeth-chattering rumble, Totty watched astonished as the Mephisto Building collapsed from top to bottom. A mile-high mushroom cloud rolled up over it, topped by a great flower of orange-tinted, smoky light.

The rumbling lasted a few moments more, replaced by the creepiest silence. The Mephisto Building was gone now, as the donut-like cloud rolled higher, darkening, then dissipating altogether.

Totty's mane of blond hair rose in a waft of warm wind. Now it was the Lycanymph who shrieked in glee. She flung her purse wildly over her head and began to dance.

GRAHAM MASTERTON
THE DOORKEEPERS

Julia Winward has been missing in England for nearly a year. When her mutilated body is finally found floating in the Thames, her brother, Josh, is determined to find out what happened to his sister and exactly who—or what—killed her.

But nothing Josh discovers makes any sense. Julia had been working for a company that went out of business sixty years ago, and living at an address that hasn't existed since World War II. The only one who might help Josh is a strange woman with psychic abilities. But the doors she can open with her mind are far better left closed. For behind these doors lie secrets too horrible to imagine.

STRANGER
SIMON CLARK

The small town of Sullivan has barricaded itself against the outside world. It is one of the last enclaves of civilization and the residents are determined that their town remain free from the strange and terrifying plague that is sweeping the land—a plague that transforms ordinary people into murderous, bloodthirsty madmen. But the transformation is only the beginning. With the shocking realization that mankind is evolving into something different, something horrifying, the struggle for survival becomes a battle to save humanity.